# SUMMER HEAT

## EDUCATION: AMERICAN GULAG STYLE

### NATALIE TRIUMPHS

HOUSE OF INDIGO

This book and its characters are fiction. Teen behavior modification programs do exist in the United States, and certain of the incidents in this book are reflective of occurrences that have all too frequently taken place in those programs. Any resemblance between the names of characters and event locations and real persons and real places is purely coincidental.



First edition February 2024

Paperback ISBN: 979-8-9887681-9-7

Ebook ISBN: 978-1-966187-00-4

*This book is dedicated to the members (current and past) of the National Youth Rights Association who have worked over the years to regulate and close down the teen behavioral modification programs AKA Gulag schools, camps and centers and to those parents who have lost their children to violent abusers in a family law system that heavily discriminates against domestic violence victims and protective parents.*

# PROLOGUE

Welcome to Hell: not the Catholic or Baptist kind where people burn in a pit for eternity. I'm talking about the kind of Hell that can only take place on Earth. This is about the nightmare that awaits less-than-perfect rich kids who don't quite live up to their parents' expectations. Only the most affluent parents could afford the thirty to one-hundred thousand-plus dollar fee for the worst nightmare of their children's lives. Some folks just have too much money. Why couldn't I have been born to a poor family? I know the poor have their own set of problems, but from my perspective, those problems are so much less traumatic. This is the abyss from which many teens return in body bags or are tortured to the point where they pray for death and are emotionally scarred for life.

I wasn't a bad kid. I wasn't wild. I didn't do drugs. I didn't even smoke. In fact, I was the best kid I knew how to be, always trying to live up to the expectations of my politically ambitious dad. Of course, I sometimes failed miserably. Now, my brother, he was perfect. He'd never wind up in Hell on Earth. As for my mother, I haven't seen her in years. I miss her. She was sweet, positive and always loving, until she wasn't there. I guess she got tired of being my dad's punching bag. I just wish she had found a way to come back for me.

How did I wind up in a situation that would make Hell in the afterlife look pretty good? It all started the day of my pre-calc final at the end of my sophomore year of high school.

# PART ONE
## CREATING THE PERFECT TEEN OR PERFECT CORPSE

# CHAPTER 1

I was on top of my subjects, expecting to get an A-plus in pre-calc. Math was my top subject and I was ready to ace the final exam. It was ten minutes before class when my phone beeped with an incoming email. It was Matt, my boyfriend, the designated love of my life. My dad had ordered me to refrain from using *Snapchat, Instagram, Tweetle, Fakebook* and all other social media on my phone, which he checked regularly. Besides, my friends and I were boycotting most of the social media sites to protest the censorship, and so it didn't hurt to comply like the good girl my dad demanded I be.

Matt and I had plans for the weekend: big plans. Not that my father would have minded. When he found out that I was dating the son of the president of one of the Fortune 500 companies, he was ready to plan out our wedding. As for me, I would have been fine if Matt's father had been a street-sweeper.

*Ten minutes to class. Do I dare look at the email? Maybe it will inspire me for the exam.*

The email was titled, "I couldn't wait until the weekend to tell you." Well, maybe he really wanted to pep me up before my exam. I opened it up. It read:

**"While we've been apart studying for finals, I realized something:**

*what kind of perfect woman I need in my life. She has to be someone who will put all her needs on hold to attend to my needs, always putting me first, always willing to give up her career, her goals and everything else to make me happy. This last week, I suddenly realized that you aren't that type of girl. It's not personal. I just do not want to continue dating someone who has her own goals. So, I am breaking up with you. I will drop off the things I have of yours next week. So long."*

*What? Right before my final exam?* I didn't realize I was sobbing until Shannon, my best friend, came over to me.

"What happened?"

I couldn't speak. I showed her the email.

"That creep. Only a real jerk would break up with his girlfriend of two years in an email during exam week and especially right before her pre-calc final."

I looked at her. I still couldn't speak. She put her arm around me. "You should send him a doormat so he will have his perfect woman. You can do much better."

The bell rang. Still in shock, I got up. I had to look normal as I went into my final. "Are you sure you don't want to go to the nurse?" Shannon asked.

I still couldn't get out any words.

Mr. Lavery looked out his open door. "Summer, please get in here before I start docking you. You are holding up the exam."

I sat at my desk. He handed me the paper with the exam questions. I pulled a pencil out of my backpack. Before I knew it, the final bell rang. I looked down at my paper. I had written my name and nothing else. Mr. Lavery shook his head as he collected my paper.

*I'll have to explain, I thought. Maybe he will let me retake the exam. It can't mean failure! It can't! After all, I have always gotten my homework in on time and have an A plus average on both my homework and quizzes prior to now. However, forty-five percent of the grade is dependent on the final. Unless I get to make it up, things don't look too good. What am I thinking? Of course, when Mr. Lavery looks over my blank page, he'll have to realize something was wrong and let me retake it. He has to, right?*

My other exams didn't go much better that day. I knew Matt wouldn't be picking me up like he usually did.

Shannon bumped into me on my way out. "Want a ride home?"

"Thanks. But I really don't want to go home right now."

"Where would you like to go? What would you like to do?"

"I don't know. I seem to have blown away my chances for the path I was supposed to follow and I don't have the foggiest idea what I want to do today, tomorrow, or whenever."

What did I want from life? I didn't have any sense of myself anymore. My mom was the last family member to ask what I wanted to be, do or have. She used to encourage me to follow my dreams, but since she had gone, my future had been chosen for me. Neither my dad nor his friends had ever once bothered to ask what I wanted. Everyone in my dad's life had expectations for me based on my being a perfect go-along showcase daughter. All that was gone now.

"Then you need to relax, forget about Matt, and go for yourself. How about we go to the beach and hang out there for a while, perhaps do a little surfing?"

"I'll watch you surf." I felt more in the mood for drowning myself.

Jimmy, Shannon's on-again, off-again sort-of boyfriend, joined us on the beach in Malibu. I generally carried my swimsuit in my school bag, mostly because I was on the New Heritage High School swim team and liked to swim when I could. I was hoping my swimming awards would give me a boost into college. At Malibu, our favorite beach, I generally liked hitting the waves, but today, nothing felt good. I mostly hung out on the shore and watched, thinking of what a loser I had become.

I had spent my whole sophomore year hanging out with Matt. *"Perfect woman!" How could I have misjudged him?* I was certainly angry, but I was also hurt. I missed the boyfriend I thought he was. He clearly wasn't that guy, but it was as if someone I had loved was dead.

"Do you want to come back to my place for a party?" Jimmy asked.

Shannon looked at me, encouragingly. "His parents are out of town until tomorrow."

"I don't know if I'm feeling in the mood for partying." I thought again. Going home and being alone with my thoughts wasn't the best thing at this point in time. "For a little while."

Jimmy was a Green Day fan. They had been really popular a couple of decades before but their songs still made for great dance music. Jimmy kept saying that we all needed to listen to the messages in their lyrics.

I watched as my friends danced and sang along with the songs and did their best to pull me into the fun. They were so natural. They never tried to fit into some politically-appropriate mold. They never had to worry about some angry, erratic overlord flying off the handle whenever they got out of line. I was once free, like them. But things changed after Mom. I wanted to be me, again, the real me that I had lost years ago, light, happy, optimistic and feeling like I could do anything. But that was a distant memory that didn't even seem real anymore. I didn't know how to get back to who I was—or thought I was.

Shannon handed me a pre-mixed glass of something pink. "Relax a little. If anyone needs a drink today, it's you," she said.

"I'll pass. I have to face my dad, and today is not the day to start drinking." I looked at the pink liquid. "What is it?"

"It's something Jimmy's dad taught him to make. It's his version of a Singapore sling, basically layered rum, instead of gin, and cherry liquor. Tastes like fruit punch."

I took a little sip and then handed it back. "It does. But I need my senses together when I get home."

"You aren't going to tell your dad about the exam, are you?"

"Not if I can help it."

"Anyone can have a bad day. They'll have to average in your final score with your other work, which was probably A-plus."

"But remember, in pre-calc, he said the final would be forty-five percent of our grade. If the A plus part is sixty-five percent, and the zero part is forty-five percent, that is still failing."

"We'll figure something out. Don't tell him, or if you do, tell him you were sick, had a seizure or something and need to retake it. They do generally allow make-ups."

"Hope so."

<hr>

As I got home, I snuck in and went towards the stairs to get up to my room.

"Summer!" It was my dad. He looked as if he had downed several glasses of the drink I had refused. Or maybe it was just one of his typical rages. His tone and the look in his eyes told me I was in big trouble. He certainly wasn't exhibiting the calm, warm, likeable image people in political circles saw. As Senator Dana Madstein's former chief of staff and as Governor Slick's current chief of staff, he received considerable respect and admiration and everyone thought he was a really charming guy. I knew better.

"Not now, Dad," I said, trying to rush on. I didn't get far. I felt my hair grabbed from behind and fell back against the railing at the bottom of the staircase, hitting my head.

He pulled me up by my hair. Using his free hand, he forced me to face him and then slapped my face harder than I had ever been hit before. I felt myself go a little dizzy as I collapsed against the stairs.

"You little tramp. I heard you and Matt broke up."

"Did Matt tell you?"

"No. His father told me."

"Really. He put it on me?"

"Matt has a future."

"Yeah, his dad is the president of one of your boss's top campaign contributors. Did it put a damper on your own career plans, Dad?"

"Don't you talk that way to me! You are going to apologize to Matt. Tell him that you are sorry."

"I will do no such thing."

"You will or I will send you to one of those reform schools or boot camps where you will learn to do what you are told."

"Really? Aren't you supposed to be progressive? Or at least that's what you are telling people. How progressive is it to send your daughter to a boot camp because she won't be the perfect slut for some corporate legacy?"

"Watch your mouth. You are on detention until this is resolved."

"Thanks, Dad. It's nice to know that all I am to you is a way to climb the political ladder. Mom's lucky she got out."

He grabbed my arm again, pulled me up to face him and smacked my face again. As I fell back, again, and hit the floor, I heard the front door open.

Pan, my brother, waltzed in and looked briefly at me before walking into the kitchen, ignoring the whole situation. I used the distraction to scramble up the stairs before my father could do more. Before I reached my room, I could hear the phone ring.

I briefly listened as I was closing my door. I could hear my dad pick up the phone located near the bottom of the stairs. Yes, we still had a landline. My dad found them more trustworthy.

"Yes, Mr. Lavery," I heard him say. "What? But math's her top subject." I didn't want to hear any more but couldn't close out the entire discussion.

I locked my door. I had to get out of there. But not right away. I turned up some music in my room. My dad came and pounded on the door.

"You hit me. I deserve a break."

"I'm going to do more than hit you. I'm going to break something!" my dad shouted back.

# CHAPTER 2

I did my best to hold it together as he continued yelling and then walked off. Inside, I was angry and devastated at the same time. However, knowing it could only get worse, this was not the night to let myself in for more.

A trellis to the side of my window was the way I had sometimes left the house at night when Matt and I had snuck out. Now, it seemed like the best way to escape. I needed to talk things out with someone because I didn't know what to think or feel about what my dad was threatening.

When he was in one of his rages, he could do anything. I remembered his bragging about destroying an intern at Senator Madstein's office. The guy had embarrassed my dad in front of the Senator.

*But I am his daughter. If he does something to me, it will reflect badly on him, right?* Of course, people would believe whatever he said.

Shannon opened her bedroom window as I climbed the tree that leaned close to it. I could have gone in through the front door, but I couldn't count on her mother not mentioning my visit to my dad.

"You don't have to put on a brave front here."

"Well, what was that old saying? Eat, drink and be merry."

"Matt didn't deserve you. It will only get better."

"Define better. Tonight, after Dad threatened me over Matt, my pre-calc instructor called him and said I was going to flunk. My dad has put me into detention for the rest of my life and said for the ninth time that he would send me away to some boot camp before I embarrassed him any further. He's so angry and so icy, I'm waiting for him to pull out the knives again. I should have hidden them before I left the house. I've never had a drink, except for that sip this evening, and I've never had sex, but tonight I'd like to have both."

"The sex you will have to get elsewhere. But I can help you with the drink part. My parents have a liquor cabinet."

There was a knock at Shannon's bedroom door. I put my fingers to my lips and stepped into Shannon's closet. I could hear the door to the room open. "All clear. It's Tiff."

I stepped out of the closet. I thought about making a joke and then changed my mind. "Hi, Tiff."

"Summer, I heard what happened with Matt. I never thought he was good enough for you."

"That's what I have been saying," Shannon affirmed. "We should have a dozen doormats sent to him in front of everyone at his summer internship. Which company is it he'll be working at?"

"Thanks, but he's the least of my problems. Actually, he's responsible for my problems."

"What?" Tiffany asked.

"Her father is threatening her with Siberia or worse."

"Right," I added.

"Over Matt?"

"My dad was expecting Matt's dad to back his future campaign for Lieutenant Governor. Now, Matt's rich daddy might pull out."

"Tell him you dumped Matt for one of Soros's nephews," Tiffany suggested. "You're way prettier than Chelsea, whose husband isn't really a Soros nephew, by the way."

"A Soros nephew? Yuck. I'd sooner die."

"You don't have to let your dad know that, and by the time he finds out the truth, the Matt thing will be ancient history."

"My dad is the Governor's Chief of Staff. Soros has been one of his top backers. Dad'll find out I'm lying by the end of tomorrow."

"How about your mother?"

"Like she hasn't bothered to see me in years. It's as if I have the plague. I mean, I can't blame her for not wanting anything to do with my dad. But did she have to drop me, too?"

"Summer, you don't know?" Tiffany asked.

"Know? Is a nuclear war coming? That would be the perfect ending to the day."

"Your parents. Their divorce is on the Net. Your mother will go to jail if she goes near you."

"What?" I lifted up both hands, palms up in disbelief. I had never bothered to look up my parents' divorce. It was too much just living through it. I knew my father was somehow given full custody. "What is this about jail?"

"Your mother said he abused her and that he threatened to kill you both. It's called 'alienation.' If one parent alleges abuse, no matter how many medical records they have or how much the police want to back them up, it's still 'alienation.' The courts don't allow the witnesses, such as doctors or the police, to testify to the abuse, and so the mere intimation that there was abuse is enough for a court to take away all parenting rights from the parent claiming abuse."

"But why didn't they ask me? I saw him beating her. His favorite response to something he didn't like was to threaten to kill us and dump our bodies in a trash can like that Broderick guy supposedly did with his wife's body in San Diego."

"I remember hearing about the Broderick case. According to one Indymedia article, in your parents' case, they wouldn't allow any testimony proving abuse. If you had tried to testify, they would have claimed that your mother put you up to claiming abuse. According to the article, your mother is not allowed to see you until you turn eighteen."

"What article?"

Tiffany pulled her minicomputer from her bag and started it up. We both had Shannon's Wi-Fi login on our computers from previous homework sessions. Tiffany opened up her browser and typed in a query to *Gagle's* search engine. "Yep. The censors are at it again. Most of the articles are gone. There used to be a lot of articles about your family linked on *Gagle*." She typed a few more keystrokes and went into Linda Sherwood's blog. In it, she found a link that she followed to the *WayBack Machine*. "Even the *WayBack Machine* is removing articles these days. But they didn't remove this one, yet."

I looked. It was an article titled "Who Cares About the Children?" The article was about children who had allegedly been given to child molesters and abusers. It mentioned a little boy named Jonah, who had been given to an international sex trafficking ring, and a couple of little girls named Lexi and Sarah. In those three cases, it was alleged that the men who had gotten full custody of the children had violently and sexually abused them or other children.

In Lexi's case, the man who got custody was a reported terrorist who had to flee the country to avoid arrest after repeatedly sexually molesting Lexi but was still able to retain custody in absentia while her mother was prohibited from seeing her own daughter. Neither parent was an American—though Lexi had been born in California. The mother was a Canadian citizen by birth, and though she was a long-time resident of the U.S., her Visa to stay in this country was revoked to prevent her from arguing that she was the only parent still in the country. Canada gave full custody to the mom and ordered the U.S. to deliver the child, who belonged in Canada. However, the American courts refused to honor the Canadian ruling. A corrupt district attorney helped the raping terrorist get back into the country so he could traffic her to Thailand, and a corrupt State Department decided to issue a passport to help him do it.

In Sarah's case, the man who got custody was a registered convicted child rapist with a long history of arrests. He was also living with drug dealers with their own long histories of arrests. In all these cases, the mothers had done nothing wrong other than to try to protect their children.

The article went on to say that the courts give children to abusers in ninety percent of the cases where there is sexual abuse and in seventy of the cases where there is non-sexual physical violence. A little ways further down the page, I saw my name.

It said my mother had been beaten severely to the point of being hospitalized in a coma. When she woke up, she alleged I was in danger. The court called her an "alienator" and gave my dad full custody. I knew about my mother's beatings and that my dad had gotten full custody, but none of it made sense. The decision made out as if my mother was the abuser. She wasn't capable of abusing an insect before she left. I knew she wasn't abusive, but she abandoned me, and I never really forgave her.

"If she loved me, if she really loved me, wouldn't she have found a way?" I asked my friends.

"I don't know. She would have gone to prison and you would have still been with your father," Tiffany said.

I was internally beating myself up for not doing my own research on my own parents' divorce. *How is it that my friends know more about my family than I do?* But I knew why. It hurt too much.

"This is awful. Women really are second—no, third-class—citizens in America. There has to be something we can do," Shannon interjected, swinging her arms across each other and then outward.

"Not until Summer turns eighteen," Tiffany responded. "Then, the court won't have jurisdiction—unless she does what that Damon kid did."

"Damon?" I asked.

"He has a site, *savingdamon.com.* He was given to a father he said repeatedly molested him. He ran away and was hidden by a bunch of courageous women until he turned sixteen. Then his mother went to, get this, a brothel in Nevada and offered two hundred dollars to anyone who would marry her son on paper."

"Did they agree?"

"No. The people running the brothel said it wasn't enough money. But one girl came up and spoke to the mother afterward and told her she would do it. She never even charged her the two hundred. After that, Damon was declared emancipated and got a paper annulment. Then, he got to live with his mother."

"I'm not getting married. I've had it with guys. Besides, I don't know if my mother wants me."

"You can't be certain," Shannon responded. "Write your mother a letter. I'll mail it. Maybe she can find a way to rescue you."

"If she even remembers me, she has gone on with her life. If she hasn't bothered to see me in years, why would she now?"

"It's worth a try. Besides, if it doesn't work, you are no worse off than now, and you will know she doesn't deserve you either," Shannon said.

I started to write. *What can I say? Will my mom care? Will she even bother to read it?* I proceeded, anyway, on what I assumed was a useless gesture.

*Dear Mom:*

*I miss you. I remember we used to have so much fun together. You were the one person I could rely on. Then you weren't there and I didn't have anyone. So, I had to be strong for myself.*

*But now I could be in trouble. Dad is really angry. He is threatening to send me away to some boot camp. I don't think he will really do that. But he is mean, crazy, and I am really scared. I need you.*

*I know you are probably afraid to contact me, but isn't there something you can do? Maybe, I can run away and you can hide me, or I can hide out and see you when you feel it's safe?*

*I need you. I love you.*

*Your daughter,*

*Spring*

"Spring?" Shannon asked, cocking her head.

"It's a private joke between my mom and me. I was born in May, but my dad felt Summer was a better name than Spring, and naturally, he got his way."

I sealed the letter in an envelope addressed to my mom at the last address I had for her. Shannon promised to mail it the next day. "I don't know if I can wait. I am going to go home, pack tonight and get out of Dodge, as they used to say in the old Westerns. I will call you tomorrow," I told Shannon.

"Call me, too?" Tiffany asked.

"Of course. You are both my best friends."

Shannon went downstairs and got us some dark hot chocolate and vegan lemon tarts. We used to celebrate my victories on the swim team with those, and it was her way of saying we would be victorious, again. I had introduced her to the vegan lemon tarts when I found out that most tarts were made with bovine gelatin. I hadn't had meat since I was a little kid. These days, I generally avoided grains because of the glyphosate, but an exception was in order. We listened to some songs and sang. I felt lighter than I had all day. I would see my mom soon— or at least I would be free of him. If my mom didn't want me, I'd find some place to go.

As I snuck back up the trellis, I told myself that this was for the last time. I pulled my largest backpack out of my closet. Whatever wouldn't fit in it was not coming. I looked at my medals I had won with my swimming. It occurred to me that it might have been vanity, but when I won those, I had felt like a winner. Those were coming. I didn't have room for the trophies. I figured I could pick up additional outer clothes, but I wanted as much clean underwear as possible. I pulled out a charm bracelet my mother had given me as a child. It was one of the mementos from my time with my mom that my dad hadn't confiscated on his monthly raids of my room. I had managed to keep it hidden away under my chest of drawers. It was the only piece of jewelry that meant anything.

I had about five thousand dollars stashed away that I put into my backpack as well. I had read that the majority of Americans didn't have a thousand dollars for an emergency, but I was a rich kid and this was nothing compared to my bank account. My mother had put money into a trust fund when I was born that my father couldn't touch. I wondered if she had any money now. My father had probably broken her.

I heard a noise in the hall. I put the backpack under my bed. The door was locked, and I had stolen my dad's key to my room on a previous occasion. I wasn't above that. But still, something was in the lock, and it was turning.

What came through the door was some big, burly guy who looked like he hadn't bathed in a week. I picked up a trophy that was on the shelf next to my bed. Before I could pelt him with it, he pulled out something that looked a little like a gun but not quite.

# CHAPTER 3

I reacted by pulling my cell out of my pocket, to which he said, "I wouldn't try that."

"I'm calling 9-1-1. I suggest you leave."

The next thing I knew, bolts of pain shot through me, and I collapsed onto my knees. I'd been tased. I pulled myself together. I had to get away. I grabbed my backpack from under the bed and headed for the window. More pain. I wasn't going to let it floor me. I turned around and started to swing the backpack.

"Good to see you're packed, but you won't need that where you're going," he laughed as he avoided my thrust.

I backed up towards the open window. All I needed was to jump. I could catch the trellis or a tree branch on the way down, I hoped. I started to back through it, but the man grabbed me before I could and thrust me to the floor. Again, I was tased, and this time, the taser continued blasting me until I thought I might die.

I lay there, writhing in pain and then unable to move. My assailant pushed me from my back onto my stomach and pulled my arms behind me. I struggled to pull my arm free, but then I felt cable ties going around my wrists. I told myself I was strong, that I could find a way out of this. Some people had died after being tased once, and I was alive and kicking after being tased three times.

But then something sharp touched my arm. A needle. I felt something being inserted under the skin. I continued to struggle, but my consciousness was wavering. I had to make it away from this man. Where was my father?

"Daddy?" I tried to call out and found myself melting into a dream. I tried to open my eyes, but they wouldn't open. Then suddenly, I could see. But everything was so distorted, I didn't know if it was real or if I was having a hallucination or a dream.

*Colors flashed before my eyes. I saw rainbows and images of school, my friends, my swim meets, my dad's raging temper, my brother's coldness, my mother holding me, telling me, "I love you. I love you."*

*"Save me!" I called out to her, but she was gone. "Mom, come back!"*

It had to be a dream. I hadn't seen my mom in years—unless she had found out what had happened and had come to rescue me.

*Next, Matt appeared. I didn't want to see or dream about him. "I need the perfect woman. If you want to be perfect, kiss my feet, make my dinner and then do a striptease for me."*

*"I don't do stripteases!" I shouted.*

*"Do it," my dad insisted.*

*"Dad, rescue me!" He turned away from me, patted Matt on the shoulder and then walked away.*

*Suddenly, I was surrounded by a dozen guys all shouting, "Strip! Be the perfect woman! You're a failure! Who would want you?"*

I felt movement. My lids were still closed. It was a dream. I tried but couldn't open my eyes. *I pictured Shannon. I called out to her. "Please help! Get my mom! I need her!"*

*"Jimmy and I will save you. Won't we, Jimmy?"*

*"Have a drink. It will make it go easier," Jimmy urged me.*

*Suddenly, there was a judge. "Beat her some more. She needs to be put in her place."*

*"No!" Shannon screamed.*

*"Unhand her!" Jimmy shouted.*

*A bailiff appeared with two deputy sheriffs. "Take them away," the judge said. The deputies tased Shannon and Jimmy, causing them to fall and land hurt on the floor. The officers put cable ties on their wrists and dragged them behind the bench and out a door behind the judge.*

*The judge turned to me. "There is no one to speak for you now. I sentence you to doom."*

*"Help!" I screamed.*

"She's waking," I heard a muffled voice say. It didn't sound like the one from my room.

"She can't go anywhere." That was the voice of the man who had drugged and tased me. I heard a loud bang, like something closing. I was too weak to stay awake and dozed off again. I fought to wake up, but I kept lapsing in and out of consciousness.

I tried to open my eyes, again. *I can do it*, I told myself. Finally, as I managed to open them, all I could see was black. I lay there trying to gain control of my senses. My ears felt like they were popping, as if I was traveling to a higher elevation. My hands were cable-tied together. So were my ankles. I tried to grasp my surroundings. I could hear what sounded like road noises under me. I was in the trunk of some kind of vehicle.

I was not going to allow myself to be helpless. I was not going to be a victim. I needed something sharp to cut the cable ties. There was the latch, but it wasn't sharp. There was the bolt holding in the spare tire. Thank goodness there were still some cars with spare tires. At least, I had hope. If I could get loose, I could find a way to open the truck from the inside when the car slowed down.

There was very little room to get the bolt into the area between my wrists, but somehow, I managed it. My wrists already felt as if I had scraped them. There was a dampness. Blood. Well, if I didn't get free, what was next could be a lot worse. I tried to rub the bolt against the ties, but it seemed to be searing my wrists more than the ties. *I might bleed to death here.* I ignored the pain. *Better to die fighting,* I told myself.

The car seemed to be pulling off whatever highway it was on. It stopped but there was nothing I could do without some freedom. It started up again. It was traveling slower, I believed, than it would have been on a regular highway, but it was still probably going too fast for me to jump and make a break for it at this point. *Aren't there any stoplights, or do these guys just know how to run them? I'm not free yet, anyway.*

The vehicle started curving right and then left. Were we on some kind of mountain road?

I continued rubbing and rubbing. I tried to pull my hands back as hard as I could, putting pressure on the bolt to snap the tie, and then it did. *Free!* I felt around. The bolt was my best bet for getting my ankles free. I felt the latch on the inside of the trunk. I could open it, but it would be suicide to jump at this speed on a mountain road with legs tied—maybe even without them tied. I needed more time.

Finally, I felt the tie around my ankles break. I unlatched the trunk and slightly lifted it—enough to get a glimpse. I was definitely on a mountain road. I saw trees, mixed in with bare patches, hills or mountains and dips. If I jumped at the wrong time, I might go off a cliff. I couldn't tell where we were. How long had I been asleep? The vehicle turned onto a dirt road, slowing quite a bit.

Now was my chance. I lifted the truck, jumped and rolled. My whole body ached, and there was a sharp pain in my wrists and ankles, but I kept going.

*Darn!* The trunk had flown wide open. I sprinted away as best as I could, using patches of trees to try to keep out of sight, while traveling counter to the direction the car had taken. But the vehicle stopped and the burly man and another man, slighter in build, got out and were running in the direction I was going. I needed to turn and change directions. The pain in my legs and my wrists had turned to numbness, and I had to fight to keep from collapsing. I moved further from the dirt road into a wider patch of trees, switching directions to backtrack towards the way the car had been traveling, hoping they would run past me.

"There," I heard the burly guy say. I had been spotted.

I saw the burly guy pulling out his taser device again. *Where is the other man?*

Suddenly, I felt a crack at my skull. I fell to the ground. I wasn't fully unconscious, but I couldn't stand. My head felt heavy, bursting in pain, as if it had been smashed against a wall. My thoughts were a scrambled mess, and I couldn't get up the strength to move again as I was put back into the trunk.

# CHAPTER 4

A part of me thought I might die. I could feel blood. It seemed to be oozing from my head. My wrists and ankles were raw and felt like they were oozing as well. I fell back into a mist of sleep again.

When I next woke, I was lying on my back. My right hand was cable-tied to my left ankle and my left hand was cable-tied to my right ankle. A chain was hooked around my waist and attached, at the other end, to a stake in the ground. I was near a fire.

Someone shone a light into my eyes. From what I could see, I could tell it was a guy, much bigger than me and heavier but shorter and less thick than the kidnapper. His skin looked leathery, like he had been out in the sun a lot. His full head of greasy dark hair didn't improve his looks. In my situation, I felt justified in classifying him as the ugliest guy I had ever seen.

"Look where your struggles got you. You've got a concussion. You are going to be nauseous and headachy for a few days."

"Are you a doctor?" Who was I kidding? But the question had just popped out.

He laughed. "Doctor? Oh, sure. Just haven't been to medical school."

"I'm injured. I need medical care from a real doctor. My dad is rich.

I have insurance. I promise that, if you get me medical care, you will be reimbursed."

"Your father is the one who paid us to bring you here."

"My father? No. This would be bad for his career. This is child abuse."

He laughed again. "Out here, there is no such thing. I am providing medical care and keeping you from injuring yourself again. We will be giving you back your cell phone to make a call. Unfortunately, the battery seems to be missing. I bet you didn't think it was removable."

"This is illegal! It's kidnapping."

Another laugh. "Not with your father's permission."

"Look. I have a trust fund. I can get you more than you were paid, lots more, if you just let me go."

Another laugh. "My friend Joe has already paid me three hundred dollars."

"Joe?"

"The man who brought you from your room."

"He took my money," I said groggily, thinking of what I had put in my backpack. With all else in there, my thoughts went to the bracelet I had saved all those years. *Will I ever see it again?*

"You mean Joe's money. But he's generous. He gave me half of the six hundred dollars he picked up in Brentwood."

"Where are we?"

"That's the question, isn't it?"

"How about an answer?"

"Well, that's the thing. You're a runner, and here, there is nowhere to run to. But the location is still a secret." He put his fore and middle fingers to his mouth and said, "Shhh."

"Who are you?"

"When we get to be friends, good friends, you can call me Claudio. Until then, I'm Sir."

"I'm sick." I started to heave. I was on my back and the vomit went right back into my mouth and nose. I tried to breathe but it was tough. I felt as if I was drowning. He turned me face down. I passed out.

# CHAPTER 5

To my surprise, I woke up again, my wrists and ankles still bound. My head felt as if it had been punched in by a sledgehammer. My stomach felt like it would take little to get it to empty itself again. I felt pricks on my legs, stomach and chest like sharp needles going into them. My face. I was currently face down, and I smelled like stale, moldy food. *At least I'm alive, but what is that sharp, prickly feeling?*

"God is watching out for me. The hot, smelly chick is awake. I was pulling for you, princess," a voice spoke out not far from me. I couldn't quite focus on anything other than the person's feet. He wasn't one of the two original men. He sounded like he was maybe my age or a little older.

"I'm not a princess. Ouch!" I said.

"No talking to the preppie, Santana." Claudio's voice scolded.

I worked to scoot my body almost onto my side and then I saw it. I was lying on a red ant hill, hogtied and helpless.

"Help! Red ants!"

Claudio chuckled. "This is not the palace, princess. You won't get the royal treatment here."

"I said, 'I'm not a princess.' This hurts!"

"Life is tough."

The pain from the ants and my head made me dizzy. There was nobody to help me, nobody but Claudio and that obnoxious Santana guy.

*Did Mom get my letter? Did I just dream that I wrote to her? My dad. Would my dad really do this to me?* The answer came quickly: *Yes!* The pain was excruciating. "Please, a doctor, a real doctor!"

"This is for your own good. When you return home," Claudio laughed. "If you return home."

"If?"

"There have been a few unfortunate incidents. But I think you will come around. Learn to loooove us. After all, we've been hired to help you."

"Help? Could you please get me away from these ants!" I screamed.

"You can't do this to her," came another male voice, sounding urgent, concerned.

"Easy. Back Jason. You know the consequences." Whoever this Jason was, he seemed to be on my side.

"I'd hate to see the smelly not-a-princess die," came Santana's voice. "She might be allergic. Couldn't you use a different indoctrination? The rack or something that will make her a little taller?"

"Both of you back up," Claudio said. "Neither of you has made blue yet. There are consequences for interference."

I didn't know if I could handle the pain, anymore. No. I knew I couldn't. I lost consciousness again. I knew I was asleep, but the pain didn't go away. It continued through my dreams.

---

I woke up in a dark room, still hogtied, but this time naked. No, not a room, a box. I could feel the wood against my body. It wasn't smooth. There were some sharp splinters that were cutting into me. I had to be careful moving. I tried to twist and managed to roll onto my side, but found that the box was closed on all sides. Everything was dark, really dark.

Who had undressed me? So far, I hadn't seen any women or girls at this place. True, I hadn't seen hardly anything of this place. There was Claudio, that nasty Santana guy, Jason, and the burly kidnapper whom Claudio called Joe. Was there anyone else here?

I would have expected to see some light filtered in between cracks in the boards. The wood didn't seem properly finished. I surmised the boards were never coated with any sealant, probably just nailed together. It must be night. I was alone. I lay there awake. At least the ants were gone. My body hurt from the angle my arms and legs were pulled into. There was nothing relaxing about it. I could hear weird eerie sounds, almost but not quite like low voices. My stomach was still weak and my head still hurt, but as I lay on my side, I thought about my mom. *Will she somehow find me? When I didn't call Shannon and Tiffany, did they realize something was wrong? How long have I been here?*

I needed to rest. I needed to build up my strength. I had been told that sleep was bad with a concussion, but I had slept quite a bit and I was still alive. I closed my eyes.

When I awoke, I was still naked and in the box. Light was slipping in through the cracks. I was thirsty, so very thirsty. How long had it been since I had been kidnapped? Was it kidnapping? Claudio claimed to have had my dad's permission and Dad had full custody of me. Where was I? Was I even still in California? I didn't think I had been given any water since I had been taken. How long had it been? Days, I guessed. Or did it just seem like days?

How long could a person survive without water? I think I had read three days. I thought about crying out for water, but all my other requests had been met with laughter or further cruelty. What kind of father would send me here? This was cruel-even for my father.

It was summertime. Would the box turn into an oven in the sun? It wasn't long until I could feel the box heating up. I remembered about the dogs that had died in closed cars. I could see what looked like bright light cutting across the foot of one side of the box. Indirect light was coming through the other cracks. Perhaps, I was partially under a tree.

As the day went on, it got hotter. It did not appear I was in direct sunlight. But if the heat didn't get me, the thirst might. Would any of the people I had met at the Democratic Party meetings ask about me? Would any reporters? My dad was planning to run for office in his own right. Lieutenant Governor. He was hoping to later be Governor and maybe someday President with the support of his current boss, Governor Slick. Would anyone ask where his daughter was? If they did, would he lie and say I was traveling in Europe?

I heard sounds outside. The voices seemed to be arguing. "What if she dies? Then there could be an inquiry." It was Santana's voice. Was he sticking up for me, or was he just against an inquiry for murder?

"Shut up or you'll get the box, yourself, or maybe the noose." That was Claudio's voice.

"The noose? You expect me to crack like Blake? What did you tell his parents? Or did you? We are required to have working phones and be able to contact our parents—at least in some states."

"And what state are we in?"

Silence. Then the voices continued.

"So, you've got the hots for the girl? Maybe if you behave, we'll let you have a little time with her. If not, maybe we can remove your ability to have time with any girl? You don't think we would do that?"

"She's nothing to me. Hot chicks are a dime a dozen. If you've screwed one, you've screwed them all. My dad's a congressman. If I can't give him grandbabies, I assure you he will close this place down."

"You think? And has he contacted you once since you've been here?"

"F— you," came the reply. I heard a sound like something had fallen. Then a noise like a chain moving. "Try to break me. My dad will have an inquiry if I return home harmed," came Santana's strained, now raspy voice.

*What have they done to him?*

A while later, I heard something touch my box and then the jingle of the chain again, followed by a bang as if it had hit something. There was a yelp of pain. I couldn't make out whether it was Santana or someone else. I heard the chain again and then another yelp of pain.

I heard movements, but no more talking for a while. Then, "Amy, sweet girl. Did you bring me some water?"

"Only for you," came the response. "What's wrong with Jason?"

"He tried to interfere with the new girl's training."

"Jason, don't worry. She needs to be broken," Amy's voice said. "If Claudio doesn't break her, she'll be pathetic forever. I used to be that way. I'm better now."

"He's torturing her." It was Jason's voice.

"Easy. Or you'll get more of what you got before. And no talking to the other campers without permission."

"What? You going to kill me? Go ahead. Then you'll have to explain my body to somebody."

"We are here to make you kids better. You think you're helping her by trying to free her, but you are really hurting her."

"You are sick."

I felt something touch the box and then heard a swishing sound, like a whip hitting something. Then more moving, groaning. *Jason?* I hoped he wasn't hurt but from the yelps, I was sure he was. He was the closest thing I had to a friend, a protector, here. He was risking his own safety for me. I hoped I would get to know him. He just had to be okay.

"Get him out of here," I heard Claudio say to someone.

"Me?" It was Santana's voice, still raspy. "Sure, man. Jason, she's just an overrated rich chick. She's not worth the trouble." His voice was moving away. I heard what sounded like someone stumbling or maybe being dragged. That was probably Jason.

"Overrated rich chick," Santana had said. What a pathetic, uncaring, egotistical P.O.S. I kept hoping Jason was okay.

"And you, Jamie, quit looking sorry for her, or you'll get the same."

---

A while later, I heard more movement.

"Aww. You know how to please me. Careful with the food."

"Oh, you don't really mind, do you? After all, I need to get up my energy." It was Amy's voice.

"Well, maybe a little. Especially since you will be leaving in two days."

"In two days?"

"Yeah, we've had an offer to buy out your scholarship. There is a Senator in Washington who liked the pictures we sent of you. I told you those pictures would help you. We told him about you." He paused. "Cooperative and eager to please."

"I'm going to Washington? I'm getting out of here?" She sounded happy. "Not that I'm unhappy here. Well, at first."

"We'll miss your extra credit. Maybe you can do a return trip sometime."

"How can I do that when I don't even know where we are?"

"Better that way. How about a last one before you hit the road?"

"To remember me by?"

*Is this a whorehouse prep school for the pleasure of American leaders*? I wondered.

# CHAPTER 6

I drifted in and out of sleep. It was dark out. Even through the box, I felt cold. The top opened. "Shh," someone said. I couldn't make out who. A cup of liquid was placed against my lips. Water, I hoped. Right then, I was so thirsty that even cyanide juice would taste good. I shivered at the thought and took a sip. It tasted like water. I sipped a little more. Suddenly, it was pulled away, and the lid of my box was closed. I heard footsteps scurrying away.

"Emily, what are you doing here?" came Claudio's voice and then a laugh.

"I was thirsty."

"Did I give you permission to get water?"

"No."

"Go ahead. Get some water, Emily. Would you like to earn some favors?"

"Please don't," I heard her say.

"Please; so polite," he replied, mockingly.

"Please, don't touch me like that. You're sending Amy to those Congressional pimps. Isn't that sleazy enough?"

"Feisty tonight, aren't we?"

"I'm going to my tent for the night. I'm sorry about being thirsty."

*So, was it Emily who had given me the water?*

Later the box opened, again, just enough for a hand to fit through. More water came to my lips. Tied up, I could only feel what the hand brought. But the hand smelled sweet, like lemons.

"Thank you, Emily," I whispered. She didn't say anything. Something was placed against my lips. It was some kind of berry. I took a bite. Then there were more berries. Suddenly, the hand was withdrawn, and Emily rushed away.

I drifted off, again, or so I thought. The next thing I saw jolted me.

*It was my mother's face. What was she doing here? No. We weren't here. We were on a teeter-totter, and she was bigger, like she had been when I was little. She was singing, "Aren't You Lovely?" her personal version of the Stevie Wonder song that she would sing to me as a kid. I knew it was a dream, but I didn't want to leave it. Suddenly the scene shifted. She was downstairs, in the living room, arguing with my dad.*

*"I'm sorry. I'm trying my best," she was saying. "Please don't hurt me!" she cried.*

*"Don't hurt you? I'm going to kill you."*

*I knew what was coming next. I yelled at my dad, "Please don't hurt her! Please! Please!" But it was as if I wasn't saying anything.*

*My dad picked up the fire poker and started swinging it at her. He clubbed her several times and she fell.*

*"Mommy," I yelled from the top of the stairs. My brother Pan had been downstairs. He walked past where my mom lay, then up the stairs and past me.*

*"Pan, please stop him!" I cried. He just kept going into his room and closed the door.*

*"Summer, get out of here! Please, go!" my mother screamed, pulling herself up and moving towards the bottom of the stairs as she spoke. My dad grabbed her, twisting her arm. It appeared to snap out of place.*

*"Stop it!" I yelled. He ignored me.*

*I went into my parents' room, picked up the phone and dialed 9-1-1.*

*"9-1-1. What is your emergency?"*

*"My dad is hurting my mom! She needs help!"*

*"How old are you?"*

*"Seven."*

*"Are you in danger?"*

*"I'm in another room."*

*"Stay there until a car gets there. We have your location."*

*I didn't stay there. I ran downstairs. My mom was unconscious. Something even worse must have happened after I went for the phone.*

*My dad had left the living room and gone into his study.*

*"Mommy, please wake up! Please wake up!" I cried kneeling beside her and trying to shake her.*

*My brother Pan came out of his room and looked at me.*

*"Please help Mommy!"*

*Looking bored and uninterested, he went back into his room and slammed the door as I sobbed and begged for him to help.*

*Mom didn't seem to be moving. I put my head on her chest. I could hear the thump, thump of her heart. I didn't know how long I lay there listening. Soon, I heard sirens, and the doorbell rang. My dad answered it.*

*"Sir, we got a 9-1-1 call."*

*"Yes, I'm glad you came. My wife fell down the stairs. I've been beside myself," he lied.*

*"That isn't what happened!" I looked at my dad and the EMTs who were entering the house, looking as if they trusted my dad's words and ignored mine. Didn't they believe what I had said on the phone? Two men and a woman dressed in scrubs took my mom away on a stretcher. That was the last time my mom was in the house. After that, my mom didn't live with us anymore.*

*"Mommy, come back!" I screamed as the dream faded. "Mommy, please! I need you!"*

I heard a chuckle. "Mommy, Mommy," I heard Claudio's mocking tone.

*Oh no.* I was still in that stupid box. At that moment, I felt certain that if my mother knew what I was going through, she'd save me. She had loved me back then. She couldn't have stopped loving me. There had to be a reason she didn't come back for me. As I continued thinking about her, the doubts started back in.

# CHAPTER 7

Another sunrise came, and then another sunset. While I was awake, I heard more voices, a lot more—girls and boys. Some sounded timid. Some were bullies. Some came across as firm and strong, but it was hard to make out more than just an impression of what they were like. I occasionally heard Jason. He offered to do extra chores if only Claudio would release me from the box. Every now and then, Santana would come by and throw insults at the box, like, "So, Stinky's still sleeping in the coffin. Maybe we should take her down to the stream and throw her remains in to float away so the air, here, will be more breathable."

I heard a lot of comments from Claudio and people in charge about, "The customer is waiting for the product, and you are behind schedule."

*Are we slave labor*? I wondered. I had been without water outside of those two drinks for at least two, maybe three, days. I hoped I lived long enough to thank Emily for the water. It was clear those Klingons running the camp didn't care if I lived or died. Maybe my dad was eager to get rid of the kid he hated and just wanted to stick with his evil clone. At least, that's how I saw my brother. Pan had to know what had happened to me. He was probably backing up whatever my dad was saying about me to explain my absence.

---

That night, very late I was, again, awakened as the box was opened and someone reached in to give me more water. The person's skin still smelled like lemons. *How does someone smell like lemons out here on the far side of hell?* I still couldn't detect whether my water-bearer was male or female, but it had to be Emily.

"Thank you," I whispered.

Instead of berries, bread was placed against my lips. I didn't normally eat bread, but I was hungry, really hungry and so I ate just a little. It wasn't an allergy thing. Weird. I was starving, and still, I reflected on my concerns about glyphosate. In the U.S., even organic grains contained glyphosate, a poison that was slowly killing the population. The time without food had also depressed my appetite, and I felt as if I might throw up if I ate more, especially more bread. I shook my head against it. The hand gave me more water.

---

The next morning, I was released. Claudio opened the box, cut my ties, poured a bucket of soapy water over me, threw me some underwear, slacks and a red t-shirt and said, "Get dressed. It's time to get acquainted with the other counselors."

*Counselors from Hades*, I figured. I was surprised they didn't call them "professors" or "saints," given that, from their conversations, I gathered they equated torture with kindness or education. I had trouble moving. Claudio pushed over the box, and I slid out. Though I was muddy now, I moved on all fours, sliding behind a tree to put on my clothes and to try to block Claudio's view of me as much as possible. Even the thought that Claudio had touched me while I was naked was enough to make me nauseous. I was sick enough already and didn't want to get any sicker. I certainly didn't want to throw up all over myself again.

It wasn't easy to put on the clothes. My hands and legs didn't want to move. I felt rigid. The days of inertia had made it seem as if someone had injected a paralyzer into my limbs. I forced myself to rise up, brushing off some of the mud and struggling to put on the outfit on while wondering if I would ever get my flexibility back.

As I pulled my slacks into position, Claudio grabbed my right arm and dragged me across the campsite to where two middle-aged guys were sitting in camping chairs and drinking beer.

"Meet Hinter and Marco," he said, pointing to the two. Joe, the burley guy who had kidnapped me, wasn't there.

"Is there another one? A female? Aren't organizations like this required to have female counselors?" I asked.

"Oh, Nancy comes here once a week. So, we're covered. We are required to have a female counselor here, and we do."

"And the guy with the taser?"

"Oh, you mean Joe. He's just a transporter, a bounty hunter. Don't worry about missing out on the taser experience. We've got plenty here."

"Wonderful."

"Now, if you are a good girl," he said suggestively, "You can earn privileges." Claudio emphasized the word "privileges."

"I've already been to D.C. So, I'm not interested in those kinds of privileges," I countered, thinking about how slutty Amy had sounded.

"So, you want to stay here with us. We could use a pretty like you." Claudio chuckled, touching my face.

I backed away. "I want to call my dad."

He handed me my cell back. I looked. The back was missing along with the battery. "This phone is electronically-challenged," I commented. Lame reaction, I knew. But what do you say to a battery-less phone? "How many other teens are here?"

"About twenty, right now. All industrious. Nobody slacks off here. Idle hands, you know."

"I didn't realize that this was a religious camp."

"Christian."

"I see." *Different kind of Christianity than I am used to.*

I looked around, hoping to figure out an escape path. We were in an area covered by large trees. There was a large picnic table with attached benches near where the counselors sat. To my left on the other side of the picnic table, I could see logs set inside a circle of stones, maybe for a campfire. A little ways in front and to the right was a big pit, maybe about four feet below ground level, with tapered sides to allow people to walk down into it. The thought of stoning the counselors and throwing them into the pit came to mind—though I had never even considered resorting to violence before.

Behind me, between where I had been in the box and where I was standing, was a very large tent that looked like it held supplies. I wondered if any working cell phones were in there. There was another large tent about twenty-five feet away to my left with purple patches. About fifteen feet beyond it I could see part of a smaller red-patched tent. Forward and to my left, about twenty feet across from the purple-patched tent, was a similarly-sized red-patched tent.

Further to my right than pit but more directly to my side was an eight to twelve person tent, perhaps a twenty-person tent, with the door facing away but the blue patches were visible. Beyond the pit and the blue tent, I could see the edges of smaller tents, maybe private ones, with gold patches on them. I suspected these were for the counselors. I wondered if I could just get away by just running past the tents. I now had a real heart-felt goal in life: to get away from here at the first opportunity.

Claudio grabbed my arm again. "I'll introduce you to some of the other teens." Being touched by him made me feel dirtier than I already felt. I tried to pull away, but he clasped tighter. He escorted me around the blue tent to a table where eight teens were working, cutting white powdery substances and putting them into capsules and then baggies, assembly-line style.

The occupants were wearing a variety of shirt colors: red, blue and purple. I was wearing a red shirt and wondered about the significance of the color scheme and whether they related to tent assignments.

"Are you guys working for the cartel or a pharmaceutical company?" I asked.

"Is there any difference?" I recognized Santana's voice. There were four boys and two other girls at the table.

"At this camp, we earn our keep. We get different contracts that require filling," Claudio said.

"Is this stuff cocaine or heroin?" I inquired, as the white chalky substance that was being cut puffed out into a powdery mist.

"We don't ask questions here," Claudio responded. "There is also no talking without permission."

"I see. Just so long as we don't wind up like Barry Seal," I noted.

Santana fixedly stared at the product as if he had lost interest in the conversation.

"You know, the CIA pilot who was running drugs. Didn't wind up so well for him," I added.

Santana chuckled. "The smelly princess has got spunk."

I glared at him. I thought about responding but then realized he wasn't worthy of any attention, whatsoever, from me.

"I saw that movie," Claudio said. I had seen it too. In fact, I had watched almost all of Tom Cruise's movies, not because I approved of the way he treated his wives, but because his movies were really good, or at least the ones that weren't just plain weird. Claudio's comment was followed by laughter from the group.

I looked at Santana as I pretended to look at the guy next to him. My observation confirmed my suspicion about Santana's age. He looked maybe a year or two older than me. He had dark hair, cut sort of Aladdin-style, dark eyes, an olive complexion and a face that could have come out of a Latin romance film or telenovela. He reminded me of those cute guys who were so in love with themselves that it was best to stay three football fields away from them. *Typical*, I thought. *Obnoxious guys are always the best lookers*. He was wearing a purple shirt.

"Hey, hottie, any chance for a date?" Santana chimed in. "I can show you a camp like no other you've seen." The attitude was so irritating. One thing for certain: he was the kind of guy I didn't ever, I mean ever, want to get to know.

"I am not 'hottie' or 'princess.' You must have come from the egotist fraternity. Maybe Skull and Bones?"

"I'm sure I'd be a legacy—if I ever make it to college, which is somewhat doubtful at this point." He looked at Claudio.

"Santana, lay off her," a guy wearing a red shirt with a smiley face handcrafted onto it said. I recognized his voice as Jason's. "She's been through enough of a nightmare. She doesn't need any of your baggage." Jason was nice-looking, blonde-haired, blue-eyed and fair-complected. I had never been into blonde guys, but I certainly liked him a lot better than Santana, and I had to admit, he was really good-looking.

"Now, chit-chat time is over," Claudio interjected.

One of the girls, appearing more like a pre-teen than a teen, was starting to tear up. She wiped her eyes with the back of her hand. The girl had a slight build, wavy chestnut-colored hair that fell below her shoulders, a very pretty face and large blue eyes that were red from crying, I assumed.

"Are you okay?" I asked her.

She looked up at me.

"Emily, don't answer. I said 'chit-chat time is over.'" Claudio advised her. He turned to me. "You'll be sharing a tent with Emily, Ariel, Hillary and Sonja. Hillary is your tent leader, and you will follow her instructions."

"Because Amy, who used to be in your tent, has graduated to the real nightmare." Santana crowed out. It wasn't hard to read him. He reminded me of a slimy, macho type. *Did I hear something about his dad being a congressman? Figures.* Most politicians I knew had their heads in the gutter. Their sons tended to be spoiled brats. And it looked like Santana was in the running to join the bottom of the barrel. I wondered if we had met at a function in D.C. My dad had too often ordered me to attend such events to build his image. They were events of the rich and famous where various members of Congress pretended to be regular guys while sipping champagne and eating caviar. They also brought their children to show off what wonderful family people they were. In public, I was my dad's trophy—at least until my relationship with Matt blew up. The faces of the celebrities and their children seemed to blend into a blur. I never cared to get to know any of them. Right now, my head was so cloudy, it was hard to think. There were four hundred and thirty-five members in the House. Who was Santana's father?

"I said, 'Shut it!' Or do you want another necktie?"

Santana glared at Claudio but didn't respond.

Claudio turned to me. "Princess, we have other work for you."

I silently grimaced, not in the mood to argue about my name any further at the moment.

Claudio took me around the back of the blue tent and closer to the supply tent where another girl was lifting boxes from the ground and putting them into a truck bed. I thought about the possibility of stealing the truck. I wish I had taken Automotive 101 instead of College Prep and found someone in the class to teach me to hotwire a truck. Pre-calc turned out to be a bust. If I hadn't been in pre-calc, I wouldn't even be here—maybe. On the other hand, even if I had aced pre-calc, I still might have been punished over the break-up.

"Summer, Ariel," he introduced me to the girl loading the truck.

"Hi," I said to her.

"Hi."

"Enough conversation. Now get to work." One word was apparently enough conversation.

I assumed "back to work" meant following Ariel's lead in putting the boxes in the truck.

"Ariel, you need to grab the last box from the culinary supply tent," he instructed. She went to the large tent. As she opened the side panel, it looked as if it had more than cooking supplies. "Princess, start picking up boxes and putting them into the bed. Laziness will not be tolerated."

I picked up a box. It was heavy, as if it had bricks or lead weights inside.

"Put it down gently," he instructed.

After Ariel rejoined me at the truck, Claudio watched for about five more minutes and then went back towards the drug or whatever table I had just been at.

After putting one of the boxes in the truck bed, I moved towards the passenger compartment. The keys were not in the ignition. *Darn.* That didn't mean they weren't in the truck.

"Hey, no slacking off!" Claudio yelled at me, apparently still watching us.

As we continued, Hinter got into the truck. Claudio went to one of the tents and yelled, "It's time. Better get out here, or you're back on kitchen duty."

A female that I assumed was Amy, walked around from the other side of the supply tent. Unlike me, she had apparently had a real shower or bath and was well made up with a dress and heels. Claudio escorted her to the passenger side of the truck. "Now behave or you'll wind up back here and it won't be so pleasant next time."

"Won't she be able to get help in D.C.?" I whispered to Ariel.

At first, she didn't answer. She watched Claudio, who seemed distracted. "She's a scholarship from CPS. It's better than the streets of Miami," she whispered back.

So, it was a camp for rich kids and CPS scholarship sex dolls. What a wonderful place. If the public knew what my dad had gotten me into, that would be the end of his career. Or so I could hope. That thought was the most pleasant thing that had happened to me since I got here.

"Princess, focus!" Claudio yelled at me.

"These don't feel like pharmaceuticals," I whispered to Ariel.

"Be careful," She whispered back. "Pharmaceuticals are the least dangerous of the things we are putting together."

"Is the government okay with this?"

"If they monitored us or objected, we'd be closed down," she replied, almost under her breath.

"No talking!" Claudio shouted.

I continued lifting and trying to look industrious. Why was I looking industrious? Here I was in a place I didn't want to be with men who rivaled Darth Vader for Evil Lunatic of the Year. Maybe worse because Luke did turn Vader back to the Light side of the Force, and that was unlikely to happen here. I had only seen the first six *Star Wars* movies on the web and didn't know what happened in the Disney versions, which my friends said were awful.

"Faster," Hinter said. "I've got to get this shipment and *the package* going." I took it Amy was "the package." Suddenly, I felt a sharp pain on my back, and I almost collapsed.

Claudio was standing nearby, swinging a chain like a whip. He looked like he was about to strike me with it again. "Consequences for slowdown. Next time, all work and no talk."

I hurt, but I moved faster, wanting to keep my body from being destroyed any further than it had been over the last few days. I was very weak, but I somehow had a surprising amount of energy for my condition. *Determination to survive,* I told myself.

After Hinter and Amy left with the boxes, we were pushed to the cooking area where what looked like rye was being boiled. We were told to drain the contents and blot them when whatever it was was finished and to "be very careful."

"Lunch?" I asked.

"I wouldn't eat it," Claudio responded.

I had taken chemistry, and I had an idea of what we might be creating. "Are we working with MKUltra?"

A slap across my face told me that questions were to be reserved for never. *Boy, would my dad be in trouble if this got out.* The thought of getting out the word gave me a reason to survive.

Ariel looked really nervous and visibly tried not to touch the mixture.

After that, we were told to throw burgers onto the fire. "I don't eat meat or bread," I said.

"Then I guess you will starve," Claudio replied. "I think I told you to cook."

"I'm fine with cooking tonight," Jason said, coming up towards the grill with Santana.

"You've already got an assignment and you are not supposed to wander off on your own."

"Just trying to help," he said. "I was taking a potty break and Santana was acting as my buddy."

"I instructed Summer to throw on the burgers. That's her job. Now get to it," Claudio said.

Under Claudio's direction, I threw some burgers on the stove. They weren't particularly cold and smelled off, like maybe he had forgotten to refrigerate the burgers when he got them a month before. I was hungry, but there was no way I was eating that stuff. I got lucky. I was told to make some mashed potatoes. I skipped using milk as I didn't like that either.

After days of almost no food, the spoonfuls of potatoes I got for lunch had never tasted so good. I was limited to three spoonfuls, but they gave me energy and I hoped that maybe, with enough energy, I could find a way out.

"The princess has an attitude," Santana said. "Oh right, you don't like being called 'princess.' How about 'Up' for 'Stuck Up?'"

"Leave her alone," Jason told him.

"Whoa, Up has made a conquest," Santana responded.

Santana and I were not just not going to be friends. We were now mortal enemies for life. "Oh, and I'll call you 'Bad Santa.' No 'Dimwit Santa.'"

Jason laughed. I heard some other snickers from a couple of the guys I hadn't realized were watching.

"I'll second that," a boy with a blue shirt announced. That got him a thumbs-up from a couple of the other blue shirts. He was blonde with cold grey eyes and an air of superiority in the way he held himself as he looked at me and Emily.

---

That evening, I chose to continue starving, except for a carrot and a hamburger bun, which I reluctantly ate. I wasn't sure if the glyphosate would do more damage than starvation, but what little food I had had wasn't enough to give me much energy.

Among the male reds were a boy named John and another named Charlie. I got the impression they were close friends. John gave me his carrot. I smiled at him, hoping that that wasn't against some rule and not wanting to call attention to it. I snapped it up and offered him my meat that I wasn't going to eat. He watched Claudio and Marco and carefully took it. I didn't think either of them were paying attention to the exchange.

"Now for the entertainment," Marco announced. A less than pleasant look went through the group of twenty or more teens. Charlie and John looked nervously at each other.

"Hey, Dimwit. No, evil Santa, ya got some Christmas presents for me?" the blonde-blue camper, who had seconded me, asked.

"Yeah. When I find a guillotine, I'll make sure you're the first to enjoy it."

"You two just volunteered. Santana and Ian, into the pit"

"Woo," Santana said. "I didn't volunteer for anything."

"Afraid?" Ian asked.

"No, I just like to fight with real men," Santana shot back.

The pit was about ten feet from the fire. Santana hesitated and Marco pushed him into it. Ian seemed more willing. As they got down into the pit, I could see why Ian was so eager. He pulled a knife out from behind his back.

"He's got a knife," I notified Marco. I didn't like Santana, but my belief in fairness overrode my disgust for him. From the look in Ian's eyes, I had a feeling Santana was likely to be leaving horizontally.

# CHAPTER 8

"Clever. I'll have to count the knives after KP duty from now on," Marco casually commented.

"Aren't you going to take it away from him or punish him?" I asked.

Everyone laughed.

"Worried about me, Up? I'll win this one for you."

"Not in this lifetime," Ian said sharply. Ian lunged at Santana with his knife in his right hand, but Santana dodged to the side and kicked that hand. Ian didn't lose the knife but sliced into Santana's shoe. They started to come at each other again, Ian watching more carefully for another dodge to the side. Instead, Santana went for the ground, rolled onto his back with his head towards Ian and kicked Ian off balance as he grabbed Ian's legs and threw him forward. Santana's move was very fast, as if he had taken some previous training.

Ian managed to cut into Santana's left leg before dropping the knife as Ian fell onto his head. Ian seemed somewhat dazed from hitting his head. Santana was on his feet, limping. He kicked the knife away and then kicked Ian in the head. Santana picked up the knife.

"Use it!" one of the other male campers taunted.

Santana looked at me.

"He broke the rules. What you going to do about it, Santana?" Marco yelled. Was this a push to get him to use the knife on Ian? Santana threw the knife up to the top of the pit and stood with his fists out. Ian got up, Santana kicked him down again, then did a secondary kick and climbed out of the pit.

"I didn't say you were done," Marco admonished him.

"I won. It's over."

"It's not over until I say it's over," Marco said.

Santana stood at the top of the pit. "I'm not a killer or a torturer. That's for you and Claudio."

Marco picked up a chain and swung it, knocking Santana back into the pit. Ian, who had come up from the pit, jumped on Santana and started slugging him. Santana seemed to go unconscious.

I didn't care that Santana was a creep. Marco had no right to do this to him. "Stop! This is inhuman! My dad is my governor's chief of staff, and he will close down this place and have you charged if you don't stop torturing people."

"Would you rather be down there? I think that could be arranged."

"F—you," I replied.

Marco swung the chain at me, but I dodged out of its way. "Ned, Don!" Marco called. Before I knew what was happening one of the male teens grabbed me and another hit me in the stomach with a branch. I fell to the ground.

Jason rushed to me, blocking the other two from harming me further. I had a protector. In an instant, the chain was swung at him and then again, first hitting his chest and then his face.

"My God. Stop! You're insane!" I screamed.

I saw a seemingly unconscious Santana being dragged up from the pit. Everyone seemed to be looking back and forth between me, Jason and Marco, and I don't think they detected Santana opening one eye and winking at me.

---

I needed to be careful. These Gulag camp operators were very unstable.

In my tent, Hillary was the only girl wearing a blue shirt. She came in briefly and then left and could be heard joking with Marco. Ariel and Emily were more or less quiet. Sonja was more talkative.

"You're new here. So, I'll tell you how to survive," Sonja said. "First, don't question the counselors. Don't defend anyone else. They really hate that, and they'll whop both of you harder if you interfere. You are better off playing up to the counselors. I figure playing up to these slimes is no worse than saddling up to some chief executive who sticks his Cubans into interns. At least, playing up to these guys might get us our freedom."

"Like Amy?"

"Amy is out of here."

"I'd rather die than give that to the counselors or some freakin' senator."

"It's not so bad. You're a virgin?"

"And I'm planning to stay that way."

"Then maybe you should be more like Emily or Ariel. They are quiet and do what they are told. But neither of them will get out of here before their time is up." She looked at them. They were both quiet.

"What about escape?"

"Don't ever say that word," Ariel interjected. "If they even suspect you are thinking of escaping, they will subject you to a lot worse than those three days in a box."

"I was there for three days?"

"I think. Time is hard to judge in this place," Sonja related. "I can't remember how long it's been since my all too wealthy father forked over the funds to have me kidnapped to this place."

"You were kidnapped, too?"

"Most of us were. Parents who pay the goons to take us here don't have the guts to do it in person."

"You're also from a well-to-do family. So, you aren't a scholarship, right?" I asked her.

"No. But I'm not a virgin, either. Didn't you ever have a boyfriend? You're pretty enough."

"He's the reason I'm here. He broke up with me after two years, right before an exam."

"That's what brings a lot of kids here. Undesirable friends. Bad grades. They embarrass their parents."

"I think my dad was more angry that he lost a future son-in-law from a top Wall Street family than that I blew an exam."

"Sounds as jerkish as my dad. Is he ambitious, planning to run for office, looking for contributions?"

"You too?"

"No. My dad is a big stockbroker. I'm supposed to go to Yale and marry some future Skull and Bones President, be happy and be the next Hillary Clinton. I'd rather create a dart board with her picture on it."

"What is it with these fathers? Mine is expecting the Governor he's working for to endorse him for Lieutenant Governor and he is looking for an inside financial edge. Nothing like a little money to buy his way into office."

"And the solution was to get you to marry Mr. Right and Wealthy; forget that he's not someone you would ever choose to marry on your own."

I nodded.

"The camp promoters probably told your dad they'd send him back a Stepford daughter. The school psychologists sell it as a place of reflection, learning and positive obedience training. Kind of like where you send your dog and get back a well-behaved animal."

"Do the school psychologists know what really happens here?"

"Some of them. But there are kickbacks. Destroy-a-kid-for-a-five-thousand-dollar bonus. Most counselors are so desperate for the extra funds that they'd gladly send kids to a place like this. I'm sure mine received a huge bonus. She convinced my parents that this was like college prep and would assist me in getting into the top universities."

"Ouch. What a bitch. She deserves a life sentence in this camp," I said. "Are there any books?"

"You kidding? I don't even think the counselors can read."

"If the bonuses are in the thousands, how much do these camps cost?"

"Twenty to thirty thousand at the low end. One to two hundred thousand dollars is common," Sonja continued. "I've heard of some parents paying a lot more."

"Judging from the egos in this camp, I'd guess that most here are in the one-to-two hundred thousand dollar or more category. And the CPS scholarships?"

"Nobodies. They won't be missed. CPS is already getting one-hundred and fifty thousand a year from HHS for every kid they snatch from parents. They place kids here so they won't have to deal with them while the one-fifty K just keeps rolling in."

"And taxpayers foot the bill."

"It's a win for CPS—even if not for the little girls and boys. The Washington beat has more perks than twenty-five dollars on a street corner. So, Amy is one of the lucky ones."

"Little girls and boys? Everyone I've seen is a teen, I think."

"They have some sites for the younger ones. I was required to run an errand over to one of them. The kids were really young."

"Are we talking about pedophilia?"

"Fancy word, but it fits."

"So, they are having sex with kids, even young kids?"

"No better way to prepare them to be the next Monica Lewinski or whatever. And some are sent to that Island."

"What do they expect of us non-scholarships?"

"Obedience and submission. Worshipping the counselors will get you points. If we make it to Washington, we'll have higher status because our parents will use their influence to get us good positions. Nobody who leaves here leaves whole. Sometimes it's best to play the game and tell yourself it's like a job or a class that you just have to do to get on with your life. If you fight it, they'll break you. Give yourself the task of getting the hell out. Would I sleep with all those creepy counselors to get out? Yes."

"Well, I'm going to find another way out."

"Best of luck." Footsteps could be heard approaching. She raised her voice a little. "And you will find yourself acclimating to the place. It's not so bad when you get used to it."

The flap opened and Hillary stuck her head in. "No talking in the tent. Or I'll have to report you to Marco." I made a motion of zipping my mouth. As she turned to close the tent, Sonja whispered. "No talking in the presence of the acknowledged tent snitch."

Hillary returned. "If anyone has to pee in the middle of the night, don't. I am required to accompany anyone leaving for those purposes and I don't like being woken up." I heard something that sounded like a lock being placed over the zipper from the outside.

"They lock us in?"

"For our safety, the tents are locked every night. We were cut some slack the last couple of nights, but that's over."

***

As I drifted off, I saw my dad yelling at me.

*"You little tramp. I heard you and Matt broke up."*

*I had to make it turn out different this time. I lied. "He said his dad had decided not to help you. That's why I broke up with him. Besides, my new boyfriend is from a much richer family."*

*My dad relaxed some. "You better be telling me the truth. If I find you've lied—"*

*"Here, I stand up for you and find a better way to help you and this is what I get? Next time, I'll stand by the guy who is screwing you over."*

*"Watch your mouth."*

*"Sorry, Daddy. A little faith would help. Haven't I always tried to be a good daughter?"*

*No kidnapping. No camp. I saw myself at a yacht party with Shannon and Tiffany. Santana was there. "How did you get here?" I asked him.*

*"You wouldn't come to me. So, I had to escape and come to you."*

*"Escape?" I reached out towards him, but what I felt was my sleeping bag and the cold air.* It hadn't worked out that way. It was just a dream.

The next morning, we were forced up at dawn. We were told to run down the hill, two at a time, to the stream and back to the campsite ten times. It was a tough run. I looked around as I ran. I could see, in the distance, among the hills, areas where the trees thinned out dramatically. I had done track in school, but nothing this strenuous. I tried to rest my third time down the hill, sitting on a large stone, partially in the stream. I reached down, cupping my hand to take a drink. Marco was nearby, watching. He picked up a fist-sized stone and smashed my right hand with it. The pain almost made me dizzy again. I looked. It was at least bruised, maybe sprained. I couldn't be sure that I didn't have broken fingers.

"Now get going. No slacking."

I started running back up again and noticed Ariel, collapsed on the trail. I tried to help her up. Marco came up behind me and knocked me away, causing me to fall against a tree.

"You think you can just lie there?" he asked Ariel. He wrapped a rope around her wrists and dragged her up the hill through brush, stickers, and rocks. Her screams were anguished.

I got up and ran up the hill. I paused and watched as they almost reached the camp. He looked at me. "You want this same treatment, or are you going to keep running?"

I went back down, half still focusing on them. He dragged her back down towards the stream as I ran up again. She didn't look conscious at that point. On my way down, I saw them on their way back up. She was awake and being pulled roughly by him.

On the side of the hill was a gorge. He dragged her over to the edge of the gorge, removed the rope from her wrists and wrapped it around her ankles. Then, he shoved her off and hung her from the cliff with only the rope tied to her ankles, keeping her from falling. Her screams filled the air.

# CHAPTER 9

As I watched, Claudio came up behind me and saw me watching Marco and Ariel. "You're new. We're cutting you some slack."

"Is that what you call it?"

"Don't mouth off to me or you will lose your advantage. Now, get going or you'll be hanging next to Ariel and I can't promise I won't accidentally let go." I continued on my way. I was exhausted and thirsty, but I didn't dare even stop for a drink from the stream along the way. I knew if I tried to drink, I might meet a fate worse than Ariel's.

---

At breakfast, several of us were singled out for dieting. Apparently, we didn't run fast enough. Those included me, Emily and Ariel. We were also denied water, though, after that run, I'm sure the others were as thirsty as I was. Were we being Stockholmed? Why hadn't we ignored the counselors and drunk from the stream, ignoring the threat? Would they dare kill all three of us?

Jason looked at me and decided not to eat. Another boy, Jamie, a blue boy who was quiet in contrast to guys like Santana, Ian, and Ian's groupies, decided to skip his meal also. I recalled that Jamie had also been admonished while I was in the box. He looked sympathetically at me.

"You guys are boycotting breakfast?" Claudio asked. "Very well then, don't expect lunch either."

---

After breakfast, I was ordered to go with go with Santana to check the traps.

"Traps?"

"For food. Who knows? You may be able to dine on a gourmet rat, Up," Santana said.

"Up yours."

"Oh, that's right. You're a vegan. Maybe we will find some nice juicy twigs."

"No talking," Claudio admonished.

"Aye, aye, Captain," Santana responded, saluting. "Besides, she hates me. Ian would probably be a better conversationalist."

"Get moving."

"I'm pretty good at checking the traps. Maybe I could switch with Santana," Jason suggested.

"Why would I send you?"

"Santana's been a real jerk to Summer." He turned to Santana "Sorry, Santana, but you have." He turned back to Claudio. "He's the last person you should send with her."

"That's precisely why I'm sending him with her," Claudio clarified.

This reminded me of a teacher at my elementary school who used to be really nice to the school bullies and awful to the shy students. It was almost as if she got a sick pleasure from watching the shy kids suffer. Except here, they even encouraged violence.

If I went with Santana, would they even expect me to come back alive? I looked at the guy who tried to save me. Jason was the tallest of the male campers, and the more I looked at him, the better-looking he seemed to get. The smiley face drawn onto his shirt was perhaps the friendliest thing I'd seen since I'd been here. The idea of him being my would-be protector was kind of endearing.

Santana and I walked higher up the hill for about half a mile. "Why are the traps so far away?" I whispered, wondering if we had been followed.

Santana talked quietly, though we were likely out of earshot. "To get the animals that are afraid to come close to camp."

I knew that if I tried to discuss animal rights, it would be wasted on this brainless wonder. "Is your dad a hunter?"

"He's a Democrat. If he is, it's top secret. It's too much work for him. He'd rather hire someone else to assassinate the animals." I got that he was making fun of my diet.

"Which congressman is he?"

"Congressman Barilla, from the Los Angeles area."

"I think I've met him."

"I met you once. It was a couple of years ago. You were hanging out with some Wall Street legacy."

"Matt. He's the reason I'm here."

"Oh?"

"Long story. Not that it's any of your business."

"Does that mean you're available?'

"Not to you. I do have standards."

"Don't like Latinos?"

"Don't like male chauvinist pigs."

"Woo. Did you learn that term from your mom?"

"Leave my mom out of this."

"How does she feel about your being here?"

"If she cares enough to find out what my dad sentenced me to, she might know I'm here. If she cares." *Why did I open up to this lowlife?* I felt my face go red, thinking of the ammo I had given the creep.

His response surprised me. "I'm sorry. My parents are split up, too. I'm the rebel in the family he couldn't tame. If I had gotten my way, I would have taken off to Venezuela or Cuba."

"Why Venezuela or Cuba?"

"Because my dad hates them. He's from Cuba and he constantly touts the propaganda about how those evil communists destroyed freedom. I guess this is freedom to him."

"Yeah. And I suppose he's chummy with the oil execs who want to overthrow the legitimately elected Venezuelan government for the country's oil?"

"Right. Wow, someone who actually knows what is going on over there."

"I'm a big fan of Jimmy Carter, who said Venezuela has the best election system in the world. In other words, its government is the most legitimate."

He looked at me and gave me a thumbs-up.

"Besides, my dad wants to go to war with Venezuela, too. His former boss made too much money from her husband's war profiteer business."

"As one non-brainwashed-from-birth protégé to another, welcome to camp terror." He held out his palm. "Truce?"

"Maybe," I said hesitantly as I high-fived him. "So, how do we get out of 'Camp Terror?'"

"I'm working on that."

"Know how to hotwire a truck?"

"Actually, yes. "

I gave him a surprised look.

"That's why my dad sent me here. My number one specialty was always getting into trouble, and I was in detention half of my life. I got good at bypassing security systems so I could keep getting out of the mansion. My dad kept having the police pick me up and bring me home in lieu of jail and then paying them to keep it quiet. If I had been poor and Black, I'd be dead."

"The police are using Latinos for target practice, too."

"Not rich Latinos. Besides, I've got a get-out-of-jail-free card. Congressional legacy privilege."

"So, you think you could steal their truck?"

"They remove the battery when they aren't attending it for any length of time. But if we could find another vehicle—"

"First, we have to figure out where we are. Or do you have any idea? We are both from California. Could we still be there?"

"California has regulations on boot camps. If this is California, they'd be in trouble."

"Ricardo Lara was the one who got through that legislation, right?"

"So, you knew about the camps before you came here?"

"Some. I didn't really pay enough attention. Didn't think I'd wind up in one."

"Surprise," Santana announced, holding his palms up and out.

"I mainly remember the bill because my dad, the guy who sent me here, made a big deal out of supporting the legislation to regulate them. It was all a show, just like everything else about him."

"My dad showed up for the press release when the legislation was signed. Most of these camps are located in Utah. There have been some in California, but—"

"But?" I asked.

"With what I've seen here, I can't believe they would do this shit in California."

"What you've seen? You are making pharmaceuticals, right?"

"Among other things. We basically do whatever work the camp director contracts for."

"Which one is the director?"

"I don't think you've met him. His name is Evan. He only comes around once in a while to check up on us. He has other camps."

"Like the little kids' camps?"

"You heard about that?"

"Does this have something to do with child sex trafficking? Like the stuff WikiLeaks was talking about?"

"What do you think?" Kind of an affirmation.

The very thought made me sick. I promised myself to uncover the full story. "What other things are you making here?"

"Like things that they would kill to keep quiet."

"Not us."

"Don't be so sure. They could say we ran away, and perhaps someday a body would turn up in some other location."

"What if the authorities were told about this camp?"

"Why do you think Congress won't follow through with regulating them? There was bi-partisan legislation long ago sponsored by George

Miller and others, but there is a reason it never passed the Senate to reach the President's desk, and I doubt any of our Presidents, then or now, would sign it anyway."

"Oh!" I screamed, seeing a fox caught in a trap. Its neck was snapped. "Poor thing." I felt sick. I tried not to let Santana see the tears that I was sure were rolling down my cheeks.

"Dinner," Santana said, pulling a sack off his shoulder, pushing apart the teeth of the trap to free the body and then feeling the tummy. "This one was pregnant."

"That's terrible."

Santana didn't say anything as he bagged it. "At this camp, there is no place for picky eaters. You'll starve."

"At least I'll be able to live with myself. There is no way I'm eating a pregnant fox."

Suddenly, I was really nauseous. Santana tried to reach out to me, but I ran up the hill. In the distance, I heard dogs barking. I ran in the direction of the barking.

"Wait!" Santana yelled. "You can't."

But I wasn't listening further. Suddenly, my head felt like it had been slit open. I collapsed.

I felt myself being carried. I couldn't focus on anything but the pain. Finally, Santana sat me down not far from the trap.

"They have frequency barriers. If you go past a border, it will knock you flat."

"So that's how they keep campers here."

"It's a good thing the truck didn't have any keys yesterday. It might have killed you trying to take off."

"You saw me checking it out?"

He smiled.

"So, we're trapped? There has to be a way."

He reached into his pocket and handed me a couple of skin-colored little somethings. "Ear plugs. You can still hear, but they jam out the dangerous frequencies."

"And you got them how?"

"A friend of mine saw a box of them and stole quite a few pairs."

"Thank you. But don't expect me to go overboard over some earplugs."

"Sí. You aren't that kind of girl. I figured that out days ago. Another thing: when we get back to the camp, we have to keep being unfriends, or they won't trust us to not talk to each other."

"That will be easy, Evil Santa," I said, holding back a smile.

"Up."

"Can't you think of a better nickname for me?"

"Snooty."

"Great," I said, facetiously. I still didn't like him, but I could use an ally if I was to escape—unless he was setting me up. I had no reason to trust him.

As we turned back, I couldn't stop thinking about the fox. My mind drifted to the little kids in the other camp that I'd never met. It was bad enough that I was here— but little kids.

"No!" I reacted as my foot snagged on a root sticking out from a bush and I started to fall. I braced myself for the landing but was caught by a hand with a scent of lemon. I turned to Santana, "You? The water?"

"Shh," he said. "We wouldn't want the counselors to think I was soft on you, not to mention it is against the rules."

"You really are obnoxious. But underneath, thank you." I felt stunned in disbelief.

He smiled. "You're welcome. But remember, I'm obnoxious. That's who I am."

"Right."

In another trap, we found a squirrel. It reminded me of stories I had heard of hillbillies getting dementia from eating roadkill. I could wish that on the counselors.

He pulled some berries off a bush and handed them to me.

I looked at them. Gooseberries. Beautiful gooseberries. I was starving after days in a box and three spoonfuls of mashed potatoes. I didn't even care to find a place to wash them. I just started filling my mouth. They were the same berries he had fed me in the box.

"Thank you for the berries when I was in the box."

"Shh," he said, again. "Careful. Don't want to leave telltale signs on your red blouse."

I kept wiping my chin to stop the juice that was pouring down. "What do the shirt colors mean?"

"Red means you are a frosh and to be watched at all times. Pink means hot to trot. Blue means you can be trusted to do what the counselors demand, including beating up anyone who gets out of line."

"And purple?"

He looked at his purple shirt. "It means that they have hope of turning you from a red into a blue."

"I haven't seen any pink shirts or tents."

"They wind up in either the red, purple or blue tents. Amy was pink. She left."

"The fight. Does that happen a lot?"

"At times, I think they are grooming us for something. I've heard they groom kids at the kids' camp, too."

"Is there a lot of Stockholming going on?"

Santana laughed. "They call it acclimation."

---

When we arrived back at camp, we were told to set the fox and squirrel on the cooking table. "Go with Jason to the river for some water," Claudio instructed Santana.

"See you, Snooty," Santana said, mockingly.

"Break a leg on the way down, Evil Santa," I snarled back.

Claudio handed me a knife. I thought about using it on him. I guess that's what being tortured can do to a person. I noticed Marco watching.

"Slice off the heads of your catch. Not much left of the necks so that should be easy. Then skin them," Claudio instructed.

"F—you."

"What did you say?"

"No F—ing way."

"Oh, Duchess, not the right answer."

"Really? What are you going to do? My dad expects me back, without any marks on me. Governor Slick will be asking where I am."

"Not exactly. Your dad just received a letter from you, telling him how much you are learning at the prep camp."

"I didn't write a letter."

"Who said one? You also wrote one to Governor Slick asking for more funding for this camp and one to your mother, telling her that you were having a great time here."

"The handwriting won't match."

"Your dad gave us samples of your work to assist with your studies."

"My studies, like how to torture innocent girls and boys. I'm going back to my tent."

"I'm afraid not." He signaled behind me. I turned to look back. "Ian and Ned, put her in the box." I held out the knife and faced them.

Something hard clunked against my back. I turned towards Claudio, who was holding a branch. I still had the knife. From behind me, I felt hands reaching around me and grabbing at my hands. I tried to turn the knife as I managed to knock away one of the hands grabbing for the knife, but another hand from behind pulled it away. I went down backward and then was pulled up and knocked against the table.

When I lifted my head a little, I could see the dead eyes of the fox.

# CHAPTER 10

"Those clothes are too good for you," Claudio said. He directed Ned and Ian, "Don't tear them as you remove them. Help her sunbathe against that tree in the meadow."

I didn't look where Claudio pointed. I was too angry about the hands pulling me up from behind and trying to remove my clothes. I tried to fight my assailants. Matt hadn't even seen me naked and these disgusting creeps were going to get a show. I kicked and clawed and even bit. "You bastards!"

"Jared, help out the boys."

"Yes, sir."

Now, presumably, it was Jared and another boy removing my clothes from behind as the other two held my wrists and feet, only moving their hands to assist Jared and the other boy.

I started to cry. "Tears, princess?" Claudio asked. "Think of us as a medical staff, providing you with a much-needed treatment. After all, it is important to attend to your medical needs, like getting vitamin D from the sun."

"My dad will kill you when he finds out," I said. Though, I had no way to know if my dad would care. After all, he was ready to sell me out to Matt.

After removing my shirt, one of the boys behind me started to reach for my breast. I leaned my head down and bit his wrist as hard as I could.

"Ow, you bitch," a voice came from behind me. It sounded like Ned's.

"Feisty," came Ian's voice. "Can't wait until you assimilate."

"Never," I snapped.

"We'll see about that," Ian responded.

I was bound with duct tape to a tree, facing the sun. I felt violated, naked, dirty. I had refused to give myself to Matt or any other boy, refused to let any guy see me naked. I was waiting for the right time and somewhere deep inside of me, I always had been hoping to find the right guy, not Matt. It was a crazy hope that, despite my being forced into a relationship with Matt, some knight, some handsome hero, would come riding up on a beautiful stallion and rescue me from Matt and the boring life I feared I'd have with him. My heart ached, desiring to be pure and innocent when the real love of my life arrived. If I had spoken about that hope, my dad would have told me to get real. I held it inside, afraid to even daydream of it.

Now, I'd never get my purity back. Sure, I had worn scanty outfits and clothes at times, but those were clothes. My vitals were always covered. Here, they were visible for anyone to see. I felt I would never be clean again. The thought of being in the box naked rushed to my head, and I pushed it away—not wanting to think of the creep who may have already seen me naked.

The berries had helped with my thirst. But it was not long before I felt dehydrated. The afternoon dragged on. I knew I had to pretend to assimilate if I was to survive this, but I was not going to slice up animals. The fox had looked so beautiful, even when dead. They could kill me first. Someday, someone would ask my dad what happened to me, and there would be an inquiry. I knew they wouldn't dare touch my face. My dad would never allow that, but I was coming to terms with the fact that my dad had intentionally sent me here.

I thought back to the bill that was written by Ricardo Lara. I was young and I hadn't paid much attention to these behavior modification programs, but my dad was photographed with the group of leaders standing behind Lara and the Governor as it was signed into law. From what Santana said, his dad was there, too. Dad had shown off the picture. but I hadn't paid much attention. He had to know what was happening in these camps and what could happen to me here when he chose to send me. If they were regulated in California, I had to be elsewhere. *But where?*

One thing I knew for sure: if my mom got my real letter, she wouldn't believe the one they sent. When I wrote to my mom, I always signed my letters Spring, as I was really born in Spring, even though my parents chose Summer for my name. If the counselors didn't know that, if my dad hadn't told them, my mom would be instantly suspicious of their letter. Or maybe he had given them copies of letters I had written before to her. Letters that went unanswered. I generally had mailed them in a public mailbox but a few I had put out for the mailman at the house. Had he been home when I did so and able to steal those out of the mailbox? I had to remember.

I thought about my brother. He had always resented me for some reason. He was cold, emotionless, just like Dad. He'd probably wind up a wife-beater like Dad. I had read that ninety percent of abusive males were from abusive families and were following in their abusive fathers' footsteps. They saw power in the abuse and wanted to be like the powerful one in the family. It was much rarer for girls to follow that path. *No wonder my dad is so popular. A lot of men probably relate to Daddy-dearest.*

I thought about the expanding number of violent men. First, you had the abusers, then their sons and then their son's sons. It's a miracle any woman ever finds a non-abusive male. But I knew many had. Shannon's dad was really nice. So was Jimmy's. Jimmy himself was a great guy, always treating Shannon respectfully.

Seeing the violence in my parents' marriage, the last thing I wanted was to ever get married. At first, I liked Matt. Later, I dated him just to appease my dad. But I had thought Matt, at least, cared. Still, I always sensed that underneath was someone different than who he appeared to be on the surface. I was never forced to face who he really was until the email. What saddened me wasn't the breakup but losing a friend who never existed. The guy who wrote that email wasn't the Matt I thought I knew. But in a sense, there was still relief, relief that I didn't have to marry that guy. If only I hadn't wound up here.

And then, there was Santana, speaking viciously to me in public, but then risking a lot to help me survive when I was in the box. His explanation that he wouldn't be allowed near me if he were nice made sense. Or was he just a sleaze saying that to impress a potential conquest? Jamie and Jason were apparently not allowed alone with me because they had been nice to me in front of the counselors. Who was the real Santana: the nice guy or the one he portrayed for the counselors? He was cute, but Jason and Jamie were a lot nicer, and they were willing to stand up to Claudio for me. If I were to form a strong friendship with someone here, it was bound to be one of the nicer guys. If I had to trust someone to get my back, it would be one of those two.

I heard Santana return and start to ask about me. Marco silenced him with the whip for speaking without permission and then sent him back to the creek and then up the hill with Jamie to check for any additional catches. The blue campers were busy creating, I don't know what, on a nearby table. The other colors were working on the far side of the blue tent.

As the afternoon dragged on, I was so thirsty. My lips and my throat were dry. I felt very alone.

"You can't do this to her. She could die." Someone did seem to care. It was Jason.

He came toward me and started to undo the duct tape. A whip smacked against his back. He turned. Ian and Jared grabbed his hands. He fought, pulling away from them.

Marco pulled out a Taser and zapped him once, twice, then three times. Jason fell to the ground, at first shaking and then pretty much motionless.

"Bring him over here, boys," Marco said, pointing to an area in the middle of the clearing between the tree and the nearest tent. "Keep him there. Watch to make sure he doesn't get away." They watched, but Jason was barely moving. A few minutes later, Marco came back with a battery connected to a box that was attached to two cables.

"This is your doing, princess!" Marco spat at me. He placed a metal band around Jason's head and attached two cables between it and a device he attached to the box.

"Please, don't!" I tried to shout through my parched throat. "Please! He didn't free me. It was my fault. Not his. Please!"

Marco ignored me and flipped a switch on the box and moved a dial on it. Jason cried in pain. Marco cut the switch. Then he turned the dial and flipped the switch again.

"Stop! Please!" I begged. All this because Jason was kind to me. This really was my fault.

Again, Marco paused the torture and then flipped the switch, and Jason cried out again, this time louder, sounding more like a wounded animal than a human.

"Please! What do you want me to do? Ask it! Just stop!" I cried. Marco cut the electricity. I saw him move the dial.

"That's so sweet, princess, but you're the one who got him into trouble. You've been very bad for him. This is to help with his character development. He needs to learn proper behavior." He turned the dial as far as it would go and flipped the switch. Jason's body shook, but this time, he didn't cry out. Marco cut the switch and removed the headband. On Marco's instructions, Ian and Jared started to carry a limp Jason back towards the guys' red tent. Jared, who had the upper half of Jason's body, paused.

"Hey," Ian complained.

"I think he's dead," Jared said. "Look at his tongue and his eyes."

"Keep moving," Marco ordered. "Get him out of here."

# CHAPTER 11

Jason was hurt, maybe dead, because he tried to help me. If he was dead, could I ever forgive myself? He was so kind, so protective of me. I said a prayer that he would recover. I didn't know if there was a God up there. But I didn't want anyone dying or even being hurt because of me.

I sat there and cried, cried for Jason and cried for myself. I was so thirsty. Part of me felt I deserved to be punished for what had happened to Jason. It occurred to me that I might die. Maybe I deserved to die. I felt something against my cheek. It was a hand. It was reaching from behind the tree and smelled like lemons. A cup of water was pushed against my lips.

I looked towards the campground and didn't see any of the campers or counselors. "Thank you," I whispered.

"De Nada," came the reply. Then the hand was gone. I knew that if Claudio or Marco found out that Santana had helped me, he would receive some terrible punishment, maybe even be killed. He had told me to play the game. But I had seen and heard him resist, too. Despite my initial dislike for him, he continued helping me. Whatever happened, at least I had an ally, an ally who, like me, knew what it was like to be expected to be the perfect showpiece and who didn't like that life any better than I did. In this abyss, an ally could mean the difference between life and death.

At sundown, I expected them to release me. I had struggled against the duct tape with no luck. I was too weak. I could smell the food, but I knew I was S.O.L. when it came to dinner. I didn't want to eat that mother whose life had been cut short, anyway. I remembered the gooseberries and my mouth started to water. At least I wasn't going to get fat here. Dieters could do a promo for this place with more merit than what the counselors told Sonja's parents.

As the night dragged on, it started getting cold, very cold. I heard something scurrying around. I didn't want to think what kind of animals might come my way. I saw cat eyes. Was it a bobcat or a mountain lion? I couldn't tell in the dark. Was it rabid? Would it attack? No, it wandered off. Maybe it knew I wouldn't harm it, so it wouldn't harm me. Maybe it cared about the fox the way I did.

I heard Claudio yelling at someone. "His father is a chief executive in Beckco. Evan isn't going to be happy."

Then Marco's voice came a little lower. "He's not the first and Evan has dealt with it before. Remember Blake? Evan took care of that. Blake's father thinks he ran off somewhere."

"And it could still come back to haunt us. If word gets around that top dollar kids are taking off and disappearing, parents might use their money to have them sent elsewhere."

Very late at night, I heard something heavier moving. Was it Claudio, come to free me? No, just my luck. A bear. Well, they'd have fun explaining my eaten body to my dad. There had to be something I could do to protect myself. I had been told that animals shared information in mental pictures. I pictured food sitting on a table up the hill. As I was trying to send positive thoughts to the bear, a hand clasped my mouth. The bear wandered off towards the heart of the camp. I heard noises as if boxes were being ripped apart. "Hey, shoo!" came a loud voice. Then I heard a shot, a howl and another shot. Then, a noise like a scuffle and a wrenching yell of pain. The bear could be heard running and howling as more shots could be heard.

"Hinter? You alive? Hinter?" It was Claudio's voice.

"I'm bleeding. He broke my leg and some ribs."

"I'll have Marco drive you to the hospital."

A little while later, the truck took off. I was still outside. I heard the camp sounds quiet down. I could tell that someone was still with me.

A second later, a blanket was thrown around me. "Bears come looking for food. They don't like to attack people unless they are attacked. It's best not to call attention to yourself if you can't frighten them away. The counselors haven't learned that yet."

"How did you get out here?" I asked Santana. "Don't you have a tent monitor like I do?"

"The guys in my tent are cooler. You've got Hillary. She's a piece of work."

"I'll say. Hitler could have used her at the death camps."

"Don't be sure this isn't a death camp."

"Have you seen anyone die here?"

"Only one since I've been here, but I heard someone died before I came—unless something happened to Jason."

"Is he alive?"

"The last time I saw him was breakfast. He wasn't at dinner."

"They gave him electric shock treatment and Jared thought he was dead."

"No," he sounded distressed. "He's a really nice guy. I hope Jared was wrong."

"Me too. It was my fault." I started to cry.

"Señorita, it's not your fault. It's these monstruos running this camp."

"He was hurt because he tried to help me. If he was killed, it was because of me."

"You can't blame yourself for what esos mostruos do. If you did, you'd be overwhelmed by guilt every day. They want us to feel guilty."

"But it is my fault."

"I'm the one who should feel bad. I've been terrible to him lately. It's an act. I don't know if he knew that. I could have been nicer to him, but I'm keeping up a front for the counselors."

"He was hurt after the pit for protecting me. Everything bad that's happened to him happened because of me. And now, I may have killed him."

"Por favor, try to go easier on yourself. The counselors will be tough enough on you. Jason wanted to be the kind of person who helped an innocent girl. It's an honorable way to go."

"Nobody deserves to be tortured or killed."

"Acordado." (Agreed)

"You said someone else died. How?"

"Tied to a tree, cooked in the sun."

"Oh, good. They must really love me."

He let out a low, sarcastic laugh. "You have to try to pretend to acquiesce. Put on an act. Be credible. They won't believe an overnight change. You have too much spirit. But let go, adjust in whatever way you can."

"I'm not going to become a slut. I'm not saying Amy was. But, if I did that, I would be one."

"Don't. Be strong in that way, but fake eating the food and pretend there is something here you find helpful."

"Tall order. But I'll try."

"I couldn't sneak much to you. And I will have to take the blanket away before morning. Here are some rolls."

"Great. Glyphosate. Roundup."

"Only the best poisons for you. After all, I'm sure your dad will want financial backing from Monsanto. He'll be running for Lieutenant Governor, right?"

"Right. And selling out is his middle name."

Though Santana continued to stay out of sight behind the tree, he fed me by hand. Nobody had done that since my mother, when I was a little girl. Behind the tree, he wasn't looking at my body. Of course, if he broke the tape and released me, they'd know someone had been here.

"Don't you have to get back? Get some rest?"

"Nice night. Beautiful girl. Snooty but beautiful. And you could probably use the protection."

"Don't get me wrong. I appreciate your help. And it's good to have a friend. But that's all it is. I'm through with men."

"Well, there's Hillary? You're more her type than me."

"Right, I took her for a dyke. Ouch, my dad would freak if he heard me use that term. I must always be politically correct, and I've known a number of lesbians and gays who are very nice. I'll rephrase that to say, she's a girl who knows what she wants."

He chuckled. "I think even most lesbians would call someone that mean by names you wouldn't dream of using. But if you want to go into politics, you should consider going the way of Hillary. The party chairman and all the committee leaders in our state are—"

"I know, gay. It's a requirement for party assignments. I have no intention of getting into politics."

"Too straight?"

"No. I don't like the corruption. But I do wish I could get into gay. It would be a lot easier than being forced into another relationship with another creepy rich guy."

"That Espeluznante imbécil rico—"

"What?"

"Creepy, rich imbecile. My Dad's undocumented housekeeper and groundkeeper speak Spanish and so I grew up switching between the two languages. My dad hates it when I do that, and that makes me do it more. That loser is probably crying his eyes out."

"Ha. He's probably searching the mail-order catalogs for the perfect Stepford girlfriend."

Santana chuckled.

"Seriously. Right before my pre-calc final, after two years of dating, he sent me an email saying he was looking for the perfect woman who would attend to his every need, and he knew I wouldn't do that."

Santana laughed and then caught himself and quieted down. "¡Qué gilipollas!"

I guessed he was calling Matt an asshole. "You really aren't so bad. You are actually really nice."

"You don't know me well enough to say that."

# CHAPTER 12

Under the blanket, I was cold but not unbearably cold. I dozed off, and before I knew it, it was daylight. The blanket was gone and so was Santana. But there were broken-off pine branches covering me with their soft needles. It could have looked like they'd naturally blown my way. But I knew better. It was as if Santana had wanted to give me back some of my privacy, a little bit of my humanity. I hoped he hadn't looked when he put the branches down.

I had to watch out. If I wasn't careful, I might actually start to like him.

I felt violated, but I still cared about my privacy—as if a part of me believed I was still whole. I knew I needed to feel completely whole to survive, but it was as if something had been stolen from me that I'd never get back.

The camp was starting to stir. Claudio came over to the tree. He looked at the branches and proceeded to cut the tape. He threw my clothes down on top of the branches and walked away.

After I got dressed and walked towards my tent, Santana bumped into me. "Why don't you watch where you are going, Snooty?" he asked as his hand slipped something into mine. Inside my tent, I saw it was antiseptic lotion. I put it on some of the broken skin left by friction from the duct tape.

We all lined up outside our respective tents and were assigned duties. I didn't see Jason anywhere. Hillary and I were assigned to bring up buckets of sand from the creek area. She was strong and sturdy but was more of a drill sergeant than a teammate. At one point, when she was looking up the hill, I reached down for some creek water. I was willing to risk dysentery I was so thirsty.

She caught my hand. "You drink when we are done."

I carried two buckets full of sand at a time up the hill and deposited the contents in a vat. I was forced to continue until I had brought fourteen full buckets. Then, I was assigned to bring stones. I piled the largest rocks I could manage into the buckets.

I was sore, tired and thirsty, but every time I looked longingly at the water, Hillary looked at me and said, "Not now."

"And if I do?" I finally asked her on the third trip for the stones.

"Then you will lose your drinking privileges."

"Are those better than what I have now?"

I wondered if there was any practical reason for the sand and stones or if this was just indoctrination into submissiveness. I started up the hill and then collapsed. I felt a hand slapping my face and then water splashing on it. My eyelids were pulled up harshly, but I was barely conscious. I couldn't focus. I just lay there, unable to move.

I thought about Ariel, hanging into the gorge. Would this be my fate? In my case, maybe they'd drop me. Jason was a rich kid, and apparently, they were okay with having killed or almost killed him.

Was it a dream or did I hear a "whoopee" up above? Something was going on. I lay there, keeping my eyes closed. I didn't have to pretend much to appear unconscious. I could hear Hillary walking away from me towards the camp. I guess I didn't need a buddy while I was unable to move.

I heard voices flowing from the campsite. They seemed cheery. It was as if a party was going on up there. I heard shouted words like "Get cleaned," "where," "new girl," "out cold," "leave her," and "five minutes."

I felt a little strength coming back. I was going to fake still being out of it until everyone was distracted with whatever was happening. If there was a way out of here, I'd take it. Maybe I could steal the truck if it was back here, get to a road and then hitchhike. This might be my only shot at escaping. When I got to safety, I'd send help back for Santana, Emily, Ariel, Sonja and the rest.

It wasn't long before I heard a vehicle or vehicles pull up towards the camp. I rolled down the hill right into the creek. It felt so good. Then I took a sip, probably a bad idea, but I couldn't go any longer without a drink.

I moved slowly up the hill, crouching down and moving from tree to tree to stay out of sight. The group was crowded around a man in a white suit. There were some other adults I didn't recognize, including a woman.

"Evan, it looks like you've done a great job with this group," the man in the white suit, whose back was to me, said to a man I hadn't seen before. So that was Evan. Mr. White Suit began speaking to the teens. As he moved, I tried but couldn't see his face from my position as the teens were blocking most of my view. "Are they treating you well?" His voice sounded familiar.

"The best." That was Santana.

"We were so lucky to be sent here." That was from a kid I recognized as Bruce.

It wasn't until the man moved past the group and turned to the side that I was able to get a better view and recognize him from behind my tree. *Senator Shemberg from New York, the majority leader. What is he doing here? Interesting that he is here without security.* My experience of him was that he was more than a bit on the paranoid side when it came to protection. Odd that he didn't have extra protection unless he didn't want anyone to know that he was here. Maybe the other man or the woman who had accompanied him and Evan to the camp was his protection.

"Alright, kids. Let's show the Senator how we prepare lunch," Claudio said. Ned and Ian put some steaks on the grill while Jarred worked on preparing soup. I hadn't seen any steaks like that during my limited time of minimal freedom. They were probably brought up fresh, just for the occasion.

I snuck around towards the new vehicles, an Explorer and a Mercedes. With the kids being watched, they might not have thought to secure them. I had to take a chance. Nobody appeared to be watching the vehicles.

I looked back at the Senator. He sat down at a table as Sonja started to approach him. "My, my, what do we have here?"

*Disgusting*, I thought. *He is old enough to be Sonja's grandfather.*

"Just a happy camper. I am hoping to be a Senate aide one day."

"Come over here," he said as he reached out and pulled her onto his lap. "What a pretty little thing. I'll tell you, we have girls your age serving as female pages, or rather aides, in the Senate. We have instructors for them so that they have schooling every day and then get to experience what it's like to work in government for the rest of each day."

"Do you really think you could use me? I'd be the best aide you ever had."

"When you graduate from here, maybe we could work something out." I noticed that Marco was not with the group. I looked around for him. He was standing near one of the tents with a camera aimed right at the Senator. He was partially hidden and I doubted the Senator had any idea he was there.

"We need to do lunch quickly. They are expecting us at the other camp and then the Senator has a flight to catch." This was from the man I presumed to be Evan.

I figured the Mercedes 300 had to be the car the Senator was traveling in. I checked the Mercedes, hoping for no alarm. Nothing sounded as I touched it. The passenger door was locked. I went to the driver's side. It was open. No keys. I felt around the seat and checked the ashtray. No keys. I heard a shout as the food was done. I pulled the trunk latch release. The Senator would need to be going back sometime and it might be my best shot at hitching a ride. There was a blanket and a suitcase in the truck. I could either hide under the blanket or in the tire well. They might notice if I took the time to remove the tire. I got in and pulled the trunk closed over me. Then I pulled the blanket over me and the suitcase past me and closer to the back of the car. I waited. After some time, the trunk opened. I hoped I was invisible. If I was noticed, Claudio and Marco would find a fate worse than tied naked to a tree for me. The suitcase moved. Ouch. I held my breath, certain I was about to be discovered. It felt as if something was put in the trunk and it closed again.

# CHAPTER 13

I felt warmth, moving warmth. A hand reached under the blanket and grabbed mine. Next came a whisper: "If it isn't a Summer's day." I recognized Santana's voice.

"Won't you be missed?" I whispered back.

"No, I told the Senator I was going to my tent for my afternoon nap. I complimented Claudio, saying he was worried about my health and had told me to take it easy until I was feeling better, making it look like the counselors actually cared about our health. They won't do anything while the Senator is here. And by the time they check, I'll be out of here."

"Smart. Was one of the other two a bodyguard?"

"Nope. There was Evan, the director. The woman was Nancy, the sometimes counselor, here to make it look like the girls had female supervision and another man who seemed to be with Evan."

Santana quieted as we heard voices approaching the car. "Do I really need the blindfold?"

*A Senator who allows himself to be blindfolded?*

I could hear the doors on the car opening. "Is the blindfold really necessary?" the Senator asked again.

"Sorry, but this is a secret location, for everyone's protection." This sounded like the Evan guy.

"But I'm a patron."

"Plausible deniability, I think you call it."

"Are we going to the other camp now?"

"As promised. You don't think I would cheat you on this adventure."

I heard the car doors close and the engine start and felt the car begin to move.

"My ears don't hurt. Is that soundwave device off?" I whispered to Santana

"Sí. He wouldn't want the Senator to think we were being held against our will. I'm pretty sure he had it off last night, too. Otherwise, the bear couldn't have come into camp."

"Why did he turn it off last night?"

"Sometimes the traps just injure very small animals, like mice and rats, and Marco takes the injured ones and feeds them alive to the dogs."

"That's sick."

"I agree. But he turns it off when he's doing that. I guess he forgot to turn it back on. You don't have your earplugs in, do you?" His voice was low, but I could slightly make out his words.

"I must have lost them around the river."

"Here's another pair." He placed them in my hand. "Keep them in at all times. It was Bruce who figured out they have some kind of radio wave thing to stop us from leaving. After he lifted several pairs from Marco, I lifted quite a few more. Marco had extra sets in his pocket. He probably figured he lost them in the woods. He's mean, but he's not very bright."

"Is Bruce some kind of genius?"

"Actually, yes, he is."

"With the barrier on, how do animals get into the traps?"

"It's a large area. The barrier is off occasionally for some to get through. Some may arrive from above through the trees or below in little tunnels. I think some small animals may be immune to the radio waves."

I could hear some barely audible chatting as the car continued down the bumpy dirt road. It sounded as if another vehicle, probably the Explorer, was also coming down the road behind us. About twenty minutes later, we pulled to a stop. Car doors opened and closed. The sun was beating down on the car.

"We're going to cook in here," I whispered to Santana.

"We've got to get out of here." He unlatched and slowly lifted the trunk lid and looked out.

"What do you see?"

"Dirt and some trees not too far from here. I don't see any people."

"Let's get out of here, at least, for now. I don't feel like being barbequed as Claudio's follow-up meal to the pregnant fox."

"But summer barbeques are the best," he quipped.

We slowly slid out onto the ground and looked around the side of the vehicle before moving towards the trees.

We could see a two-story cabin across from the parking area beyond some more trees. "Your choice," he offered. "Stay here or check it out."

"Let's see what they are up to."

As we snuck closer, I could see the female counselor who had been at our camp. She brought a little boy, perhaps six years old, into the cabin. We crept up on the cabin and looked into a side window.

"That's Nancy," Santana whispered.

"Cute. My dad sent me to a real class operation."

The Senator was sitting on a couch as the little boy approached him. Laughing and smiling, he pulled the boy closer.

"Look." Santana pointed to an inside balcony.

From where we were, we could see a camera lens pointed at the Senator.

"You can see the top of the cameraman's head. I think that's the guy who accompanied Evan and the Senator to camp."

"You got a better look at him than I did at the camp."

There was a sound of movement towards the front of the cabin and we headed back for the trees. We continued watching.

A little while later, Nancy left with the little boy, who was crying. She returned shortly with another little boy.

"Do you think we could take them?"

"If you have some superpowers I don't know about," Santana replied. "Our best bet is to get out of here and send back help."

"The Senator will deny everything. I regularly saw my dad cover for Senator Madstein when she did, not this, but other stuff she wasn't supposed to do."

"My dad gets out of a lot of stuff, too. He's got a team of people covering for him."

"So, what kind of cars did you steal?"

"Mostly my dad's. He's got a collection of classic cars. I was doing him a favor. By testing their top speed, I was really making sure they were safe. My dad should have paid me."

I started to laugh and then caught myself. "So, your father sent you here because you took his cars out for a spin? What a jerk."

"Not as much as yours. Did he really send you here because of your breakup with that Gilipollas?"

"Gilipollas. That means AH, right?"

"Sí."

"Good description. That was the biggest part, I think. He was expecting the AH's father to finance his win in the Lieutenant Governor's race, and now the AH's father's financial support is in question."

"Wouldn't it be nice to come from a poor, non-political family?"

"At times, I've wished that too. But poor families have their own problems. The banks are taking their homes and then the police ticket them for being homeless and steal their belongings because they have no place to keep them safe."

"Sucks. But at least their dads don't have the money to send them up here," he pointed out.

"I doubt people paid to have their kids in this place. These kids are too young to embarrass their parents."

"Where do you think they got the kids?"

"Didn't you ever read *WikiLeaks*?" I asked.

"Too time-consuming. I saw Lee Camp talk about it when I was younger."

"Have you heard anything about Pizzagate or pedo rings?"

"Of course. Links were all over *Fakebook for* a while—until it was censored and the posters were banned. I know Zuck sold out to the CIA and/or Deep State, but it's got a lot of subscribers who managed to forward out real information before the links were taken down. So, this is what Pizzagate is all about?"

"Something like that. Why does it have to be our Party that is so heavily involved in covering it up?"

"Cheer up. The GOP is probably running the rings that the Democrats frequent. Isn't their moral code 'Grab em by the pussy?'" He paused. "Hey, don't look at me like that. I didn't come up with the line. When have you known the Republican leadership to have any morals?"

"The difference is they don't pretend to be the good guys."

"Well, the Democrats aren't pretending convincingly anymore. Everyone knows our Party has sold out."

The second boy left. Next, came a little girl. "I don't want to watch anymore if we aren't going to do anything to save them at the moment."

"I think our camp is over there," he said, pointing halfway up one of the hills. "It's hard to be certain of the route from traveling inside the trunk."

"So, do you think you can hotwire one of these cars?"

He smiled. "These are a little harder than my dad's because they are newer than his classics, but give me a screwdriver and I'll have one running."

"I don't have one on me."

"Maybe we can find something that will do. It looks like he's going to be here a while." We walked around the area, making sure we stayed out of sight of any camp guards. Like at our campground, there were tents, but these were larger. They had posted someone outside each tent.

"Can't have the little assets running off," I scoffed.

"And that's how they see them," he acknowledged.

There were some bins that looked as if they might have some supplies. "If we go in there, we'll be spotted," I warned.

"Muchacha, I have talents."

Santana picked up a rock, walked back through the trees to where the cars were in sight. Then he threw it against the side of the SUV. The car alarm went off bigtime. People started running in the direction of the vehicles.

"Won't they come looking for the culprits?"

"They'll assume it was an animal?"

"I don't see anything here," Evan said.

"It's probably a squirrel," another man responded.

We circled back through the trees toward the kitchen area. One of the counselors was still there. "Miscalculation. I thought I could get them all running."

"Why didn't the Mercedes alarm go off when we got in?"

"It wasn't locked. Careless driver. We need another distraction, perhaps behind the tent."

"Won't they figure it out?"

"Mischievous squirrel."

"You're hoping."

As we started to move around the backside, we heard something that changed our plans. It was the vehicles taking off. We started to run towards them, but they were gone.

# CHAPTER 14

"Now what?" I asked.

"We get back before they notice we've taken off."

"That car drove quite a ways from the other camp."

"That's because it took the road. We can travel through the trees. It can be a bit of a climb and take some stamina, but we could probably make it back in half an hour. Look." He pointed to the outdoor cooking area as we passed it. "Security's gone. Let's grab some food and water for the trip."

"Like any squirrel would do."

"This squirrel's hungry. I skipped the steaks, too."

Santana got some fresh root beers out of the cooler and some donuts out of a box.

He offered me a donut.

"Round-up? Gee, just what I need."

"Picky, picky."

I grabbed a donut from his hand as he smiled. *I guess, if you're hungry enough, you'll even consider eating poison.* I took one of the root beers too.

As we walked, I asked. "So why are we going back to the torture chamber?"

"So, we will be free to escape another day."

"Unless they kill us or beat us into paralysis for running off."

"I got out of having to use the knife on Ian by pretending to be out cold. That sometimes really does work. You collapsed towards the bottom of the hill, unconscious, and they left you."

"And so you went for the car—some friend."

"After I saw you slide into it."

"Oh." He definitely piqued my curiosity. "You said your father sent you. How did your mother feel about it?"

"She hasn't been in the picture for years. My dad has remarried. His new wifey doesn't particularly like me."

"Cinderfella."

"Hey, I'm walking back to camp with a princess."

"My name is Summer."

"Admit it. You like Princess better than Snooty."

I shook my head. "You're a lunatic."

"Thank you."

"Where is your mother now?"

"She remarried. She wasn't allowed to see me, and so she married someone else and started a new family."

"She wasn't allowed to see you?"

"Alienation. That's the latest in child stealing. A woman gets beaten and the guy who beats her yells alienation."

"You too?"

"Your mom?"

"Same. But I don't know if she's remarried. Pardon me for saying this, but the odds are in favor of your being a wife-beater if your dad was."

He looked down and away. "I've heard that. I'll have to watch out for that for the rest of my life. Find myself a woman who won't cut me any slack on that one."

"It seems like there is a dramatic increase in domestic violence. Why do you think that is?"

"Because they can. Nobody stops them. Fathers are organized and women don't have a chance when they get to court."

His comment surprised me. "Most people, particularly guys, think the opposite is true."

"Only the ones who haven't been to court. I saw what my dad did to my mom. The worst part was the court let him control the finances and violate the law whenever he felt like it. If my dad had asked for my mother to be buried alive ten feet under, he would have gotten it." He looked sad. "He canceled my mom's health insurance during the divorce while she was in the intensive care unit in need of surgery that she then couldn't have. That's illegal, but courts let men do that all the time. In the end, my mom gave up on me. I miss her, but I will never forgive her for not fighting longer."

"I didn't think mine fought until a friend looked up my parents' divorce. Now, I don't know. I sent Mom a letter before I came here. Maybe she doesn't care. She hasn't come to rescue me."

"How would she find you?"

"True. But it still hurts."

"I didn't even write. I figured mine gave up on me."

"I'm sorry."

"Me, too, about your mom."

As we came to a stream, a little wider than the creek I had been gathering water at, I jumped in. It was cold, but I didn't care. The earlier dunking hadn't completely rid me of the horrible smell that I didn't want to get used to. "I know I smell, and I can't even breathe around myself."

"I wasn't going to say anything." He smiled.

"Thank you, but I still have a nose." Five minutes later, I was a whole lot wetter and colder but much better smelling as I emerged. Santana took off his shirt and suggested I wear it until we got close to camp.

"Turn around," I insisted when I was ready to take off my shirt and put his on. He quickly complied.

As we continued on, I noticed he had a nice build. He didn't have bulging muscles but he was solid.

"You just wanted to go shirtless," I teased.

"That's what I get for being a gentleman?" he teased back.

"Gentleman was the last thing I would have called you when I first came to camp."

"And now?"

"Not so creepy."

He laughed.

We followed the stream part way towards where we thought our camp was. As it diverted away from where we were going, another stream cut in from the side, joining it, and we crossed that. Finally, we got to our creek and then moved along it towards our camp but on the opposite side in case we were caught and had to run. I made Santana turn away again as I switched back into my shirt. We both had our earplugs in, just in case the sound barrier had been turned back on.

As we crossed the creek, we saw no sign of immediate danger. As we got to the other side, Bruce came towards us with four buckets. "Fill yours fast, bro. I've been covering for you." From Santana, I knew he was on our side. But wow, he was actively helping us without hesitation.

"What do they think happened to me?" I asked.

"You've got nowhere to go. So, they thought they'd leave you where you collapsed. I told them we were having to step over you." He turned to Santana. "And get this! The SUV. It brought more hydrazine."

"Acid," Santana remarked.

"I saw the rye heads the other day," I added.

"Did you see any more of the surroundings?" Bruce asked.

"We found the kids' camp. I can tell you why our leaders aren't regulating us nationally," Santana responded.

"I saw him with Sonja," Bruce stated.

"Marco was filming that," I informed them.

Bruce nodded and then changed the topic. "I've been studying the height of the sun and the constellations. I think we are somewhere between twenty-five and forty degrees north of the Equator."

"California, Nevada, Arizona, New Mexico, Texas," I started.

"But it also isn't too humid. So that rules out Texas and east of there. I'm going with California, Nevada, Arizona or New Mexico," Bruce said. "Glad to have you on the team, Summer."

"Team." That sounded promising. "I guess I need to look disheveled if I've been crashing all day," I said.

"I've got an idea." Santana reached for me, and I backed up. "Trust me. We're on the same team now."

"Team." That same word. Maybe we really could have a revolution here.

Santana lowered his voice to a whisper. "Look unconscious." He placed his hands on my sides and lifted me over his shoulder. I pretended to go limp. Bruce filled two buckets with water and handed them to Santana, who somehow was able to hold both them and me. Bruce filled the other two and carried them up alongside us.

"We got tired of stepping over the trash, and so I thought I'd bring her up here," Santana told Marco.

"Maybe she will improve after another night by the tree."

"She seems really messed up. It might be heatstroke. Perhaps if we let her sleep it off in her tent, we can work her double in the morning," Bruce interjected. "It seems the most logical solution."

"It does?" Marco asked sarcastically. "Maybe we should tie her to a tree and still work her double tomorrow."

"She'll be worthless in this state. We could use the help tomorrow," Santana added. "She's got to be good for something besides getting herself tied up."

"Alright, but no finished work means no dinner," Marco responded.

I guessed I was going to be dieting again.

"She looks as if she'll be out until morning," Santana told him.

---

I heard the tent flap open and felt Santana put me down inside on a sleeping bag. I opened my eyes to see him wink at me as he finished closing the tent flap on his way out. Fortunately, the tent was only locked at night.

I could smell the dinner cooking. This time, it smelled like vegetables. Of course, they would cook something I could eat when I was closed up in the tent. I listened to the voices. Actually, it sounded as if the main banter was coming from the group I had labeled "the bullies," the ones with the blue shirts. "What do you get when you mix a Mexican with a Vietnamese?" It sounded like Ian's voice.

"I wouldn't know. I'm neither Mexican nor Vietnamese. But I'm sure that mixture can drive better than you," came back Santana's response. It was becoming very clear that the nastier and tougher you sounded, the more likely you were to survive here. I had heard that about prisons, too. My dad was into prison reform—or at least he paid lip service to it while asking for donations from the prison industrial complex as well as from the military industrial complex that Eisenhower had warned Americans about.

I could hear the truck pull back to the camp. "I understand we have a late night, early morning run." It was Marco's voice.

"We sure do," Claudio said.

"Everyone, this is Jake, Hinter's temporary replacement."

"Hi, Jake," several voices said in unison.

"Is this everyone?"

"Except for Snooty. She was depressing the camp. So we made her stay in her tent. Can we send her back where she came from?" That was Santana.

"They don't want her either." That was Claudio's response. The air was lit with vicious laughter.

*Maybe my mom would want me,* I told myself. *Shannon and Tiffany care about me.* I thought about how it was now summer vacation. My friends were probably enjoying yachts and boys and might, I hope, be wishing I were with them. I heard a scraping noise against the bottom of the tent near my sleeping bag. Something poked through and then the hole became a little larger. It was a knife. Next, a hand came through with a cup of mixed vegetables and another with some slices of bacon. It was followed by a cup of water.

"Thank you, Santa."

"Not Evil Santa?"

"No, just Santa."

As I took the cup, he put his hand around mine. "Be careful, Chica."

"You too, Santa."

With that, the hand was withdrawn.

# CHAPTER 15

I finished the veggies in a couple of gulps. I wasn't about to eat the bacon. Santana knew I was a vegan. I wondered if he gave me those strips to bribe someone in an emergency. I hid the cups and the bacon in my socks under my sleeping bag. I could sneak them back out in the morning.

I heard Santana's voice. "What do you mean you are personally locking our tent tonight? We've earned privileges. I thought locking all the tents was our monitor's job."

"Don't speak back to me. If you mouth off, you'll be hogtied and locked down nightly from now on," Claudio said.

So, the purple tent wasn't necessarily locked at night. I wondered what they had to do to earn that privilege.

Later, after Emily, Hillary and Ariel were all in the tent, seemingly sleeping or faking it like me, Claudio let Sonja into our tent and locked it.

I heard voices from outside the tent. "Sonja is ready. Let the Senator know we have that pretty package he wanted."

It was a way out for her, but not a pretty one. Maybe, if she was lucky, she would escape when she got to D.C. I could hear the truck driving off in the distance. A few minutes later, I heard the tent's lock opening.

"You're getting out of here. Consider yourself lucky, babe." It was Claudio's voice. "But first, how about some fun for all of us? You can change in the supply tent."

Sonja picked up some clothes. "Good luck," I whispered. After she left, the tent was locked again.

"All right. Now for the fun," I heard Marco say. He must have thought we were asleep as he wasn't trying to be quiet.

"So many of you for the goodbye!" Sonja exclaimed.

"We're letting you go. The least you could do is give us a taste," Claudio bantered, cheerfully.

"Wait! You expect me to give it to all of you and this group of blues?" Sonya asked with a shaking voice.

"What do you think you are going to be doing in Washington?"

"Perhaps saving the world. Let me go, and I'll be back with bonuses for all of you."

"Just something so you don't forget us. Or are you really ready to leave? Perhaps you'd like to stay here for a few more months."

"No. No. Please."

"I think the proper response is: 'Yes, yes, yes.'"

"No! Stop! I don't want this."

I moved towards the front of my tent. We were locked in. A light from outside provided a dim glow through the wall of the tent, but the wall wasn't transparent, and I could only imagine what was happening out there. It was after bedtime, and Santana and Bruce were apparently locked in, too.

So, who was out there? Ian, maybe Ned and Jared. Possibly also Grayson, Harv, Dan and George, rounding out the bully gang. Additionally, Marco, Claudio, and Hinter's replacement, Jake. No. Claudio couldn't mean that many. I hoped it was nothing like that. Even if it was just a couple of them, it was a couple too many. I needed to help her.

"Stop!" I yelled. I started shaking the tent. Emily started to help me shake the tent.

"Stop, you idiots," Ariel demanded of us. "We don't want them coming after us, too."

"They are raping her!" I exclaimed.

"She's our friend," Emily pleaded.

"She said she was okay with sex," Ariel responded harshly.

"Even girls who are sexual have the right to say 'no,'" I pointed out.

"Summer's right," Emily agreed. "That could be any of us out there."

"No. We don't parade around the guys like we want some," Ariel countered.

"And if we did, they still wouldn't have the right," I responded.

The screams got louder.

"Go to sleep," Hillary demanded.

I shouted in the hopes I could be heard outside. "Stop! You're hurting her!"

I felt something heavy and hard hit my head from behind. I almost fell against the wall of the tent and barely steadied myself.

Emily screamed, "Hillary, no! You hurt Summer!" Next, Hillary grabbed me, turned me and started punching. I collapsed on the floor as she jumped onto me and continued hitting me. Emily tried to pull her off and got knocked back. I was too weak to fight effectively, and Emily was no match for Hillary. Ariel watched as we struggled.

Hillary picked up one of her boots and smashed the heel against my cheek as Emily tried to rush her again and was, again, knocked away. I felt numb. Before I knew how to react, Hillary grabbed some long, thin cords and tied them around my wrists. I pulled them forward and punched her in the face with both fists together.

Hillary picked up a metal box from next to her sleeping bag and tried to hit me with it, but I dropped and rolled away. Emily continued to try to struggle with Hillary, but Hillary was much stronger. I stood up again, and Hillary went for me. She may have been strong, but I was motivated as I blocked and kicked. Eventually, Hillary stopped attacking me, and Emily sat down.

The screams outside the tent continued and got louder and louder. As I turned towards them and started back towards the entrance, trying to tear the flap to get at the lock, I heard a "No!" inside the tent from Emily.

Before I could look, the metal box smashed against my head. I felt dizzy and collapsed. I couldn't even lift my head. I was locked in with no way to help Sonja. Emily helped me into my sleeping bag.

"Let's just believe that somehow she will be okay," Emily whispered. "They have us locked in here with Eva Braun."

"Emily, go back to your sleeping bag," Hillary ordered.

"You just beat up one of our roommates. And you are letting them rape another," Emily stated, standing up. "I think it's you who should go back to your sleeping bag. You may be tough, but you are outnumbered in this tent." I started to rise, weekly, out of my bag. Both Emily and I stared down Hillary.

"I am reporting both of you in the morning."

# CHAPTER 16

I snapped awake at the feeling of a rat running across my chest. *Wonderful.* I covered my face and lay there, briefly frozen in terror. I remembered the rats in *1984*. The rat, on top of everything else, freaked me out. It should have been no surprise that my father would do this to me, but part of me still didn't want to believe that he had stooped so low. Emily was still sleeping. The rat was heading her way. I had to get brave. I moved towards her, swinging my blanket to scare it away from her.

What had happened to Sonja? The night before came back to me, along with the screams and sounds of sex and more sex with all those sick men.

"Rise and shine, ladies." It was Claudio's voice.

Emily stirred. "What time is it?" She and I were alone in the tent. Hillary had probably already reported us. Ariel was gone, too, perhaps not wanting to engage in a confrontation.

The flap opened, and Claudio stuck his head in. "Did I authorize you to ask questions? We need water and some filler. You know what that means?"

"Close the door," I retorted.

"Shy? Now, there are privileges for those who cooperate. Sonja is already out of here. You could be, too."

"Is she alive?"

He paused. "She was when she left here." There was something about his look that said he was holding something back. He changed the subject. "You need to stop fighting us. Become the kind of girl your father could be proud of."

"Somehow, I don't think my father would approve of my being forced into group sex. So, what's it like to be a pimp?"

"What do you think your father is?" I couldn't argue with that one, but it didn't change how disgusted I was.

"Door, please."

"Please," he repeated. "You are learning."

He half-closed the tent flap. I got back into my sleeping bag and changed into my dirty clothes. My eyes spotted the hole Santana had cut the night before. Inside a napkin were berries and a sealed baggie, not with drugs but with bacon. I quickly stuffed the berries into my mouth and added the bacon I had put into my socks the night before into the baggie and stuffed it into my pocket. Santana knew I didn't eat meat, yet he had left me bacon twice.

Emily started crying.

"It's okay," I said, going over and giving her a hug. I knew it wasn't okay, but Emily didn't need more reason to worry. "Maybe she really is on her way to D.C."

"No talking," came Claudio's voice from outside.

As we left the tent, Claudio handed us each two buckets. I wondered whether we could disable him with a blow to the head with the buckets.

"Don't think of it," he said, almost reading my mind, as he stepped back and picked up his chain. "Now get your butts moving."

---

As we approached the stream with our buckets, I saw a wild dog. It wasn't a wolf but had the appearance of a dog that had been abandoned in the wilderness. He looked like a combination of mastiff, pit bull, shepherd and Rottweiler, rolled into one.

"Hey, baby," I said.

"Don't," Emily reacted. "He could be rabid or hungry."

I remembered the bacon I had in my pocket. I was still hungry, but I was certain bacon was more his thing than mine. I couldn't help wondering if Santana had snuck it to me as some kind of defense against wild animals. But for some reason, this dog didn't scare me.

"Here, girl," I said, holding out the meat. The dog moved slowly towards me. I put it on the ground,

"It's not a girl," Emily observed.

"Guess I'm blind. Come here, boy," I said.

Slowly, the dog moved forward, limping a little, and took the bacon. I kneeled down so as to look non-threatening. I had always been told to look ferocious, but my heart told me the dog was more afraid of me than I was of him. His left rear leg was bleeding. I reached out my hand, palm up, and let the dog sniff. He ducked his head and I petted it. I took out some of the antiseptic cream Santana had slipped me for my wrists after the duct tape was removed. I tore a piece off my already torn left sleeve and smeared the cream on it. I started to bring the makeshift bandage towards the dog's leg, but the dog let out a growl and backed away. "It's alright, boy." I held out the cloth to show it was nothing dangerous. The dog came forward. I petted him some more until he seemed to get that I meant him no harm. Then, I reached around and wrapped the leg. I made sure to tie the cloth tight as I wanted it to hold for at least a day. I pulled my arms close around the dog and hugged him.

"You've got guts," Emily said. "That dog could have ripped you apart."

"I love dogs. Humans are much more dangerous. I'm sure Sonja would agree with me this morning."

"I will agree about the humans, but wild dogs scare me. I've heard stories of pit bulls attacking and even killing people. He does seem sweet, though. I wonder if he used to belong to somebody."

The dog started to follow me back towards the camp. "Stay here, baby. The humans at the camp are much too dangerous for a sweetie like you," I cautioned him.

As I brought the water up to the campsite, I noticed the purple and red groups mixing white power with something that looked like cornstarch and putting it into baggies. The appearance was more like I would have expected cocaine to look than LSD. Hillary, on the other hand, was inside one of the service tents with what looked like chemicals, blotter paper and a distillery. I noticed a bottle labeled hydrazine on the floor of the tent. It fit. Were they servicing some drug dealer, or was my sarcastic remark about MKUltra correct? I had read about Harvard's LSD experiments. What kind of people was my dad connected with? I looked around the tent a moment longer and saw some bottles of sulfuric acid. I figured it was probably used in connection with the drugs, but I hadn't studied drug-making. It wasn't part of the college prep classwork I was taking.

Jamie, a somewhat reserved blue male who had been nice to me, was freaking out in a corner of the supply tent. "What's wrong?" I asked him.

"It's none of your business," Claudio said from behind me. "It used to be that when someone couldn't stop talking, they would cut out his tongue, or in your case, her tongue."

I turned around and glared at him.

"Well, well, looks like someone else didn't like your chatter."

I hadn't looked in a mirror since the fight with Hillary as there weren't any mirrors in the campsite or the tent. I probably had a black and blue badge of courage. Not the red kind Stephen Crane had in mind, but here, I was like a soldier fighting this insanity and not giving into being Stockholmed.

Holding my head up, I said, "I brought up the water. What do you want next?"

"How about a foot massage?"

The thought of touching any part of this thing's body, including his feet, grossed me out. But his feet weren't as offensive as other parts of his body, though they were probably filthy.

"Well, if you want a real foot massage the way I usually do them, I will need some warm water and soap." *Boiling water would be better*, I thought. "I mean, even Jesus washed the feet of his di— I mean friends." I figured he might react to the word disciple. This might be a Christian camp, but I doubted whether any of those running it had ever read any *Bible*. My dad claimed to be a Christian, but he beat his wife and sent his daughter off to be tortured.

"You just brought up some water. Take it to the camp stove and warm it up." As I warmed it up, I allowed myself to think of all the things I'd like to do to Claudio, including getting some of that sulfuric acid out of the supply tent and dissolving his feet in it. After heating the water, I brought it to where he was sitting and poured it into a little plastic tub. I added some soap from the supply tent. I was surprised that they had any soap at a place like this. Sitting tied up in the sun, I had been forced to pee in place, not to mention what I had had to do in the box.

I sat the tub in front of where Claudio was sitting. I still didn't want to touch any part of him—not even his feet.

"First, stick your feet in the water," I said.

He pulled off his shoes. "You really are starting to come around."

"I'm tired of being the odd one out. I want to be part of something," I said as sweetly as I could.

"That's what I like to hear. There's always been something special about you. That's why we pushed you so hard."

"You were trying to make me into a better person." I hoped he didn't pick up on my lack of sincerity.

"Now I'm seeing that better person emerge."

The truck pulled up and Evan came into the camp looking at me and Claudio. Claudio waved me off.

"I got some splinters in my feet," he told Evan. They both looked at me as if they wanted me to disappear. I went around the corner of the blue tent as if planning to go over to the table on the other side. Instead, I stopped to listen.

"What?" Claudio asked.

"She bled out. What did you guys think you were doing? She wasn't a scholarship. Her dad is going to be wondering about her. Senator Shemberg will be asking about her."

"We'll do what we did with Blake. Move the body out of state and claim she ran off. If they find her, we'll claim no connection."

"Except the Senator saw her yesterday. He knew she was taking the early morning flight from the base straight to D.C. If he talks to her dad, there will be an inquest."

"We got a lot of footage on Shemberg yesterday. Why don't we tell him she had a change of heart and ran away? Insist he keeps silent until she is found. If he mentions he saw her here, the footage goes viral."

"We don't want to do that at this point. Blackmailing an ally isn't the best way to keep him on our side. He may be silent, but he may find another way to stab us in the back."

"The guys were just having a little fun. Who knew there would be so much blood?"

"She was fourteen. She was a virgin."

"What? That slut? She slunk around like she had slept with everyone in her hometown."

"It was an act, a performance. I'm going to send you to our Utah Three Camp until this blows over. Hopefully, Marco and Jake will be able to handle the teens until we get more backup."

"Utah?"

"Sex is freer there. You should like it."

"I've been there. I couldn't wait to get out. How long do I have to stay?"

"Depends on whether there's an inquiry."

# CHAPTER 17

I wanted to race off and tell Santana, but I didn't dare. Poor Sonja. A virgin. Her flirting was all a performance to get out of here. She must have been really desperate. While somehow holding back the tears that kept trying to fall from my eyes, I went around the other corner of the tent towards where the blue and purple kids were putting wires and timers into boxes.

"Well, look who's joined us," Ian mused. "Care to hang out with a real guy?"

"I came to tell you 'Up yours.'"

"Hey, aren't you 'Up' and doesn't that make you mine?"

"Shove it. Evan's here, and I'm sure he would love to know how you made Sonja scream last night."

Ian turned almost white. "Why would you say that?"

"I think everyone could hear you from miles away."

He didn't say anything as I walked away, taking a roundabout path towards the river where Emily was now preparing to carry up stones.

"Why didn't you ask me for help?" I inquired.

"Marco had that creep Dan helping me, and then they said Ian needed his help with fuses."

"Fuses, as in bombs?"

"Who knows? They make some weird stuff here."

"Drugs and bombs?"

"We probably should keep our noses out of what they are making. They are getting more and more vicious," Emily said.

"That wasn't why I was looking for you. I overheard Evan and Claudio talking about Sonja."

"She flew to D.C., right?" Emily asked, holding her breath. I had to decide whether it was worth it to be honest, even if that hurt.

I shook my head, trying not to cry. From the tears in my eyes, she knew. She started crying, herself, and we held each other for a minute.

"Did you know she was a virgin?"

"I thought it might be an act." Emily started really sobbing. "She was kooky and said some crazy stuff at times, but she was really a good, sweet person. Why did this have to happen to her just as she was about to escape?"

"I don't know that it would have been better in D.C, but there would have been more places to seek help and telephones, real telephones."

"What are we going to do?"

"We're getting out of here."

"How?"

"I don't know, but more than you and me want out."

"I'm sure everyone, but the blues, wants out."

"We need to be careful," I cautioned. "We can't trust anyone who is so afraid they'll turn us in." I was thinking of Ariel with that comment.

"Right."

"Let's get these stones up on top, and we'll talk more later."

We carried the stones up the hill as Evan assembled everyone near the food table.

"Emily and Snooty," Santana said, approaching us. I looked away, not wanting him to see the tears in my eyes. "Maybe, if you come down off your cloud, you'll find us more enjoyable," he continued. The others were focused on Evan. "You've been crying," he whispered.

I wanted to tell him, but I couldn't. I feared I'd break down, sobbing uncontrollably.

"Any news about—" He didn't have to finish. I nodded and had to cover my eyes to prevent anyone else from seeing the tears.

"Oh, no," he said, almost under his breath. "We need to talk. Tonight."

# CHAPTER 18

That night at dinner, Jamie still looked under. I wondered if he had been a friend of Sonja's. Except for a few of us, everyone thought she had just gone away. Jamie played with his food. He took a bite and then ran off to throw up. Jamie, being a blue, was in Ian's tent, something I wouldn't wish on any decent person. Maybe he slipped out of the tent and saw what was happening last night. I noticed that John and Charlie looked more nervous than usual. Ariel was pretty quiet. She seemed to be avoiding me and Emily. It looked as if she and Hillary had made a connection. Ariel was probably the only girl who could tolerate Hillary. I didn't know how I would get out of the locked tent or how I was going to slip past Ariel and Hillary tonight. But if there was any way, I wanted to speak with Santana.

Marco assigned me, not Charlie, to go with John to the river that evening to pick up extra water. On the way down, John spoke quietly to me. "I heard what they were doing to Sonja last night. That happens a lot in places like this."

"It does?"

"Both Charlie and I were in another program before. If not for him, I wouldn't have made it out with my brain intact, such as it is. He's the closest thing to a brother I have."

"What was it like?"

"It was a school without books. They hogtied and beat anyone who got out of line. Girls were raped. There was waterboarding. We sometimes went for days without eating or drinking water. A couple of campers died because they were forced to drink their own vomit while being hogtied. A couple died of dehydration. Someone blew the whistle on it, and they transferred us here."

"What brought most of the kids to that school?"

"Supposed drug problems for most of them. But I'm sure they did more drugs in the camp than on the outside. They didn't have a choice. Sometimes, there was a reaction, and they died. They never have real medical personnel or any real teachers at any of these camps or schools."

"George Miller had hearings about the camps, years ago. I saw a video of one hearing on the Internet when I was old enough to understand."

"You're pretty well informed."

"My dad was chief of staff to Senator Madstein and now to the governor of my state. I hated my situation, and I sometimes looked at videos recommended by the National Youth Rights Association to find out what was really happening in the world. So, what happened to the school after it was investigated?"

"Nothing much was done. I understand that school has reopened and is as bad as before."

"Some of us have parents who are politically connected. What about you?"

"Charlie and I may be exceptions. My dad is a banker, and my mom works for a defense contractor but doesn't do anything really important. Charlie's dad is with a pharmaceutical company."

"That's not an exception. The defense contractors and pharmaceutical companies pretty much tell our leaders what to do."

"I guess."

To my surprise, Evan assigned Hillary to the "culinary supply tent," which housed a distillery, among other things, for the night. As far as I could tell, it held a lot more than cooking supplies, such as those heavy boxes we packed in the truck days ago. "I believe you have some work to finish," he murmured to her.

Ariel, who was sitting near Hillary, asked, "Could I help Hillary? Two can work faster than one."

I couldn't really blame Ariel for playing up to the tent monitor. Hanging by a rope from the cliff must have put a major scare into her. But this was excellent luck. With them gone, it gave me some space to talk to Santana and maybe Bruce. Now, if I just knew how to pick a lock from inside the tent.

After Emily and I turned in, I heard Evan tell Paul to lock the tent. I hadn't had much interaction with Paul. He was a blue. I was guessing he was one of the gang of rapists. After Emily and I entered the tent, I heard someone, presumably Paul, playing with the lock.

I gave Emily a hug. We sobbed in each other's arms. Then, she went to lie down in her sleeping bag as she continued sobbing. I figured I'd fill her in later on anything I found out. It was best if she didn't take any risks. She was so young, though just a couple years younger than me. She had such an innocence about her. It made me angry that someone had sent her here.

A short while later, it sounded as if the other teens had turned in. About an hour after that, with my ear to the wall of my tent, I heard Evan and Jake speaking quietly. They were standing near our tent and speaking in low voices, probably assuming Emily and I were asleep. "I'm going down to the base. I have to drop off Claudio, and we have a new camper flying into the airfield."

"When will we get a replacement for Claudio? Some of these kids are trouble."

"Claudio says they are acclimating, even the Tanner girl."

"With all this shit lying around, we could use more security."

"We're out of the way. No one would think to come up here."

The next part of their conversation was too garbled to understand.

"Claudio's replacement won't be here until next Sunday. You'll have to handle it until then. It's time to go."

I heard Claudio say bye to Jake. Either Jake responded non-verbally or not at all.

After I heard the truck take off and it sounded quiet outside the tent, I went over to Emily's sleeping bag. "Hey. You awake?"

"I can't sleep. I keep thinking of Sonja. What I said last night. That could have been any of us."

"Right. We have to get out of here. I think we are going to have a strategy session tonight."

"Locked in here?"

"Santana seems to be able to get past the watchers," I whispered.

"Santana? I thought you two didn't like each other. Isn't he with the bullies?

"He's a purple and different in private. He's really a good guy."

"You and Santana?"

"It isn't like that. We're all in this together."

"Did you notice how, suddenly, Ariel is hitting it off with Hillary?"

"Claudio put the fear of death into her. I don't know if I could have handled what she went through without cracking. If you would feel safer staying in the tent, I'll let you know how it goes."

"No. I want to be part of it."

---

I lay awake until I heard a noise near the hole. I went over to it.

"Santa?"

"Shh."

"It's only Emily and me."

"Emily?"

"She's cool. But we're locked in."

"I'll see what I can do."

I went and tapped on Emily's shoulder.

"I'm still awake. Who can sleep?"

As we put on our shoes, I heard the lock rattle. Then, the zipper was pulled open.

Emily and I moved towards the opening. Santana was leaning in with his right forefinger to his lips. We followed him out and down the hill, careful not to make any noise.

"I guess you're a good burglar," I said as we reached the creek.

"The best, but the tent was unlocked. I just had to slip out the lock."

"Is that how they usually do it?"

"No. It's generally locked."

"Paul was supposed to lock us in. Do you think it's a trap?"

"Don't know. But, if so, he's likely onto me and Bruce as well. He's the blue monitor for our tent and he never locks it. He's a sound sleeper, unless he's not. Let's keep our eyes open."

Footsteps approached. I recognized Bruce's shape: sturdy, not muscular, neither slender nor heavy, essentially an average build and about 6 feet tall. Bruce had dark hair and dark eyes.

"They killed Sonja," I told him.

"Santana told me." He shook his head.

"We need to find a way out or we could be joining her on the other side," Santana pointed out.

"Did they mention whether she died in the hospital? There will be a report if she did," Bruce noted.

"They took her somewhere. Evan said she bled out. They were also talking about disposing of the body out of state."

"They don't want her found in this state. That may mean something," Bruce figured.

"Probably they took her to a private facility with doctors who are receiving kickbacks from those drugs," Santana's justifiable cynicism continued.

"Wouldn't even doctors on the take worry about covering up a murder?" I asked.

"Not all doctors are reputable," Bruce responded, seemingly agreeing with Santana. "Like the ones over-prescribing drugs for the pharmaceutical companies or pushing dangerous drugs or vaccines on their patents for kickbacks."

"Is there anyone, anywhere, we can trust?"

"Individuals, not classifications. There are good and bad cops, good and bad doctors, good and bad politicians," Bruce answered.

"I know about the politicians," I mused. "There is a lot to be said for going off to some island and becoming a hermit."

"Only if there are fast cars there," Santana interjected.

"I just want out of here," I responded.

"Did you get any clue about our location from their discussion?" Bruce asked.

"There is a base not far away."

"I heard them mention that tonight, too," Emily noted.

"They are flying in a new victim," I said. "The camp is going to be short-staffed until next Sunday."

"Then, we need to find a way out of here by then," Santana responded.

"Does anyone know what day it is?" Emily asked.

"If they had Sunday worship services, we'd know," Santana remarked.

"Well, I left late night on a Friday or rather very early on a Saturday morning. I don't know how long the drive was but I was in a box for three days. That was almost about three, almost four days ago."

"Before the box, you were in the ground, hog-tied and asleep until the ants woke you up," Santana reminded me.

"Then this could be Friday or Saturday night," Bruce threw in.

"He said next Sunday, not this Sunday," Emily noted.

"Right. So, we probably have close to a week," I added. "What's the plan?"

"The little kids' camp is down the hill, easier to walk to than from," Santana pointed out.

"But did you see any vehicles other than the one we were in and the SUV?" I asked Santana.

"There has to be a real road somewhere we can walk to," Santana remarked.

"But we could get picked up by someone tied to this operation."

"Summer's right," Bruce joined back in. "If you look at the chemicals they have us working with, this could be a big operation. Maybe the Cartel, Blackwater or Serco?"

"We could, also, wind up like Sonja if we try to get out," Emily said.

"If we don't take the risk, we won't be able to get ayuda for every-one," Santana pressed.

I knew that was the word for help.

"We'd need proof. Otherwise, they'd just move the operation," Bruce pointed out.

"I saw them taking video of the Senator. If we could get their video stash, we might have some proof," I related.

"Don't forget that they have people covering for them. My dad sent us here and he's not going to want the truth to tarnish his career," Santana said.

"My dad's been known to cover things up, too," I noted.

"My dad works with HAARP. You think he's telling people anything about their activities?" Bruce asked.

"How did you wind up here?" I inquired.

"My school career counselor convinced my dad that attending a behavior modification school would help me get into MIT. Also, I blew up my high school chem lab."

We stared at him.

"How was I supposed to know what ethyl alcohol and silver nitrate would do heated up together—until I checked it out personally?"

"Somehow, I think you knew," I responded.

"Okay, but I didn't realize the explosion would be that big. I guess I used just a little too much silver nitrate."

"You were at a school before you came here?" I asked.

"No books. Lots of torture. Tech skills were unappreciated. They felt this camp could better rein me in.

"Some day you'll have to tell me what havoc you caused at the school," Santana stated.

"I'm glad you're on our team." I chuckled. "So, we have the scientist, the car thief and lock breaker, yours truly who seems to have a nose for getting into trouble and—"

"Me. What can I contribute?" Emily asked.

"Actually, you can contribute the most. You're pretty quiet. You're the last person they would expect to make a break for it. Keep your ears open, and see what information you can pick up," I told Emily, putting my arm around her shoulder.

"Wow," Bruce said, starting to back up. I turned. It was a dog, my dog, growling at Bruce.

"He's safe," I assured him. "Here, boy. Really, Bruce, it's alright."

"He's wild."

"He's my friend. He won't hurt you."

"I'm not so sure. He's looking at me funny."

"Oh, don't be a cobarde," Santana said, reaching for the dog. The dog barked menacingly at him.

"Uh, tell him I'm your amigo," Santana nervously implored me.

"Don't worry." I knelt down, reached into my pocket and pulled some meat from dinner I had saved for him. The thought of eating meat made me feel sick, but my dog seemed to love it and the alternative was throwing it in the trash. One day, I'd make the dog a vegan—if he and I got out of here.

"Boy, these are friends of mine. Be nice to them. Santana, give me your hand." Hesitantly, Santana gave me his hand and I petted the dog with it. "Now, you, Bruce."

"I'm fine here."

Santana chuckled. "Cobarde."

"Right, when it comes to killer dogs, I am a coward."

Santana turned from Bruce to me. "If you're going to keep that dog, how about coming up with a better name for him than Boy?"

I thought for a moment. "Hope."

"That's a girl's name," Santana chided.

"So, girls have the lock on hope, huh?" I asked rhetorically.

"Hey, do you really want to be called Hope?" Santana asked him.

I pulled some meat from my other pocket just as Hope barked. The timing was perfect, given Santana's question.

"I'm not going to argue with that," Santana said. Then he noticed the meat. "Cheater."

Bruce got us back on track. "It would really do some good to narrow down our location. I came from Fairbanks. It was a nine or ten hour flight. I didn't come directly here. I went to a school first. From there, it was about a three hour flight here. I was blind-folded both times."

"Did you hear any airport noises, cities mentioned?" I asked.

"I'm pretty sure I was taken by private plane both times. Nothing was announced. Santana?"

"I was taken by air from SF. I was there with my dad, embarrassing him in front of the mayor, and that night, I was taken from the hotel room, blindfolded. There was a stop. Claudio came on board and the plane lifted off again and flew for maybe fifteen or twenty minutes. The total time, including the stop, was maybe an hour or an hour and a half. I was blindfolded the whole time. So, I don't think any legitimate airline would have flown me."

"You might be surprised," Bruce said. "Emily?"

"It was long—hours. I lost track of time. I came from my parents' vacation home in Florida. I think I was also flown private—from some-where near Orlando."

"Summer?"

"I don't recall a plane. But I was unconscious much of the time and can't be sure. I came from Brentwood. I mainly remember being in the truck of a car. I could have been on a plane and not realized. I was unconscious when I arrived."

"A 90210 girl," Santana remarked.

"Close, but Beverly Hills is down the road. If only that old show accurately depicted my life."

"How does the chief of staff to the Governor live in the Los Angeles area?"

"My dad flies back and forth between Los Angeles and Sacramento. While working for Madstein, he regularly flew between D. C., Frisco and Los Angeles. He was gone a lot. We don't like each other, so it was the perfect situation until he sent me here."

"The best indicator is an hour and a half with a stop-over from SF," Bruce analyzed the situation. "You could have reversed directions after picking up Claudio, Santana, but the weather isn't cool enough for Northern California. Let's say that Summer doesn't remember a plane because she wasn't on one. That means we could be driving distance from Los Angeles. That could place us in the Sierras, maybe the San

Gabriel or Tehachapi mountains, possibly California, Nevada or somewhere off Highway 40. The climate is wrong for Central and Southern Arizona. I'm guessing the planes landed at a military base. Fewer questions."

"And what bases do we have in these areas?" I asked.

"Near Los Angeles, we have Edwards. Arizona has Luke, and Nevada has Nellis. If they went to New Mexico, we could be looking at Kirkland. There are also bases in the San Diego area. With this terrain, we can't rule out that we are east of El Cajon or perhaps in the Cleveland National Forest."

"I guess you studied geography," I responded to Bruce's analysis.

"With my dad's job, we traveled a lot."

"So, tell me, HAARP Legacy, is it true that HAARP created the earthquake that sent the tidal wave towards Fukushima? Sorry, I saw a video by a Lauren something or other, and she insisted that's what happened."

Santana laughed. "Conspiracy theorist. Remind me to get you a tin foil hat."

"Not so fast, Santana," Bruce corrected.

"You're kidding," Santana responded.

"According to HAARP's patent, it is capable of creating an effect similar to an atomic bomb. I'm not saying that's what happened. But it is capable of creating something as powerful as an earthquake."

"Holy Caramba! No wonder they wanted to make sure you were under total control."

"Well, my scientific knowledge may help us out. Marco said something about my working on what sounded a lot like building drones."

"Perfecto. The drones can tell us where we are."

"Only if they let us add in a camera, get one airborne, and watch what it shows."

"With all the explosive materials they have here, I wouldn't be surprised if they are planning to use the drones to keep the masses under control and—"

"My thought's exactly," Bruce interrupted me. "Remember that killer robot in Texas? Well, imagine a killer drone that could fly into your window or onto your car."

"Armed drones have been legal in some places for a while," I said.

"But with explosives, they could fly it into a stadium, blow up the people and blame it on the Arabs or the Venezuelans," Santana suggested.

"If Venezuela's weapons are as good as their prisons, that prisoners just walk out of, who would believe it?" I asked. "They'll blame it on the Russians."

"And how much of our DNA would they find on whatever remained? Notice that the counselors are really tight with gloves. They use them on toxic materials while we have none." Bruce pointed out.

"So, if we get out of line, they fly us to an event, kill us so we don't talk, expose our fingerprints on evidence and claim that we were lone bombers," Santana picked up the thought.

"We're getting out of here by Saturday, aren't we?" Emily, who had been taking in our conversation, asked.

"That's the plan," Santana answered her.

"The good thing about the drones is I might get access to battery material."

"The phones!" I said, hopefully.

"Unless they are otherwise disabled or we are out of a service area."

"All that aside, there's no way we're legally in California," I remarked, getting back on the subject of location. "California has regulated these camps. A significant number of kids died in these camps in California within a one-year period a while back, and Ricardo Lara used that to push through the legislation to regulate these places in the state. My dad was there at the press conference when the Governor signed it."

"Torture is illegal. Child abuse is illegal. And murder is illegal. Whether we are in a state where they are regulated or unregulated, they have no compunctions about breaking the laws on the books," Santana pointed out. "What's a little violation of education laws?"

I had to admit he was right. When it came to breaking the law, the wealthy and corporate executives seemed to have a get-out-of-jail-free card. "If this is California, that may be why they want to move Sonja's body out of state."

"Let's get back up there before someone checks on us," Santana suggested. "We can hash this over again when we have more clues about our location."

I gave Hope a goodbye hug. Santana escorted me and Emily back to our tent so he could slip back in the lock. He snapped it shut in case Marco found it open and took added security measures in the future. *Why hadn't Paul locked it? Was it a set-up, a slip-up or was he secretly cool?* I wondered.

# CHAPTER 19

The next morning, Jake assigned me to sort wires and circuit boards into large baggies inside the storage tent to be handed out to the blue crew at the side of the tent. Out the other exit at the dinner table, Jamie was assigned to put the capsules that others were working on into smaller baggies and then pack the baggies into boxes. Suddenly, he opened one of the baggies he was packing, poured the capsules into his hand and lifted them to his face as if he was preparing to swallow the whole bunch. Just as he was about to put them into his mouth, Santana came up behind him, knocked the pills out of his hand onto the ground and asked, "What are you doing, man?"

"I can't. I can't do this anymore."

"Hey, hermono." Santana put his arm around Jamie. "It's okay. We've all had to do stuff we hated."

"You don't understand."

"Let's walk," Santana suggested. They moved away from the table but closer to the tent where I was putting together my assigned set of baggies.

"I'm gay."

"I know. It's okay."

"It's not okay with them. They insisted I join, saying it would make me a real man. I just wanted them to stop pressuring me."

"What are you talking about?"

"I didn't want to hurt her. But when we were done, she was bleeding so badly."

"Sonja?"

"Tell me she's alright."

Santana didn't say anything for a minute. "What you did was wrong, man, but it was them. Everyone here is trying to survive. How many others were there that night?"

"There were eight of us. They rushed her off in the truck."

"I know."

"Tell me she's alright."

"I can't do that, man, but I can tell you that you weren't the one who was responsible."

"I really liked her. She was my friend. She will never forgive me."

"Honor her by surviving and never doing it again to anyone."

"I can't. I've been trying to tell myself that I had to do it. But I didn't. I could have refused. Like you refused that night in the pit with Ian."

"Learn. Do different next time."

"Sonja?"

Santana didn't say anything.

"God, she can't be—" Jamie didn't say anything further. He started to go back to where the pills lay on the ground, but Santana grabbed him.

"What happened to these pills?" Jake asked, coming up and seeing the pills on the ground.

"It was an accident. My accident," Santana said. "I bumped into Jamie. I'll clean them up and bag them."

"See that you do," Jake said.

Jake didn't seem as bad as Claudio. Or maybe he was giving us a temporary reprieve until everything about Sonja calmed down. There were the counselors and the blues to deal with. I wondered if, somehow, we could simply take over the camp.

There seemed to be a temporary lull in the cruelty. The remainder of the day, Santana and I gave each other knowing looks but avoided talking to each other, except for the insulting banter that seemed to characterize our official camp relationship.

# CHAPTER 20

"They are having us hollow out the insides of the drones," Bruce said when we met up later that night. "We are putting in the wiring and connections to allow them to fly, but they aren't giving us any batteries or power. They trust us with the drones but not with the batteries to make them fly."

It was late night, and the four of us campers were sitting below a tree near the creek. Hope was lying across my legs. Once again, my tent had been unlocked when Santana came for me and Emily.

"Could you put a message into the hollow space in the drone? Something like, 'Help?'" I asked.

"Maybe. But they'll open it up, again, when they slip in the batteries." Bruce replied.

"Have you seen the new recruit?" Emily asked, changing the subject.

"She is in a box in Claudio's former tent," Bruce informed us.

"It's a very slight improvement over being left outside, but it's still torture," Santana remarked. "At least, the tent is fully shaded. And I saw Jake going in there with water."

"Bet she was grateful for the water. This is how mind control works. They make you grateful for what they owed you all along and especially when they eventually release you from torture as if they are being good guys," Bruce said.

"I must be immune to gratitude," I commented.

"Mind control only works on a certain percentage of the population. That's why the Nazis killed so many people. I'm not talking about the Jews. I'm talking about the professors, the reporters, the dissidents," Bruce noted.

"I think I saw them move Marco's tent right against Claudio's before we went into ours," Santana informed us.

"Much worse. Marco's a psycho and it makes it hard for any of us to sneak her food and water," I said. "We don't know whether Jake is giving her actual water or just teasing her with it."

"At least, Marco will have to put up with the smell. Jake's new tent is upwind," Santana joked.

"She's better off outside in the box than in Marco's clutches," I noted. "Emily, did you notice anything else unusual today?"

"Last night, you mentioned silver nitrate. Well, I saw some boxes marked 'AgNO3' when I went into the supply tent, this evening."

"It's also used to seal wounds," I noted. "I once used it to stop a rabbit from bleeding to death."

"Then, it's either for an explosive or first aid," Santana elucidated.

"There were boxes of it," Emily said. "How many wounds are they expecting?"

"The quantity is suspicious, but they could be over-reacting from Sonja bleeding to death," Bruce suggested.

"You don't really believe they care about our health, do you?" I asked.

"We are valuable. They've already lost at least two assets, maybe three."

"Assets?" Emily asked.

"That's what they call us when we aren't around," Bruce continued. "They might be able to explain one or two. However, if they lose too many of us, there will be questions."

I thought about Jason, hoping he was somehow still alive.

"Any luck on finding where they store the cameras?"

"I think they are currently in Jake's tent," Santana said.

"How are we supposed to go in there?"

"Very carefully. He keeps it locked during the day. And at night, he's sleeping in it."

"Does anyone know where they keep the keys? Maybe we can help the new girl, too."

"Jake usually has them on him," Santana answered me. "And it's harder to spring the lock without getting caught in the daytime."

"So, we are S.O.L. on getting the evidence or on helping the latest victim. When they find we've walked out of here, the kids will be gone, the drugs will be gone and the drones will be gone. It will be as if we were never here," I lamented.

"If they leave here, they'll have to go somewhere," Santana pointed out.

"Here's another theory," Bruce suggested. "What if this camp really is about us and everything they have us doing is nothing more than a distraction designed to subvert our morality, prepare us to follow whatever orders come next? MK-Ultra conditioning camp. *Manchurian Candidate*-type stuff."

"But what about the drugs and the chemicals?" I asked. "I was bagging parts for the drones today."

"The drones are missing the critical parts, and without batteries, or some sort of power or catalyst, they will never be operational," Bruce commented. "Maybe the drugs aren't real either. Would any of us even recognize LSD or cocaine if we saw it? What we are putting together looks pretty suspicious, but drugs aren't my area of science. I never did drugs."

"Me neither," Emily seconded.

"I'll pass," Santana said.

"Not my thing," I chimed in. "Even at the vet clinic, where I interned, I never gave the injections or handled the drugs."

"What about the hydrazine and the silver nitrate?" Santana asked.

"Those are labels. Most any similar looking materials could be inside," Bruce said.

"Isn't this whole thing elaborate for just a hoax or a way to entrap or brainwash a bunch of teens?" I questioned.

"Like they've said, we are the 'assets.' Let's say we follow in our parent's footsteps. Santana goes into politics. And you, you'll probably have support from all the people tied to your dad, Summer. You might even become President, a step for womankind, or a First Lady."

"Eww."

"Emily, what do your parents do?" Bruce asked.

"My dad is in land speculation, and my mom is an attorney."

"Do either of your parents serve in any organizations?"

"My dad's on the CFR. Barack and Michele Obama used to be on that."

"The CFR?" Bruce asked, leaving his mouth hanging open for several seconds.

"Counsel on Foreign Relations. He's the chairman," Emily casually noted.

"Sh-t," I uttered. "They're the ones pushing all these wars."

"So, here you are to learn to accept your place in the family order," Bruce surmised.

"And you, Bruce," I said. "If HAARP is really that bad, you could be called on to continue your dad's work in ways that would bring the world to its knees."

"We aren't just rich kids. We are very well-connected rich kids."

"And with their video cameras, they are getting evidence they could use against us or our parents at any time they want to blackmail us or turn us into patsies," I said.

"Are you saying this is all just mind games?" Emily asked.

"Of course, it's mind games," Bruce said. "The question is whether what we are doing is just part of the game or whether it has a secondary purpose."

"With the secondary purpose being getting drugs for distribution or the explosives to use on someone or something," I agreed. "Either way, they are grooming us, and eventually, they will find a way to use us. Or maybe we'll be the next patsies in some false flag. Maybe they'll have a dirty bomb drill turned false flag and produce our bodies to say they squelched the threat."

"We have a week or less left," Emily noted.

"Tomorrow night, two or more of us ought to go back to the kids' camp to see if there is something we can use to escape. Maybe there's a car we didn't see or a telephone," Santana suggested.

"If the bullies didn't support the counselors, we'd have them outnumbered," I said. "Let's make a pack. If one of us gets out, we'll find a way to rescue the others."

I put my right hand out. Santana put his hand on top of mine. Bruce added his, and Emily put hers on top.

"Mañana por la noche." (tomorrow night)

"How long will Hillary be in the food tent?" Bruce asked.

"At most, one more night," Emily replied. "I heard Marco lecturing her about being too slow. He said that if she didn't finish fast, he'd find somebody else to finish for her. She is getting so frustrated that she had an argument with Ariel about it today. Ariel doesn't like to argue as she doesn't want to offend anyone in the power structure, but Hillary was so nasty, today."

"Hillary was really mean to her the other day," I recalled.

"This time, it was more hot-tempered. I don't know if she's getting any sleep. There are sleeping bags for new campers, but I haven't noticed any on the ground."

"If Hillary comes back to my tent, I won't be able to escape tomorrow night unnoticed," I advised.

"Get some rest tonight. We'll figure something out in the morning," Santana said.

"How do you two get out past your monitor? Paul is the monitor for your tent, isn't he?" I asked Santana.

"Sí. But he is the soundest sleeper I've ever met."

"And why has he left our tent unlocked?" I asked, pointing between myself and Emily.

"Maybe he likes señoritas hermosas."

"Or maybe they know what we are planning and are monitoring our actions, kind of like O'Brien was monitoring Julia and Winston in *1984* before they were carted off to the Ministry of Love."

"I think this is the Ministry of Love," Santana responded to me. "Paul is hard to read. He's a no-nonsense Establishment type, but he's not cruel like most of the other blues."

"Jamie's different, too." Whatever he had done, he had been kind to me.

"I think he was trying to fit in but found that fitting in was against his morality. Now, he's suffering, and he should," Santana stated.

"We're all being subjected to mind control. They are trying to find ways to get us all to crack," Bruce remarked.

"Like with Winston and the rats," I said.

"Something like that," Bruce responded.

In the morning, I awoke to find Marco in my tent, staring at me. "I'm your partner for this morning."

"What about the other teens?"

"Jake is watching them. Ian and Paul have been moved up to assistant counselors. It's something you should strive towards. We could send back a report to your dad saying your behavior has improved and you are taking a leadership position."

"While I'm here, maybe I can meet the son of some future campaign donor for him. That would impress him more than anything."

"Are you playing me? Don't."

"No. That's why he sent me here. Or I think that's the main reason. I broke up with someone he had selected for me."

"There are a couple of boys here your dad might approve of, but you don't seem to like them."

"It's kind of hard to get to know people when we can't talk to each other."

"Make it into a leadership position and you'll have some opportunities for talking. Today, we work. Build up those muscles."

"If I make assistant counselor, will my tent be unlocked at night?"

"That's not one of the benes. Tents are still locked."

*Okay, Paul must be special if he is in charge of locks and isn't locking his own or my tent,* I thought.

Marco, holding an ax, accompanied me up the hill. It gave me shivers. I kept picturing him in a *Friday the 13th* Jason mask. We came across a fallen tree, and he chopped up the branches. "Arms," he instructed. I held them out, and he placed so many broken pieces in my arms that I thought I was going to collapse. "That's good. We can come back for more."

"Aren't you going to carry some?"

"That's not my job," he said, slinging the ax over his shoulder.

When we got back to camp, Hillary and Ariel were arguing. "You do what I tell you to do."

"I just want gloves. I don't want to destroy my hands. Please!"

"You little elitist. No. You will fall in line, even if it means roughing up those pretty hands."

"They aren't pretty, anymore."

Marco seemed to be smiling at the interchange. I watched to see if he was going to do something, but instead he took a seat as if this were a theater and the girls were the stars.

"Who's in charge, Marco?" Hillary asked.

"I am. But Ariel is your ward today."

"Thank you."

Hillary looked around the camp. She went into our tent and brought out a toothbrush.

"Is that mine?" Ariel asked.

Hillary looked around the ground. A few feet away, there was some poop that had probably been dropped by one of the animals during the night. She went over and rubbed the toothbrush in it.

"I'm going to need a new toothbrush," Ariel said.

"This one will do. Now, brush your teeth."

"Drop dead," Ariel responded and started to walk off.

Hillary looked at Marco. "Does she get away with disobeying a direct order?"

"No, ma'am. You're a tough lady."

Ariel continued walking towards the woods. "You aren't allowed to wander off without a buddy," Marco said. "You know the rules." He turned his head and called, "Ian."

Ian came up quickly.

"We have a situation. Bring back Ariel. She is disobeying the rules and a direct order."

I had observed that the rule about not walking off without a buddy was enforced selectively. I had even been allowed to evade it a few times under Claudio's and Marco's watch.

Ian kicked Ariel in the back. She turned. He grabbed her wrist and dragged her back as she was trying to push him away. She used her free hand to slug him in the side. He responded by grabbing her throat and squeezing. She struggled, but she was losing the fight.

"That's enough," Marco said when it looked like she was losing consciousness. Ian let go, and she fell to the ground.

Hillary came up and stuck the toothbrush in her mouth, turning it as Ariel grabbed Hillary's hands and tried to push it away. When the toothbrush was pulled out, Ariel started to throw up.

# CHAPTER 21

"That's disgusting," Marco said, apparently referencing the vomit.

Ian took a cloth that was lying on the ground and stuffed it into Ariel's mouth. She was lying on her back, clearly gagging and choking on her own vomit, and looked as if she was asphyxiating. She started to convulse, almost going into an epileptic fit.

I rushed to her and removed the gag. Hillary slugged me, knocking me down. Ariel was still convulsing on the ground.

"Are you going to kill another camper?" I asked. Several teens standing nearby heard my question, and whispers went through the crowd.

Marco moved quickly to Ariel, turned her over and pushed her on her stomach. She vomited repeatedly and then started gasping for air. A minute later, she was lying on the ground more peacefully, alive but very weak. "We don't kill campers. Nobody has died."

That was apparently the final word on the subject. I looked at the others. There was doubt in their eyes as if they knew he was lying.

Hillary went back into the supply tent as Ariel lay on the ground, breathing but still appearing too weak to do anything except lie there.

"Too unpleasant for your elite eyes, Snooty?" Santana spouted at me. I knew it was an act, but it still hurt.

"F—off," I said to him.

"Woo. You've still got an attitude." Was he trying to get me in trouble? "Marco, I'd like to volunteer to check the traps."

"You need a buddy." Marco looked at me and then back at Santana. "I suspect she'll talk if you break any rules."

"Her again? This is unfair. Couldn't I get someone more pleasant?"

"You've been assigned. Do it. Enemies make good buddies. Be glad you aren't going with Ian."

Out of earshot of the campers and on the way to the uphill traps, I said, "Ariel could have died."

"I know. I was afraid you'd be next. It took a lot of courage to step in there. You were impressive, but your courage scares me. I really don't want anything bad to happen to you."

"Is this like Hillary Clinton's speech about one way to talk to Wall Street bankers and another way to talk to the voters? Except here, it's one way in front of counselors and another behind their backs?"

"Maybe, but you'd have to be out of your mind to think I approved of what went on down there. When we get free, we can send back help for Ariel and the rest."

"So, what do we do if Hillary is back in my tent tonight?"

"Stuff your bag after she falls asleep. I'm looking to spend the night alone with the hottest chick in camp."

The comment freaked me out until I realized he was kidding. "In your dreams. This is just the business of escape."

"Yes, ma'am."

The upper trap was empty today. "Maybe the other animals noticed how horribly the pregnant fox died. I can't believe you ate part of the remains."

"Starvation isn't my thing. I bet you've lost a lot of weight in the last week."

"Probably."

"You look thin, good, but thin. When we get you out of here, maybe I can help fatten you up?"

"For my dad to slaughter?"

"I'm sure mine will slaughter me first if I go back to him.

I picked up a stick and started writing Shannon's cell number in the dirt. "If you get out without me, here is my best friend's number. Let her know what is happening. Her name is Shannon. If she contacts my mom, tell her to tell my mom Spring sent you—"

Santana took the stick from me and traced the number. "Spring?"

"It's like a private code between me and my mother."

"And you gave it to me. I'm honored." He erased the number from the dirt. "I've got it. But if you think I'm leaving you behind, you can forget it. You can call Shannon yourself."

"Just in case."

When we got back with only a large rat from the second trap, Marco shook his head. Jamie was wandering around, seemingly in a daze. The blues were putting baggies with some kind of chemicals into the drones. It wasn't clear what the chemicals were. But if they were acidic, they would probably eat right through the bags. I thought of Timothy McVeigh and Oklahoma City. An indymedia replay of the TV news from the day of the Murrah bombing showed they were pulling bombs out of the building, casting doubt on the official story. But now the world knew, from the alleged official cause, that certain mixtures, such as fertilizer and bleach, could theoretically bring down a building.

"Jamie, go back to the other table," Marco's caustic voice demanded. "If you haven't fixed your attitude by the end of the day, you're back to a red shirt."

Jamie came at Marco as if he were going to attack. "Other table, where we are making what? Drugs? Doesn't anyone here have any morality? We raped her, all of us. She was sweet. She never said an unkind word to me. She never cared that I was gay. Gay is okay. Rape is not."

"Jamie, stop carrying on, or we'll have to put you in the box for a new learning experience."

"Torture. You will torture me into enjoying being a rapist like my other proud blue friends."

Santana went over to him. "Marco, I can handle this."

"Because you're gay, too," Ian chided. That hadn't occurred to me.

"Because Jamie is one of us, and he's hurting."

Now Santana was doing what I was doing earlier, trying to protect another camper. *Dangerous.*

"Ian, back to your table," Marco said. Ian made a hand gesture, indicating Santana was gay and then walked off. "Santana, see that Jamie gets in line, fast," Marco ordered, starting to walk off.

Jamie continued to focus on Marco. "I can't do this, anymore. I can't do anything, anymore. You can torture me, kill me, but I cannot do this, anymore. I don't want to be an evil person, and you are turning me into a rapist, a killer. Is Ariel better, or did you kill her, too?"

"Ariel is fine," Santana said. "She's probably back in her tent. Is she, Marco?"

"She's sleeping," Marco said. "We went easy on her."

"When I get out of here, I'm going to talk. This whole camp needs to come down. We should all die for what we did."

"You want to die?" Marco asked.

"No. It was a figure of speech," Santana said. As much as Santana tried to hide it, I could see the worry in his eyes. "He doesn't know what he is saying. Let him calm down, and I'll talk some sense into him."

"We'll see how eager you are to die." Marco turned towards the supply tent, "Hillary, bring me a ladder. And a chain."

She did so, and Marco set up the ladder under the branches of one of the trees.

"No, man. Look, he just needs to calm down!" Santana shrieked. Santana had known Marco longer than I had, and if he was scared for Jamie, I should be, too.

"Paul," Marco shouted. "Get Santana out of here."

Paul came from the blue table around the far side of the culinary supply tent. He grabbed Santana. The two started fighting. Marco took the chain from Hillary, pushed Santana face down, and, with Paul's help, wrapped the chain around his wrists and held it together with a cable tie. Santana managed to use the chain to break the cable tie. Marco responded by pulling a lock out of his pocket. "Paul, lock his wrists in the chain." Paul did as told.

"I need another chain, longer with a hook at each end!" Marco yelled at Hillary. She went back into the supply tent and came out with a longer chain with hooks.

Paul sat Santana up as Marco fastened the new chain around Jamie's neck. It wasn't a slip knot. It was fastened like a choker with a clasp at the end. Marco stood the ladder under a tree.

Paul looked uneasy, but he continued watching. "Marco, this could be dangerous. Make your point another way."

Marco ignored Paul. "Now, climb," he bellowed at Jamie.

Jamie stepped onto the ladder like a soldier on his way to his grave.

"Jamie, don't!" I pleaded and grabbed his arm.

"Ian!" Marco called.

I hadn't noticed that Ian was back. Ian grabbed my arm. I shook my arm to try to rid myself of him, but he pulled it, twisted it and flung me down.

Hands chained behind his back, Santana got up and rammed into Ian's back. Ned came up and assisted Ian in keeping us down. As the three of us were struggling, Jamie continued climbing the ladder. Marco threw the other end of the chain over a tree branch, then wrapped it around the tree trunk and fastened it to itself.

"Accidents happen. This is a really bad idea," Paul told Marco. "We can't afford another incident."

"Who put you in charge?" Marco turned from Paul to Jamie. "The choice is yours. You can come back down, and I'll take it off your neck. You can choose to live and join us in celebrating the opportunities here. Or you can jump. The chain isn't tight enough to kill you unless you jump. Now cut this out, and let's get on with the afternoon."

At that moment, Jake came running in. "What's going on here, Marco?" The distraction turned our attention from Jamie, but when we looked back, he had jumped.

"Get him down, now!" Jake ordered. Paul was already unhooking the end of the chain from around Jamie's neck. They lowered Jamie and placed him carefully on the ground. His head flopped to the side. Marco tried to shake him. Didn't they know not to shake someone who might have a broken neck?

Other campers came running. Most were silent. "Oh my God!" Emily screamed.

# CHAPTER 22

"I swear. I didn't think he'd do it," Marco professed. Paul looked pretty shaken. Santana managed to get up and rushed over to Jamie, putting his head on Jamie's chest.

"Unchain Santana. Everyone, go to your tents," Jake said, placing a couple of fingers against Jamie's neck, seemingly to feel for the pulse and then leaning down, pushing Santana away and putting his own head to Jamie's chest and listening. Jake started trying CPR, but we all knew Jamie was beyond that.

"Go," Marco shouted at us. He ushered us in the direction of our tents. He opened the lock on Santana's chain. Santana looked like he was going to speak out in anger and then punched a tree on the way into his tent. Most of us were in shock as we moved.

In the tent, Ariel was lying on her side on her sleeping bag, messed up with vomit. She was staring at the far side of the tent.

Emily and I sat on our sleeping bags in silence, neither of us knowing what to say. Emily was pale as a ghost. Tears were burning in my eyes.

Emily started sobbing. She was visibly trying to stop but couldn't. Finally, she got out, "First Sonja. Now Jamie. We're all going to die."

I put my arms around her. "No, we're not. I won't let them harm you."

"You and Santana couldn't save Jamie. Nobody can stop them."

"This may sound harsh, but Jamie wanted to die. I might have been able to save him from Marco, but it was himself he needed saving from."

"They did this to him. They took away his will to live."

"We have to be strong. No matter what they make us do, we can't let them destroy us." I didn't know if I was faking my resolve and optimism or if I was just getting stronger, more determined.

"Sonja thought her dreams were coming true. She wanted to live, to get out alive. How can she be dead? How can Jamie be dead? He was my friend." Emily continued crying, and I knew tears were also running down my face.

"I didn't know Jamie well, but he had a conscience, and he really felt bad about what he had done to Sonja. What eight of them had done to Sonja."

I could hear Ariel whimpering, too. I went over to her. "Ariel, no matter what they said, they didn't have the right to do that to you."

She didn't say anything. She just lay there.

---

Sitting on my sleeping bag, I thought about my father. Was he tricked into sending me here? He wasn't that ignorant. He knew what he was doing? My dad wasn't someone to be fooled. If I survived, I wasn't going back. If I did, I'd be making this all okay. He expected gratitude and subservience. Right now, I wanted to tear him apart, piece by piece. *What my mother must have gone through. No wonder she left without turning back.*

About half an hour later, they called us out. We had skipped lunch. An early dinner had been prepared. It was some kind of vegetable soup and sides of sausage. I pocketed the sausage and tried to eat the soup. None of us had any real appetite.

During dinner, everyone was quiet. The usual sniping and fighting were gone. I knew I would have to sneak out tonight and hope not to get caught. Hillary had volunteered to work through the night in the supply tent on whatever she was doing. Ariel would be staying in the tent with me and Emily.

It would be hours before it would be safe to leave, and so I decided to rest until Jake and Marco were asleep. With Ariel in the tent, there would be a risk. Again, I heard the tent lock going into its slot. I didn't hear a click but I might have missed it.

I closed my eyes.

*My mom and I were in a motel room. "We are going where you will be safe," she assured me.*

*"I'm so glad you are better and I'm with you again. I don't like Dad after what he did to you."*

*"Has he hurt you?"*

*"Some, but I'm fine. Let's go where he can't find us."*

*She hugged me. "I love you. I'm going to protect you."*

*There was a knock at the door. I knew this was a dream. But it was also a memory. I had to change it. Maybe if I changed my dream, I could change my life.*

*"Please don't answer it. It's some really bad men."*

*"Mrs. Tanner, this is the police. Open the door."*

*My mother stood there, not seeming to know what to do. I looked around. The windows opened onto the front of the motel and there was no back way out. There was no escape.*

*"Here's the key," I heard someone say.*

*"No," I cautioned. I had to stop it from happening, but how?*

*A second later, the door opened. A police officer was there with two men who used to hang out with my dad. I knew them. I hadn't known them at the time, but I had met them later. They were on the security detail for Senator Madstein.*

*I jumped in front of my mom but she pulled me to the side and then behind her.*

*"You can't take my mom. I need to be with her!" I shouted.*

*"Officer, I just got out of the hospital. I wanted to stay somewhere private and my daughter was visiting me. There is nothing wrong with that. Her father and I are still married."*

*"You accused your husband of putting you in the hospital, is that right?"*

"That doesn't matter, right now. We are spending a nice evening together."

"I'm going to have to take you in for questioning. These men will take your daughter home."

"No. I need to accompany her!" I pleaded.

"That's not the way it works."

I held tightly onto my mom. "I won't leave her."

"You wouldn't want your mother to get into trouble."

"Please. Let her go," my mom said, as the men grabbed me.

"We're just taking her home. You wouldn't want her to be dragged down to police headquarters with you, would you?"

"I want her to stay with me. You can't have my mother! Where she goes, I go!" I protested.

The officer addressed my mom. "This matter isn't appropriate for a child. You'll have to settle this issue with Mr. Tanner, later. In the meantime, these men have to take her."

The security men worked to remove my arms from around my mother and to pull me away. I kicked and punched at them and tried to re-clasp onto my mom. My would-be captors pulled me back as the officer pulled my mom out the door and held her back, keeping her from reaching out for me as I was carried away. She was crying. I was crying. That was the last time I saw my mother.

# CHAPTER 23

I awoke, realizing that I had been crying in my sleep. I looked over at Ariel. She was still asleep.

I heard a rustling and noticed a hand reaching through the hole near my feet. I touched it. As I went to the door, it was slightly opened and two hands gave me a log and then some rags. I used them to stuff my bag. Then I went out and followed Santana into the night.

We crossed the creek and headed towards the little kids' camp. As we got to the stream, Santana lifted me up and started carrying me across. He stumbled and we both fell into the cold water. We laughed. as we scurried to the other side.

"What are your plans for when we get out of here? Cuba or Venezuela or to your mom's?" I asked.

"I'll try to contact my mother, my real mother. I don't think she wants me, though. I guess, I could go to Florida and take a boat to Cuba. My dad hated Fidel and Raul and he doesn't like the new guy any better. I might have some relatives there I don't know about. I am thinking of asking for asylum and then doing a live press conference from Havana."

"If my mother doesn't help me, I guess I'll hide out until I'm eighteen. Cuba wouldn't be so bad."

"I think I can make room for you on my boat."

"No. I think I'll make room for you on mine." I teased. "I hate to be a downer, but how will we get money to buy a boat?"

"Señorita, I have talents. I have accounts and I know the passwords to all my dad's online accounts. And I have friends who just might be willing to help me relieve him of his funds."

"They won't be happy if they get arrested."

"With fake ID's and double online transfers, my dad won't know what hit him until everyone's out of the country."

"Did you ever see *Sneakers* where Robert Redford broke into in the RNC account and gave their money to Green Peace? I saw it at a retro film festival."

"I have other talents that are much more impressive than those of Redford's syndicate friend. So do we hang together?"

"For a while, maybe. At least, until we are safe."

Santana high-fived me. It was really great to have him cheering up the night. I felt pinpricks in my stomach thinking about how I would miss him when we finally parted. Given how much I had hated him, it didn't make sense that his leaving would bother me.

When we arrived, the truck was at the kids' camp. That was a plus. There was also the SUV with the alarm system. "Think you can hotwire the truck?"

"Piece of cake."

"That's an old expression."

"Okay, piece of tiramisu?" he joked.

As we approached, we could see we didn't have a clear path. Outside the vehicles, Evan and Jake were talking. "How did this happen?" Evan inquired.

"Marco is a bit of a loose cannon."

"Jamie's father is the deputy chairman of the Federal Reserve. We were supposed to straighten him out, not kill him."

"He's not expected home until he's straight. We have time to figure out a plan," Jake said.

"We could have the authorities breathing down our neck. We need to change some of our plans in case of problems. I'm taking tonight's video with me and flying it to Utah. What's that over there?" Evan asked, pointing in our direction. I had thought we were hidden. Evan pulled out a gun and headed toward our location. Santana and I backed up.

"Go that way," Santana said, pointing in the direction from which we had come. He went the other way, making noise, drawing the attention away from me.

I passed the camping area we had been by before. I had to divert attention from Santana. I knocked the propane stove over, turning their attention in my direction. I continued on in the same direction, but they were running close on my heels. Two other men armed with assault rifles came up behind Evan. I went behind a tree and Evan came forward.

Another minute and he would likely find me. The four split up and were preparing to circle both sides of the tree I was standing behind. Just when I thought I'd be nailed, the injured bear limped through the campsite. Evan fired a shot at the bear as it took off.

Evan turned and headed towards the truck, got in and started it up. Jake and the two men looked around and then went towards the cabin. A man came out. I couldn't believe my eyes.

"Dick, it was just a bear. You can relax. Go back in," one of the men, said.

*A former VVIP. Guess he's found another hobby besides shooting his attorneys.*

As he, Jake and the remaining men went into the cabin, the truck turned and took off—with Santana on the back of the tail.

# CHAPTER 24

I waited a while and saw the two armed men escort the VVIP out of the cabin to the SUV and drive away. I started to walk back.

In the distance, I heard some loud sounds, maybe firecrackers or gunshots or a vehicle backfiring. I couldn't tell, as it was a ways away. But a chill went through me. It didn't sound like they came from the exact direction in which Santana and the truck had taken off, but I couldn't be sure they hadn't turned in that direction.

*He's okay*, I told myself.

As I crossed the stream, I heard movement on the other side. I paused, wondering if I should proceed. I backed up and waited. Maybe it was an owl or a raccoon. I continued on. A little while later, there were more sounds, both behind me and in front of me. I backed against a tree. I heard fast running footsteps coming towards me and then saw the wag of a tail.

"Hope," I said leaning down and giving him a hug. "I'm so glad it's you. You scared me."

For Hope and the bear to have made it down the hill, it occurred to me that either they had forgotten to turn on the protection barrier or intentionally had it off for the VVIP.

As Hope and I made our way past the creek, I gave him a hug and whispered to him, "You stay here. I wish I could bring you with me."

He whined a little.

"Wait, I almost forgot." I reached into my pocket and pulled out the sausages from dinner. He took them from my hand, tail wagging. "Just wait until you taste some good vegan food. You'll never want to touch that stuff again." I gave him another hug and said "Goodnight."

As I got to my sleeping bag, everything looked dark and calm. I pulled the log out of my sleeping bag and took it outside and placed it on the ground. I put the extra clothes under the bag. I tried to put the lock on but it was too difficult as it required the zipper be closed. I laid it on the ground, near the door, hoping they would think they forgot to put it on.

A couple minutes later, the tent was unzipped. I'd been caught. It was Ariel who stepped in. She zipped the tent back up.

"Have a nice rendezvous?"

"I just went for a walk."

"Alone?"

"Who else would go? Emily's sleeping and everyone is locked in."

"That's not what I saw."

I didn't answer her.

"I thought you and Santana didn't like each other?"

"Did you see me coming back with anyone?"

"I wonder how much trouble you will get into if I talk."

"If they believe you."

"I guess we can find out. Unless you take me with you."

"What?"

"You are planning an escape, right?"

"I thought you were afraid of escaping."

"I can't be here anymore."

*She has every reason to want to be out. But she had been playing the game with them. Can she be trusted or is she a mole?*

I sat down. "Fine. Right now, I am looking for a way out. But I don't even know where this camp is. I need more information if we are to get out."

"That's easy. We're in California."

"How do you know?"

"Because I heard Evan tell Jake he was going to Edwards Air Force Base the other day. My dad is with NASA. I know where Edwards is."

"We never left California, wow."

"I wasn't in California. I came from Houston."

"Okay, when I get out, I'll include you. But you need to keep quiet about everything you saw tonight. And as for Santana, maybe I just gave him payback for all those insults."

I lay back in my sleeping bag. I felt sad and I felt guilty about feeling sad. I should be happy. Santana got out. Maybe he would call Shannon or send help. I found myself missing him. The odds of my seeing him again seemed slim. He deserved to get away. He was a good guy. He tried to save Jamie and he had risked his safety for me as well. He was pretty resourceful. If anyone could make it and avoid capture, it was him.

Morning seemed to come too soon after I fell asleep. I was exhausted. The tent was locked again in the morning. Had we been caught or had someone thought it was a mistake that it was unlocked and remedied the situation? Something was different. Jake gathered us together for breakfast.

The new camper joined us. Her name was Abigail. She was tall with a Twiggy figure and her head was shaved. I had a feeling that the shaved head wasn't her idea. Jake had Hillary take her down to the creek to clean her up. When they returned, she was in fresh clothes with her head and face washed and smelling a lot cleaner. Jake fed Abigail large portions of eggs and hash browns for breakfast.

"Why does she get so much food?" Ian complained. "We only got two scoops of hash browns." He looked at me as if I was responsible for his not getting more.

I suspected Abigail hadn't eaten in days. She looked questioningly at her food and then downed it in seconds.

After breakfast, we sat in a circle and Jake handed out *Bibles*. That was new. These were the first books they had given us. Claudio may have claimed it was a Christian camp, but I could have sworn that these guys were closer to Satanists than Christians. Santana was noticeably missing.

"Paul, where is Santana?" Jake asked.

"He's got a fever. I left him in the tent. He's going to be useless today."

"Work is good for fevers," Marco spoke up.

"I think we can cut Santana a little slack, today. No reason to have any more losses," Jake pointedly replied to Marco.

I listened to the exchange. Paul was in charge of Santana's tent. There was no way that Santana was lying in his bag with a fever. Paul had to be covering for him. I thought back to the nights when the lock was in place on my tent but unlocked. It was Paul who was supposed to lock it. He was a blue shirt and they were trusting him, like Ian, with extra duties. I wondered what his story was. It could have been an accident that he had left my tent unlocked or maybe he thought it didn't matter if I couldn't remove the open lock from the inside. This morning, he could have just decided to cut Santana a break after yesterday and just left the tent without checking on him, or maybe he was covering so as not to get in trouble for Santana's escape.

"Where are John and Charlie?" Ian asked.

"Charlie is in a time out," Marco said. "John left for another camp."

There was something about the way he said it that concerned me. I didn't see Charlie by the tree. Maybe he was in a box in Marco's tent. But I hadn't heard any exchanges about John leaving camp until then. I probably had missed a lot. Maybe this happened when Santana and I were out.

Bruce picked up the *Bible* he was handed, seemingly eager to dive into it. I was certain it was an act. "May we do more *Bible* verses at lunch?" he asked.

"I think that would be an excellent idea," Jake said.

"Oh, aren't we being sweet, Christian, loving," Abigail ridiculed. "I've been gagged in Abu Ghraib and starved for days, and now I'm in Christian Sunday School. Is this the second coming?"

She had character. I instantly liked her.

"Did my daddy threaten to bomb you? Oh, wait, he's the one who had me kidnapped to this concentration camp."

"Sometimes, it takes some strong measures to get kids off drugs," Jake responded.

"I wasn't a drug addict. I want my hair back." The more I heard from her, the more I knew I was certain we were going to be friends.

"It was green. Unhealthy."

"I like it that way."

"Now, would you care to pick up your *Bible*, Abigail, and join in the morning study or just listen in and join us when you are ready?" Jake asked.

Everyone acted as if we had been doing *Bible* verses since the camp began. The deaths had probably scared the counselors. Maybe, Sonja's father was looking into things. Maybe, other parents were starting to ask questions. The counselors might need our support if there was an inquiry, later. I couldn't imagine anyone but the blue gang giving them a good report, no matter how many *Bible* verses they threw at us.

Later that morning, much of the blue group continued its curious work. Hillary stayed busy with chemicals in the culinary tent. Ian assisted her. Pairs of purples and reds walked hand in hand towards the traps and down to the river.

After lunch, Evan drove up in the truck. "Is everyone well, up here?" he asked.

"All except Santana," Jake replied. "He's asleep in his tent with a fever."

"Let me take a look at him," Evan said.

*Is there a distraction I can manifest?* Ian came up alongside of me.

"Stop pushing me!" I shouted at him.

Evan turned towards Ian and harshly scolded, "Part of the reason you boys are here is to learn to treat women with respect." I almost laughed, considering how well they treated Sonja. "I mean it, Ian. I want you to apologize to Summer."

"You're kidding. She's lying. I didn't touch her."

"Really!" I reacted. "How many times have you grabbed me? The whole camp has seen you put your hands on me, again and again."

"Ian, I want you to apologize and promise Summer it won't happen, again."

I rolled my eyes.

"I didn't."

"Ian."

"I'm sorry for the times I've touched you, bitch."

"Ian. Go to your tent for a time out," Evan instructed.

This pretense at teaching the campers respect was almost hilarious. It occurred to me that Evan might really be scared of what was coming. If I were staying, I might enjoy seeing him sweat. But I intended to be out of here before anyone else died.

As we sat down to lunch, I thought about Santana. Had he contacted Shannon? Had she contacted my mother? Was help on the way? How much did Ariel know? She had seen Santana. She didn't seem to know he was gone. She didn't know about Bruce. I meant it when I told her we'd take her, but I didn't want to clue her in too much in advance, in case she was planning to use the information to get in good with our captors.

"So, what have you been learning today?" Evan asked the campers.

"*Bible* verses," Ned told him.

"John 3:16," Jared crowed. "For God so loved the world that he gave his only begotten Son that whosoever believeth in him shall not perish but have everlasting life."

"Very good, Jared," Evan congratulated him.

Abigail mostly gave eye rolls. "I've got a good one, my dad's favorite: 'An eye for an eye and a tooth for a tooth.'"

"I see your dad has taught you the *Old Testament*," Evan noted, missing the gist of her comment, probably on purpose. "Perhaps you could lead one of the later *Bible* studies."

A hushed murmur of chuckles went through the group.

It was only then that I noticed a camera recording us. Marco was holding it. I wondered if this video of our wonderful Christian camp would be going to our parents.

"Well, I have to be leaving," Evan said. "It looks like things are going pretty well here. I'm sure your parents will be happy with the progress you all have made."

Despite the propaganda value of the video, I breathed a sigh of relief that Evan seemed to have forgotten about Santana. Perhaps I breathed it a little too soon. "Before I go, I want to check on in our sick boy," he said, feigning a look of concern.

I had already done a distraction. I couldn't pull the same thing, again. As we walked in the direction of the purple tent, Bruce tripped over who knows what, maybe his own feet. But it was enough to call attention away from the tent. Evan looked in Bruce's direction and then turned back to the tent and told Paul, "Open it up."

*What is the worst that could happen?* I told myself. *They'll find Santana has flown the Gulag. Or maybe Evan will suspect that there is something else Marco and Jake are keeping secret. If Santana isn't here, he can't be punished.* But they could send out a search party, lock down the airports, put out an APB on him, and make it harder for Santana to get away clean.

# CHAPTER 25

Evan marched into the tent. "Santana, do you need medical help?"

"That's rich," Bruce whispered, noticing my nervousness. "I wonder what condition the doctor would say the shirts and log have."

I held back a laugh but continued to worry.

"Oh, no. I'm starting to feel better," came a groggy sounding response.

I almost collapsed in shock and then breathed a sigh of relief. It was clearly Santana's voice. "I just need a little more rest if that's okay."

"Well, we only want the best for you. I'll have Paul bring you in a plate of food." They were really faking being nice today. I noticed the camera was still recording.

"Thank you."

I was pretty sure I hadn't dreamed his riding off on the back of the truck. Maybe he had gotten off before it got far. Perhaps I should have waited a bit before coming back.

Santana deserved to be free. I shouldn't be feeling joy at knowing he was back. Yet, I felt my heart leaping. Maybe it was because I felt I had an ally, a friend, I thought I would never see again. I didn't have the right to feel that way. *He shouldn't be back here,* I told myself.

I glanced at Bruce. He looked as stunned as I felt. As Paul walked by me, he said, "You look like you've seen a creature from outer space."

"Yes. This camp. The complete turn-around from a torture chamber to a *Bible* institute."

"Don't let Marco hear you talking like that."

I moved over to Bruce and whispered, trying to keep my lips in a smile and not move them. "How do you think he got back in there?"

"I don't know. I could swear he wasn't there when I got up, but I didn't actually check. I didn't want Paul to notice."

"Maybe he really does have a fever. But the last time I saw him— Let's talk later." I changed the subject. "I am really liking Abigail. I hope they don't kill her." My comment took me aback. It was a tasteless remark when I thought of how two, probably three, teens had actually died here since I arrived.

Bruce ignored my impropriety. "She's a kick. I wonder who her dad is. Perhaps some general."

"Side-talking," Paul said, quietly enough that only we noticed. "Rules."

"Hey, Green," Ian loudly called to Abigail. "How about joining the blues? We could use some gallows humor."

"Ian, watch your mouth," Evan reacted.

"Hardy, har. The mindless Nazi thinks he's got something to say," Abigail responded, looking Ian's way and then dismissing him with her eyes as if he was of no interest to her.

Abigail was giving Ian his due and hadn't let the camp break her. She was wearing a red shirt. That meant I might have a new ally in my tent.

Evan got into the truck and drove off.

"I wonder if this means the pit fighting will be on hold for a while," I whispered to Bruce.

"You didn't see the worst of it," Bruce noted.

"Wonderful Christians," I commented.

"Summer!" Jake called.

"Sh-t," I uttered under my breath.

"Show Abigail how we collect water for the stove."

I picked up the buckets and nodded towards downhill. "Sure thing."

"So, are you my Kapo?" she asked as we headed towards the creek.

"What?"

"Death camp inmate trustee."

"That would be Hillary or Ian. I am likely slated to be one of those who is about to die. I could kill my father."

"Could you get mine, too, while you're at it?"

"Who is your father?"

"Secretary of Defense. Didn't like his little girl rebelling, living it up at parties, creating scenes, getting in the tabloids. And yours?"

"Chief of Staff for the Governor and formerly for Senator Dana Madstein."

She laughed. "If they could do this to their own kids, imagine how little they care about lives in the rest of the world."

"Exactly."

"So is Hillary the blonde with the attitude?"

"You could say that. She is the eyes and ears of the—" Abigail had clocked the name of the place right. "The death camp administrators."

"And Ian?"

"He and his gang are nasty. Watch your back around him."

"Does everyone spend a year in a box when they come here?"

"It seemed like a year. I understand I was there for three days. I think you were there for two."

"Has anyone died here?"

"Two, maybe three, since I came a little over a week ago. All rich kids. I think they're scared about the deaths. You made it here for the first *Bible* study."

"I guess I was just in time for the religious indoctrination."

I laughed. "So, what's with the green hair?"

"It was my independence, my way of saying my body belongs to me. They shaved it off." Her expression changed as my dog approached. "What's this?"

"This is Hope." I pulled some bacon out of my pocket and gave it to him.

"Hi there, Hope. You're a pretty one," Abigail said. "My dad has Rottweilers. He's part pit bull, isn't he?"

"I think he is."

"Well, you won't talk when I blow this place, will you?" she asked Hope. She turned to me, "So, how do we blow this place?"

"I knew we would hit it off. I'm looking for a way out, myself. They generally put a lock on the tents at night and we are supposed to be on a buddy system when we go to pee or do anything else outside the camp site."

"Well, I'm not locked up now. Hope you don't get in trouble." With that, she took off.

# CHAPTER 26

But not far. I saw her bending over in pain on the other side of the creek. I rushed over to her and helped her back to the camp side. My earplugs protected me. Her pain seemed to lesson and then let up.

"It's auditory," I said. "There is some kind of radio wave barrier around the camp. Earplugs suppress it. I might be able to get you some."

"Not waiting around," she responded. She picked up leaves, wrapped them around some wet sand, stuffed them in her ears and took off, this time, making it out of sight.

I went back up to the camp with the water.

"Where's Abigail?" Jake, who was holding a small stack of wet rags, asked.

"She's not back? She wanted to rush back to do more work. She's pretty industrious. I mentioned something about food traps. Maybe she went up the hill to help out or maybe she got lost. There's nowhere to go."

"She's not supposed to be on her own. Neither are you. Take these wet cloths to Santana and put them on his head while I look for her."

"Why are we babying that jerk? Can I stuff them down his throat?"

"Just treat his fever and dump your petty differences."

"Hey, are you really sick?" I asked Santana as I put a cloth on his head. His head didn't feel hot.

"Florence Nightingale. I think I've got this fatal condition. What do you call it when a patient falls for his nurse?"

"Yeah, right. How far did you get?" I whispered, smacking his arm.

"Lancaster. That base he mentioned might be Edwards."

"Well, I could have told you that."

"Don't BS me."

"Really. Ariel told me last night. She overheard them talking about it. So, we really are in California? Someone should notify the authorities."

"I left an anonymous message I'm hoping will get through to the authorities."

"Why did you come back?"

"Well, I stole this car and I was thinking I could make it to the coast, learn to surf and become a beach bum." He looked at me.

I waited for more.

"But then there was this girl that I just couldn't leave, and so I drove back towards the camp."

I made a fist and shook it. "Don't blame me."

"Can't help it. It's amore."

"That's Italian," I said, showing him my fist, again. "And we are not each other's type."

"Who said it was you? I was thinking Hillary. She could take on an army."

I started to laugh and then caught myself. I didn't want Marco hearing me happy around Santana.

"Anyway, I was so proud of myself for stealing the car that I didn't bother to check the gas gage. After it died, I pushed it into a clump of trees and made it back up here while you guys were having breakfast."

"Paul said you were sick when he checked you before breakfast."

"The log may have been sick. Probably was dead."

"So, what we need is gas and we can take off."

"If nothing else, we've got hydrazine."

"Yeah. Maybe it will help the car blow up. You shouldn't have come back."

"There are four of us. We're a team."

"Five. Ariel is demanding in. I don't trust her, but she saw us last night."

He looked skeptical. "Fine. Five. But don't tell her any more than you have to."

"She doesn't even know about Emily and Bruce, just you and me. And I pretended I was just getting revenge on you last night."

"Let's keep it that way."

"We've got a new girl. Or rather we had. She just ran off."

"Wise girl."

"What's that?" I asked, distracted by the sound of snarling dogs.

I went to the door of the tent. Marco was having them sniff some clothing. They looked like mastiffs, hungry mastiffs. I went over to Paul, who was across from Santana's tent. "Where did the dogs come from?" I asked.

"They keep them up the hill at a distance from the campers and just use them in case someone tries to run."

"Who?"

"None of your business. Now, back to work and make yourself busy."

"I'm on Clara Barton duty," I said, going back into Santana's tent.

"Did you know they have tracking dogs?" I asked Santana.

"I've heard them at times in the distance. That must be where Marco keeps running off with the meat that's better than what we get. I thought he was just gorging himself to be a sumo wrestler?"

"I don't think they'd dare kill her. Her dad's the Secretary of Defense."

"Kreskin's daughter is here?"

"Was. Do you know her?"

"Don't you ever look at the tabloids? She makes Lindsay Lohan and Paris Hilton look like tea-toddling nuns."

"Summer!" Jake called to me from outside the tent. "Hillary needs some help moving some items in the cooking supply tent. Then, I need you to help with lunch." Jake looked in the opening and asked, "Santana, do you think you will be able to make it to lunch?"

Santana started to sit up and then groaned and held his head. "Could someone bring me in a bowl of something? I promise I'll be better tomorrow."

Hillary had something boiling in what looked like a distillery in the cooking tent. She was not attending it though. She was sitting near the open side of the tent in a chair, looking tired. Maybe she had been up all night.

"Summer, we've got cans of vegetable soup, just for you. They are behind the stuff in the back of the tent. I need you to move everything in front of them over to the side wall," she said pointing to the wall opposite her.

Moving items around a supply tent seemed like one of the more normal things they could have us do. In front of the back wall, there were bags of fertilizer. Some containers marked in large letters read "Hydrazine." Some other containers were marked "Nitric Acid," "Silver Nitrate" and "Pseudoephedrine." With all that pseudoephedrine, I'd never have to worry about stuffed sinuses. There were also some heavy boxes. There were so many containers in front of the tent back wall that half an hour later, I was only part way through. It occurred to me that this was all indicative of supplies for bombs and drugs.

After I had lifted the more dangerous looking chemicals, I came across some wrapped bricklike substances that looked like packed white powder. As I carried a couple to the side, I discovered the packing was loose. The powder came out in a puff and spread all over me.

I turned around to try to explain to Hillary and saw the telephoto end of a camcorder pointing right at me through the opening of the tent. Someone was video recording me.

# CHAPTER 27

My mind went to the subject of extortion. Maybe they would use it against my dad, try to tarnish his reputation. If that was their plan, I might be willing to join in and help them. Or it could be to set me up as some kind of patsy, like that Paddock guy who was blamed for the Vegas shooting—even though it would have been physically impossible for him to have done what they claimed.

"If you have a broom, I'll clean up this mess your supplies made, Marco," I said, assuming he was on the other end of the camera. The flap was mostly closed and so it was hard to see.

"What have you been up to?" Good guess. That was Marco's voice.

"Moving your supplies like you asked," I said.

"Why did you bring that stuff to the camp?" Hillary directed her comment at me.

"These are your supplies and I'm leaving your tent," I said.

The lens was down at this point. I pushed my way through. Marco grabbed me and slammed me to the ground. I sat up and tried to stay calm.

"I thought you were out looking for someone."

"Found her. Abigail's in your tent, resting. Jake is with her."

"What did you do to her?"

"Tried to help her. It seems some wild animals attacked her. But she'll be alright."

"Wild animals, like your dogs?"

"Don't go spreading rumors about dogs."

*Was the video to shut me up about the dogs? Or was it standard camp procedure to set us up for blackmail?*

"Like the rest of the campers didn't also see and hear your attack dogs."

"If you don't stop mouthing off, maybe you would like to spend another day and night with the tree."

"Is that the Christian thing to do?" I got up and stalked off towards my tent.

"I didn't give you permission to leave."

I turned back to look at him.

"Summer, get back in here," Hillary demanded form the opening of the tent.

Still looking at Marco, I said, "No, but your camera did. Send it to my dad. Let him know what kind of camp he sent me to." I turned away, again, and went to my tent.

Jake was with Abigail. "Oh my—" I reacted, lifting hands up to my face in shock. There was an extensive amount of blood on the floor. Her body, from her feet to her neck, was covered with a blanket. "She needs to be taken to a hospital," I demanded.

"Who gave you permission to enter?"

Ignoring him, I went over to Abigail. "God. What did they do to you?"

She appeared to be in too much pain to answer.

"Are you sadists going to let her bleed to death, like you did Sonja?"

"Be more respectful," he cautioned, glaring at me. He turned back to Abigail. "Her wounds have been sealed. The bleeding's stopped."

"What about a transfusion?"

"I don't think she'll need one."

"With all this blood on the floor?"

"Believe it or not, I've had some training. I worked in a hospital for a while. I used a medical grade form of superglue that works better than stiches."

"She needs fluids. What training did you have in the hospital? Janitorial?"

"You aren't helping."

"You're afraid that, if you take her to a hospital, they will come and close down your little torture operation, complete with attack dogs, hangings, pit fights to the death and gang rapes?"

"That will be enough. You need to leave."

"Not with her in this condition. You've already tortured me. Unless you're planning to kill me, you're not getting me away from her." He looked angry but was holding it back more than Marco would have.

"Very well. Keep an eye on her." He handed me a bottle of water. "See if you can get her to drink."

"What about antibiotics?" I asked.

"What?"

"If she survives the blood loss, an infection could get her."

"I'm not sure we have any."

"I'm allergic to—to pen—penicillin," Abigail murmured, barely able to get out the words.

"I'll see what we have."

As Jake left. I sat down beside Abigail. "I didn't know about the dogs," I said apologetically. "I had heard dogs out there, but I didn't know they were using trained attack dogs."

Tears streamed down her cheeks.

"I and some others will get you out of here, and you'll be okay. We'll find a way."

"They wouldn't stop biting."

I removed the blanket. There were bloody bandages covering part of her left leg and the right side of her abdomen. Her right arm was also bandaged, and her bandages were also covered with blood.

"They glued it under the bandages?" I asked.

There also were marks and scratches all up and down her torso.

"I guess," she whimpered, grimacing and gasping. She was clearly in tremendous pain.

"Did they give you anything for the pain?" I asked, re-covering her.

"I heard Jake say painkillers would thin my blood. I wonder if they have alcohol here. I could use a drink," she said through almost clenched teeth. She scrunched her face and cried out in anguish.

I wished like anything I could find a way to make the pain go away. "Maybe. They have everything else. See if you can sleep," I suggested.

"Thank you," she breathed.

"For what?"

"For being the first person in a long time who cared about me."

"We all deserve better. Somehow, some way, we'll get you out of here."

I heard some low voices outside the tent. I moved closer to the wall of the tent. "Evan is going to shit in his pants." It was Jake.

"Let's not tell him." I recognized Marco's voice.

"And if she doesn't make it? We can't take her to any regular facility." It was Jake, again. "Abigail's face has been over the news. What about that clinic doctor who tried to save Sonja?"

"We had to pay her twenty thousand bucks to shut her up. If she recognizes Abigail, it will be a million dollars, just for starters."

"I sealed the wounds with superglue and covered them with bandages. She's lost quite a bit of blood. Do we have any antibiotics?"

"I'm sure there's some in the supply tent. We had to treat a case of clap a few weeks ago."

The voices moved away. I went back and sat down.

---

A while later, Marco brought in a couple of bowls of vegetable soup. "Today's your lucky day."

"I feel so lucky," I said sarcastically.

"You need to be more appreciative," he advised me.

Marco produced four pills from a bottle. "Antibiotics," he said.

Abigail groaned and then opened her mouth and he put them in. I gave her some water to wash them down. It was only after that that I looked at the label. I grabbed the bottle of pills. "Are you mad? It says 'Penicillin' and calls for one pill four times a day."

Abigail started trying to choke them up, but it looked like she was too weak.

"Get her some epinephrine or Benadryl fast," I said. I had used Benadryl for allergic reactions to bee stings in dogs when I had assisted at a vet's office back home, but didn't know if it would work for Abigail.

Jake came in, apparently having heard my reaction. I turned to him. "She needs a doctor, a real doctor. He just gave her penicillin. She's allergic."

Jake looked at Marco.

"It was all we had," Marco said.

"The penicillin could kill her. Please, this has gone beyond the point of hoping and praying. You guys don't have the foggiest clue how to treat an injury."

"Do you think you could do any better?" Jake asked.

"I'm not a doctor and I wouldn't pretend to be one. At least, get some hydrogen peroxide to help her throw up the pills."

Jake and Marco went out. Jake came back in with an unopened hydrogen peroxide bottle and an empty cup. I poured the liquid into the cup and got Abigail to drink a little. Abigail somehow managed to vomit. I had hoped she had gotten them all out.

"Benadryl or an epi-pen! We need something!" I insisted as he left.

I waited as nobody returned.

"Have some of the soup and water. Maybe it will dilute what's left of the penicillin." I knew I wasn't going to be able to eat my soup, as upset as I was, but she needed the fluids. I intended to see that she got some into her. I spooned some of the soup into her mouth. She coughed. I didn't want to pat her back, making the injuries worse. When the coughing stopped, I helped her drink some water.

"I'm going to die here, aren't I?"

"Not if I can help it."

She needed to get her mind off what was happening. "Abigail, tell me about your favorite things. What do you like to do for fun?"

"This one party, we had some volunteers dress up to mock the President and his Cabinet, including my father." She paused to gasp in pain and then pushed herself to continue. "They handed out some soft tomatoes and we threw them until the entire group of mock leaders was covered in red. Then one of my friends pulled out some fruit punch and poured it on the ground and the imitators laid down in it. The rest of us posed near the bodies for pictures and sent them to the papers. Nobody printed them, but we all got copies. It was so much fun." She gasped, again.

"I'd love to do that to my dad and the people he's worked with, especially the Senate Majority Leader."

"He's awful."

"I know. He voted for all the wars and the attacks on our rights, and he dared to call himself progressive."

"There aren't too many Dennis Kuciniches or Ron Pauls around. And they got defrauded by their own parities. Too honest. We need them back in Congress."

"You're a fan of theirs too?" I asked. "I sent Dennis a letter asking him to run for President again. My dad saw it and burned it. So, I emailed him."

"My dad flipped out when I spoke at a dinner about how all politicians should be honest like Ron Paul."

"Then there's Cynthia McKinney," I noted.

"She's got courage. She keeps putting her life on the line to stop the wars and genocides, particularly the ongoing one against the Palestinians."

"It's funny. You and I are probably from different parties, but we have more in common than we do with our party leaders."

"That's for sure."

"I thought your dad had flipped back and forth between the two parties."

"He faked it. He's always been a NeoCon." Her speech was stumbling and sounded pained. "Daddy?"

"What?"

"I'm starting to see things, weird things."

"You need to rest." I felt her forehead. "What kind of reaction do you usually have to penicillin?"

"Usually a rash," she lightly uttered, closing her eyes. As far as I could tell, the rash hadn't settled in yet.

I started singing an old Green Day song, "On Holiday," to her that I thought would make her feel better. It was about our country's psycho war policy. By the end of the song, she appeared to be sleeping.

I got up and looked out. Paul was just outside my tent. "Is she going to make it?" he asked. He seemed genuinely concerned about her and that surprised me.

"I don't know. They aren't doing anything to save her. On top of the loss of blood, and the likelihood of infection, Marco just poisoned her."

Paul looked upward. "That idiot. If I had a way to get her to a doctor, I would."

"Better watch out. They might force you to wear a purple shirt or even worse, a red shirt."

He shook his head and grimaced.

"If you could find some Benadryl, it might help with the allergic reaction to the drug."

"I'll see if I can find some. Just so you'll know. I wasn't one of the gang that raped Sonja."

With that, he walked off. I thought back to the unlocked tent and his covering for Santana. I wondered if he knew about my rendezvous with Santana.

I started counting numbers. There weren't enough of us reds and purples to overcome both the bullies and the counselors—especially since the counselors were in charge of the weapons and dogs.

---

Later that afternoon, Marco forced Santana out of his tent. "So do I get to meet this new girl?" he asked Marco. "I mean Snooty is getting kind of dull. We need someone to liven things up."

I knew he was putting on an act, but I found myself reacting, anyway. I came out of my tent. "Would you call getting torn apart by dogs, bleeding practically to death and being poisoned lively enough?" I punched his shoulder and turned to Marco. "If you don't get her proper care, now, there is no place you can hide from her father!"

"Is she getting worse?" Jake asked. My overly loud comments had apparently brought him into the area and every head nearby turned my way.

I didn't care. I was angry. "She'll be lucky to survive your brutality. We all will."

As Jake went into our tent, Marco growled, "You need to chill out. Ian, Dan, take Summer down to the creek for some chilling out."

Santana turned towards Ian as he came at me and knocked him to the ground. Dan, another blue who had been part of Ian's gang, jumped on Santana's back. Santana managed to lift himself, doing a one-eighty degree turn, throwing Dan off his back onto the ground and then turned to face Dan.

Ian grabbed Santana's arms from behind as Dan got up and punched him in the stomach. Marco approached Santana from behind and kicked him.

I ran into Marco knocking us both down. "Sonja, Jason, Jamie and now Abigail. You don't get to kill us."

Nobody else joined for the moment. It was just Santana and me facing down Marco. Then Dan and Ian went at Santana at once, again, knocking him down and kicking him. Marco pulled my hair and slammed my head against a stone. I was dizzy.

Through my blurred vision, I saw Ian sitting on Santana and Dan twisting his arm. Somehow, I got up and kicked Dan off balance. He grabbed my leg and twisted it, causing me to fall.

As Dan and I were on the ground, Harv, another blue, took his place twisting Santana's arms as Santana struggled and Ian continued to hold him down. Marco pulled some cable ties out of his pocket and used them like handcuffs to bind Santana's wrists. Santana tried to kick but his attackers grabbed his legs and cable-tied them, too.

I got up, and ran back over to Santana and kicked Marco, but Harv and Ian grabbed me, and they and Dan carried me down to the creek. I was on my back on the edge of the creek. My head was being pushed under water.

# CHAPTER 28

How long could I hold my breath? I counted to sixty. I hadn't been prepared. "Hang on," I told myself.

When I thought I was going to die, they brought me up. "You going to behave?" Ian asked.

"Never," I responded as I released a breath and then took one on the way back down into the creek. They said that waterboarding never worked with terrorists. Would I survive? I wondered how they would explain my drowning at camp. Swimming pool injury? I counted to one-hundred and twenty. I was still going strong, or so I told myself. They brought me back up. I gasped. "Go ahead. Kill me. There will be an inquiry and you'll get LWOP."

"What's LWOP?" Ian asked. This gave me a little more time to catch my breath.

"Without possibility of parole," I said exhaling. I took another breath just before going under again. Forty, sixty, one hundred. Twenty counts later, they still weren't releasing me. One-fifty. I was still under. Was this the end for me? One-eighty. I started slowly letting some of the air out of my lungs. Two hundred. Could I last much longer before I started breathing in water?

As if a miracle occurred, they suddenly released me. I clasped onto a stone on the bank and pulled myself up, hearing screams as my ears came out of the water.

It was Hope. He was attacking all three of them. Bleary-eyed, I could see Harv putting his hands to a large gash in his neck and falling to the ground in pain. Ian picked up a rock and prepared to hit Hope with it. I grabbed Ian's legs and pulled him off balance.

Dan, who was now being attacked by my canine rescuer, was doing his best to fight Hope off without much success. Hope bit a chuck out of one of Dan's legs. Dan collapsed on the ground, bleeding and crying in pain, leaving me and my hero to fight Ian.

Ian punched me and Hope came at his throat. Ian fell back, hit his head and stopped moving.

"Good boy, Hope." I gave him a hug. "Now, get out of here before you get into trouble. Go! Please!" I pointed up the creek. I pictured the counselors with pitchforks running down the mountain after him. If dogs could pick up on mental pictures, maybe he would understand the danger. Hope whimpered and then took my direction as he disappeared around a tree. I wondered if he knew how to stay away from the soundwave barrier or if he had a natural ability to handle it.

Dan was now looking upwards toward the camp, crawling, hurt and bleeding, in that direction. "That stupid dog. I'm going to kill it."

Ian started coming to and was grabbing at his own throat. There was blood coming out, but it didn't look like Hope's teeth had hit any arteries. Ian tried to talk but seemed for once to be having trouble getting out the words.

I got up and went up the hill as my water-boarders continued focusing on their wounds.

---

I didn't see Marco when I entered the campground. Santana's wrists and ankles were cable-tied and he was held by a rope to a table. I went over to him. "There's a knife in my pocket," he whispered. As I reached in, he said, "Nothing like getting beaten and tied up to get a girl to touch me in the right places."

"Ha," I responded as I cut his cable ties. I helped him untie the rope. We went into my tent. "We've got to go, now." Santana said.

"I can't. Not unless we can take Abigail."

"We could all die. If we go, we can send back help."

"You can go. There is no way I'm leaving Abigail. Look at her."

"They'll know you let me loose. And we've blown our cover of hating each other."

"That's nothing. Hope took out Ian, Harv and Dan. They're in worse shape than you and I are."

"Good dog."

"With all the injuries, maybe they'll radio or call Evan. Then, we can create a diversion, put Abigail into the bed of his truck and steal it."

"James Bond. I'll go for that. Hope we live long enough. Not a reference to your dog."

Outside, we could hear Ian's and Marco's voices. They must not have realized we were back in my tent.

"That girl's like that Altaira character in *Forbidden Planet*. One of your attack dogs came up, and she got it to attack us." Ian's voice was hoarse, but he was pushing it.

"Then it let her hug it," Dan added. "Really, it did! We aren't making it up. And Harv can't talk, yet."

"Your minds are wacked from your injuries. We don't have attack dogs. It must have been a wolf."

"It looked like one of those attack dogs you sicced on the new girl. We all saw and heard them."

"It must be your imagination. I wouldn't mention it to anyone else. There are a lot of wild animals out there. Next time, be more careful and don't fight with wolves."

"When I get my hands on that bitch. Do you know where she went?" Ian croaked out.

"I don't know, but she's probably the one who released Santana," Marco said.

"Santana was released? We've got to find him. He's trouble. If they're together—"

Ian's concerns were interrupted by Paul. "I released him. He's in our tent. He's still sick and Evan doesn't want any more deaths."

Paul was covering for me and Santana. *Why?*

"And the bitch? Where is she?"

"She's been nurse-maiding Abigail. You two are going to get this camp closed down. You need to control yourselves," Paul responded.

"Who are you to try to take charge?" Marco demanded. "This is the second time you've tried to pull that."

"Who am I? The fact that you are asking that instead of knowing the answer should tell you something."

It sounded as if someone walked off. "His last name. What is it? Only you and Jake know the last names," Ian said hoarsely.

"I can't discuss that with you," Marco said. I heard more footsteps walking off.

I whispered to Santana. "Paul's your tent leader. What do you know about him?"

"He's pretty cool for a blue."

"He just covered for us, and I think he intentionally covered for you earlier. He's also the one who hasn't been locking my tent. Think he's watching us?"

"If he were watching us for Evan or Jake, we'd have been busted by now. Especially with me taking off last night."

"Has he told you anything about his family?"

"Just that his father is a dick—not Dick—but a dick."

"What about this? We're in California. What they are doing is totally a violation of the law here. Maybe he's been sent here by someone investigating the camp?"

"Well, if he's one of the good guys, he's done a lousy job of protecting Sonja, Jamie, Jason and—" He waved at our sleeping friend. "Abigail. If he were with the government, this place would have been busted a long time ago."

"Except, if they're flying on and off military bases, maybe they have military clearance and approval. How long has he been here?"

"He was here eight weeks ago when I arrived."

"Eight weeks. How did you finish your—what year are you in school?"

"Junior. They supposedly issue grades in these camps. Mine's probably an F-minus," he said with a chuckle.

"Move over. We can start a bottom of the class scholastic club," I joked. "I wonder what subjects my camp report card said I studied with no math, no English, no history, no academic anything."

"Torture 101, terrorism prep, water-boarding and street drug manufacturing."

We both laughed. I held my hand over my mouth to hush any noise.

Santana seemed to be good at laughing almost inaudibly. "I wish I could have stopped them from taking you to the creek."

"I survived with a new skill. They started *Bible* study, this morning, and so you can add that to your list of subjects," I informed him.

He laughed again and then looked towards the opening. We both hoped our conversation was quiet enough to not be heard. "I guess they are into the story of Lot. Remember, he slept with his daughters?"

I thought about the little kids at the other camp. "I personally prefer the *New Testament*. Fewer Divine-sanctioned wars and less child-killing and incest," I commented.

"Well, those little kids down the hill are getting to know their leaders in the 'Biblical' sense. No separation of Church and State there. It shouldn't only be the Priests that are getting it on with kids."

"Sick humor. I don't even like thinking about it."

"I think about the kind of person my dad is. He's not that great with his current wife, either. My mom was right to leave him."

"My dad hospitalized my mom. And then he managed to make her the bad guy. She wasn't allowed to come near me."

"I'm sorry. Did he beat you, too?"

"Some. After she left, I was his substitute punching bag. But what he did to me wasn't anywhere near as bad as what he did to my mother. If she had stayed, she probably would have died. After she got out of the hospital, we were in a hotel. The police sent me back to my dad and arrested her. I don't think she was formally charged, though. My dad wouldn't have wanted the scandal."

"And that monster is the guy who sent you here. Our society is upside down and backward. The bad guys run everything, and the good guys have to fight for mere survival."

"If we survive, if we get out of here, we need to go public and fix things so that no more kids go through what we are going through."

"I'm with you."

I smiled at his statement.

"I mean, I'm really with you. You are the bravest, most kind-hearted girl I've met. My dad used to try to match me up with girls who would make a good addition to his entourage. They were mostly phonies. You, you're real, and your looks would put all of them to shame."

"That's really sweet." I was afraid I was going to regret saying this, but I charged through anyway. "When I thought I'd never see you again, I missed you." Santana started to lean towards me. He took my shoulders in his hands. He was going to kiss me, and I was going to let him. At that moment, Abigail stirred.

"Hi. You must be the infamous Santana."

"One and the same."

"He's the one who is going to help us figure out how to get out of here," I told her.

"After that, can you help me plan a revolution against my father's government? I'm okay with involving the Russians," she joked.

"You seem to be feeling better."

"I'm feeling weird. The soup did help diminish the pain."

Santana and I looked at each other. *Did they put painkillers in the soup and not tell us?* The lack of ethics of this camp would shock Bluebeard. In fact, I didn't think they had ever heard the term "ethics."

"And that Paul guy came back and gave me something he said was Benadryl," Abigail related.

"A blue with a heart," I mused. "But I'm not letting down my guard with any of the blues."

"Wise," Santana noted.

# CHAPTER 29

At dinner time, everything seemed to have blown over. The campers were milling about, rather lethargically. Maybe the events of the last few days had gotten to everyone. Harv and Dan, both bandaged up, were helping each other move around. Hope hadn't done as much damage to my assailants as Marco's dogs had done to Abigail but his impact had been felt.

Hillary gave us some tea. Tea wasn't my thing. Again, they served vegetable soup with sides of bacon. I took the soup and slipped the bacon into my pocket. I wasn't hungry but managed to save my dinner for Hope.

"Excuse me. I need a personal potty break," I said.

Hillary looked up. "I'm not done with my dinner." I noticed she was having extra bacon, had barely touched the soup, and maybe hadn't eaten any of it.

"I'll go with her," Emily offered.

We walked down closer to the river. I held my soup bowl at my side and noticed Emily was doing the same. My appetite was gone.

She dumped hers into the river.

"When I heard those shots last night, I was afraid they had gotten you and Santana."

"Shots?"

"There were several of them."

"I thought I heard something but wasn't sure if it was shots or a car backfiring."

"I'm just glad you and Santana are okay."

I pulled out the bacon. "Hope," I whispered.

My rescuer from earlier today came running. I leaned down and fed him the bacon. Then I gave him some of the soup to lick up. He licked a little, then started moving oddly and suddenly stumbled. I picked him up. He was breathing, and his heart was beating.

"I think there's something in the soup," I said.

"And almost everyone ate it. I'm allergic to carrots. So, I poured it out."

"Did you see if Santana or Bruce had any?"

"I wasn't watching them."

"It could be a sedative or a hallucinogen. Maybe some of that acid Hillary is making."

"You think she's making acid?" Emily asked.

"She's been busy making something. After eating some soup this afternoon, Abigail's pain went down and then she thought she saw her father."

"If we do get out of here, how do we get past the creek? When I've tried, I get a terrible headache."

"I think they have some kind of frequency barrier control, like for the radio dog controls."

"But we don't have collars."

"I think it's auditory. I have some extra earplugs." I handed her one of the extra sets Santana had given me. "Abigail stuffed her ears with crunched up leaves and sand and that blocked it."

Though Hope had just taken a little of the soup, I could see the strong effect it had on him. He got up from where he had fallen and started charging at invisible things that weren't there. I knew it was dangerous to go near a dog that was hallucinating, but I reached out and petted Hope, anyway, saying, "Good boy. You just had one lick. You are going to be better."

Finally, he went into a down position and started licking my feet like a needy dog who was desperate for approval. I figured it took longer to affect humans and likely had a different effect. They had given the campers two doses today. Maybe for humans, it required two doses and more time to do whatever it was supposed to do.

"Hey, did you fall in?" It was Jake's voice. He was still up near the camp where he couldn't see us, I hoped.

I took a mouthful of water. "I haven't gotten dysentery yet. Maybe there were some rapids going into this creek," I whispered to Emily as I lowered the bowl to my side and subtly dumped the remainder of the soup in case he was watching. Looking up and not seeing him, I quickly rinsed the bowl and we went back up to the camp.

As I entered my tent, Paul handed me some Benadryl, which I gave to Abigail, hoping the two doses would be enough to prevent a reaction to the penicillin.

That night, I woke up to see Hillary and Ariel getting up from their bags and exiting the tent, looking as if they were sleepwalking or in some kind of trance. Abigail was trying to get up. I held her down. She needed to be kept still. She seemed to be hearing something. I couldn't hear anything, but from looking at Abigail, it was as if the night was whispering something to her. I remembered that night in the box when it seemed as if words were being sent into my brain but were almost under the threshold of my hearing and barely audible. Now, I couldn't hear them at all. I wondered if the earplugs had cut the sound. The leaves were missing from Abigail's ears. I popped a set of plugs into them, and she settled down again.

Emily wasn't responding to the sounds either. I figured she was wearing the earplugs. I went over and whispered to her, "We need to go out and play along. Show off your acting ability."

We walked out as if in a trance, just as the others had. One by one, everyone had to go into the culinary supply tent. I noticed Charlie was there, back from his timeout, looking as if he were in a trance state.

Santana and Bruce seemed to be under the same spell as the rest. I knew they had plugs. *Were the plugs enough? Did they eat the soup?* I didn't know. *What about the tea? I wasn't paying attention. I was too busy thinking about Abigail.*

A man I didn't recognize was escorting everyone one by one into the tent and then back out. Those who had come out of the tent stood in attention around the nearby picnic table. I was last in line. When it came my time to enter the supply tent, I walked blandly as if I were sleepwalking. I pretended to be oblivious to my escort.

"Sit down," Jake said.

So, this was a Jake operation. The unknown man was watching.

I sat down, trying to resemble one of the people in Nicole Kidman's *Invasion* movie in my movements and focus.

"We hear you are planning an escape."

Santana, Bruce and Ariel had come in here first. *Had they said anything?*

"Escape. Yes. I've talked about it."

"With whom?"

"Ariel," I said.

"What did you plan?"

"Nothing. We didn't have a plan yet. She was afraid."

"Afraid of what?"

"Getting killed."

"What about Santana?"

"He doesn't like me."

"I've heard otherwise."

"We are trying to get along for the sake of the camp." My voice was flat, without emotion. "But we hate each other." I knew Santana and Bruce had been in there, and they could have talked. I didn't know if they were controlled, but I could only hope they hadn't had any soup.

"One more thing. Have you learned anything in the morning Bible studies?"

"We went over John 3:16 this morning."

"You like the studies, don't you?"

"Of course."

They excused me, and I walked outside. Ariel had seen me with Santana but hadn't been in any of our discussions. Had she talked?

Santana looked as "Body Snatched" as I was pretending to be. I hoped was just acting. If he talked, we'd all be in trouble.

Whatever Hillary was working on must have been perfected. She appeared to be in a trance, though I hadn't seen her eat the soup. Maybe she ate it after I went to the creek, or maybe it was also in the tea, or maybe she was faking it. Did she know if they had used it on her, too? Eventually, we were all gathered around the picnic table.

Marco went over to Charlie. "There is a fly on your hand." Charlie looked and waved his hand around. "It's still there. Put your hand on the table, facing up."

Marco handed Charlie a knife. This is a rubber fly swatter. Take it and push the end against your palm as hard as you can." Charlie shoved the knife through his palm. Blood spurted out. "Your hand looks better now. Give me the swatter and keep your hand there." Charlie complied. "You look happy." Charlie smiled as the blood continued to flow.

I had to retain the appearance of a trance. This was the hardest thing I'd had to do so far.

"I'm going to put an anti-insect potion on your hand and wrap it. Keep it on for a couple of days and no more flies will land on it."

"Thank you," Charlie said, sounding appreciative. If he was acting, he had better self-control than what G. Gordon Liddy was rumored to have had. Liddy had once reportedly said, after intentionally burning his hand, that the trick was in not minding.

With gloves on, Marco spread superglue on Charlie's hand as he pushed the skin together. After the superglue dried, he put a bandage around it. Everyone seemed to stay in their trance, as if Marco was just doing some mundane task, like putting a letter in an envelope.

Marco went back into the supply tent and pulled out a fork. Marco was definitely off my dinner guest list, I told myself, trying to remain light about the insane situation to calm down my panic about what could come next.

"Paul, take this fork and stab Ian," Marco commanded. Paul walked over to Marco, took the fork and stabbed Ian in the shoulder. Ian did not react, but blood started oozing out of his shoulder.

Next, Marco came for me. I wondered if I would be required to slash my own throat. I acted as if he was just some boring political friend of my dad's as I held my trance. Nothing to worry about.

"Santana, come over here. Knock Summer down and kick her."

I braced myself but tried to look loose and unconcerned.

Santana walked around the table to where I was and pushed me down. He kicked the ground in front of me, costing him momentum prior to making contact with my side. He continued his kick up into the air after barely connecting with me, with the result being that it didn't really hurt. Was he faking it? He did do as told, more or less.

"Now, Santana. Stand Summer up."

With both hands, he pulled me to my feet.

"Now kiss her."

Santana moved in, mechanically, emotionlessly and then his lips met mine, and I knew. Outwardly, it may have looked like he was following instructions, but it was the best kiss I had ever had. It almost knocked me out of my trance state. Santana hadn't drunk the soup. What surprised me more than his kiss was that I was kissing him back and I really liked it.

# CHAPTER 30

"Now stop," came the instruction. Santana pulled back mechanically, leaving me, working to recover from feeling wobbly and aching for more. I did my best to look unmoved, emotionless. I started reciting math equations in my head to distract myself.

The next thing that happened horrified me. Marco held out a gun and put it on the table. "Ian, pick up this gun and shoot Harv."

I, again, braced myself for what was next. *Another death? Are they crazy? Was Harv a scholarship, someone they weren't worried about?*

Ian, still bleeding from his shoulder, picked up the gun and pulled the trigger. It clicked. Apparently, the chamber was empty.

"Very good, Ian," Marco said. "Harv is dead." Harv was still standing there. Ian nodded and looked at the ground where Harv would have fallen if shot. "That's a Russian imposter standing in his place. Hit him with the gun."

Harv just stood there frozen, emotionless, waiting to be hit. Ian lifted the gun as he approached Harv and whacked Harv across the temple. Harv fell to the ground and hit his head against a rock.

I reflected on how badly the day had gone for Harv. First, he was bitten and then was smacked with a gun just before his head hit a rock.

I didn't like him, but for some weird reason, I hoped the rock wouldn't seriously injure him.

Jake came out of the supply, or rather, inquisition, tent. "Go back into your tents now." We walked body-snatched style back to our tents.

I had to walk past Paul. As I did, his eyes dropped just for a second to mine. He wasn't controlled either.

Inside the tent, we stood by the opening, waiting for further instructions. Emily started to look at me. I quickly shook my head, uncertain about Ariel and Hillary. Nobody appeared to be watching in there, but Hillary or Ariel might have been instructed to report back later. Apparently, realizing he had forgotten the final instruction, Jake said, loud enough for everyone to hear, "Lie back down and go to sleep."

Hillary and Ariel complied. I lay awake. It wasn't long before Emily scooted over to me. "The zombies are asleep," she whispered.

I looked over at Abigail. She was still breathing. Even if she had wanted to comply and join the action outside, she was not physically capable of it. I got up and went over to her. She had a fever. It was dark in the tent, but it felt like welts had formed over her skin: possibly an infection or an allergic reaction to the penicillin. The Benadryl hadn't been enough. Emily and I moved to the far side of the tent from Hillary and Ariel, far enough to be out of whisper earshot. I could hear a vehicle, presumably the truck, taking off.

"What did they ask you?" I quietly inquired of Emily.

"They asked about you, if you were planning to escape. They also asked if you and Santana liked each other. I told them I thought you and Santana hated each other and you didn't trust me enough to confide in me," she whispered back.

"Ariel must have talked."

"Or Santana."

"Santana was faking. I don't know about Bruce, but I know he has earplugs too. So, we can hope."

"I caught Bruce starting to open his mouth like he was in shock when Paul stabbed Ian. I think he was also faking it," she told me.

"You had your ears plugged, too, right?"

"Yeah."

"That must be part of it. You know who else was faking it?"

"Who?"

"Paul. I wish I knew his story. He's covered for us more than once. And I think he's the one who has been leaving our tent unlocked."

As I listened to the lock slide into place and lock, voices were audible from outside. We were supposed to be asleep. They probably thought we were too far under to hear them as they were not keeping their voices down.

"What did you get on Garrison?" It was Marco.

"Nothing much. Just what his file said. He got in some fights in school. His parents wanted him in a strict environment. Like the others, he hates his parents," Jake said.

"Evan pushed him for team leader and to have extra duties, saying he had leadership potential and his parents expected him to come out of here ready to go into government." Marco paused. "You think he's a plant? Evan doesn't exactly trust us?"

"I asked Evan. They never met until Paul came here. Paul claimed to have come here voluntarily so as to prepare for government leadership when he was questioned. But his answers were really vague."

"As if he had been programmed before coming here?"

"Maybe."

*If Paul wasn't under, they didn't get anything out of him. What if someone else is programming him and that's why he is helping us?*

"Is everyone locked in?"

"Yes. Even Paul's tent."

"Any word on when that new counselor is coming?"

"They moved it up. Three days."

That's how long we had to escape, I figured.

---

A few hours later, I awoke to an argument. I recognized Evan's and Jake's voices. I suspected they probably figured we were still sleeping off the drugs. Leaning against the door, I looked at my tent-mates, all asleep. The ones who were drugged were sleeping very soundly.

"Marco is a bit of a loose cannon," Jake said.

"You were supposed to reign him in. How could you let that happen?"

"The dogs got out of control."

"Her father could close us down, have us all prosecuted."

"The Feds haven't regulated these camps."

"This is one state that has regulations. Even if this state was unregulated, it wouldn't help. Attacking a child with dogs is a crime, anywhere."

"She's recovering."

"Did you give her antibiotics?"

"We only have penicillin, and she's allergic to that. There was nothing else, so I only gave her one dose."

"I'll bring Clindamycin here in the morning. I heard the experiment went better this time. The observer was impressed."

"The campers were like the walking dead, willing to attack their friends or do whatever we told them to do. The ones they attacked just stood there. They didn't try to run or duck."

"I'll let our sponsors know the experiments are coming along. We may need to move the camp. Jamie's dad called and wanted to know how his son is doing."

"What did you tell him?"

"What do you think I told him? I told him, 'Jamie is doing fine.'"

"Did that satisfy him?"

"He is planning to meet us and Jamie in Aspen next week for a face-to-face."

"I thought he agreed to wait until the Jamie is straight."

"He's not a guy you tell to wait. I had enough trouble putting him off until next week. We have a little more time with Abigail. Her dad wants a completely new girl. But if she dies, we'll all be running for cover."

So, tonight wasn't about us. It was an experiment for some sponsor. Who? Watching Ian strike his friend Harv was like watching a remake of *The Manchurian Candidate*. We were being groomed to do their bidding at a later time. Ian had killer blood in him from the beginning. Charlie didn't even feel pain when he stabbed his own hand. So, it might not have been that much of a stretch to control us when our careers got going. Santana and Paul were faking it. Even faking it, Paul was willing to stab someone with a fork.

From what I had heard from the other campers, the deaths, the hog-tying, the striping, the raping, the beating, the dehydrating, the electric torture and the hangings were common for Gulag schools and camps. But this was something more. We were more than kids whose parents paid to get them fixed. We were the next leaders of the free world, all being programmed to do the bidding of psychopaths.

The tent was locked tonight. I figured Santana's was locked too. Because Paul was in Santana's tent and was supposedly under, someone else would have locked it. That was the one tent that was rarely locked. Would it be that way for the next two nights? Did the three days include yesterday or start with tomorrow? If they moved us before we got out, we'd have to start from scratch, having no idea where we were. They might even send us to different camps.

I laid back in my bag and thought about home. I missed Shannon and Tiffany. At school, everyone accepted me because of who my father was. Children of producers and top stars would talk to me. But there was this status thing. Shannon and Tiffany weren't invited by the other connected students, even though my best friends were knock-outs, and their families were well-to-do.

I remembered one day in the hallway outside AP U.S. History, when I was passing Janet Clayton, whose father had starred in several movies, overhearing her speaking rather coldly to Shannon. She asked, "What makes you think you deserve to go to Chuck's party?" This was a reference to Chuck Holiday, whose father was a writer for a TV series.

I had been invited but was planning to stay home. I turned to Janet and declared, "Because I invited her to come with me. Shannon's my best friend. So don't talk to her that way." After that, we really became best friends. Shannon introduced me to Tiffany and the three of us became almost inseparable.

Shannon always had a positive solution whenever anything went wrong. Tiffany was a bit of a brainiac, knowing all kinds of information that most people should know but didn't. Tiffany knew who was who in politics and would have instantly recognized Santana, Jamie and Abigail. She might even have known who Sonja was. If Shannon had been here, she would have helped me come up with a solution to free us safely. Here, I was alone.

But somehow, I didn't feel alone. Abigail was a kindred spirit. I had really gotten to care about Emily as if she were a little sister. Bruce was like a male version of Tiffany.

And Santana: wow. That kiss had really affected me. I had never felt so intrigued by any boy before. I had dated Matt because my father wanted me to. And we did have fun. I convinced myself that there was no such thing as true love for me and that loving someone was a matter of commitment and duty. But I had always wanted to pull back whenever he kissed me. In fact, his kisses were actually pretty yucky. Thinking back, kissing Matt was like an unpleasant duty I owed to him in the life that had been chosen for me.

I knew that nothing with Santana would last after we got out of the camp. We were allies at an important time. If and when we eventually all got away, we would likely just go our own ways, promising to write but never really doing it. As I fell asleep, I keep reliving the kiss that I couldn't get out of my mind.

# CHAPTER 31

Morning came and my tent was unlocked. Abigail was still breathing. She had spots all over her visible areas. Marco leaned in and handed me some pills and water for her. "Not penicillin," he told me. I took a sip of the water to test it for her. It tasted okay. How could we regain our strength if we couldn't trust the food or water?

Outside, we lined up again for *Bible* study. Ariel enthusiastically said, "I love the *Bible* studies. I look forward to these, every morning." I watched her face and listened for the sarcasm but didn't detect any. Was she being facetious, acting or brainwashed? If she was brainwashed or a sell-out, she was probably the one who told them about Santana. Fortunately, she hadn't seen much and I hadn't told her much. But she did know that we had gotten out one night. Maybe that's why we were all locked in last night.

After breakfast, remembering the berries, I offered to go look at the traps. "Send Emily with her," Santana said. "I'm so tired of having to deal with that witch."

"I wish I were a witch. I'd turn you into a frog."

"I think that's reason enough to send you two together, again," Jake said. "We need our campers to learn to get along."

When we got out of earshot, I said. "So, you didn't eat the soup."

"After watching Abigail, I lost my appetite for soup."

"And you warned Bruce."

"He was already suspecting something with all the drugs. Actually, he's worried this will turn into a remake of 'Gianna.'"

"Paul was faking it, too."

"Interesting."

"Why?"

"After covering for us yesterday, I am wondering if maybe he really is investigating this camp."

"He could certainly get in trouble for stabbing another kid with a fork," I stated.

"If he hadn't, they'd have known he wasn't under."

"And of course, that kiss was to also convince them you were under their control. You're a good actor."

"You were pretty convincing yourself when you kissed me back."

"Did I? I don't remember. Guess it wasn't that eventful," I said, nonchalantly.

"Wasn't eventful!" he reacted. "How—" He cut himself off, grabbed my shoulders and pulled me into another kiss, wrapping his arms around me. I thought the kiss last night was the hottest of my life. It was nothing compared to this kiss. His lips were soft but firm. He tasted like wild berries. His body was strong and warm as he gently held me close. I felt a tingling from my head to my toes as I melted further and further into the kiss. The camp, the torture, all the pain, all my fears were suddenly gone and all that existed was Santana and me.

# CHAPTER 32

When he released me, it took me a minute to remember where I was.

"Was that eventful enough?"

"There's room for improvement," I responded.

"Improvement!" He rebutted and then smiled, getting that I was putting him on. "I guess we'll have to try it again, then," and he did just that. This kiss was the best yet. I half collapsed into his arms. Continuing the kiss, he lowered me to the ground.

A twig snapped near us. The sound didn't register for a minute, I was so lost. Even after our lips separated, I still couldn't focus on anything but the feeling of euphoria that had centered over me. The sound got closer.

We tilted our heads to look at what was beyond. A bobcat. "Get your own girl," Santana said as he pulled me to my feet. I had heard the trick was to stand tall and roar at it. Apparently, Santana had heard the same as that's exactly what he did. It looked at us and took off.

"If we take too long, they might suspect those rumors about us are true," I said.

"Rumors?"

"I think Ariel talked."

"What did you tell them?"

"That I didn't like you but was trying to get along for the sake of the camp."

"Good. If Ariel ratted us out, that explains why Jake also asked me about you."

I looked and waited for him to continue.

"I told them you were hot but too mouthy for me."

"I think she also told them we were talking about escaping. But I did mention the idea the first night in the tent when I was speaking with Sonja. Ariel definitely heard me then and Hillary may have as well. I confessed to that."

"The less Ariel knows the better."

"Right."

We came across the gooseberries, again. I stuffed my mouth, my pockets and the inside of my shirt. Santana did likewise.

"You never know when the camp's gourmet cuisine will be safe again," I said.

"I think I'll avoid it until we're out of here," Santana responded.

"I heard Jake and Evan talking. They don't want any more deaths, but Evan is planning to move us in the next couple of days."

"We've got to leave before then."

"We'll have to carry Abigail. It's best if Evan's truck is here."

"We could time it for when they plan to move us. He'd have to bring the truck or something bigger to transport all of us. We hijack it and free all the campers."

"What if he chains us up before the transfer to make sure we don't do that?"

"Good point." He paused to think about it. "We'll figure something out."

As we approached the upper trap, I held my breath. There was a squeal, a horrid one coming from it. It was a dog. Not Hope. It had to be one of Marco's dogs.

Sensing her pain, I put my hands to my face. "We've got to free her."

"Remember what the pack did to Abigail," Santana reminded me. "I'm all for dogs, but somehow having my side, legs and arms practically bitten off is not part of my life plan."

I offered the dog some of the berries and spoke softly to it. I was afraid to get too close. I pictured myself feeding it warm food, hoping it would sense my thoughts and that I was its friend. I pictured a white light encompassing me and the dog and extending through Santana and into space. Hope had come around quickly, possibly to my positive thinking or imagery. Maybe this dog would, too.

We had a leather bag with us for any animals retrieved from the trap. Santana pulled it out of his pocket. He came up behind the dog, not an easy feat, as the dog kept trying to pull from the trap to turn towards him. I distracted it from the front. Santana managed to pull the bag over its head to keep it from biting but not shutting it tight enough to cut off its breathing. Then, Santana used a headlock to keep it from getting free and attacking. "Are you strong enough to pull the trap open?" he asked.

"I'll try." It was a very heavy trap, but with some effort, I opened it and removed the dog's leg. The dog lay on its side, writhing in pain.

"We better get out of here before she recovers," Santana said. I left some of the berries and took off with the dog, trying to work its head out of the bag. "We'll need an explanation for losing the bag."

"The truth. Marco may be mad, but we saved his dog. Maybe he'll go up and attend to it."

"Marco seems more the type to shoot a fallen dog."

"You're right. Okay, so we lie and say we saw a mountain lion and he nipped at us and got the bag instead and we let him have it and ran."

"Miss Honesty."

On the way to the second trap, we picked up some more berries. The second trap had a raccoon. I felt bad seeing the animal killed in such a horrible way, but I felt even worse for Santana, who had to carry it.

When we got back to the camp, Hillary was back to mixing chemicals in the supply tent. Emily and Ariel had gone down to the creek for water. The blues were studying their *Bibles*. The reds were mixing what looked like cookie dough. This was a far cry from what had been going on the previous days.

"I need to check on Abigail," I told Jake. He nodded and let me go into my tent. I gave some gooseberries to Abigail, ate a few more myself and put the rest in my sleeping bag. She was weak but more awake.

"Do you remember anything about last night?" I asked quietly

"I was having a really weird dream and had the urge to leave the tent. I don't remember much else." She had picked up my cue and, like me, was talking in a hushed volume.

"I held you down. You weren't in any shape to leave, anyway."

"It was as if my father was calling me to come out, ready to forgive me."

"I think they drugged the soup with hallucinogens or some kind of mind control substance. Hillary has been mixing something for several days in the supply tent."

"So, what happened?"

"It was like a *Body Snatcher* movie. Did you ever see 'Return of the Archons?' It was a *Star Trek* episode."

"One of my boyfriends was a Trekie and forced me to watch all the episodes, again and again. That was the one where everyone was under the mind control of some computer."

"I think they are using some kind of subliminal or radio waves for mind control. I put some earplugs in your ears. Do you still have them in?"

She touched her ears. "Yeah."

I handed her some more. "Santana gave me some extras for backup."

"I wonder if my father is involved in this."

"Your father?"

"Why did he select this particular camp for me? He could have sent me to any boot camp that tortures kids. He used to be in the CIA. I'm sure he knows what they are doing here." She touched her head as if she had a surge of pain and had pushed past her energy limit. Then she continued, weakly. "He could even be funding this project."

"Take it easy. We need you to get stronger. If we get out of here, we probably should avoid going home. My dad would just send me back," I said.

"Well, my mother won't. She tried to stop him from sending me here. He kept telling her it would help me. If she knew what was going on, she wouldn't let him send me back." Then she seemed to catch herself and an even more pained look crossed her face. "No. I want to believe that. She might not care. She could have stopped him if she really wanted to."

"They are getting video and pictures, maybe for later extortion. They photographed me covered with white powder. They have a little kids' camp where top officials get to do their thing with little kids. I think people are being blackmailed."

"I've heard bits and pieces of conversations about the pedo rings. I'm good at listening at keyholes. Much of Washington is involved. The last thing they want to do is fix the problem."

I heard footsteps and raised my voice. "So, I really want you to get better because this is a really interesting camp with daily *Bible* studies," I said more loudly.

Emily came in. "Nobody's behind me. Tell me, again, about those *Bible* studies."

"Jake and Marco probably never touched a *Bible* in their lives before yesterday," I continued and then we laughed.

I signaled for Emily to get close. As she moved close to me and Abigail, she said, "I talked to Bruce. He's okay."

"I think Ariel squealed about me and Santana. She didn't know much, but she told them what she knew."

Emily zipped her mouth. "Got it. Not a word to Ariel. She may be a ringer."

"Right, we need to be careful around her. She's watching us. Oh, here," I pulled some of the berries out of my sleeping bag. "We have to eat something to keep up our strength. And these also serve as a drink. They may be the healthiest thing to eat until we're out."

"Beats brushing our teeth with dog poop."

"What?" Abigail asked.

"They did that to Ariel," I informed her. "She's had it rough. And she's terrified of what they will do if they catch her."

"That doesn't excuse her telling," Emily said.

"She was under mind control. Charlie stabbed his own hand and you saw what they made Ian do to Harv. He would have killed him if there had been bullets in the gun."

"I almost wish there had been. Harv is awful," Abigail remarked. "Call me whatever you like, but the blue group is more than psychotic. They are homicidal psychopaths."

"Maybe that's it. They are ferreting out the killers from those of us who aren't."

"Looking for the next Adam Lanza, Dzhokhar Tsarnae—you remember, the Boston bomber—or Stephen Paddock," Abigail commented.

"Meanwhile, the government is using all these high-profile attacks to take away everyone's rights," I noted.

"They are microchipping and euthanizing our pets, trying to take away guns, monitoring our emails, censoring our online discussions— all so that those who are in charge remain in charge. If my dad is involved, he belongs here, not us," Abigail said.

"Your dad?" Emily asked.

"I'm Abigail Kreskin."

"You? You're so much more normal in person."

"No. It's the rest of the world that's crazy. They cut off my green hair."

"I sometimes thought about dying my hair blue," I said. "But I did whatever my dad wanted, even dated a real lowlife just to please my dad. Managed to convince myself he was the love of my life—even though he was a terrible kisser. I couldn't have been a better daughter. And here I am. At least, you had fun on the way here."

"I did. And I plan to, again."

More footsteps approached. "Emily, Summer, out!"

# CHAPTER 33

I put most of the remaining berries back into my sleeping bag, put a few into my pocket and joined Emily outside my tent.

"Chit-chat is not allowed in this camp," Jake said.

"We were just making sure that Abigail was getting better. We weren't chit-chatting," I said straight-faced. Unless someone was listening before the footsteps, we were speaking too low for him to hear our actual words.

"Well, now that you've seen her, we need some more water from the river. You two are assigned."

---

Down at the river, Hope came up, more meekly. "Here, Hope." I gave her some of the berries. "Sorry, I don't have anything you like better. I know you like bacon, but you should see what they do to pigs in factory farms. Let's get this straight. One day, I'm turning you into a vegan."

"Think they are planning a repeat, tonight?"

"Last night, they said they had run the experiment before. When I was in my box, I got an impression of spoken words but I couldn't make them out. Did anything like this happen then?"

"I remember one night I was sleeping and then I heard some irritating sounds like an out-of-tune radio. I stayed in my tent with a headache, wishing whatever it was would go away."

"Maybe they tried the mind control without the drugs and it was a failure."

"When we get out of here, we're going to be pretty hungry."

"Better than a fat farm," I quipped.

"Except none of us is fat—well, none of us except Hillary, that is, and she's just bulky."

"What are you going to do when you get out?" I asked, looking towards the hopeful future.

"I can't go back home. They're the ones who sent me here. I am actually a pretty good artist. Maybe I can self-educate, hang around some beach and get paid to draw little kids or pets."

"Off the grid?"

"Sort of. Of course, I'd have to change my name. How about Emmy Love?"

"I like that."

"Do you think you and Santana—"

"No. I mean, here we're allies. But it's all situational. I am sure he'll take off to find his friends the moment we're out." The thought that lingered in my mind was, *He came back. He could have kept going.*

"I've seen the way he looks at you when he thinks nobody is watching. And I've seen the way you look when you talk about him." Her comments put a little fear into me. I hoped Marco and Jake hadn't observed what Emily had.

"This isn't like the real world." I rolled my eyes at the phrase as I had never lived in the real world that regular teens experienced. "Where we have millions of options. When we escape, we probably won't want any reminders of what it was like in here."

"Emily, Summer, what's taking you so long?" Jake called. I shooed Hope away with my hand.

"We're on our way up," I replied.

When we reached the top, I told Jake, "We're a little sluggish today. Last night's sleep wasn't all that restful for some reason. I slept all night, but I'm exhausted. Weird, isn't it?"

He didn't respond.

He pointed to the group seated for more *Bible* study. We were treated to the parable of the Prodigal Son, about a boy who went off and messed up, but his father still loved him when he came back. We were supposedly like wayward children, learning to be good citizens. We might have learned to become model citizens if Genghis Khan and Richard III hadn't been our instructors. We were expected to go back to our parents and seek their forgiveness, not the other way around.

Hillary joined our group for the pretense. She seemed especially agitated. She kept fidgeting and appearing unfocused during the *Bible* Study. A little later, she dropped her lunch. She seemed frustrated about something while also coming across as really spacey. "I have to finish my work," she told Jake repeatedly. "We need more supplies."

I thought back to the supply tent. Maybe she was making hallucinogenic mind-control drugs. Or perhaps it was nitroglycerine, for all I knew.

"Relax," Jake told her. "You need to be calm and steady."

"How can I when I am so far behind? Evan will be mad."

Observing that the rest of the group was acting normal, I didn't think they had pulled out the drugs, yet, today.

*Why is Hillary so worried?* It finally hit me. She's scholarship. She was worried about succeeding, here, to acquire some high-power internship somewhere. She may have been a looker, once, and maybe even still was to some people, but now, she was stalky and her skin was looking tight, dry and a little gray. Well, she had certainly shown she had cruel drill sergeant skills. *They could use her torturing abilities at Guantanamo.*

---

After lunch, it got weirder. They had us singing, "Jesus loves me." It struck me that these were memories, they wanted us to take with us if we got out. As if they could brainwash us or scare us into forgetting the rest.

Ian was particularly agitated. Harv was wandering around with a terrible headache he didn't know how he got. Dan was worried he might have gotten a snake bite on his shoulder. He kept asking for antivenom. Jake gave him a cup of what looked like water and said it contained antivenom. After drinking it, Dan relaxed a little. Maybe, he was still drugged or maybe the water was drugged.

Jake repeatedly insisted that we stay with a buddy at all times when we went to the bathroom or for a chore—as if we hadn't already been following that rule sufficiently. Was he afraid of rebellion?

I wasn't alone with Santana, again, for the rest of the day. At dinner, they had us roasting marshmallows. I knew from discussions with the campers that they didn't do marshmallows at the other camps. Outside of some or most of the campers at this camp being connected to people running the country or the world, the regular camp activities were apparently pretty normal for the various behavior modification programs where thousands of teens were sent every year.

Abigail remained in our tent. I brought her some soup but encouraged her to eat the berries instead. I pointed out that, in the wild, they were probably organic.

That night, after dinner, a fight broke out between Harv and Dan. Harv accused Dan of smacking him on the head and Dan accused Harv of getting a snake to bite his shoulder. They slugged it out. Several members of the blue team joined Dan in beating up Harv, who was now being called, "Harv the snake man."

---

I figured our tents would be locked again. But when I checked late that night, mine wasn't. The lock was only attached to one side of the closure. Hillary was in the supply tent, distilling whatever she was distilling. Emily was getting some much-needed rest. Ariel appeared asleep but I fluffed up my bag in case she woke. Then, I went outside to the creek. Santana was there. We sat down and looked through the trees at the stars. He pointed out his favorites. Bruce came down and joined us.

"What does cocaine smell like?" I asked.

"You planning to use it for perfume?" Santana teased.

"No, some packets of that white stuff broke all over me."

"It smells like nail polish or paint thinner," Bruce said. "It's a very distinctive odor. You can't miss it."

"It didn't smell like much of anything. More like flour, as in cooking flour."

"The white stuff we were packaging didn't have much of an odor, either."

"So, this is possibly a set up? They photographed me. If they use the right caption, boom."

"What?" Santana asked.

"They had a camera taking pictures or video as I was moving the containers and wound up covered with white powder."

"Extortion. To keep your mouth shut or maybe to control your dad," Santana guessed.

"Did it have any medicinal or vinegar smell?" Bruce asked.

"Not really. What would that be?"

"Heroin," Santana and Bruce said in unison.

I looked between them. "Obviously, there is something missing in my drug education."

Bruce ignored my comment. "Did you know that Bayer used to market heroin as a cough suppressant for children?"

"Did you know Bayer merged with Monsanto?" I asked.

"Does that mean that aspirin will now contain Roundup? Get rid of your headache with free carcinogens. Step right up," Santana quietly announced.

I smiled. "They could be making a fast buck by selling diluted or fake drugs."

"Business wouldn't last," Bruce surmised.

"But the users wouldn't talk to the police. They could move on to another locale. By the time they are done, they could make millions," I noted.

"Millions are nothing compared to what they are getting from our parents. I think the mind control thing will net them a heck of a lot of the missing Pentagon money," Santana said.

We silently agreed.

"Maybe we should just walk out of here," Bruce suggested. "You made it down to the kids' camp. The road has to go somewhere."

"You guys prepared to carry Abigail? I'm not leaving her," I made clear.

"I can design a makeshift stretcher," Bruce replied.

"So, then, we aren't waiting for a vehicle to split?"

"This camp is getting too crazy. And I'm getting hungry for something besides those garbage berries Santana keeps bringing me."

"I like them," I said, making a mocking face at him.

"Tell Emily to prepare for tomorrow night."

"What about Ariel?"

"She's wacked," Santana said, making a crazy sign. "We'll send somebody back for her."

"See you tomorrow," Bruce said, getting up to leave.

Hope came up and Santana gave him the bacon from dinner. "The counselor's favorite meat," he said.

"You don't think they poisoned the bacon, do you? Or rather, any more poisoned than normal?"

"I've been meaning to tell you. It's not bacon, it's *Soylent Green*."

We both laughed. "I feel bad about not taking Ariel with us. She's been through a lot."

"We can't trust her."

"I know."

He got quieter. "I don't want to talk about Ariel. I want to talk about what happened earlier today."

"The dog?"

He looked up. "No. Not the dog. I was thinking of this beautiful golden-haired girl with stunning green eyes that I haven't been able to get my mind off since I saw them drag her into camp less than a couple of weeks ago."

I felt my heart fluttering. I didn't want to read too much into his flirtations. So I changed the subject. "I don't know how you've managed it here for eight—"

"It wasn't easy. But it wasn't as hard as staying away from you for the last week and a half."

I could barely catch my breath. When I did, I said, "We're in a traumatic situation. We're friends. And we need each other. It's easy to misinterpret that for something more. When we say goodbye, we'll promise to stay in touch—but then, we won't. I'll probably see you at some big Washington event with some hot redhead on your arm and—"

He leaned in and kissed me even more passionately than this afternoon, though I never would have believed that was possible. A brief fear of getting really badly emotionally hurt hit me, followed by the peace of being in his arms. When our lips parted, I lay in his arms, next to the creek.

"I've dated a lot of girls," he said.

"I'm sure." I tried to brush off the situation. "We are allies in a foreign world."

"That's not what I meant. I've never met anyone like you. The other girls were nice, but I wasn't really into them. Most of them were shallow, concerned with which party we'd go to next or who we would see where. A lot of times, I thought they cared more about my money or who my father was."

"I know how that is."

"What I keep trying to say is that, when we get out of here, I don't want to go my own way. I want to stay with you." With that, he kissed me again. I felt tears coming into my eyes. Why did I have to go into hell to find the closest guy to a saint I had ever met?

I curled up against him with my head against his chest, wishing we could stay like this forever. He had his arm around me, warm, soft, giving me the first real sense of belonging I had since my mother was taken away.

We started sharing our hopes and dreams. Santana talked about his dream of racing cars. I talked about my dreams of becoming a veterinarian. "Years ago, I had a dog who was so beautiful but she got sick. My mom was gone and my dad refused to pay for the vet to treat her. I went to the vet anyway and I begged and begged the vet to treat her and promised I'd pay double his rates when I could. They threw me and my dog out because that's what my father wanted. She died. I kept wishing it had been me who had died."

"I'm sorry about the dog. Your father was a monstruo."

"Everyone who ever cared about me has gone away or died. My mother left. My dogs died. My grandparents died."

"I'm not going to die. I'm going to save both of us. And I'm going to stay with you. I promise."

He kissed me again.

"Well, well, what do we have here?" It was Marco's voice.

# CHAPTER 34

"I told you they were together." It was Ariel.

I looked at them, frozen, not knowing what to do. A sense of fear swept through me. Arial's betrayal wasn't much of a surprise, but it stung.

"I'm guessing you have stopped hating each other," Marco said as Santana helped me up.

"Amazing how that happened," I said. "Well, if we can just get back to our tents."

"Rules. You aren't allowed to leave the tent at night. You aren't allowed to have secret, how do you say, tete-a-tete's?"

"It won't happen again."

"It won't happen before we pack up."

I tried to brush past Marco, but he grabbed my arm.

Santana yelled "¡Hijo de puta!" and shoved Marco back. Marco pulled a gun. I couldn't tell if it was the real thing or some kind of taser or stun gun. He motioned us up the hill towards the camp. Ariel had a smug smile on her face. Marco marched us towards the supply tent.

Hillary was in there, seemingly going crazy, trying to cook something on the distillery. "Hillary, take a break. Help out," Marco told her.

He took us out to the tree where I had previously spent the night. "Sit down, opposite sides of the tree, hands back around the trunk."

Hillary pushed me down. Santana started to react and Marco pointed the gun at him.

After Santana did as instructed, Marco pulled out, not zip ties, but actual handcuffs. "Ariel, put the cuffs on them." Following Marco's instructions, she locked my right wrist to Santana's left and Santana's right wrist to my left. "Now you get to be together."

"¡Bastardo! ¡Vete a la mierda!" Santana shouted at Marco as he and Hillary walked off.

A clearing in front of our tree was close to the dirt driveway that led to the side of the supply tent. From where we were cuffed, I could see the back and a side of the supply tent and the back and side of the blue tent, as well as a part of the center of the camp. To the back of our tree was a cluster of large pine trees. The blues were definitely not going to save us and anyone else trying to rescue us would wind up attached to our tree or maybe electrocuted like Jason. A sense of doom washed over me.

As Marco and Hillary stood in the side opening to the supply tent, Ariel leaned towards us and whispered, "This is what happens when you decide to leave me behind." Then she left, joining Marco and Hillary who were staring at her but out of hearing distance of her whisper.

The sun started coming up. Santana's side of the tree was facing away from the clearing, and my side was facing toward it, with the sun closing in on me.

"Let's slide around and switch sides. I've got more melanin and can withstand the sun better than you," he encouraged.

"So, I can't handle it because I'm one of those fair-skinned gringos," I teased.

"Seriously. You were pretty badly sunburned the other day. That had to hurt. You're still pretty pink. Let me take some of the sun."

"How about this? We'll take turns, so we both burn a little less. At least, we have our clothes this time."

"I should have killed him for what he did to you."

"With Hillary, Ariel and his gun, you'd be the one in the ground. At least, everything that burns this time will be above the neck."

"Chained to the prettiest girl I know, and they forgot to take off our clothes," Santana joked.

"It could be worse. Our friends are safe. For now. You heard what he said about packing up?"

"I did. !Esos bastardos!" he swore. "We've got to get out of here."

"Aren't you the lock expert?"

"Not when my hands are cuffed without any tools nearby."

"Then, I guess it's up to our friends to figure something out."

We started switching about once an hour. Then twice an hour. The bark scratched as we rotated. It hurt but I didn't want Santana to stop switching, leaving himself in the sun.

"I'm sure this isn't what you had in mind when you said you wanted to stay with me," I joked.

"I'd rather be chained with you than free without you," he responded.

I had to admit to myself that a guy who could be romantic when facing possible death was kind of special.

After a while, I found myself dozing off. I had been awake for most of two nights and I couldn't keep my eyes open any longer. When I awoke, it was late afternoon and I realized I had missed a number of my turns in the sun. "I'm sorry. I fell asleep."

"I know. I would have woken you if I needed to switch."

I thought about calling him a liar. "Let's switch now?" I didn't wait for him before I started moving. "Why did you come back? You were away. You had your freedom."

"I meant what I said about not leaving you."

"That was before we kissed or anything."

"What kind of guy would I be if I left the girl I was falling in love with in a *Friday the Thirteenth* Camp."

I was handcuffed against a tree and somehow, I felt more lifted up than in all my dates with Matt. A guy I barely knew said he was falling in love with me. Even if he was just saying that, his comment was pulling my heartstrings more than anything Matt had said or done in all the time we were dating, when he was pretending to be my future.

"Santana, if you can't get me out, I want you to escape."

"Not without you. Not today, not ever."

"They are armed. Two, maybe three campers have died. You can at least get the truth out."

"Caramba. Is this some kind of martyr complex? Lo siento. No room for martyrs. We leave together."

"I'm not planning to sacrifice myself. I just want the truth to get out. I want people to know what is happening here."

"The truth isn't going to change anything. Miller had a hearing. Greg Kutz of the Government Accounting Office testified about a bunch of deaths. And it didn't make an ounce of difference. The House passed a bill but the U.S. Senate never took it up. I wonder how much they got paid to kill it."

"The Senators could have been blackmailed. But this time, they've killed some of the children of our country's leaders. Somebody will care."

"Will your father?" He paused. "Lo siento," he said more solemnly. "I'm sorry. That was low. I just know my father won't care. He will run for cover, trying to protect himself. He won't want anyone knowing he willingly sent his son to a torture chamber. Anyone who would do that is politically dead if word gets out."

"You're right. It will be the same way with my dad. He'll do whatever it takes to prove he only sent me to a warm, fluffy camp."

"So, when I get out, we're both getting out."

I thought about Santana's insistence on getting me out. I had always lived my life for others. I didn't even dare talk to my dad about my secret desire to be a veterinarian. I didn't dare even dream of that possibility as I figured my dad would never let it happen. I had assisted in a veterinarian's office while in high school but pretended it was part of college prep so my dad wouldn't object. If I got out, when I got out, I was going to live the life I wanted to live and the heck with my dad.

And no matter how nice Santana was, I wasn't even going to let my attraction to him control me. I had let my former boyfriend wreck my life, such as it was. *It is not going to happen again. No matter how much Santana makes my heart flutter, my responsibility to Santana ends with getting him free. If necessary, I am getting out of the country. I may be fifteen. But I'm not going to risk being kidnapped again.* That's when it hit me.

"I'm sixteen. My birthday should have been the day before yesterday or maybe the day before that. I forgot all about it."

"Happy Birthday." He lightly sang me the Ringo Starr song, "You're Sixteen."

"You've got a great voice, but I'm not anyone's yet."

As the day dragged on, I got hotter and thirstier. This time, Santana wouldn't be bringing me water. All this talk about escape might be academic. We might die out here. I didn't blame Emily or Bruce for not intervening. If they tried to help, they'd be joining us in handcuffs or worse. I could only hope they were watching our captors and planning their own escape.

---

As the sun started to set, there was more frantic rushing around. Hillary's freaking out was getting very audible, all the way to our tree. All I could figure was they gave her a work assignment that was too much and too complicated for her to handle. Her rants finally seemed to calm down. Across the clearing, I saw Bruce. He put his hand to his throat as if he was making a sign that he expected to be killed next.

I could smell dinner cooking. Would there be more drugging? Currently, Santana was on the side facing the woods. I could feel him moving a little as if something was happening on the other side of the tree.

Next, a hand came around and gave me a cup of water. "It's creek water." It was Emily's voice. "I think they are planning to drug us again and then take off. All the tents, except for the supply tent are being cleared out as if they plan to pull them really soon. Bruce and I are faking eating and drinking and also faking being really sluggish."

"What's that over there?" Marco yelled. He started moving across the clearing as Emily hopefully backed into the woods. He didn't get far. An explosion in the supply tent rocked the campground, throwing Marco off his feet.

# CHAPTER 35

Heavy smoke filled the air, coming from the front side of the supply tent and, to a lesser extent, out of the side opening. I heard loud screaming and wailing. It was Hillary. She came out of the supply tent and ran around blindly, screaming in horror.

Even from our distance, it looked like part of her face had been seriously damaged. Some of the blue team campers watched and a couple of them, Ian and Dan, laughed.

Marco pulled out his gun and fired. Hillary fell. Her body twitched and then stopped moving. I had despised the way she treated Ariel. But now I felt only pity. She had been shot like a wounded animal being put to sleep.

I had always felt sorry for animals who were euthanized, instead of loved, until their last breath. I never understood why someone would kill a sick dog when they wouldn't kill their own sick or injured child. But Marco had done just that. In cold blood, he had killed an injured child for whom he was responsible.

I realized I was sobbing so much I couldn't see through the tears. Between my sobs, I whimpered, "He killed Hillary. He just killed her."

"Take it easy. You don't want him to hear you and turn the gun on us," Santana cautioned.

I continued sobbing. I couldn't help myself.

Through thick smoke, Jake and Marco started pulling things out of the side opening of the supply tent as the front of the tent became more engulfed in flames. They carried boxes and bags towards the truck that had just pulled into the campground, not far from where we were tied to the tree but stopping a distance from the fiery tent. They were filling the back of the truck when the tent exploded again, larger and louder than the last time. The trees close to the tent, the picnic tables, and everything around them were on fire. Marco pulled out his gun again and held it on the campers who were standing around, watching, while Jake cable-tied the blue group's wrists, mostly in front of them. Then Jake injected each of them with something. Whatever it was, they were still able to stand. The other campers stood awaiting their enslavement. With the gun pointed at them, nobody of any color was daring to move. The forest, itself, had started burning.

Marco and Jake were ignoring us. Were we going to be left here to burn to death as the fire continued to spread? I started thinking of all the goodbyes I would never have a chance to say. I shifted somewhat to the side to give Santana and myself both a view of what was happening.

The blue group was being escorted to the truck. Of course, they would save them first.

The truck bed had already been loaded with supplies and the blues were placed on top of the boxes. Marco put a tarp over the blues and supplies and went back to the camp to join Jake who was pointing the gun at the next group. I wondered if he was going to layer the prisoners.

"Did you notice? There was somebody missing, from the blue group?" Santana noted.

Santana rotated himself back towards the woods. That was the side most likely to catch fire first as the flames were now spreading through the trees. I tried to resist Santana's sacrifice. All I knew was that nobody was looking at us. Even if one of the blues escaped, it wouldn't help our cause.

I felt something interacting with the cuff enclosed around my left wrist. I couldn't see who was doing what with it. My left cuff opened and I heard Santana's right cuff open and then my right cuff. I looked around the tree. It was Paul. He opened Santana's final cuff as well.

Santana and I got up. "Get out of here, fast!" Paul exclaimed as we moved behind the tree.

"Not without Abigail," I replied firmly.

"Your friends are down by the creek. Now get out of here!" He put his jacket around me and said, "Take this. It will keep you warm tonight."

"Why?" I asked.

"Sí. Why have you been helping us?" Santana inquired.

"Evan is my father," he informed us very quietly and quickly. "He had me use my mother's name to get in here without the counselors knowing. I was to be Evan's eyes and ears to make sure the counselors were getting things done. Instead, I awakened. I saw things that were inhuman. I couldn't, I can't let him continue this. Just get out of here. I'm going to save as many as I can."

Marco had cabled-tied the red group of campers and Jake was injecting them.

"Someone's missing," Marco said. "What about the Kreskin chick?"

"Leave her. We can explain her death more easily than those dog bites," Jake replied.

Santana and I moved behind the tree and into the woods, checking the approaching fire to make sure we could get away before it reached the closest section of trees. Nobody seemed to be looking at us.

"Come on," Santana said to me, but instead, I paused to watch as Paul went for the truck. Paul got into the driver's seat. I saw a blue, who had escaped from the back, come up to the cab, yielding a knife.

"Scoot over." Ian's slurry voice was loud enough to carry.

Instead of moving on, we stood, watching.

"I'm getting you out," Paul told him.

"I don't want out. Here, I'm somebody. I'm going to the new camp."

"Where they will torture you?"

"You are a traitor." Ian sounded loud and drunk or drugged. From where I was located, I could see Ian's knife-yielding hand plunge into Paul's body. Ian pushed him over and started backing the truck away from the approaching fire. Paul rose up next to him in the seat. They struggled. The truck backed a ways into a tree. They continued struggling as one or both of them apparently stepped on the gas and knocked it into drive away from the tree as the wheels turned away from the camp. Through the side of my vision, I could see Santana stiffen up. I knew he wanted to help, but like me, he knew that would only make things worse. Next, I heard what was either a gunshot or a tire blowout or both. Then another one. Maybe they were warning shots from Marco or Jake, aimed at the truck.

The truck kept moving, spun, and went across the dirt road into a dip or small ravine. Next, we saw and heard an explosion coming from the ravine. This explosion was even worse than the one at the tent.

We ran through the trees on the outside of the clearing towards the truck. It was difficult to get through the smoke. A second, a third and a fourth explosion encouraged us back away from the scene. When the explosions appeared to subside, we continued towards the ravine to see if we could help Paul. When we got there, we could see that what was left of the truck, including the bed, was in flames that were spreading out. There was no sign anyone was still alive.

# CHAPTER 36

All I could think was that everyone in the truck had perished. Feelings of guilt rushed over me as I thought about how I had hated some of the blues. I never wanted any of them dead. I found myself overcome with anguish about Paul, who had only tried to help, and now, he was in pieces, incinerated. The explosion couldn't have just been from the gas tank. It had to be from the supplies they had put into the truck, possibly triggered by the shots.

Marco and Jake were running towards what was left of the truck. With the smoke billowing into the air, I hoped they didn't see us.

"We've got to get out of here," Santana said, grabbing and pulling me, breaking my frozen state.

We fled down the road, circled back towards a higher section of the creek and then started walking along it toward where it flowed below our campground. I looked down for snakes and such as we walked along the creek. It wasn't a snake that caught my attention as Santana was looking up ahead and to the side.

"Don't look!" Santana exclaimed as if I wouldn't check out what he was seeing. I couldn't turn away. There was something, someone, lying face down in the dirt. Santana went over to the body and turned it over. "John," he said. "Shot in the back."

"He was really nice. We can't just leave him here," I blurted as I started to kneel down.

"We don't have time to bury him. He probably objected to Marco boxing up Charlie. "Good thing Charlie isn't a blue."

"Maybe we could put John in the creek so he doesn't burn and his family can give him a proper burial later."

"Good idea," Santana said, looking up as if to try to hold back his feelings.

We picked John up and moved him into the creek. As we got closer to the camp, we looked for our friends along the creek. They were nowhere to be seen. "Where do you think they are?"

The fire was getting close to the creek. We lightly called "Bruce, Emily." Nothing. We continued calling. We didn't dare call any louder as we didn't want ourselves or our friends to be discovered. I wondered whether we should turn back and run through the burning trees or cross the creek.

"They probably went on to get away from the flames," Santana coughed out. The flames and heavy smoke were coming pretty close to where we were standing. "Bruce is probably analyzing the spread of the fire and keeping everyone safe."

"He's a good guy. I'm glad he's part of our group." Despite our positive comments, I still worried.

We continued across the creek. The fire was casting a bright glow through the woods. The smoke was searing my lungs. Santana tore off the bottom of his shirt and then tore it into two pieces to try to keep the soot out of our noses. I was feeling light-headed, but I didn't want to slow us down. As we walked towards the kids' camp, we tried to stay out of sight, sticking close to the trees, ready to hide among them in case anyone came looking for us. My foot caught on something and I tripped.

"Look," it was a piece of a shirt.

Santana gazed down. It was a ripped apart red shirt. We looked around. "Oh my God," I shrieked. It was a large bone. We started sifting through the leaves and rocks. More bones. Santana picked up what was left of the shirt. It had part of a smile drawn onto it. "Don't look anymore," he said. I was shaking and crying.

"No. Not a smiley face!" I exclaimed. I had known that Jason was probably dead, but I had kept hoping that he had faked it and escaped. "I kept telling myself he somehow got away," I sobbed.

Santana held me. "I'm sorry. He was a great guy. He drew that smiley face on it to help lift all our spirits." He raised a hand to his eyes and quickly wiped them to seemingly hide his own tears.

"It's my fault," I cried, collapsing against Santana. "He was only kind to me. He's dead because of me. I killed him," I was shaking, sobbing uncontrollably.

"They killed him. They killed him. Not you. They." I could hear the anger and resolve in his voice.

"I did it. They tortured him because of me, because I was thirsty."

"They were torturing us long before you got here," he replied softly. "Nothing that happened here is your fault."

Santana steadied me as he moved me onwards. I tried to pull back, but it was as if my energy had been zapped. I just wanted to lie down and die. The hope that Jason had somehow survived was gone. *Someone died because of me; someone died because he tried to help me.*

Santana put his arm around me and helped me continue on toward the kids' camp.

---

About half a mile later, I heard a "Hey." It was Bruce. "Santana, do you think you could help me with these women? Wait, what's wrong?" He looked at the tears on my face.

"Bodies," Santana got out.

"They killed Jason and John," I choked out. "And Paul perished, along with the blue team."

Emily looked fallen, sad. She was shaking. I took Paul's jacket off and put it on her, fearing she might go into shock. As I wrapped it around her, I felt something in the pocket. I pulled it out. It looked like some kind of diary. I showed it to Santana.

"Won't do much good without Paul," Santana said. "If it has anything relevant in it, they'll claim we wrote it."

"But it might give us some useful information."

"They are going to kill a lot more of us if we don't get out of here," Abigail pointed out. She was lying on top of a sheet with the sides wrapped around some branches. "Oh no," Abigail groaned as the sound of dogs rang out. They were quite a distance but clearly coming in our direction.

The four of us picked up Abigail's makeshift stretcher as we prepared to run in the direction of the kids' camp, hoping to find a working car.

As we crossed the stream, I was bolted over by a dog jumping on my back, apparently happy to see me. "Hope!" I cried out, floundering in the water. I got up. "We've got a fifth for our team."

I would have thought Abigail would have been weary of dogs. But her response was, "Welcome. We could use an extra friend."

We walked a ways down through the stream in an attempt to throw off the scent for the dog pack. As the stream diverged from our path, we stepped out and continued toward the kids' camp.

Approaching the camp, we could see the tents were gone. We went to the building. It was empty.

"Maybe, there's some food," Bruce said.

We looked at him, "Camp food?" There was running water and we each took a drink.

"At least we have shelter here," Emily stated.

"This will be the first place they'll look," Bruce warned.

"Think there's a cellar or a hiding place?" I asked.

"We don't know how many people Evan will have swarming this place," Bruce replied. "Our best shot is getting to civilization."

We headed for the road. "This will get us out of here but it's a long walk," Santana advised. "This area is covered by trees but further on, the trees are more sparse. On the back of the truck, it still took close to an hour to get to Edwards, weaving though these mountains."

"If he went there, he clearly has an in with the military. We should avoid the base," I recommended.

"Listen," Abigail held her hand to her ear.

"What?" I asked.

"Can't you hear them?"

We shook our heads, "No," I said. But I spoke too soon. The dogs were still coming and were closing in. They had not lost our scent in the stream. We ran.

"Emily, Bruce, climb," I said, pointing to a tree. "Santana and I will distract them."

Bruce helped Emily up and climbed up himself and reached down as Santana and I lifted Abigail into his arms. Then we grabbed the parts of the make-shift stretcher, retraced some of our steps and went further down along the side of the road. Along the way, we dropped the stretcher, hoping that would catch their attention. If it did, it was only briefly. As we continued on, the dogs were coming nearer and nearer. Santana helped me up a tree and then Santana lifted Hope into my arms. Next, Santana joined us. But it was too little, too late.

"You thought you could get away. Dogs, get them!" Marco's voice boomed.

# CHAPTER 37

Marco was standing there with his gun cocked and pointed in our direction. The dogs were growling at us and snapping at our feet. We had made it just above their biting reach and were trying to pull ourselves higher as the dogs came closer with every jump. Santana pushed me against the trunk and positioned himself in front of me as if to try to shield me with his body from Marco's aim. Hope barked at the other dogs and seemed to be communicating with them.

"So, there you are," Marco said. "I thought you were dead, Rollo."

*Hope was one of Marco's?* Hope looked at me and then snarled at Marco. The other dogs were barking at us, ready to attack.

My first thought was to delay until we formed a plan. "Just out of curiosity, how did you get the dogs past the creek?"

Marco sounded thrilled with himself when he stated, "There's an off switch to the frequency barrier. It's only on for you campers, not for us."

What happened next was so fast, it was hard to take it in.

"Get down or get shot," was Maro's ultimatum.

Hope jumped from the tree onto Marco biting his gun hand. Marco's gun went off, hitting the pack dog closest to the tree as he knocked Hope away. The remaining dogs turned and snarled menacingly at Marco.

From out of nowhere another dog came up limping on three legs with a fourth one hanging. The limping dog managed to bounce off his back legs, grabbing Marco's gun, along with some fingers in its mouth.

The snarling dogs leaped forward and went for Marco's throat, his limbs, and his torso. The major injuries Abigail had received seemed minor compared to the holes they were chomping in Marco.

Marco must not have tasted particularly good, as they stopped at some point. Then they looked up at us, and I wondered if we were to be their next meal.

Hope moved away and barked, grabbing the attention of the other dogs and then led them back the way they had come.

When we thought it was safe, we got down off the tree and returned to our friends.

"Where's Hope?" Abigail asked.

"I think he rejoined his family," I said, with mixed feelings of relief and sadness. "So we decided to rejoin ours."

"I wish I could let you." It was Evan with another gun.

It hadn't occurred to me to pick up Marco's gun.

"But this operation is very important, more important than the son of a Congressman, the daughter of the Secretary of Defense or the daughter of the Governor's Chief of Staff.

"Don't forget me," Bruce reminded him. "Son of a HAARP scientist."

"We could really use your scientific brain," Evan said to Bruce. Santana got behind me for once. Maybe he was tired of taking the heat. "But you three seem unredeemable. Do you have any last words?"

"Only one," Santana who was standing from behind me, responded. Just out from behind and to my side, a shot rang out and Evan dropped his gun, his hand squirting out blood.

I turned and looked at Santana.

"Of course, I picked up the gun. We're dealing with killers."

"You won't get away," Evan said, blood rushing from his wrist.

Santana pointed to Evan's gun. "Bruce, pick up the gun."

Bruce complied.

"Now, you are going to sit down. And before we leave, it's your turn to listen. You never deserved an hijo like Paul. He was a thousand times the man you are." Santana's words caught Evan off guard, almost speechless.

Evan looked at the ground. Maybe In his cruelty, there was an ounce of love for his son. "You don't have the right," he shot back.

"I'd say we do. It was Paul who saved us. Unlike you, he's a great leader," Santana chastised him.

I hugged Santana, making sure not to disturb his gun-hand, but letting him know he was right on target with his comments. He put his free arm around my shoulder.

Bruce reached into Evan's coat pocket and pulled out some cable ties and keys. Then he strapped Evan's right hand to his left foot.

"Now, shall we? Everyone?" Santana asked.

We hadn't gone more than a few feet when we heard Evan on a radio or cell phone, saying, "They're getting away. They must be stopped. Shoot on sight."

"¡Estúpido! I should have emptied all his pockets," Santana said.

"You mean, I should have," Bruce responded.

"You did good," Santana assured him.

We took off running while carrying Abigail. We didn't know who or how many we could expect to be coming for us. When we got to the road, we saw Evan's car. Bruce unlocked it and we jumped in with Santana in the driver's seat and me next to him. Abigail was resting on Bruce's and Emily's laps, behind us.

We raced down the windy road as fast as Santana dared to take the car, which was a lot faster than I drove on most highways. Above, we heard a helicopter and then we heard shots.

# CHAPTER 38

Then, more shots. One, no, two of our tires had been shot out. Santana handled the car like a pro. We were on rims in the back. The rear window was blasted. Santana pulled off the road and tried to create a new path under the cover of the trees. It was hard to tell what direction we were going. One minute, we were going down and another minute, up and then down again. Finally, the car was stopped in a muck of plants. We tried to back up, but we were stuck.

We got out and Santana checked the trunk. We already had two handguns from our interactions with our captors, and we found a rifle in the trunk.

"I hate to tell you this, but I don't really know how to use a gun," I confessed as we continued with Bruce carrying Abigail.

"Let me be honest too. I don't either," Santana said. "Cars were my things, not guns. Besides, I'm a Democrat. We're supposed to be for gun control."

"What do you call it when the government has the guns and the people have none?" I asked.

"A police state. But don't let your dad's friends in the Senate or the Governor's office hear you ask that," he advised, lightening the mood.

"Senator Madstein and the Governor hired lunatics and contracted armed protectors but they didn't want us to have guns."

"Hey, you two. I used to score big at the shooting gallery at Disneyland before we moved to Alaska," Bruce bragged. "I'll take the rifle. I can handle both it and Abigail. She's light."

*Starved was probably more like it.* "Santana, let's be honest," I said. "You shot a gun point blank out of Evan's hand. That's no amateur feat."

"It is if you are aiming for his chest."

I looked at him and wondered: *did he really try to kill Evan or is he just saying that?*

As if hearing my thoughts, he continued. "I didn't plan to kill him, but I wanted to make sure I aimed for the largest part of his body."

I gave him the same look again.

"Seriously. It was a lucky shot," he insisted.

Bruce handed me the pistol. For all I knew, I'd be more likely to accidentally shoot myself than someone else with it.

Sirens were audible in the background.

"Theoretically, the firefighters are the good guys," I said.

Santana and I hid our guns and Bruce stuffed his rifle behind his back as best he could. We made our way out onto the main road and flagged down a fire truck.

The firefighter driving got out and came over to us, and some of the other firefighters pulled him aside and out of our hearing started discussing something and pointing at us. "Just a minute," the driver told us. He went to the radio as we moved in that direction to listen. "I have those kids you've been looking for," I heard him say.

"Someone will be right there," came a voice over the radio.

"Why would they be looking for us?" Bruce asked in a low voice. "Only the camp would be looking for us."

"Maybe they think we started the fire," I murmured.

"¡Mierda!" Santana quietly swore and then looked at me. "Sorry. We need to get out of here," he whispered.

"It will be just a minute," the fireman informed us. "I'm Captain Lorel."

"Pleased to meet you, captain," Bruce said. "I've always admired firefighters."

A police car was coming towards the fire truck with sirens on.

# CHAPTER 39

Captain Lorel looked towards the police car and waved. When he turned back, we were gone, right into the fire engine. Bruce had carried Abigail into the cab, followed by me and Emily. Santana took off driving with several firemen running after the truck. The police car gave chase, after we nearly rammed into it on our getaway. The fire truck continued racing down the highway.

"We may not have set that fire," Bruce said, "but now they have us on—"

"Grand theft fire engine, evading arrest and interfering with fire-fighters. If we crash this, they'll also have us on destruction of govern-ment property and have further reason to nail us for that fire we didn't set." Santana finished for him.

The police car, which had been joined by other police cars, continued giving chase. Sirens were blaring in the background. Some police units were blocking the road, and we curved off the road onto a dirt road.

"Oh, no," Santana spouted.

"What?"

"This is leading us back to the camp."

"Well, we don't have much choice. They need the fire truck up there, anyway. At least, our stealing the truck is a good thing," I rationalized.

We couldn't get close to the camp. Everything was blazing. The fire was spreading through the trees and down the hill. Police were on our tail. We drove past some burning trees and continued on, finding ourselves surrounded by smoke and flames.

"At least this isn't like those other California fires where the porcelain and steel in the houses melted while the trees were fireproof," I commented.

"Right. Those fires defied the laws of thermodynamics," Bruce noted.

"It's called 'Prelude to land grab,'" Santana remarked.

A tree collapsed across the road behind us. It blocked our way back, and we couldn't go forward into the fire. We stopped. The blaze was hot. As we sprayed ourselves down with water from the truck, we looked around to see if we could find a way out.

Above, a plane was dumping water and who knows what else. We ran along the path it was spraying until we were out of the main fire zone. Our path was partially invisible because of the trees. But lots of water and probably toxic chemicals were coming down over our heads and we were choking from the inhaled fumes.

We were lost. If we had crossed part of the creek, I couldn't tell. Maybe the heat had evaporated the water. We weren't close enough to the camp to recognize the area. Finally, we hit the stream. We dunked ourselves in it, hoping to cool ourselves and rinse off any chemicals that may have been dropped. We didn't know exactly where the steam led after the point where we had previously parted with it, but we followed it downhill a way, carefully heading away from the kids' camp into the unknown. Finally, we stepped out of the stream onto dry land. I picked some berries I saw along the side but speed was important and so we didn't stop to eat. I hoped they hadn't sprayed this area yet with retardant.

"We're going west, I think," Bruce stated.

There may have been search parties out there for us but the fire was a distraction that kept the authorities busy, probably helping our escape.

"We've got to rest," Emily finally said. It was daylight. We were a ways from the blaze. The trees had thinned out and there were just patches of trees here and there.

"How many people do you think they have looking for us?"

"With the drugs and explosives and mind control, we may be running from the CIA, the NSA, and the Maf-I-A, not to mention the police, the firemen, the FDA and the DEA," Santana replied.

I pulled the berries out of my pocket and shirt. "But eat drink, and be merry, as they say. Berries are a food and a drink."

Santana winked at me.

"Mexico is looking pretty good," Bruce said.

"They have extradition agreements with the United States—unless they charge us with a capital crime—which they won't because of our age," I pointed out.

"LWOP," Santana said.

"They won't let us go on trial," Abigail responded. "They'll just—" she paused as if she were about to pass out, "Shoot us."

"Are you alright?" I asked. I felt her forehead. "She's burning up. We have to get her to a hospital."

As if heaven sent, rain started coming. "Well, at least something will be preserved from the fire," I said.

"Not necessarily," Bruce countered. "This was a chemical fire. Water won't necessarily put it out."

We kept going downhill, as the rain continued pouring. I slipped, falling in the dirt, rolling and winding up in what seemed a soft bed of what had turned to mud. I tried to push myself up grabbing onto a bush, feeling as if I was in quicksand. Fortunately, it only went down to my waist. As I tried to move out of it, I pulled up what felt like a branch. It wasn't. It was a bone, an arm bone, much smaller than Jason's arm bone, but it clearly was either the radius or the ulna of a small human. The wrist bones and a small hand were attached to it.

# CHAPTER 40

Santana helped me up and shook his head as he took the bones from me and sat me down on an area with smooth rocks, next to where Bruce was setting down Abigail. I couldn't handle more.

Bruce and Santana started mucking around in the mud, pulling up more and more bones, all small, looking as if they belonged to little kids. I leaned back, with mud covering my lower body and my arms. I just lay there, looking at the rain that was coming down. I felt numb. Bruce's and Santana's speech drifted in, but it was as if their words were disconnected. Emily lay down on my opposite side from Abigail and put her arms around me. I knew I should be strong for her, but she was being strong for me. I could feel the tears on her cheeks as she put her face against the side of mine.

Bruce and Santana remarked something about "graveyard," and "dozens of children." I couldn't handle more deaths and yet they kept coming. It was too much. Paul, Jason, John, Jamie, Sonja and now these kids. I wanted to just die, too, go to another universe where this wasn't happening. I got more and more soaked. I couldn't feel the temperature of my surroundings. I couldn't even feel my feet.

"You're in shock," Santana said. He took off his shirt and put it over me as Emily moved a little. "Are you holding up okay, Emily?" he asked.

I could feel her head nodding against me. His shirt and Paul's jacket were cold and wet but the gesture was warm. I was still too stunned to speak. Emily straightened up.

Santana picked me up and carried me. Bruce continued, carrying Abigail, with Emily clutching one of her hands.

I didn't know how far we went before the rain stopped. I could still see flames. They seemed to have lessened, but they were still blazing brightly. Santana put me down under a tree as our group paused to rest. Bruce put Abigail on the ground next to me and sat next to her. Santana laid down beside me holding me tight against him. I signaled to Emily to join us, and I held onto her while Santana held me close until the sun came up.

"Can you walk?" Santana asked me.

I nodded. He felt cold. It must have been cold last night, in spite of the nearby fire, and, still, he had only seemed to care about keeping me warm. "Thank you," I said, starting to cry. He held me against him. I pulled back and gave him back his shirt. "I know I'm not pulling my weight."

"Shh," he said. "You're fine."

Bruce picked up Abigail. She reached out and took my hand as he lifted her. "I'd tell you it will be alright," she told me. "But it won't. Eventually, you just feel numb. When I saw pictures of the kids my dad had bombed, I wanted to throw up and die. Then I decided to just rebel, drink and party, until it all went away. It didn't."

"You're the strongest person I've ever met," I responded.

"You're strong, too. You kept me alive," she said. "Now, don't go flaking out on me. If you do, none of us will survive."

I figured she was just being sweet, but it helped. She was clearly in considerable pain, and yet she was concerned about me.

"Thank you," I said. As I got up, I reached out and gave her a hug.

We walked, not even knowing where we were going anymore. It

wasn't long before we hit a road. "Is this the one you took to Edwards?"

"No. We are way off that route. I think we are going the other direction."

We walked along the side, ready to duck if we saw a car.

Several black cars with dark windows passed as we got down and hid in the bushes. It was hard to see who was inside as they drove by.

"No license plates," remarked Santana. "They've got to be government. Only they could get away with that."

"Whatever happens," Abigail said, "with you four, I've had more love and support these last couple of days than in my entire life."

"It's going to be alright," I responded. "And years from now, we'll be sitting around joking about our adventures." I hoped my words came true.

I hugged Abigail, again. Emily joined for a group hug.

"I think our home lives were all awful. That's why we're here. I know people say they are going to keep in touch and then don't. Please, let's not be like that," I implored them.

"Forever," Emily said.

"Forever," Santana joined in, holding up his fist. Emily and I met his fist with ours. Abigail weekly raised her fist to ours for a fourth.

"I'm in," Bruce said joining ours with his fist. "Well now, if this lovefest is over, let's keep walking before they start searching this area."

We got up and continued a little ways from the side of the road, avoiding cars. We figured that this would lead to a larger road, hopefully without any encounters. Our guess was that most cars we saw going toward the fire were probably either authorities or the bad guys. So, we made sure to stay out of sight. We saw a roadblock up ahead. Definitely nobody else was getting though. We moved further away from the road into a ditch.

The sun had dried the grassy hill, though some of the mud had dried on me, Santana and Bruce. We watched as we passed the roadblock and saw that they were checking everyone coming through. We continued on for another fifteen minutes. My legs started giving out.

Emily didn't look like she could go further. "Let's rest a little," I suggested.

We moved even further away from the road—though keeping it in sight. I sat against a tree stump. I kept telling myself we could make it. But I was exhausted and sore and definitely not sure I could continue on.

Santana moved his head to indicate he wanted a private conversation. "We'll be back in a minute," I told the others.

"The lovebirds talk," Emily teased as I wandered off with Santana helping me stay on my feet.

"Abigail's fever feels dangerously high. I can't believe she is still lucid," he quietly pointed out.

"We need more water, or we will have to stay in the shade until dark," I responded.

"I don't know if she will make it that long."

"If we could get to a phone, we could call for help."

"If they think we've escaped, they'll be monitoring our mothers' phones. If we're lucky, they'll assume we were lost in the fire."

We made it to the far side of the roadblock. At least, we were past the authorities checking who was who.

As we continued on, we came across a closed, deserted coffee shop. It was boarded up. Bruce and Santana pulled the boards free on the back side, leaving the front looking undisturbed. We went inside. There were rats scurrying across the floor. I checked the kitchen faucets. There was no running water. The fridge was empty. In one cupboard, there was an old six pack of soda that looked about a hundred years old.

"Well, the corn syrup will have glyphosate in it," I said.

"I'll take the roundup over dehydration," Santana reacted.

"Me too," I agreed.

"You realize that we are sitting ducks here," Abigail warned. At least, she was still lucid enough to give us advice—though I could tell she was straining to speak.

"I know. In the movies, they always find an abandoned place, and then the bad guys show up," I responded. Try to get some rest while we look around."

We opened every door, cupboard and drawer. In a walk-in supply closet, we found a first aid kid that had been abandoned. All the bandages were gone. There was some antiseptic, some Motrin and two icepacks that you rub to make work. Bruce was focusing on a radio he had found. It was dead and the coffee shop's electricity was clearly off.

I tried smashing a cold pack against a wall and then rubbing it until it cooled off. I took it over to Abigail who was lying on a cushioned bench seat. "Let's put this against your head. Take the Motrin." I handed her the pills and she swallowed them and took a sip of soda to wash them down.

Emily was sitting next to her. "I'll hold it against her head. We're sisters now."

Abigail let out a little smile.

When my mother left, I kept wishing I had a sister. I had this brother who didn't like me and a father who only wanted to hurt my mom by taking me away from her, even though he didn't love me. It was quite some time after that when I found Shannon and Tiffany. I missed them, but this new family gave me a real sense of belonging.

"The three of us, sisters," Abigail said weakly and then seemed to drift off into unconsciousness. Maybe she was resting. I was hoping that the fever wasn't doing any damage.

"At least she missed eating rats and foxes in the camp," I noted, trying to lighten things up.

"That was awful," Emily said. "I did eat some meat and I hope it wasn't rat. I tried not to eat any rodents."

"I do miss Hope. I hope she and her pack escaped the fires."

"Dogs have a way of surviving," she assured me.

I looked at Abigail. "There has to be someone out there who cares enough to give us some help. I sent a letter to my mom before I came. I was hoping she'd find me and somehow rescue me. It was that hope that she still cared enough to find a way to pull off some impossible feat that kept me going when I was in that box. I guess, it was asking too much."

"How would she have found you? We didn't even know where we were?"

"And my dad never would have told her."

"My mom wouldn't have even come looking."

"Like we said, we really are each other's family now."

"Abigail's just got to get better," Emily worried, her eyes tearing up.

"Does anyone have their cell phone?" Bruce asked, coming up to us excitedly.

Emily and I shook our heads.

"Darn. I think I have a way to get them powered up."

"What about Santana?" I asked.

"He doesn't have his either."

"I think I can make a battery to at least power up the radio," he said.

I went to the front of the coffee shop and sat with Santana looking out through a crack in the boards. "Abigail is passed out. I'm really scared. I don't want to lose her."

He put his arm around me. "You asked if I believed in God. We survived the camp, the dogs, Marco, Evan and being chased by all kinds of people wishing us harm and we're still alive. That's a pretty good confirmation that someone up there—" He pointed to the ceiling, "Is watching out for us. ¡Mierda!"

A black car pulled into the parking area. We rushed to our friends.

"We've got to get out of here," Santana advised.

"Hold this," Bruce handed me a plastic bag with aluminum foil, an old radio, an unopened soda and some other supplies that I didn't have time to inventory.

He picked up Abigail and we moved quickly out the back of the coffee shop as we heard someone breaking in through the front. I grabbed Evan's gun, which I had laid on the table. We ran to a dip in the ground about twenty-five feet away with trees surrounding it, just in time to see men, coming around towards the back with guns, big guns, drawn.

# CHAPTER 41

They were looking through windows on the sides of the coffee shop, frequently turning to glance at the surrounding area. We watched as they went through the back door into the coffee shop as other men came out through the back door.

We started to circle uphill, backtracking our former direction, so we could get a better look at the men we had left behind. We hid between a couple of smaller hills near a tree.

"At least they don't have dogs," Bruce said.

"Maybe they've learned that dogs can turn on them," I reminded him.

"Remember the term 'famous last words?'" Santana commented.

"Good point."

Their search appeared to be moving down in the direction we had been going, before our stop, not crediting us with backtracking.

"What kind of assault rifles are those?" I inquired.

"They look like M-16s," Bruce responded. "Military issue."

"Military? So what, we have the army after us now?"

"Probably afraid to risk another Chelsea Manning. I suspect it's contractors."

"Like the one doing the mind-control experiments on us?"

"The Pentagon is missing a lot of money. Maybe the taxpayers are picking up the tab for contractors to do this. ¡Mierda!" Santana responded.

"Bruce, you said you were at a gulag school?" I asked.

"I found a way to short out the electricity and I was sent to Camp MKUltra."

I smiled at his nickname for our camp. "So, ours isn't the only one using shock treatment?"

"No, that's pretty standard from what I read online when I was researching what the counselor was trying to sell my dad. After I saw how evil she was, I emptied her bank account online. Gave the money to several youth rights coalitions."

I gave him a high five.

"It didn't help. My dad was convinced my internment would turn me into a top scientist ready to follow in his footsteps."

"What would you like to do, I mean professionally?" I asked Bruce.

"Start my own business, countering the online government spying operations."

"Our own Edward Snowden. You do know they want to execute him and Julian Assange, don't you?"

"They'd have to catch me first. I'm really good."

"We would make a pretty good team. You could do the hacking. Santana can do the driving. Abigail, Emily and I could do the field investigations and suspect questioning."

"They're getting back into their vehicles," Emily observed. We watched as the men drove off in a downhill direction.

I looked at Abigail. She was still unconscious. Bruce stoked her hair. I could tell he really liked her.

"Okay, let's break out the bag and see what is being said." From the bag, Bruce pulled out the soda, a plastic cup, aluminum foil, some wires and some metal forks he had wired together to turn them into grippers. "I stole some of the coffee shop wiring that they were no longer using from their walls."

"Nice," I said. "You are really industrious and a better searcher than I am. I wouldn't want to challenge you to a scavenger hunt."

Bruce worked to rewire and power the radio. He attached some aluminum to it, presumably to assist with the reception, and somehow used the soda to supposedly strengthen the signal.

"I'm so glad we have Scotty with us," I remarked.

"Scotty, beam us up," Santana mused.

"Still working on it," Bruce said. "You don't believe me?"

It wouldn't have surprised me if he had turned out to be *Star Trek's* miracle worker. Pretty soon, the radio was working. Bruce switched frequencies. I was expecting music, but he had somehow tapped into the police bandwidth.

First, we heard a detailed description of ourselves from various speakers.

"If you find the kids, you must turn them over. The series of arson fires they have started across state lines makes this a federal matter."

"Will do."

"One of them was injured by wolves when setting the fire. We will be putting her under custody in a guarded hospital room."

That channel went silent. He moved the dial around.

"Five arsonists are suspected of starting the blaze that has claimed several lives. If anyone sees five kids, one injured by wolf bites while setting the fires, please contact the police. They are believed to be armed and dangerous."

"Well, everyone is looking for us. Even the hospitals will turn us in," I said.

"We need more transportation," Santana remarked.

"Armed and dangerous," I repeated.

"'Armed and dangerous' is code for 'shoot on sight,'" Santana pointed out. "I'm definitely not giving up my gun."

"Neither am I," I added.

"And I still have the rifle stuffed up my back under my clothes," Bruce acknowledged.

I laughed. "Our Party would love us gun-totters," I quipped to Santana.

"I'm going to register as a Green," Emily asserted.

"My dad's a Republican," Bruce told her. "But I'm going to be a Libertarian."

"Well, the four major parties are well represented here," I said.

"You guys aren't planning to shoot your way out?" Emily asked. "Someone might get killed."

"I freaked out when I saw that dead fox," I replied.

"We left Evan alive. But we didn't stop the dogs from having their way with Marco," Santana recalled.

"It must have been pretty horrible," Emily said, appearing to shiver from the thought of the dogs' last meal.

"And still I wish we had those dogs at our side," Santana remarked. "Super dogs, rescuing teen campers."

I laughed. "We need to get moving. I'll carry the radio."

"Let me carry Abigail for a while. Give you a rest," Santana told Bruce. "Save your strength to help her later."

Bruce complied.

"Death by arson is murder one," I noted.

"Except, we're minors," Emily said.

"They'd bind us over to be tried as adults," Santana pointed out.

---

We continued on in the direction that we believed was away from the camp, staying away from the road. As much as we had been turned around at times, I wasn't sure which way we were going. We went up a hill and down into a valley.

We were mostly out of the forested areas and moving along grass. Cattle were grazing but they paid us no mind.

We came across a tractor in a field.

"No!" Santana cried, grabbing our attention. He put Abigail down. He started giving her mouth-to-mouth and then started pumping her chest.

Emily started sobbing. "Please, God!" she cried.

I prayed that there was a God who cared enough to save Abigail. After my experiences, I didn't know if I had enough faith to believe in anything. Bruce took over the mouth-to-mouth while Santana continued to do the chest compressions. Emily and I watched, wishing there was something we could do.

# CHAPTER 42

"Santana, continue the mouth-to-mouth and compressions," Bruce instructed. He looked at me. "Battery, give me the battery I put together."

"I don't think it's strong enough," I said, suspecting what he had in mind. He looked at the tractor, pulled some more wire out of the bag and put two coils on each side of the tractor battery.

"Santana, can you hotwire the tractor?" he asked.

Santana switched off with Bruce and managed to start the engine. "Much easier than a car," he muttered.

They switched again as we pulled Abigail closer to the tractor. Bruce grabbed the wires and used them like a defibrillator to try to restart her heart.

Santana continued to compress on her chest and Bruce gave her oxygen between defibrillation attempts. Finally, on the fourth try, Santana, who was listening to her chest, said, "I think we've got a heartbeat."

Bruce continued breathing into her mouth, until Abigail's hand came up and waved him away. She drifted back into unconsciousness.

They loaded her onto the tractor's seat next to Santana. Emily and I took the back bumper and Bruce lay on the hood, watching Abigail closely. We moved forward until we hit Interstate 5 and then traveled alongside it. We finally reached a lake, Pyramid Lake.

"I know where we are," I said.

"Halfway over the Grapevine," Santana noted. Cars drove by but we didn't dare call attention to ourselves. "We need a car we can hotwire. We need to go across the highway to the parking lot."

In the lake parking lot, Santana found and started an older model car and we climbed in. Someone came running. "That's my car!"

I saw the man holding and speaking into his cell as Santana sped us away.

"They'll make us fast," Santana stated as we headed north on Interstate 5 towards Bakersfield and Highway 138. The last thing we needed to be on was a major highway in a reported stolen car.

"If we can make it to Lancaster, we can find a 24-hour clinic somewhere," I noted.

The sun had set. That made it more difficult to see the license plate, I hoped. We stopped around a curve and covered the license plate with dirt. The trunk contained a case of unopened bottles of water. Bruce managed to briefly rouse Abigail, who took a sip and then lapsed back into unconsciousness. We split a few bottles, using most of the rest to cool Abigail and create mud to put on the car.

We continued on towards Highway 138. Suddenly, blue and red lights were visible behind us.

We were speeding and for a moment, I was sure we were caught. But then, the highway patrol vehicle pulled around us and continued at top speed. We pulled off around another curve and took a road that ran along the side of the highway.

We saw lights flashing behind us, again. We went down an incline and pulled off the road following a curve, turning onto a dirt road and then departing from that and turning off our lights. It was already dark. We saw more flashing lights coming our way on the road we had taken and then going past us.

We continued on the dirt around a curve until a large rock, in the road, hit the underside of our car. "I think it got the oil pan," Santana informed us. The car continued for a while and then white smoke started coming out the back. It didn't stop us. Eventually, the car chugged and quit. "Sorry," Santana lamented.

"You got us this far," I commended him. "We'll just have to keep on."

Santana checked the glove box and found a couple of Hoffman's Cup of Golds. I remembered those were my mother's favorites long ago. Abigail was still out of it. We split the two candy cups five ways and saved a piece for her.

We walked back to the paved road, with Santana and Bruce carrying Abigail. We moved along the road, hoping to find another car we could steal.

"Now, mind you, I was a law-abiding kid before being sent to the Camp," I told them.

"I only stole my father's cars," Santana noted.

"So, you weren't a real car thief," Emily pointed out.

"But right now, we've committed more felonies than most criminals commit in a life of crime. This is the effect of the teen behavior modification camps. Go from a boring, regimented life to a life of crime. Sign up here," Santana joked.

We continued on, hanging onto the last of our water in case we didn't find new transportation soon.

"Well, at least I've got you, Clyde," I said.

"And I've got you, Bonnie," Santana replied.

"'Just because we came in one car doesn't mean we have to leave in the same car.'"

"Hey. That's my line," he scolded.

"At least we see the same old movies."

"They both died in the end," Bruce interjected.

"That's the part I didn't like," I acknowledged.

"The woman who was injured in the movie survived. That would be Abigail," Bruce recalled, smiling at the girl he was holding.

"Yeah, but I'm sure Abigail doesn't want to wind up like her. Estelle Parson's character sold everyone out," I recalled.

"Did anyone see the remake?" Emily asked.

Nobody responded.

"Guess Hollywood shouldn't waste its money on remakes," she said.

"With the exception of Nicole Kidman remakes."

Santana and Emily looked at me.

"Come on. *The Invasion* and her *Stepford Wives* movies had feel-good endings, much better than the originals."

"I remember *The Invasion* with people lining up to get the vaccines that turned them into alien zombies. My mom didn't vaccinate me for anything," Bruce said. "She and my dad said the vaccines had too many poisons."

"And they are scientists," I noted. "That's significant."

"So maybe I'm immune to having my body snatched," he bragged.

"We all passed the snatched test at camp," I responded.

Emily and I high-fived each other. Bruce and Santana, who were busy carrying Abigail, nodded in agreement.

"And yet your dad still sent you to a Gulag Camp?" I inquired of Bruce.

He shrugged. "Maybe my dad's own vaccines warped his mind."

"Now, who besides me saw any of the GAO report at George Miller's hearing from 2007? It was before I was born but later, it was on the Net on video when I was old enough to understand it," I commented.

"I only heard about it," Emily replied.

"Greg Kutz, the head of the GAO, spoke about a number of the in-camp deaths. He talked about teens brushing their teeth with toilet water, being hogtied, raped, dehydrated, forced to drink their own vomit, starved, hung and a lot of the other mierda we saw happening at the camp," Santana recalled. "I saw it on video when my dad was backing Lara's legislation."

"But most of those schools he spoke about were private, not tied to the CIA, right?" I asked.

"Right. But how do we know for sure? Why didn't the Senate regulate them?" Santana inquired.

"The small number of kids who have escaped have generally been caught and sent back to those or similar torture chambers. Our leaders know and aren't rescuing them." I noted.

"Have you ever heard of the National Youth Rights Association?" Emily asked.

"I have," I said.

"I joined," she bragged. "It was before they sent me to the camp. They were trying to get these schools and camps closed or at least regulated. The horror stories they told were similar to what we experienced. The moment I was taken from my room, I knew what was coming."

"You were kidnapped too?" I asked.

"It's S.O.P.," Santana said. "All except the most gullible were. Would anyone go there willingly?" Santana asked.

"Maybe the kids who are convinced of the lies their school counselors tell," Bruce said.

"Maybe that's why we survived. We never bought into the lies," I surmised.

"So many died," Bruce noted, sadly.

"We wouldn't be here if not for Paul. He stood up to his father and his father's thugs and died trying to end the nightmare," I added.

"That idiot Ian wanted to stay. If he hadn't grabbed the wheel, he, Paul and the other blues might still be alive," Santana said angrily.

"It's called Stockholming. I saw it with my brother. He didn't care about the beatings my mother took. He was older and could have done something. But he was just fine with my mother nearly being killed. He had no problem with the idea of my dad sending me to the camp. I was going to run away the night I was kidnapped and taken there."

"Technically, it's not a kidnapping if the custodial parent authorizes it," Bruce pointed out.

"Kids and women need more rights in our society," I remarked. I looked at Santana.

"I agree. I'm not female. But I'll be the first to admit my mother didn't get a fair shake in the courts."

"Both my parents should die, Menendez-style," Abigail chimed in.

"Good to see you coming to," I said.

"You gave us a real scare," Emily told her.

"You're the celebrity in our team. You've got to be here for the next act," I stated.

"The next act?" Emily asked.

"Going public with the truth," I elaborated.

"I'm all for going public. But we are wanted for far more serious crimes than Bonnie and Clyde," Santana said.

"Especially if they throw in the forest fire, we didn't start and the deaths of the blue team," Bruce elucidated.

"On the radio, they didn't mention our names," I noted.

"They know them. If Evan is government, they have to have our full files," Santana pointed out.

"They are protecting our evil parents," Abigail said. She was still weak and clearly in pain. Being carried along the road probably wasn't helping.

"I am beginning to understand where the Menendez brothers were coming from," Santana declared.

"They were heroes. They should be canonized," Abigail remarked.

"When we go public, you can call for their canonization on TV," I proposed.

"I don't want to burst your bubble, as bonita as it is, but nobody is going to believe anything we say. We don't have the videos. We don't have any evidence," Santana pointed out.

"Right, those videos either caught fire or are in Evan's possession, ready to prove we are drug dealers and terrorists," I responded. "Maybe we can get asylum in Russia."

"Russia is already getting heat over Edward Snowden and he's a national hero, here, " Bruce noted. "Except to the Administration. Add in the Russiaphobia and they'll say Russia sent us."

"True. The last thing we need is more grounds for World War III. My dad's former boss was eager to have her husband's company supply the weaponry to annihilate the planet and now the whole Senate is getting kickbacks for war."

"And we've probably lost our access to those underground cities where our parents expect to survive the planetary annihilation event," Santana joined back in.

"Well, we might be able use my dad's ID codes to break into a base, arm ourselves to the teeth and then blast our way into those cities and close the entrances behind us." Abigail's voice was getting more weak and pained. "Let them see what it's like to survive World War III with the peons," she pushed out.

"Genia. Access codes? Can you help us break into Edwards?" Santana asked.

"How many crimes are we adding in here? I think Abigail is in enough danger," Bruce attested. "And Abigail, I don't want you to strain yourself." He was becoming more and more protective of her as we continued. I found it very touching. I wondered if this would lead to something special after we were out of this situation. We were all young. But going through the camps had aged us. We had gone through more torture in our short time there than most people go through in their lifetimes.

I kept trying to figure out how to get Abigail medical treatment without some doctor or nurse alerting the police. There had to be a way. I put my arm around Emily. I wanted to make sure she knew how much we appreciated her, as well. She might only be thirteen, but she was as mature as any adult. Miraculously, she had retained a real innocence about her in spite of what we had been through. I only wished I could protect her from any further heartache.

Santana joined in, putting his free arm around me, making it a threesome. Despite having been brought back from the dead or near dead, Abigail was still in danger and there was no way to know if any of us would survive the night.

I had to stop thinking pessimistically. I started to sing an old Chicago song, "Nothing Can Stop Us Now." Santana joined in. Soon, Bruce and Emily joined us. Emily had a strong soprano voice.

"Where did you learn to sing like that?" I asked.

"My mother got me music lessons when I was young. I used to sing in school and church choirs."

"You sang in your church's choir and they still sent you to camp?"

"My parents didn't go to church except when they wanted to look religious. So, they didn't care. They thought I was getting involved with a guy they didn't approve of. We weren't romantic, just friends, but they didn't believe us. Anyway, one night, someone slipped some kind of drug into my drink and I was a mess. The camp was their solution. The counselor sold it as a great opportunity for turning me into the perfect young lady and putting me at the top of my class in school. And then that ugly bounty hunter."

"Joe?" I asked.

"He didn't tell me his name."

"Someone ought to Menendez your counselor," I said.

Our conversation was cut short by a set of headlights coming towards us on the road. We went over to the side and ducked down. The car started to go by. I pulled myself up.

Santana tried to grab me, but I freed myself and ran into the road, waving and jumping up and down. Santana raced onto the road beside me and tried to bring me to my senses.

"Stop, stop," I yelled, though I figured the driver wouldn't see me behind the car.

I was wrong. The car stopped and backed up. I ran up to the front passenger-side door. It opened and outstepped my mom. I threw myself into her arms. "You came."

# PART TWO
## CENSORSHIP, EXECUTION-STYLE

# CHAPTER 43

My mom hugged me for what seemed like an eternity, but it may have been just a few minutes. "Can I join in, too?" Shannon asked, stepping out the driver's door.

I broke free and ran over to hug my best friend. "I love you, Shannon. I mean, I really love you. How did you two find us?"

"This guy named Santana called."

I pulled back and stared at Santana. "You called?"

"Isn't that why you gave me the number, Spring?" he teased. "I couldn't go back to the camp without notifying someone."

"Your mom and I were already trying to figure out where you were and then he called. His information was sketchy and I had to wait for my parents to leave for the Bahamas before I could go looking. We've been driving around these mountains for days."

"As soon as I got your letter, I started looking for you. Your dad wouldn't tell me anything. If it hadn't been for your Santana friend, we never would have found you."

"My Santana friend is awesome." I ran and jumped into Santana's arms.

"I definitely plan to get to know your young man," my mom said.

"My young man saved my life over and over again," I gushingly told her.

"Bye, bye Matt," Shannon joked. "Hello, Santana."

"Matt, who?" I responded.

"I hate to be a killjoy," Bruce said. "We need to get out of here before we're spotted, and Abigail needs a doctor."

"Oh, right. Mom, this is Bruce. The girl he's helping is Abigail, who is awesome, and this is my good friend, Emily."

"I'm pleased to meet you all," my mom marveled with a smile in her voice.

Bruce, Abigail, and Emily squeezed into the back passenger seat of the car, while my mom scooted in next to Shannon. As I started to squeeze in next to my mom, I heard a familiar bark.

I rushed back out and hugged Hope as she ran up. "You followed our scent all this way. We're going to have to make more room for my dog."

My mom got out and looked curiously at my canine friend.

"Mom, Hope, Hope, Mom." I took my mom's hand, and together, we petted Hope, letting Hope know my mom was okay. "Shannon, I'm glad you have your parents' car. We never would have fit in yours."

"I don't know where you are going to fit the dog," Shannon stated.

"We'll handle it." I sat on Santana's lap, with my mom sitting on the outside in front. Hope was straddled across my lap and my mom's.

My mom looked at me on Santana's lap and said, "I can see I've missed way too much of your life."

---

We headed, this time, toward Los Angeles. The odds of finding help for Abigail seemed better, there, and we would not be expected to get that far. On the radio, there was an all-points bulletin looking for five kids who had started the forest fire with a brief reference to possible deaths.

"Yep, we could get nailed for felony murder," I said.

"We can't fry in California, but they can still give us LWOP, for what would be a capital offense if we were older," Santana pointed out.

As we traveled, we filled my mom and Shannon in on the nightmare, the torture, the deaths and the escape. "They are going to cover it up," I warned.

"I don't want to speak ill of your father, but he will probably help them with the cover-up. I tried to—"

"I remember. When I was in camp, I had time to remember."

The radio continued with detailed descriptions.

"It doesn't matter where we go. They'll find us. They are describing Abigail's injuries. The moment we enter a hospital, they'll recognize us," Emily warned.

"I know it's substandard, but let's start at the veterinarian clinic I volunteered at," I suggested. "Dr. Hobbes is one of the few good vets in Beverly Hills. That will give us a little extra time to find someone who will help and not tell."

"Won't he call your dad?" my mom asked.

"I don't think so. I know the nighttime techs. And they have handled cardiac problems in the past. That clinic's much more reputable than the one that killed my dog."

"Your dog?" my mom asked. "Cynthia?"

I nodded.

"I've missed too much."

We went to the side entrance. The code I had previously used to get into the clinic hadn't changed and worked to get us in. Jeff, one of the techs there, greeted us. "Summer, what are you—" He paused as Bruce carried in Abigail. We had decided it was best for the others to wait outside.

"Look, we can't go to a doctor because of a lot of things we can't talk about. But Abigail will die if we don't get her help," I told him. Jeff and I had been good friends and I trusted him not to rat us out to the police.

"Bruce, put Abigail down on a table," I instructed.

"Dr. Hobbs should be notified. I don't know if I can handle this."

"That could put him in trouble. Please help us. I know you're a good, kind person, and Abigail's good and kind, too. Please, treat her." I started to cry.

Jeff reached out and gave me a friendly hug. "Please don't cry. For all those times you covered for me when I had to take off, I owe you. But she looks like she needs real help."

I calmed down. "You know my family has money. I realize it's a risk to you, but I'll make sure you have enough money to cover your college tuition through graduate school if you help us."

"You don't have to do that, but I won't refuse it. Here's the thing. If, after I examine her, I determine I can't treat her, you'll have to take her to a real doctor."

I nodded.

He felt her forehead. "She's burning up."

"Right. She needs antibiotics, not penicillin. It says she's about 120 pounds," I said, looking at the scale attached to the table.

"I've lost weight," she announced with a pained expression on her face.

"Clindamycin?" he asked. She nodded. He pulled out a vile of something, drew it into a needle and injected her with it. Then he pulled some pills out of the drawer and handed them to me. "She'll have to take these four times a day."

He pulled the bandages off her patched-up bites, poured betadine on her injuries and re-bandaged them. He looked at an instrument close to the table and moved it closer to her, scanning her body. "When was she microchipped?"

"What?" Abigail asked. "I've never been—the camp, when I was unconscious?"

"How about me?" I asked. Sure enough, it detected I was microchipped, too. So was Bruce.

"Camp? What was this, a prison camp?"

"Not for crimes, but for being teenagers," I informed him.

The reader seemed to indicate the chips were in our wrists.

"We have to get them out," Bruce said.

"Why would someone want to track you?"

"We are dealing with some really evil people," I explained. "Jeff, you remember all the stuff you said about nine-eleven. Well, this is as insane as that. If they find us, they will kill us."

"Call me crazy. But I believe you," he said. I gave him a hug for that one.

He pulled out a scalpel and made an incision into Abigail's wrist. He pulled out something the size of a very tiny pill. He scanned her, again. Nothing.

"You're lucky they just put one this size into the wrist. Now they are putting nano-chips into drugs like Abilify and it's a lot harder to pull them out of where they wind up."

Jeff proceeded to stitch and bandage over the incision. He did the same to my wrist and Bruce's. I had Bruce go out and get Santana and Emily. Jeff found and removed both of their chips and then rescanned us. "You're all clean."

Santana was visibly bothered in learning that he had been chipped. He made a couple of fists as if he wanted to go back and punch what was left of Marco.

"Would you check Abigail's heart?" I asked. "She had a cardiac arrest earlier tonight."

"That's over my head." He pulled out an EKG machine. After he looked at the monitor, he said, "I don't know if there is a problem, but I think you should get her to a hospital. You wouldn't want her to die. My college tuition is not worth someone's life."

"We will get her medical help as soon as it's safe, but we don't want to risk her life. Even if you can't help, I'll make sure you get that money," I assured him.

"Wait," he urged. "My sister Susie has the same medical plan as I do. Use this name. He wrote down his sister's name, date and place of birth, driver's license number and her Blue Shield number."

"Thank you," I gave him a kiss on the cheek. "Oh, what's your mom's name?"

"Shana Morrison. List me as the emergency contact. Here's my number." He wrote that down as well.

We decided that Cedars Sanai was the best place to go for quality treatment. I walked in there with my mother and Bruce. Santana, Emily and the others stayed in the car, again. My mom pretended to be Shana Morrison. She told them her identification had been stolen earlier that evening.

"We'll have to report these injuries."

"Already reported," my mom said. "Is Charlene Rose still here? We used to be close friends when I lived in the area."

"I'm afraid she's passed away."

"I've been out of touch."

"Her sister Janet is working here."

Because we had told them about Abigail's cardiac problem, Abigail was brought into the back quickly.

A nurse with a tag, marked Janet, came in and connected Abigail to an EKG machine. "I understand you knew my sister."

"I did. She was a wonderful person," my mom said. "I'm so sorry she's gone. I guess I've been out of touch."

Janet looked Abigail over. "I've got to report these animal bites."

"They've already been reported," my mom said.

"Look," I interceded, hoping I wasn't messing things up. "I know you don't know me and my friend from anything, but we need the help of someone we can trust."

My mom joined in, "My former husband put our daughter in a teen wilderness camp where they went through a form of torture that no kids should endure. If she were your child and she came back this way, what would you do? If you notify the authorities, she'll go back to the camp, and this or worse will happen, again."

Janet looked at us. "I've been there. Not that way, but my former husband abused me and my daughter. Still, I can't break the rules. Oh heck, nobody helped me and my daughter, and I never understood why someone didn't take a risk on us. I take it her name isn't really Susie."

My mom didn't say anything.

"It's fine. I'll do what I can. The EKG doesn't look great. She is going to need to be here for at least a week."

"A week?" I asked, picturing the authorities closing in. "She could be in real danger. Look, they tortured us. They sent the dogs after her. Look what they did to her."

"I'll take care of it. I'll put my cell down as the contact and take care of the records. I'm taking a risk here. Call it a favor for a friend of my late sister."

"Thank you," my mom said. I gave Janet a hug.

Before we left, Bruce insisted on coming in and spending some time with Abigail in her hospital room.

I went back to the car to wait. My mom came out of the hospital with a concerned look on her face.

"Is Abigail okay?"

"The same. Janet is taking care of her. I just talked to my neighbor. The authorities are at my house."

# CHAPTER 44

"Your phone," I said.

"Phone?"

"They can trace it unless it's a fresh burner phone," Santana advised.

She pulled out her smartphone and looked at it.

"Pull the battery," Santana suggested.

My mom tried to open it up. The battery compartment wouldn't open. Shannon pulled out her own cell battery and then got a small tool kit out of the back of the car. Using a micro-mini-Philips head screwdriver, Santana opened the back of my mom's phone and took out the battery. As he did so, Bruce came down and we filled him in.

"Where is your home?" Bruce asked.

"Crescent City."

"They may not be saying why they are there, but we know they're looking for us," Bruce stated.

"If they're searching Crescent City, there must be a statewide dragnet search for our group. We need to watch our backs," I noted. We looked up at the camera in the middle of the street.

"They may know we're in Los Angeles, now," Bruce acknowledged.

"Or maybe just that my mom is looking for us. You didn't tell your neighbor anything did you, Mom?"

"No."

"We may have some time," Bruce noted.

"We can go back to my place," Shannon said.

"My dad knows you're my best friend."

"Jimmy," she responded.

"Isn't he at home until his college starts?"

"He wanted freedom his last summer before college. So, he got his own place, where he can hang out with me. Isn't that sweet?"

I turned to the others. "Jimmy's cool."

---

"Summer, you've looked better," Jimmy remarked as he greeted us at the door.

"Thanks. Felt better too." He moved back as I entered with Shannon, my mom and my new friends.

"Parties are fun. Anyone bring the refreshments?"

Shannon punched his shoulder.

We sat down and let him in on the happenings of the last couple of weeks.

"Wow, this sounds like Deep State stuff."

"We need some identification," Santana said.

"I take it you mean fake identification."

"Three sets apiece. Can you help us?"

"Why three?"

"In case we have to compromise one or two of them," Santana responded.

"It's going to cost."

"I'm good for it," Shannon said. "I'm sure, Summer will repay me when she gets her name cleared."

"I do have a lot of money in the bank that I can't access," I noted.

"I have some money, but I want to avoid using my bank cards," my mom told us.

"They'll be watching you," I pointed out.

"I know a guy. He gets fake driver's licenses for all my friends who want to drink before turning twenty-one. It's uncool to make us wait until we're almost out of college to drink."

"Agreed. So he can help us, Jimmy?" I asked.

"I'm pretty sure. You need driver's licenses?"

"And passports," Santana said.

"I've lost my daughter once," my mom stated. "I'm not losing her again. We'll need a new ID for me as well."

"How about a different look?" Emily asked. "Our descriptions are all over the news."

The idea of new looks caught on fast. Emily, my mom and I all got our hair blackened with a temporary die. Shannon cut and curled my hair and Emily's so we both looked like sisters.

Santana looked at me. I sensed he hated it.

"You look different. Good but different." At least, he was nice about it, even if he did hate it.

"Which me do you prefer?"

"I prefer you any which way I can be with you."

"Smart answer," Jimmy stated.

---

Shannon purchased some thick reading glasses and sunglasses for us at a twenty-four-hour drugstore. "You'll only need them when someone is ID-ing you. Also, for regular daytime, wear these polarized sunglasses."

Jimmy took us to a bar in Venice where he had previously met up with a guy who could help.

"Hey, you kids can't come in here," the bouncer bellowed. Jimmy showed the bouncer his fake ID and said he had some business with Antonio. We were told we were to wait outside around back.

About half an hour later, a door opened and an African-American male, in possibly his early twenties, stuck his head out. "This better not be a sting."

"Believe me, it's no sting, bro," Santana assured him.

"They need passports and licenses," Jimmy noted. "Three sets."

"Antonio's not my real name, but it will do. How soon do you need them?"

"Tomorrow," Santana replied.

"And the lady?" He motioned to my mom.

"These are my daughters and my sons. And there is another daughter. Please give us IDs that reflect that."

"Well, the girls and the one guy fit, but the Latino will need to be a half-brother to the girls, a little older, previous marriage."

"Make me and him over eighteen," Santana said, pointing to Bruce.

"Three sets a piece. Planning a heist?"

"Nothing like that."

"No problem. I have a no-questions-asked policy."

After Antonio escorted us into a back room and took our pictures and obtained a sizable cash deposit from my mom, we went back to Jimmy's.

"I've been doing the economics. If we're going to disappear, we need a lot of money," Bruce said.

"I've got several million in an account. But, if I don't have my real ID, they wouldn't give it to me and if I went as myself, they'd arrest me the moment I went into a bank," Santana responded.

"You have online account access?" Jimmy asked.

"I did."

"Unless it's been revoked, we transfer thousands to another account," Jimmy said. "Perhaps using one of the fake IDs to retrieve it. Pick some money up here and the bulk in Mexico. Less security."

"Do you think your father has put a lock on your account?" I asked.

"He doesn't have the password. And he knows I don't have ID."

"Rumor has it, he is money-hungry," I said.

"My grandfather set it up for me before he died. My dad isn't a trustee or anything on the account."

"So, we're going to need some serious internet when we get to Mexico." Bruce noted.

"I can sell you one of my computers," Jimmy told him.

"Jimmy!" Shannon scolded him, with a glare and her hands on her hips.

"Or give it to you."

The next morning, Bruce and I were surprised to find Abigail had been transferred into intensive care when we went to see her. Santana and Shannon waited in the car. Abigail's name was still listed as Jeff's sister Susie.

"Her blood work showed a major infection, and we are very worried about her, given the cardiac arrest you reported," Janet told us.

Bruce, my mom, Emily and I were allowed in briefly to see her. There was a two-only rule. First, Bruce and my mom went in. My mom was still pretending to be Abigail's, or rather Susie's, mom. Bruce stayed as my mom switched with Emily.

As Emily came out, they let me go in. "We're trying to get passports to get out of the country. Shannon will help you get out when you're better if that's what you want," I informed her.

"What are you talking about?" Bruce asked. "I'm not leaving without her."

"No. Go," Abigail said. "I'll have an easier time getting out without you guys. With these injuries and you, they'll spot me for sure."

"No," Bruce stated, firmly.

Abigail glared at him. "Do you think I'm lying? If you don't believe me and go with the others, then we have nothing further to talk about."

# CHAPTER 45

"How will you get down there?" Abigail asked.

"Shannon and Jimmy will help us cross," I said. "Their descriptions aren't being circulated."

"I don't want to leave you," Bruce insisted.

"Listen. We're all a family," Abigail told him. "You need to make sure my family is safe and waiting for me when I arrive. I'm counting on you."

"How will you know where to find us?" Bruce asked.

"Shannon and Jimmy," I interjected.

"Bruce, if you care about me, you'll do it," Abigail pushed. "I'm safer crossing without you guys."

"If you aren't down there in a week, I'm coming back."

"I'll be there."

"Summer, can I have some time alone with Abigail?" Bruce asked.

"I'll be waiting outside." I gave her a hug. "Sisters, remember."

In the car, Shannon and Santana were listening to music and laughing. I was almost jealous. I stood outside a while.

Santana turned his head, saw me and jumped out of the car. "Shannon was having me listen to your favorite Green Day song," he said, hugging me. "She was telling me about the time you went to a party and danced on a table to the *American Idiot* soundtrack."

"I should have danced to it on the Governor's desk during a press conference," I said, " while wearing a lampshade, of course."

He leaned in and kissed me. I don't know why his kisses always made me a little dizzy, but I loved them.

"Wow. I can feel the heat," Shannon said as he helped steady me afterward. "But if you ever hurt my best friend, I'll make you wish you were back in camp."

That afternoon, back at Jimmy's place, Shannon and I had a long heart-to-heart while the guys went to the beach to chat. We had picked up burner phones with Mexico access that we were not going to use for anything but talking to each other. She handed me a packet and asked me to wait until Mexico to open it. "It was all the money I could scrounge up from my college account. I know you will pay me back when you can."

"You don't have to."

"Yes, I do. I love you. Besides, I expect twenty percent interest."

"Loan shark," I joked. "When I went to camp, what I missed most of all was you."

"I missed you every day you were gone," she told me. "Wherever you go, when it's safe, I want to come there for vacations, at least twice a year."

"Make it four times. Twice in the summer and Christmas and Spring breaks."

"Deal. I have a surprise."

"A surprise?" Sometimes her surprises were a bit much. She opened up the front door and in popped Tiffany with a bottle of champagne.

"I've never tasted champagne," I confessed. At that moment, my mom walked into the living room from the bedroom we had been staying in.

"I didn't see it." I knew she meant the alcohol. "And I don't want to see it in the future. Hello, Tiffany," she said, walking into the kitchen.

"How did she know who you were? She left before I met you?"

"I called to say I was coming with champagne and she okayed it."

My mom was full of surprises. The best surprise of all was that she still loved me and was willing to give up everything to protect me.

The champagne was too bitter for me, but it didn't matter. Tiffany and Shannon and I laughed like there was no tomorrow.

Emily came out of the bedroom and started to go back in, "Excuse me. I didn't mean to interrupt."

"Emily, join us," I encouraged.

"While I was missing the two of you, Emily helped take care of me. She kept me sane and alive. I want us all to be one happy family."

"Welcome to the family," Tiffany told Emily.

"There's another girl too: Abigail. She's in the hospital, but she's brave and witty like you are Tiffany. Shannon has met her."

"She's really nice. I liked her, right away," Shannon said.

"He's adorable!" Tiffany exclaimed as Hope ran into the room. As she reached out to hug Hope, my dog barked approval.

---

Jimmy, Bruce and Santana returned. "I couldn't stay away from my girl for long," Santana related.

"Your girl," I commented. "I don't recall being anyone's girl."

"Let me rephrase that. The only girl for me," he said and then kissed me. Shannon and Tiffany were all oohhs and aahhs. I introduced Tiffany to Santana and Bruce.

"If this is what you meet in camp, when do I get to go?" Tiffany asked.

I shook my head.

Shannon whispered something to Jimmy, and he went into the kitchen. A minute later, someone turned out the lights. I looked toward the kitchen door, through which a glow was moving toward the living room. Jimmy was holding a cake with candles.

"Organic," Shannon professed. "You didn't think we forgot your birthday, did you? We just couldn't find you to celebrate."

I gave her a hug and blew out the candles.

"I have something for you, too," my mom said. She handed me a little wrapped box. Inside was a pendant on a chain. I opened it and saw a picture of my mom holding me as a baby.

I was so overcome I couldn't speak at first. "I love you, Mom. Thank you. I love all of you."

"One more present," Santana said. He handed me a slightly larger wrapped box. Inside was a service vest for Hope. "We don't want anyone treating him like a dog."

I gave him a hug. I wanted to kiss him, but I noticed my mom was watching us closely. "Thank you for the present and for saving my life."

Later that night, we picked up our IDs. Early the next morning, Santana transferred most of his money to a Swiss account, and then opened a new bank account under one of his fake names. With Bruce's help and a VPN, Santana transferred almost all the funds remaining in his old account, depositing thousands into a new account Santana had set up under one of his fake names and an account in a fake name Jimmy had used, both at branches of the original bank to avoid a delay.

I was surprised at how trusting Santana was of my friends after being around so many untrustworthy people in the past. I worried as they picked up the transferred cash at the bank, but it went smoothly. Between the two of them, they were only able to access ten thousand dollars that day. I was surprised the bank let them have that much. Jimmy planned to help Santana transfer more money from the Swiss account when needed.

We discussed leaving the States through Tecate. The security was less intense than at Tijuana. Mexicali could function as a backup if anything looked funny. Shannon pointed out that it would be easier to get lost in the crowd in Tijuana as long as we didn't call attention to ourselves.

"There are APBs out on us," I noted. "Even with the hair change, they might recognize us with all the cameras there."

"You realize that the Real ID Act isn't to keep Mexicans out but rather us in. They are closing the borders. We've already been microchipped," Santana remarked.

"You mean we were microchipped. Past tense," Bruce pointed out.

"Right. We are freer now, but—" I jumped in.

"But?" Bruce asked.

"I am a little concerned about future surprises."

In the end, we decided to leave through Tecate.

Shannon drove me, Santana, Bruce and Hope in her car. Jimmy had my mom and Emily in his car. Before reaching the border, my mom and Emily switched with Santana and Bruce. We thought it would be better if we split up and confused anyone looking at street images of the passengers. Santana was using his second ID, as the one used for the bank might be compromised. Emily and I were using IDs showing that we were minors, though we had IDs with older ages, too.

We dropped Shannon off at a coffee shop on the American side to wait for Jimmy to return. "Goodbye to my car and my best friend, her mom and my new friends. I'll catch you all later," Shannon said.

"Until we meet up below the border. Thank you for rescuing us, for everything."

"Admit it. You would have done the same for me."

"True." I gave her a goodbye hug as did Emily and my mom.

At the American side of the crossing, the border patrol checked our passports. "Just a minute," the officer advised. He went into his booth and talked to one of the guards. He came back. "What service does your service dog perform?"

My mom replied, "My daughters both have limited vision. The dog is for Tobbie, but I plan to get one for Tulla at a later time." I was Tobbie and Emily was Tulla.

"May I see the dog's health certificate?"

My mother presented the health certificate, our computer expert, Bruce, had created for Hope.

"Very well." He waved us through.

We went to the other side, turned right and waited for an hour at the nearest coffee shop along the road as we had pre-planned. We waited and waited. The boys were a no-show. I was getting nervous. *They had to have made it through alright*, I unconvincingly told myself.

# CHAPTER 46

I started rubbing my hands, panicking. "I have to go back to the border. They should be here."

"It will only be worse for them if the authorities in the States see you, too," my mother cautioned.

"I –I," What had happened to me? Protecting Santana, keeping this boy I had met less than two weeks ago meant more than my freedom, maybe more than my life. I had never felt like that about anyone. But it wasn't just Santana, I was ready to sacrifice myself for my whole group of friends, if necessary.

"I know. You really care for him," my mother said.

The door opened and the guys walked in. I ran over and gave Santana a big hug. "Not that I was worried about you."

"Of course not, Up," he joked. "More seriously," he said, "We wanted to wait until after a change of guard so they wouldn't make the connection, and we took a taxi across so as to not connect Jimmy to our escape. You've got some great friends. Jimmy said that he and Shannon will join us in a wink if we need them."

"I have really been lucky in the friend department," I replied, smiling.

"And the boyfriend department," he quipped, pointing at himself.

"Hmm. You're pretty sure of yourself."

"No. I'm pretty sure of you."

---

The six of us and Hope drove away from Alta California towards Caborca and from there to Los Mochis, where we checked into a hotel. We went to an Internet café and checked reports. Now, they had at least one name for a patsy. Santana's first fake identity of Carlos Marimba had been flagged as one of the five fire-starters. We suspected they got that from the bank. Our descriptions were still out there but not our real names. We wondered if, the names we used crossing the border had also been flagged or if just the branch where Santana had withdrawn the money had flagged him.

Our planned destination in our Mexico travels was actually Mérida, though we were taking a circular route. Online, we had found someone who specialized in assisting people out of Mexico. Bruce did some checking to make sure the person wasn't connected to our government. It turned out he was Columbian and probably a drug lord. Judging from what was happening at the camp, we might be wanted by the drug cartels.

"So, you guys really want to go to Cuba?" Bruce asked. "Aren't you worried about losing your freedom?"

"Are we free now?" Santana answered with a question.

"Cuba has an undeservedly bad reputation. They have better doctors than the U.S. and I want to go to a veterinarian school. Besides, it's a safer place for us to veg out until this thing blows over," I said. I thought about my words. Before camp, I knew my dad wouldn't approve of me becoming a vet, and so it was out of the question. But now, looking at Hope, I knew that was the career I wanted.

Emily was rather passive, willing to go along with whatever travel plans the rest of us decided.

"I don't want to leave Mérida until Abigail joins us," Bruce declared, definitively.

"That's why we're taking such an incredibly round-about route," I said. "As you know, instead of going directly to the Gulf Coast, we are following the West Cast to Petatlán, then backtracking a little and traveling northeast to Toluca and then southeast to Oaxaca and eventually winding up in Mérida, about a half-hour drive from the Gulf Coast. Let's hope that's enough time for her to be able to travel to us."

Santana related that "Jimmy did further checking online just before we left and found out that some smugglers often frequented a bar in Mérida and that we needed to speak to a guy named Arturo. Our route there may change depending on what happens on the way."

"Have any of you heard about all the gangs of killers in Mexico?" Bruce asked

"Are they any worse than the gangs of killers we escaped in the United States?" Santana responded. Similar banter continued between them. There had been no word from Shannon or Abigail for some time. We hoped that Abigail and my friends back home were all right.

Everything went smoothly on the ride to Oaxaca. Santana would put his arm around me in the car when my mom wasn't looking or was sleeping. As she turned our way, he'd pull it back.

"Caught," she said, chuckling about the fourth time he did it. "I was young once, believe it or not. So you don't have to wait until I'm not looking."

"I love you, Mom," I told her.

The people in Mexico were more relaxed and friendly than in our country, and I hoped Cuba would be as warm. From Oaxaca, we backtracked a bit towards Puebla. In our room, I noticed a dark car pulling up in front of the hotel. Some men in suits got out and went into the office.

# CHAPTER 47

"Time to take off," I said as calmly as I could—though inside I felt my heart racing. The last thing we needed was more panic.

We moved through a back window with our luggage and rushed to our car, which we had had the foresight to always park in nearby lots each time we stopped for the night. We never felt safe. From there, we went to Minatitián and from there up to the Coatzacoalcos on the coast. I was starting to feel more at ease and relaxed.

It had been a while since we had had good internet. We finally got a good connection at a small restaurant. From the international news, we learned something major was happening in Washington. It was some kind of funeral.

"Hopefully, it's for whoever is behind those Gulag camps," I said. There was a picture of the Secretary of Defense. "Abigail's dad," I reacted. "Did something happen to him?"

He started speaking, and so I guessed not.

*"I remember when Abigail was born, the most beautiful baby I had ever seen. I took joy in all her activities. She was a little wild, but aren't all kids? She was a good person with a good heart."*

"Why is he talking about Abigail in the past tense?" Bruce asked.

A tinge of fear went through me and I worked to dismiss it.

Knowing what he did to her, anger took over my mood and I wanted to throw something at his face on the screen.

*"I remember when she got her first tooth, when she first attended school. I walked her there myself, so proud, so very, very proud. After school, we would play ball together and I would take her to the playground and push her on the merry-go-round. That was her favorite ride."*

"I wonder who wrote this nonsense," I snapped. "He was never there for her. He only cared about his own career. And what kind of father is willing to have his daughter tortured because she won't live up to his expectations?"

"Ours," Emily said. She was right. Our fathers had sent us there, too.

*"She meant more to me than my own life. I would have done anything for her."*

"Ha!" Santana and I exclaimed in unison.

*"We will always miss her."*

"She won't miss you," I told his TV image.

*"Her death is the most tragic catastrophe that has ever happened to our family."*

"Death?" Santana questioned. I could see Bruce make fists with both hands as he turned pale. Emily opened her mouth in shock as my mom put her arm around my younger friend.

I shook my head. "No. He's lying or they lied to him. She was fine when we last saw her." I reacted. I didn't want to express my fears about what could have happened after we left the country. But terror ran through me. *We never should have left her.* "There must be some mistake. Maybe, they thought she perished at the camp with the other kids."

"When she left the camp, she was coming home. We were about to get our daughter back when this tragedy struck."

# CHAPTER 48

Bruce shut off the computer. "I'm going back."

"This may be a set-up. She wasn't critical. I don't believe Janet would have turned her over to be killed," my mom reassured us.

"This guy lies on a daily basis and the camp counselors were lying to the outside world about everything going on in the camp. My mom's right. It's probably a set-up." I was trying to look calm but inside everything was swirling and I felt like throwing up.

Bruce went outside and Santana followed to speak with him. When they returned, Bruce agreed to accompany us to Mérida before heading back for Abigail. We were about to leave to go out to our car, which was at the side of the building, when we saw a black car pull in.

Santana spoke to the waitress. "Los hombres del padre de mi amor." He pointed to the front. She showed us to the back door, more than willing to help a romantic couple get away from a pursuing father's thugs. Santana gave her a hundred-dollar tip.

"Good line," Bruce mused as the waitress went back in.

All but Santana went to Shannon's car. He went to the black car, which the men had left to go inside. Santana knifed the tires and then ran back to join us."

"A little slowdown," he said. We took off quickly. "You realize, we should ditch the car and pick up a new one,"

"Just so long as Shannon's car doesn't get trashed." I had taken Shannon's money and I didn't want her car damaged or stolen.

At Villahermosa, a more inland town along the main highway, we put the car into long-term parking at the airport.

"I'll send Shannon a note letting her know where to retrieve it," I told the group.

We walked off with our backpacks, hoping for a miracle. As we started from the parking lot, we saw black cars with blacked-out windows pulling to the front of the airport.

Bruce looked at a jet leaving the airport. "Too bad we don't know how to fly a plane."

"Um, I've had flying lessons," Emily informed us. "I've never flown a big plane, and they've never let me fly solo. The airports have been freaked out about anyone under sixteen piloting a plane, even with an instructor on board, for any distance since Jessica Dubroff's plane crash before I was born."

"But how do we get control of one of the planes?" Bruce asked.

We had Mom watch the outside of the airport and stay out of sight while we slipped into a side entrance and asked about the private planes. Santana said his pilot father was debating on which airport to store his plane at. One of the baggage claims guys gave us details about the private hangers and costs.

I looked up and noticed there was a camera pointing in our direction. *Great,* I thought.

We collected my mom and walked out to where the private planes were located as we saw more black cars arriving and men in suits leaving the vehicles and walking towards the front of the airport.

As we rushed to the private plane section, we saw an open hanger and ran for it. Inside was a man rubbing down his plane.

"We'd like to rent your plane for an hour," Santana said.

"All of you?" He spoke perfect English, a plus.

"We're doing a movie."

"Movie?"

"Yes. Don't you recognize Lana Marshall?" Bruce asked, pointing to my mom.

"I don't watch many movies, but you girls certainly look like you could be movie stars."

"You can be in it, full credit, if you like," Santana told the man. "What's your name?"

"Jaime LaRosa."

"Great name for an upcoming star," Santana responded. "And the product placement of your plane, could boost your business."

Jaime looked at Hope. "No dogs."

"He's an important part of the movie. Laddy is playing an amazing service dog that just saved Trudy's life and he's going to help her as Tisha flies her to the hospital."

"I don't know."

"Look, the plane we were supposed to use for the movie had a bad engine and we're on a time schedule. But if you don't want the money —" Santana pulled out a stack of hundreds. He counted to ten.

"Give me another five," the man said. He looked around. "Where's the camera equipment?"

"Really. This must be your first time. Cameras are already in place around the airport and along the route. We have people on the ground who will be filming from outside as it takes off and lands. After the first landing, we'll be picking up an additional cameraman to film the inside shots. Then the special effects crew does its magic."

Emily sat in the pilot's seat.

"You're a child."

"I've been trained for this."

"She's been flying in rehearsals all week until the plane we were using developed engine problems," Santana told him. "You'll be the co-pilot who assists her."

We saw the black suits coming on foot towards the hangar as Emily rolled the plane forward onto the runway.

"You aren't all belted in," the pilot said.

"That's part of the movie. So are those guys," Bruce said pointing to the men, resembling American federal agents, who were rushing towards the plane.

As Emily opened the engine full throttle, starting the takeoff, the radio blared, "Stop! You are not cleared for take-off. We need to search the plane."

# CHAPTER 49

"That's good. They got the line down perfectly," Bruce fabricated. "Now, as we keep going, those men are supposed to fire blanks at us."

Sure enough, as the plane hurtled toward the end of the runway, shots could be heard. It actually sounded as if the bullets hit something connected with the plane. The pilot looked worried.

"They've got the special effects down pretty good," Bruce bragged.

Emily took off in a northeastern direction and then turned southward once in the air.

"So, how is the dog helping her?"

"He's a wonder dog. Telepathic," Bruce said. "Tisha, Charleen's character, has supposedly never flown a plane before, even though Charleen, the young actress here, has flown across country several times. Laddy is supposedly feeding brainwaves into Tisha that allow her to fly planes, drive cars and later rocket into outer space."

"When will I get to see this picture?"

"It will probably be in post-production until Christmas. It takes a while to perfect the special effects."

"How far are we going before we turn around?"

"We need to fly into the landing spot and then pick up the camera crew."

"Where will that be?"

"Southeast, just outside of Palenque."

"I don't know if there is an airport there."

"The studio has it all set up. I can't believe you didn't recognize Lana Marshall after that Academy Award speech she gave a couple of years ago. At least you recognize Tracey Gardner, don't you?"

I waved at Jaime.

"You know, I do think I recognize you. You starred in that killer robot movie. Am I not right?"

"You saw it! Did you like it?"

"Great movie."

"Thank you. A lot of people didn't like it. I was afraid it would destroy my career."

"No. You were good."

I smiled. Supposedly, if you tell someone something enough times, it will create a memory. At least it worked on Jaime.

We flew for about half an hour. Santana was looking for a road not far from some cars he could borrow. From out of nowhere, a plane approached and started firing at us.

"¡Mierda!" Santana swore. "They're making it a little too close." He looked at Jaime. "They were supposed to make it look real. but they weren't supposed to get this close."

"On the road?" Jaime asked, in surprise, as Santana pointed down and advised Emily to land.

"Not here," Bruce said matter-of-factly. "The other photography crew is in the trees a ways up ahead."

"Are you sure that's safe?" Jaime queried.

"If not, the studio could get sued for millions."

A second plane approached, joining the first in pursuing us.

The second plane fired what seemed like a missile at us. Emily, headed down and then around the back side of what looked to be some kind of power plant, which took the hit. I figured it must have been one of those old heat-seeking missiles. Behind us the complex exploded. We looked back and couldn't see the second plane through the thick smoke but a secondary explosion could be heard.

"I hope they got the shot of that one-take explosion," Santana related. "Good work with the pyrotechnics."

I thought I heard a third explosion. The first plane seemed to have disappeared, as well, and I wondered if it thought the missile got us or if the first pilot had also been unable to see through the smoke and his plane was the third explosion.

We continued following the main road to a side road, leading into a woodsy area. "Set down there," Santana advised Emily. "Isn't that where the crew said they would be waiting?"

Emily picked up on it. "I think so. It looks like the picture they showed us of where we were supposed to land." She pulled down onto the side road, using it as a runway. Fortunately, there weren't any cars on it at the moment. That probably wouldn't last long. From the road, she slowly taxied the small plane into an area below a canopy of overhanging branches and stopped.

"We should be back in about an hour with the equipment," Santana informed Jaime.

"Unless they got the other plane working," Bruce added in.

"Here," Santana gave Jaime an extra five hundred. "Wait for us."

From there, we fled with our backpacks and our dog, heading in the direction of Mérida.

After about a half hour of walking, we came across a farmhouse and saw a truck in the driveway. "That's our transportation," Santana said. It was an older truck. Seconds later, Santana had it running. We were expecting someone to run out of the farmhouse, but nobody did.

---

We continued on and stopped in Campeche on the Gulf Coast. There, Santana traded our truck for a car we found on a backstreet in an area with warehouses. On we continued to Mérida.

"So, who do you think was in those planes?" I asked Santana.

"How about the CFR?" Santana queried.

I looked at Emily, who appeared uncomfortable.

"Counsel on Foreign Relations?" my mom asked.

"Who do you think is behind most of these imperialistic wars? Michelle and Barack were both on the CFR before he became President. He expanded us from two wars to seven," Santana pointed out.

"I thought your dad was a Democrat," my mom commented.

"My dad sent me to a Gulag Camp, just like Summer's, Emily's and Bruce's fathers."

"It might not be the CFR. The President is just a puppet doing the bidding of the PMIC," I said.

"Pharmaceutical-Military Industrial Complex?" my mom asked. My mom had once told me about seeing Eisenhower's speech on the subject.

"Well, one of them is undoubtedly controlling the Presidential strings," Bruce surmised. He turned back to Santana. "So, you think the Council on Foreign Relations was tied to the camp?"

"Santana!" I warned, seeing Emily shaking.

"Go ahead. I need to know the truth," Emily said.

"I'm sorry. I was being insensitive. Summer could be right," Santana softly voiced.

"We're just speculating," I told her. "Besides, the CFR would more likely use one of those directed energy weapons I've seen ads for?"

Santana looked at me.

"My dad had to analyze the military funding requests for Madstein. She automatically approved them with lots of extras for unknown projects and nobody cared."

"Directed energy works better on stationary or slower moving targets, like houses or cars," Bruce said. "One minute they're there and the next, they're a puff of smoke. Or one minute, it's raining and the next there's a wildfire that burns bricks and cars but not trees."

"It could be the PMIC or some other government program tied to some bad stuff. Maybe MKUltra," Santana surmised. "If they were programming teens to kill, think of all the hits or school shootings the drugged teens could pull off."

"Sirhan Sirhan claimed to have no memory of shooting RFK," I noted.

"Thomas Namaguchi said he didn't do it. That's why Bugliosi

didn't call him as a prosecution witness. How often does the prosecution fear calling the coroner in a murder case?" Santana responded.

"What do you think they are saying about us?" Emily asked.

"Apparently, we're teen terrorists, but not under our real identities."

None of us had spoken about Abigail since we left Coatzacoalcos. I still hadn't been able to contact Shannon. Bruce had also tried his burner phone, but we weren't in good reception areas when he did so. We were all too devastated and afraid but still hung onto the hope that she was fine. I was praying the claims of her death were greatly exaggerated. I thought about how much courage she had and how much she had survived. She was a real fighter. A part of me was sure she was out there, somewhere.

"No matter what happens, this is the best time of my life," Emily said. "It's scary and I could get killed, but I am on the run with people I care about, and we are doing something important. Nobody is telling me that I don't live up to their expectations."

"And nobody is forcing me to date someone I don't like," I noted.

Bruce didn't say anything.

"After you go back and find Abigail alive and she has to be healthy and fine, we'll be expecting you to join us," I told him.

Bruce nodded.

"I will say this is more adventurous than stealing my dad's cars. I could use a little less adventure and more relaxation. Perhaps when we get to Cuba, we can hit the beach and surf."

"You surf, too?" I asked.

"Not yet. I guess my surfer girl is going to teach me," Santana said. "Jimmy says you're pretty good."

"I'm okay," I said. I turned to Emily. "You were talking as if you didn't have any skills. I've heard you sing and you have an incredible voice. I wouldn't dare fly a plane, and you flew like an expert. You are awesome."

"We've got the scientist slash computer hacker, the athlete, the pilot and, when Abigail rejoins us, the party girl. We could be a team of superheroes, running around saving the world," Santana suggested.

"Don't forget the all-important car thief," I added to Santana's list.

"Just make sure you superheroes eat your breakfast," my mom joked.

"Abigail has a lot of talents, too, besides partying," Bruce noted.

"Of course, she does," Santana acknowledged.

When we got to Mérida, we went to a bar named Fuente, near the warehouse district. Per Jimmy's information, we were looking for a guy named Aurturo.

I was surprised by how my mom was holding up. She let us lead and never once questioned our judgment. Perhaps the fact that we had escaped from a Gulag camp gave her a clue that we could handle ourselves. Also, with the likelihood that our government was shooting at us, it was clear that we were on our own.

On the television in the bar, it said that police were looking for the terrorists who had blown up a power plant, causing a blackout. I couldn't make out all the words, but I did recognize the word "terrori-sistas," "explosion" and "peligro." The announcement gave the names we had used on our passports crossing the border and traveling in Mexico.

"Sounds like I am down to my last passport," Santana said.

Next, what we saw was a picture of us at the airport. Same clothes. It was a bit fuzzy but, with the clothes, we might be recognized. A few people were already staring at us.

A man, looking very Zorroesque, walked in the door. "He's cute," Emily said. He sat down at the bar. Another man came through with sunglasses and a hat covering most of his head. "You think?" Emily asked.

"Maybe," I responded.

"Well, so far I'm not on the wanted list," my mom said. "I'll go ask him." Her quest was cut short when two officers walked in the door and slammed the second man against a wall. We turned away from the man as my mom walked back and sat at a nearby table, watching the ruckus.

After the second man was dragged out, my mom went to the bar.

She was close enough that, even though she spoke lightly, I could hear her ask if the man taken away was Arturo. The bartender didn't respond. My mom looked concerned.

As she pulled away from the bar, the Zorroesque-looking guy said.

"Who wants to know?"

"And who are you?"

"That depends."

"I have some packages I need delivered somewhere."

"Don't know him."

"Guess I got the wrong information," my mom said.

While the bartender and the man were still focused on my mom, we got up and went just outside the door as we were wanted and she wasn't. Mom quickly joined us. There was something going on across the street. The police appeared to be looking at the car we came in. We headed for an alley that went alongside the bar.

As we got about twenty feet down it, the Zorroesque guy came out the side door. "You said you were looking for Arturo."

"Are you Arturo?" Santana asked.

"I am who I am," he responded.

*An evasive answer*, I thought. His evasiveness could mean he was Arturo, a friend of Arturo's or one of the bad guys.

Emily boldly spoke up. "We need safe passage to Cuba."

"The travel restrictions have been lifted for twelve categories of people. Why do you seek Arturo?"

We didn't answer.

"I sense some trouble."

We still didn't answer.

"Arturo doesn't need any hassles." We remained quiet. "Go to the docks at Progreso and bring money. Not the cruise boat section. Check out the private fishing boats off Calle 148." He bowed to Emily and then left.

"I think you have an admirer," I told her.

"He's a little old for Emily," my mom said.

"But he's cute, and it's flattering," Emily replied.

My mom started to say the line, "I understand. I was your age once," but cut herself off after the word "your."

"We need a new car," Santana pointed out.

"Or a train," Bruce said, looking at a train about to load.

"Public transportation might be risky with our pictures splashed all over the place," I noted.

I texted Progreso docks, Calle 148, in code to Shannon on a new burner phone I had picked up along the route. The code involved going up by one letter for the first burner and up one more letter each time I got a new phone. I still had the original one at this point and had been texting her information about our progress on the second one. I hadn't heard anything back from her. I didn't know if it was our poor reception or something to worry about.

"I wonder if they hacked into the burner phone I was using," I worried.

Santana said, "May I?"

I reluctantly gave the old one to him and he broke it as well as the one I had just texted on. I knew I could get another. I hoped Shannon would visit Cuba before the end of summer. Since she wasn't wanted, she didn't need all the cloak and dagger and chases that we had undergone. She might be able to just hop on a plane and show up in Cuba, under the educational, religious or athletic category.

***

We picked up some new clothes and sombreros and avoided looking directly at anyone as we boarded the train to Progreso. The conductor reacted to Hope until I pointed out the service vest. Our sombreros hid some of our features.

Once we boarded the train, we split up among two rows. My mom sat next to me and Santana. Hope sat on the window side of Santana. As Santana napped, I turned to my mother. "Mom, I really missed you."

She hugged me. "I love you, darling. There wasn't a day I didn't want you back. I hired attorneys. They took my money and did little or nothing. Your dad got an order preventing me from seeing you. He said that, by reporting abuse, I had committed alienation and the court agreed."

"He was the alienator."

"That's not how the courts see it. If a mother claims abuse, she is classified as an alienator, no matter how bad the beatings."

"You almost died. I dreamt about the night you went to the hospital and the night they took you from the motel."

"My doctors and the paramedics were not allowed to testify. The dispatcher who got your 9-1-1 call wasn't allowed to testify. Without evidence being allowed, there was no proof that I was telling the truth."

"Tiffany told me that was common in family law courts. Dad never cared about me. He sent me off to be tortured. A lot of parents are doing that."

"I looked up the information on the camps after Santana's call. What happened to you was the subject of hearings in Congress. Everything you've told me is similar to what came out in those hearings. A lot of kids die in the schools and camps. The ones that do come back are usually messed up for life. One of the parents who testified at the hearing said he couldn't even recognize his son's body. His face was smashed in. Your dad was Chief of Staff for Dana. He had to have known what they were doing to kids there."

"He was angry about Matt."

"Matt? Was that that boy you were dating? I saw your picture in a magazine."

"Daddy wanted me to date him. I never felt for him what I feel for —" I caught myself. I shouldn't be talking to my mom about my feelings for Santana. I wasn't even sure where our relationship was going.

"It's okay. I see the way you look at him," she whispered. "And I've seen the way he looks at you. He's really handsome."

"I know."

I looked at Santana and could almost swear I could see a smile, as if he had been listening to our conversation.

"How long do you think you can stay with us in Cuba?"

"As long as you're there."

"But your career?"

"You come first. Besides, maybe Cuba could use some good paralegals."

"I understand they have free college."

"Maybe I'll get my law degree and go back and kick some butt."

"I want to be a veterinarian."

"You were really good with Cynthia. Hope clearly loves you. Did they allow you to bring her to camp?"

I laughed. "I found her there. She ran away from a pack of attack dogs, the ones who attacked Abigail." I reflected on how the relationship between her and Bruce had grown. "Bruce has become really attached to Abigail. I don't think he'll be able to handle it if she is really—" I couldn't say the word. There was no way I could handle it if Abigail were gone.

<hr>

At the next station, we saw some policemen boarding the front of the train. We didn't know if they were looking for us, but we didn't want to take any chances. Bruce and Emily were chatting playfully as if they were a brother with his little sister. I tapped Bruce and mouthed "police."

We headed for the back of the train. As we noticed someone moving forward from the back, we all stepped into the train restroom. I thought about making a joke about how many people you can fit in a Volkswagen, but I didn't want to be heard. Someone tried to push in on the door, without any luck. Even if we hadn't locked it, it wouldn't have been possible to open it with us pushed up against it. As the footsteps moved away, we moved as best we could to clear the door and then opened it. The train was starting to move. Quickly, we went back a car.

I had heard of people dying from being thrown off trains, but what were the options? We jumped.

# CHAPTER 50

Hope was heavy, very heavy, but I picked him up in my arms as I leaped and rolled, trying not to squash him as I landed, scraping my arm.

"Ouch," Emily said after connecting with the ground. "It didn't look like it was going that fast."

"It hadn't gotten up to speed yet. If it had, it would have been a lot worse," I noted. "Are you alright?" I put down Hope and went over to her.

She shook her arms and legs. "Yes. Sore, but alright."

I gave her a hug. "I'm sorry that it hasn't been easier."

"It's easier than camp," she lilted, smiling briefly.

I nodded, thinking about how little I had seen of what she had gone through.

"I never want to do that again," my mom stated. She also appeared to be alright as did the others. I gave her a hug too, and then Santana came over to me and almost gave me a hug but then looked at my mom and held back.

Now, we were on foot, miles from our destination. We walked through the night. I thought of what Abigail would be doing if she were here. She'd be singing morbid camp songs or perhaps songs about revolution. So that's what we did. Then, Santana and Bruce started telling ghost stories. They were one-downing each other to see who could create the scariest one.

My feet were hurting from all the walking we had done since leaving the camp. I was wearing soft, padded tennis shoes, and my feet still ached. "May we stop for a while?" I asked.

"Thank you," Emily sighed. "I didn't think I could walk another step."

As we sat, we talked about a code to use in case we got separated. We didn't have any burner phones left and didn't know how easy it would be to get a phone in the middle of the night or in Cuba. I suggested *FakeBook*. Santana pointed out that the CIA was monitoring it and was even using artificial intelligence and Israeli agents to analyze every word everyone posted. I noted that they would have to know who we were and break down our code. I suggested that to tell each other our phone numbers, we list each digit one lower than the real one. We discussed what fake names we would use. Santana suggested we use *Twittle* as a backup in case we got locked out of *Fake-Book* or in case it wasn't available wherever we wound up. Bruce reminded us that that was being monitored, too, and suggested a couple of other backup platforms, including *VK*.

"Going to Cuba, talking about using a Russian social media platform. Maybe, we are Putin puppets," I joked.

"I'll tell them my dad turned me into one," Santana quipped back.

We got up and continued towards Progreso. When we got near our destination, we took a taxi to within a mile of the docks. Then, we walked the rest of the way. Arturo was correct about avoiding the cruise section. The authorities were in full force checking people heading towards the cruise boats. I wondered if they were looking for us. The sun was coming up. Progreso had beautiful beaches and lots of natural swimming holes. Eventually, we made it to what we assumed was our destination.

As boats left without any sign of anyone interested in taking on passengers or fishermen, we decided it would be best to look like casual tourists. We went down to the beach and sat in the sand, occasionally checking the docks in case Arturo or someone, we could deduce was one of his contacts, arrived. Being fugitives, we needed to be careful.

The day dragged on. Workers came and left. Nobody looked like someone likely to assist us to Cuba. We weren't sure what we were looking for but one word to the wrong person and the authorities might be called in.

The night settled in. We went back to the docks and looked to see if anyone in any of the boats might be about ready to embark for a fishing trip or to give stray passengers a ride to Cuba.

As we walked by the second berth, I felt a knife in my back. We were suddenly surrounded.

# CHAPTER 51

"Whoa!" Santana reacted.

I turned as Hope grabbed the knife-holding hand with her teeth and the knife fell. "Easy Hope; let him go for now." Hope didn't obey. The man was howling. I pulled Hope free and stood in front of him. The other two men who had accompanied the knife guy pulled out their knives.

"That dog is dead," the first guy fumed.

"He was just protecting me."

Santana spoke for us and as he moved between me and the knives. "We come in peace. En paz."

"So do we, but we belong here. You guys look like trouble," a second guy grunted at us.

"We're kids," Bruce pointed out.

"And that prevents you from being trouble?"

"And we brought our mother," I said. "Who in their right mind brings their mother when they are planning to get into trouble? Where I live, kids lie to their parents and tell them they are going to study or to a movie and then go do something their parents wouldn't approve of."

"What say you, Mommy?" the second man asked. "Are these buenos niños?"

"The best."

"Well, that's trouble, too," he said.

"We're looking for Arturo," Santana explained. "Would we be looking for him if we were trouble?"

"I don't know. You could be con immigración," the second man said.

"Believe me, we are not with immigration," Santana retorted.

"I've seen your faces. And you've got the dog," the third man observed. "These are those kids everyone is seeking."

"Is there a reward?" the first one asked, holding his injured hand and appearing in some pain.

"The reward is they'll kill you if they think we've told you anything," Santana advised them.

"What don't they want us to know?"

"We have information that could bring down a lot of people."

"If that's the case, I suspect a lot of people would be willing to pay lots of dolares to anyone who silences you." The first man pulled another knife from behind his back and pointed it at Santana's throat.

"They may offer, but then they will kill you," Santana assured him. "We were told we could meet Auturo here. If he's not going to show, we'll leave. That way, you don't get into trouble for knowing what we know, and we don't get into trouble because you delayed us here."

They didn't drop the knives. I was scared, but I kept telling myself we had been through and survived worse.

"Let them go," came a voice. I turned. It was the Zorroesque-looking guy.

"Arturo?" I asked.

"You gringos have someone really scared. They are looking for you, everywhere."

"We should turn them in. Collect the reward," the first man said.

"Dé jalo ir," the man I assumed was Arturo ordered the men "You don't want me turning you in."

"Arturo?" the first man reacted.

"Besides, she's adorable," Arturo said, turning to Emily.

"And too young for you," my mom declared. I tapped her with my foot, sort of a "Mom, shut up."

"Gracias," Emily responded.

"Queremos ir a Cuba," Santana told Arturo.

"Either you like places that are hot and muggy in the summer or you don't want to be extradited."

"Whichever answer will get us there is the right one," Santana responded.

Arturo laughed.

"Let them go, boys." He turned to us. "Go sit beside that warehouse." He pointed at a building. "Until the fishing boat is back."

"Gracias." Santana turned to Bruce. "Well, I guess this is it for a while, bro."

"Are you sure you don't want to come with us?" my mom asked as we walked towards the warehouse. "You can go back later for Abigail when things settle down. When we get to Cuba, my daughter will get in touch with her friend and find out how your girlfriend is doing."

"It's less risky," Santana pointed out. "Abigail would want you to stay safe until she joins us."

"I can't do that, and you know it, Santana. If it were Summer, would you be leaving for Cuba?"

He looked at me. "You know I wouldn't."

My mom clasped my hand, a sign that she was impressed with what Santana had said.

"The Feds are looking for you in Mexico. Everyone is looking for you in Mexico." I told Bruce. "They believe Abigail's dead. If you find her, you could put her in danger, just by being in her presence."

"I've been thinking about that. But they are looking for us as a group. We wore heavy glasses for the passports we used at the border. I'll change my appearance again. I'll use the one without the glasses. I have two passports left."

Santana reached into his bag. "You'll need this." He gave Bruce a stack of hundred-dollar bills. "And you know how to reach me once we get new burner phones."

"Do they even have those in Cuba?"

We all shrugged, not knowing the answer.

"Bruce, I'm really going to miss you," I said. "Remember, we're family. You're like the brother I always wished I had."

"You're my brother, too." Emily lamented. "If I had grown up with a brother like you, I'd never have wound up in that camp."

Santana lifted his fist and tapped it against Bruce's. "When you rejoin us, we'll do all those things hermonos do."

"I wish I had a son like you," my mom told him. I realized this was a well-deserved slight against my brother. It must have been hard for my mother to realize that her son had turned out to be an abuser-in-training. My brother was so brainwashed that there was little hope he would change. He had never once tried to help my mother when she was hurt, and he had let my dad send me to the camp. I thought about how much better my mother's life and my life would have been if she had had a son like Bruce.

After quite some wait, we saw a fishing boat pulling up. Arturo went to greet it and spoke to the men on board. Then, he came over to us. "It's time."

Bruce walked us onto the boat. "Stay safe," he said.

"You're not going?" Arturo asked Bruce.

"He's got a girl," Santana explained.

Arturo nodded. "It will be two thousand American dollars now and one thousand more when you arrive. The four of you and the dog are going to be below deck. We have removable floorboards you can go under in case we get boarded."

I smiled, remembering the removable flooring in *Star Wars*. Santana paid Arturo and Bruce walked us down below. We each hugged him.

"It's not goodbye," Santana stated. "It's so long."

Above, we heard Arturo. "Who are you?" We couldn't hear the response. "No, we don't have any passengers."

Then came a voice I recognized. "We were told they would be going with you."

I ran up the steps onto the deck. "Jimmy!" I exclaimed, running and hugging him.

"Don't I get a hug?"

I turned and hugged Shannon, and then reacted, "Oh my God!" as I saw Abigail.

Bruce, who had followed me up on deck along with Santana, picked up Abigail, whirled her around, and kissed her passionately.

# CHAPTER 52

"Well, hello," Abigail said, joyfully.

"We heard that you—" I started.

"I know. Rumors of my—have been greatly exaggerated. I look pretty good for a ghost, don't I? They even had a funeral for me. And also, for you."

"What? I'm dead too?" I asked.

"We all are," she informed us.

"She's supposed to take it very easy," Shannon said. "The hospital was a little reluctant to release her, but she insisted on getting to you before you left Mexico."

"I've even recovered enough that I was able to walk across the border."

"You walked?" Bruce asked.

"Since we were going to be driving her through Mexico, we thought it would be easier to cross separately so they wouldn't be looking for our car if they later realized who she was," Jimmy informed him.

"That was risky. What if they had grabbed her when she crossed?" he scolded.

"With the wig, contacts and fake passport, we thought she'd defeat facial ID and it would take some time for them to figure it out. Jimmy and I were prepared to create a distraction if anything went wrong." Shannon said.

"You look so much better," I told Abigail. I threw my arms in the air, excited about her massive improvement.

"Dead feels pretty good," she joked.

"The boat has to leave," Arturo informed us.

"I guess we'll discuss this later." I turned to Shannon. "Thank you. I love you. I still have your money."

"Hang onto it. You never know if you'll need it in Cuba. I'm still expecting that twenty percent."

I laughed and gave her and Jimmy a group hug. Arturo escorted me, Santana, Bruce and Abigail below the deck as we waved goodbye to my best friend and her boyfriend.

"Abigail!" Emily exclaimed, when we got below. "I was praying and now you're here."

"Of course, I am, little sister," Abigail said.

Santana patted Bruce on the shoulder and gave Abigail a loose hug, apparently not wanting to hurt her. "Welcome, hermana."

We settled down for the trip. Whatever else was wrong, we were all alive and safe for now.

"Buena suerte," Arturo said.

"You aren't coming?" Santana asked.

"Already seen Cuba. Enjoy the trip." He turned to Emily. "If you return to Mexico, you know where to find me."

We thanked Arturo. As he went above deck to leave, Emily looked a little fallen. It was kind of cute: Emily's crush on him.

---

The new problem for me was that nobody on board spoke much English outside of our party. Santana had to do most of the translating. In addition to the captain or skipper, the other occupants consisted of a helmsman or navigator who was steering the boat and three fishermen I presumed were Mexican. I wasn't sure what they were fishing for, given the heavy oil from American spills in the Gulf.

Below deck, there was a little cabin where there were two small beds There were four of us females, including my mom, and two guys. There was no way my mother would allow us to sleep three and three. Two of us would sleep at once while the rest used the second bed as a couch.

Though we occasionally went above deck to look at the stars or at the Gulf, we mostly hung out below deck, talking about our plans for Cuba. Our understanding from Arturo was that we were to be dropped off at Vista del Mar, a resort harbor, where we could slip in unnoticed. I had concerns about being in too public a place, given our notoriety, but Santana seemed to feel that the U.S. news was more censored in Cuba.

Guantanamo was at the other end of the Island from where we headed. Hopefully, we were not going to accidentally wind up there. Occasionally we could hear planes overhead. That made me more than a little nervous. I felt safer when we were below deck.

We found a deck of cards in a drawer, and Santana taught Emily, me and Bruce how to play poker. We used little pieces of paper for chips. My mom turned out to be surprisingly good at it. Abigail whispered, apparently not wanting my mom to hear her, that the only poker she had previously played was strip poker.

My mom taught us how to play bridge. She made me her partner. I was getting to know my mother all over again, and I really liked her. I could see why my dad had married her. I couldn't see why he stopped loving and started beating her. One thing I was certain of: the problem was him, not her. As badly as he also treated me, I wondered if it was a misogyny issue.

I thought about reading Paul's diary but it felt too personal. Our boat trip would be about two hundred miles, but the boat was going slowly, maybe to make it appear more as a legitimate fishing boat. We had taken off at night and it was night again. I was dozing next to Abigail with Hope at our feet when suddenly I heard a lot of ruckus. The engineer was screaming something about the radio at Santana.

"We've got to go," Santana said.

"What? Are we there?"

"There's a problem. On the radio, they said they were looking for five kids on a boat. They are searching everything. The captain wants us to leave."

"What? Swim to Cuba?"

"We're close to shore and they've got a raft," Santana tried to assure me. "We're going to take it to shore and then walk inland towards some place called Viñales. The captain plans to land a few miles south of the road to the town and suggests we move away from the shore for a day or two. If they don't find us on a boat, tonight, they might check the coastal towns."

We grabbed our backpacks and followed one of the fishermen to the raft. The captain handed each of us females a bag of fruit and the guys some bottles of water. We all put on life vests and fastened one around Hope. The Captain also handed us some blankets. I couldn't make out all of what they put in the raft as it was dark.

They lowered the raft into the Gulf and then we climbed in and departed, not far from land. It was nighttime on the open sea but the air felt warm. Santana and Bruce manned the oars.

The physical labor in the camp had likely strengthened their arms or maybe they were strong all along. We were near the coast and they rowed very quickly to land. We pulled the raft on shore, deflated it and hid it in some brambles below a tree.

"Look," Santana said, pointing at the fishing boat. Some kind of military boat had pulled up alongside it. Some sort of commands were given over a loudspeaker in Spanish. Because of my limited knowledge of Spanish, I couldn't make out much. Men in uniforms from the military boat started boarding the fishing boat.

"We just got off in time," Santana pointed out.

We couldn't see all the details at this distance, but floodlights from the military boat lit the fishing boat up like daylight and we were close enough to get a good idea of what was happening. As we watched, it looked like two patrolmen were going down below the deck of the fishing boat with the captain and the fishermen.

"I wonder if they'll tell them where we went," I queried.

"They might," Santana replied. We continued hiding among some trees and watched.

A minute later, we saw a plane that appeared to come out of

nowhere. "Do you think someone tipped them off or are they just suspicious of boats going to Cuba?" I asked.

"Maybe one of those guys in Progreso made some extra money by reporting the boat," my mom suggested. "They didn't seem too reputable."

"On the radio, it said that they were looking for terrorists who had fled Mexico and left on a boat. Five kids," Santana informed us.

"So, Cuba thinks we're terrorists?" A shiver went through me. This meant danger. We might be shot before we even had a chance to tell our story. "What about my mom?"

"As far as I know, there was no mention of her."

*Thank goodness for that,* I told myself.

We started to turn to move in the direction we believed was Viñales but were shaken by a pair of loud explosions. We looked back. What had been two boats had been replaced by pieces and flames dancing on the water.

# CHAPTER 53

"My God, at least seven more dead!" I exclaimed.

"Plus, anyone left on the patrol boat," Bruce stated, angrily.

"They are going to blame this on us too, just watch," Abigail advised, coolly like someone who was all too used to injustices.

"So, what do we do? Do we ask for asylum here, or do we head for the U.S. Consulate and tell them who we are?" I asked.

"Did any of you see any markings on that plane?" Bruce inquired.

I shook my head. Nobody responded in the affirmative.

"Isn't it odd that there were no markings?"

It had been dark, but the patrol boat's floodlights had reflected off the plane.

"Think it was the people we were working for at the camp?" Emily questioned.

"Remember 9/11?" Santana asked.

"What does that have to do with this?" I responded, almost irritated by the distraction. "I'm not that old, and we don't have time to go into conspiracy theories."

"The planes that hit the World Trade Center weren't 757s, and they didn't have any markings," Santana continued.

"Are you actually comparing the people after us to those who did 9/11?"

"My dad works for HAARP." Bruce's comment silenced us. "Most people think HAARP is a conspiracy theory."

"Well, whoever they are, they don't have a lot of respect for life," my mom said. "We need to get you kids out of danger."

I had serious doubts that "out of danger" was a possibility.

---

As we approached Viñales, I was in awe at its beauty. "I wouldn't mind settling down in a place like this," I said.

"If they figure out we weren't on board, they may track us here and go door to door looking for us," Bruce pointed out.

"How would they know? Are they going to count the submerged body parts in the water?" I asked.

"They have devices that could have done that from the air before the boats blew. Seriously," Bruce stated.

"Well, if they knew we weren't on board, why would they have blown the boat sky high?"

"Eliminate witnesses," Abigail said. "They must be afraid of something we know or they think we know. Otherwise, they'd just want us locked away."

"If they really are looking for five kids, we better arrive separately at any hotels," Bruce encouraged.

"A mom and three daughters and their dog and also two guys on summer break. We'll pretend to meet at the hotel," my mom suggested.

"Hotel?" Emily asked.

"We've got to get some rest before going on to Havana," my mom noted. "You five have been through a nightmare nobody should have to endure in a lifetime."

We continued walking to Viñales. Though it was early, Cuba was significantly hotter and muggier than California, where I was used to dry heat.

We couldn't use credit cards. All of us had switched to secondary passports and in Santana's case, his final passport. My mom pretended she lost her credit card and needed to pay in cash. As we should have suspected, given that Fidel Castro had thrown out the mob corporations when he came into power, the standard corporate policies of American hotels were not in effect in Viñales, making it easier to get a room without a hassle. The desk clerk at the Playa de los Viñales was so charmed by this widow with three daughters that he gave her a special discount and didn't even nail her for a deposit.

We said we wanted to go souvenir shopping in Viñales and the clerk gave us a map of the layout of the town. We actually went clothes shopping for stuff that hadn't fit in our backpacks. Back at the hotel, Emily and I decided to go swimming in our new baiting suits we had picked up. Abigail put on a blouse and loose pants with a sequenced design that she found in one of the shops. Her wounds weren't ready for swimming.

As Emily changed, I saw the welts on her back. "You never spoke about those. I'm so sorry."

She started to cry and then hugged me. "It was awful. They brutalized us all."

"I plan to make sure that never happens to you, again."

"It's great to have a sister." We hugged again.

"Two sisters," Abigail corrected, joining in for a group hug.

"Instead of gaining one daughter, I've gained three. All beautiful," my mom said. We surrounded her with a hug, as well.

Emily put a little top over her bathing suit so her welts didn't show. We all went down to the pool.

There, we caught up with Santana and Bruce. "Why, hello, beautiful girls," Santana said loud enough for anyone listening to think we had just met. "I'm Ramon."

"My name is Charles," Bruce said, walking up and sitting down next to Abigail. "Does this beautiful girl have a name?"

My mom looked at Abigail, who replied, "Sierra. Pleased to meet you, Charles."

"And my name is Alejandro," said a teenage boy who had just walked up. "Do you mind if I join you?"

"Just don't steal the one I'm looking at." Santana pointed his head towards me.

"What's your name?" Alejandro asked Emily.

"Marie."

"Marie. *Tú* eres muy bonita. ¿Tue habla español?"

"Un poco."

"Ese es bien. I've been learning English in school. My parents also speak quite a bit of English."

"You are doing really well," Emily said.

"Are your parents here?" My mom asked.

"Sí. We're here, celebrating my parents' anniversary in Viñales. Will you be in Viñales long?"

"Tomorrow, we'll be going on to Mariel."

"That's part way to where my family lives. We're closer to Havana. Would you and your sisters like to join us for dinner tonight?" he asked my mom.

"Daughters, but gracias," my mom replied, realizing that Alejandro was being polite. "Don't you need to ask your parents, first?"

"We're a gran familia feliz. I mean a big, happy family. They'll welcome you with open arms."

"Mom, I'd like to go," I said. Joining a big family seemed like a good cover.

"So how old are you, Alejandro?" my mom asked.

"Fourteen."

"My sister Marie is thirteen," I noted.

"Fourteen on June seventeenth," she said.

"That's mañana. Que tenga un dia marvillosa en su cumpleaños," Alejandro replied. "May you have a wonderful day on your birthday."

"That's why we're here, celebrating," I said, though I had had no idea tomorrow was her birthday or what day it was until just now. *Why hadn't I asked her?*

"So, will you join us tonight?" he asked.

"Please," Emily implored my mom.

"With my daughters so enthusiastic, how could I say 'no?'"

Emily excitedly jumped up and hugged my mom.

---

The seven of us had lunch together at El Olivo, a restaurant that served vegan options. After that, Alejandro and Emily did some sight-seeing as my mother, Abigail and I went shopping for dresses.

To our not surprise, we ran into Santana and Bruce shopping. "Well, there you are again. It's so nice to see you Señora, I didn't get your last name," Santana remarked to my mom.

"Sutherland. Isabel Sutherland."

"I must say your daughter, Jalena, is very, very beautiful," he said, looking at me. "I hope we'll keep bumping into you."

"Gracias."

"And Sierra, it's nice to see you again," Bruce greeted Abigail.

"So, will we see you tonight at the party?" I asked.

"Charles and I wouldn't miss it."

"See you later," I responded, smiling.

"Esperando ansiosamente. Sorry. Anxiously looking forward to it."

"Likewise," Bruce said

Abigail waved goodbye to Bruce and I did likewise to Santana.

I picked out a green dress with a full skirt to match my eyes. Abigail got a silver and black dress and we purchased a pink dress for Emily. I also selected a gold chain to give to Emily for her birthday.

When we got back to our room, Emily seemed like a little kid about to get a pony. I was a little worried about being discovered and thrown out of the evening celebration, but I didn't want to put a damper on anything that had Emily so excited.

"Alejandro is so nice. We went bike riding and he gave me a shell he had picked up on the beach." She showed me a beautiful blue and beige oyster shell he had given her. "I hope we will see him after tonight."

"I was going to wait until tomorrow to give you this." I handed her the box with the gold chain.

"It's beautiful," she said, opening it.

"That shell will go perfectly on it." We strung the chain through the shell. Abigail pulled out a curling iron and make-up she had purchased and did our hair and make-up. Instead of curling Emily's hair, she straightened it. The temporary black die had come out of our hair, and it was a good thing, given that the pictures they were showing of us had black hair. Abigail was wearing a blonde wig to match my hair, making us look a little more like sisters. Emily's light chestnut hair fell into a page, making her look more elegant.

"You look like a princess out of a movie," I said.

"Do you think Alejandro will think so?"

"I'm sure he will."

"Emily, we're just here for a night," Abigail interjected.

"She deserves a little joy," my mom noted. "You all do."

# CHAPTER 54

The boys were waiting at the bottom of the staircase as Abigail, Emily, my mom and I descended. Santana drew in a breath as he looked at me. "Espléndido. I've never seen anything so beautiful," he said. As I looked at him, the hotel and everything else seemed to disappear and all I could see was Santana.

Abigail jolted me out of it. "Come on, lovebirds."

Bruce took Abigail's arm, "Come, Miss America. I want to escort you to a dance."

We walked down to the hotel ballroom where Alejandro's family was celebrating. He introduced us. "Papa, this is my girlfriend Marie and her familia." That would have seemed like an overly bold introduction if Emily hadn't been glowing.

"I'm so pleased to meet your family," Emily said. The rest of our party nodded.

Alejandro's mother took my mother's hand. "Alejandro says you are on vacation, celebrating your daughter's birthday. We hope it will be a wonderful birthday."

"Gracias," my mom said. "It's so nice to meet your beautiful family, and it is very nice of you to let us join you for your celebration."

"We are very happy to have you. I know that Alejandro hopes we will see a lot more of you. My name is Juanita Martina. If you need anything, we will be happy to accommodate you. Marie is the first girl Alejandro has brought to meet the family."

"He seems like such a nice boy. He and your family have really made Marie's birthday special."

Music filled the room as people took to the dancefloor. "That's ballet folklorico," I noted. "I learned to dance that in grammar school."

"I remember," my mom said.

"Please, join in," Alejandro's mother encouraged.

I ran out to the dancefloor. I had always loved dancing, and I picked up the routine very quickly. After we finished, Santana and I did a slow dance. I noticed my mom dancing with someone I figured must be part of Alejandro's family.

Towards the end of the dance, Santana escorted me towards an outside door. "It's all I can do to keep my hands off you," he whispered into my ear.

His remark gave me goosebumps. I was excited and very nervous at the same time.

As we stepped into the moonlight, I said the most dangerous thing I had ever said to a guy. "Maybe I don't want you to keep your hands off me." This was the boy I had started off hating at camp, and now, it seemed like it had been years since the day I first saw and hated him.

He smiled, pulled me to him and gave me a kiss that made my heart almost stop. How could his kisses keep having that effect on me? Afterward, I had to catch my breath. I was certain I looked like an idiot.

"I love you," he said softly. "I've never said that to anyone, before, but I love you. And I'm never going to let you go," A teasing smile crossed his face. "Except when your mother is watching. I don't want her to kick me out the door."

"She won't."

"Remember that old Dr. Hook song, *Silvia's Mother*? I always wondered if I would wind up being the one Silvia's mother lied to on the phone."

I laughed. "I ran away with you once, more than once. I'll do it again if anyone tells me not to see you." I knew I wasn't playing hard to get, but tough. I had tried not to fall for him and had failed miserably. Every time I was with him, my stomach seemed to drop, and I felt like my insides would jump out of me.

He took my left hand in his and put his right arm around me as we walked in the moonlight. "Years from now, when we're old and celebrating our fiftieth anniversary, let's come back here."

*Oh my, is that like a promise of a future proposal or some kind of commitment?* I wondered. "Fiftieth anniversary? Aren't we skipping a few steps?"

"I know how I feel, and it's not going to change. We can take our time, but someday, well, we will have lots of time for that conversation. I just don't want to spend my life with anyone else."

I turned and we kissed, again. I had never felt so loved or even thought that I could feel so in love. Heck, I had never before felt even a fraction of what I felt every time I looked at him—every time he touched me. But somehow it was hard for me to get the words out. I didn't want to lose what we had or jinx it by throwing myself at him— even if he had just kind of opened up and thrown himself and our future at me, but I was losing the struggle.

"I don't want anyone else either," I said.

We sat down in the grass and looked at the stars. They were more beautiful and brighter than I had ever seen them. In my whole life, this was the most perfect night.

As we returned, we saw Emily and Alejandro outside. They appeared to be having fun. Alejandro leaned in and gave Emily a kiss. It was quick and uncertain, but she looked so happy, smiling. I suspected that was her first kiss.

---

Alejandro and Emily walked back in and we followed. I didn't look at the time. But as soon as they started singing "Feliz cumpleaños," I knew it was midnight. Alejandro's mother had ordered a special cake with Marie's name on it. We laughed, danced and celebrated.

Emily looked so sad when the night was over. Alejandro promised to see her in the morning before it was time to leave. His father invited our pseudo-family to travel with them to Mariel, where we told them we were heading. We felt that it was best not to mention our planned final destination was Havana nor to reveal our real identities or plans to request asylum. I looked at Santana. He nodded. Earlier, we had decided it was better to pretend to split up and travel separately the next day, and I was hopeful he and Bruce could make it there safely.

"This was the best birthday of my life," Emily gushed, whirling around with excitement and awe when we got back to our room.

"Alejandro is really sweet and it was so nice of his family to invite us to travel with them," I said.

"What about Santana and Bruce?" Emily asked.

"We'll pick a hotel in the morning and meet up there. It will be safer that way." I turned to Abigail. "You and Bruce seem to have really hit it off."

"He respects me. Other boys liked to see how far they could go with me at parties, or they wanted to impress my father. The latter ones were the guys I dumped without a second thought. Bruce likes me for me. He's a real gentleman."

"I've missed so much of my daughter's life," my mom told me. "I'm glad you are dating a nice boy like Santana. But remember, you are only sixteen."

I felt uneasy talking about boys with my mom, but I was able to say, "I really, really like him. I don't think I'm going to change my mind about him when I'm older."

My mom hugged me. She seemed unusually happy. I wondered who the man she danced with was.

---

The next morning, we agreed to meet up at Hotel Mariel. We said goodbye to Santana and Bruce and rode with Alejandro's family. Alejandro and Emily were in Alejandro's parents' car. Abigail, my mom and I rode with his uncle Alonzo, whom it turned out was the man I had seen my mom dancing with the night before. He was a widower who had thrown himself into his work some time back and was glad for the distraction.

Alonzo had a joint legal practice with Alejandro's father. Alonzo was a criminal defense attorney, while his brother was a civil attorney. He explained that the Cuban legal system was very different than ours. Defendants didn't have the right to an attorney during questioning, and instead of jury trials, defendants were tried before a three-judge panel. My mom, who was a paralegal, said it sounded archaic and void of rights. Alonzo pointed out that Cuba was no longer using the death penalty, making the United States, which still had it, less advanced than every other country in the Western Hemisphere. My mom agreed with him on that.

"This is probably a little out of your way, isn't it?" my mom asked. "It is very kind of you to drive us."

"Consider it a pleasant diversion," Alonzo replied.

When we arrived at the Hotel Mariel. Alonzo took in our bags. Alejandro said that, after he went home, he wanted to come back and take Emily to dinner. My mom officially gave him permission but asked if it was a bit far for him to come back.

"My uncle said he would bring me."

"Alonzo?" my mom asked.

"It would be my pleasure." Alonzo smiled. "Perhaps you would join me for dinner as well."

She looked at me. I approvingly nodded and patted her on the arm, and she accepted his offer.

"Your whole family is welcome to join us."

"Sierra and I were thinking of just wandering around on our own," I told him. I didn't want to crowd in on my mother's date.

"If you change your mind—" Alonzo started to say.

"Mom could probably use a break from us," I responded.

I saw Bruce and Santana hanging out by the pool, but we avoided talking to them at that point in order to avoid raising suspicion.

After Alonzo and Alejandro left, planning to return at dinner time, we went up to our room to find it had been invaded.

"Fancy meeting you here," Santana, teased, taking off his shoes and lying back on one of the beds.

We turned on the TV. English subtitles were available. It seemed that most of the stations were carrying news. There was a picture of us as we had looked back when we hijacked the firetruck. "Maybe we should have kept wearing the thick glasses and hair dye."

"We looked like a mess back in those pictures. I don't think most people would mistake us for those disheveled kids with soot and dirt all over their faces, and they are not identifying us by name," Santana said. "I don't think they want us recognized as they don't want us talking. Besides, the real us-es are supposed to be dead. It says five terrorist teens torched the camp in Utah and later escaped to Cuba."

"Ouch," I said. There was an out of focus picture of four of us from the inside of the airport showing our disguises. "We had the chips removed."

"Facial recognition," Bruce surmised. "Disguises generally don't defeat it. The bad guys know who they are looking for and they undoubtedly are keeping tabs on us."

"Which means the bad guys have access to all kinds of government tracking data," I responded. "But Abigail was in bad shape when we left the camp and she didn't cross with us. For all they know, she really did die."

"I crossed at Mexicali and you guys crossed at Tecate. That must have thrown them a bit," Abigail said. "Just not enough."

"Double ouch," I gaped, wincing. There was a picture of Abigail in her wig crossing the border.

We went back to watching. The TV was flashing through pictures of the campers. "That's Paul." The pictures kept flashing on the screen with names. For the first time, we learned the last names of our campmates.

"What's that about a plane?" my mom asked.

"It says it crashed, there," Abigail reported after reading the subtitles. The TV was showing a field with some debris.

"I don't see any wreckage," Bruce observed.

"They say everything was incinerated," Santana translated.

"Bullshit," Bruce said. "This is just like the Pentagon. No real plane wreckage there either on 9/11 and they wanted us to believe that a 757 hit the Pentagon."

"Nobody in their right mind believed that one," Santana chimed in.

"Look, more pictures," Emily said. We watched as our faces and names appeared on the screen—but not the images from stealing the truck or crossing the border or the airport. These were our pre-camp photos.

The camera flashed to Abigail's father who was speaking in English. *"My daughter and the other kids were on their way to Washington to speak before a Senate subcommittee about how helpful the camp had been and to encourage them to oppose any attempt to impose restrictions that would make it impossible to operate those camps."*

"Like hell I was," Abigail said. "When I speak out about the camps, you and your torturers are going down, Daddy Dearest."

"I was wondering how we died," I said. "I figured it was in the fire."

"They said that the details hadn't been released," Abigail informed me.

"They needed time to set up our demise," Bruce surmised.

*"When she boarded the plane in Salt Lake City, she was happy, smiling. None of the campers ever expected the plane to be blown out of the sky over Ohio."*

I sat on the bed open-mouthed. Santana got up. "This is crazy."

Abigail's father continued. *"I feel bad for Victor and Elizabeth Hattan, Congressman Santo Barillo and Marcus Tanner, Governor Slick's Chief of Staff, who also lost their children in that terrible crash. This is not a time for partisan divide but for unity and strength. Our country will expend every effort in bringing those five terrorists who planted the bomb on the plane to justice."*

"Wait," Santana said, "This is hilarious. We just killed ourselves by blowing up the plane we were on."

"I'm glad I survived the plane explosion," I quipped, trying to make light of the situation.

"We're dead," Abigail mused. "They can't arrest dead people for terrorism."

"Well did any of you expect the afterlife to look like this?" I asked. That got a smile out of Santana.

"Look, there's Ariel," Emily said. "It says her last name is Duggans."

The screen flashed to Ariel. *"Summer was my friend. She was so happy about the experience. We often collected water together for cooking, and we learned how to do so many things at camp. She was so excited about telling the Senators how much she loved being there. She said she was personally going to hug her father to show her appreciation when the plane landed."*

"The bitch," Santana jeered her. Then, he looked at my mom and apologized. "Sorry."

"I especially liked how you got us chained to that tree, Ariel," I said, facetiously.

"Shit, it's my dad." Santana covered his mouth and looked at my mom, who stayed focused on the TV.

"With my dad," I said.

*"In their memory,"* Santana's dad announced, *"We must keep these camps open, give them federal funding and encourage all troubled teens to attend them. We also encourage everyone to report any kids who may be the dangerous Utah Five."*

"The parents of the Utah Five have names. Could they be Tanner, Barillo, Kreskin, Hattan and Jenkens?" I reacted. "And I've never been to Utah. Too Republican—though I might join the Republican Party, just to spite you, Daddy."

"So, all we have to do is go public and tell everyone we're alive," Emily suggested.

"Unless they think we are just the Utah Five and not ourselves," Bruce contended. "The fantasies on the MSM are always more believed than anything provable."

"Fortunately, we have my mom to verify who we are."

"Good thing they haven't been tracking her," Santana said.

"Remember what they did to all the witnesses on those boats?" Bruce rhetorically asked.

"You're kidding," Santana said, continuing to watch the news.

"What?" I was almost afraid to ask.

"They say the firetruck we hijacked was trying to save any survivors of the crash."

"At least we're off the hook for the fire in California," I remarked, trying to see the bright side.

"Maybe we were in two places at once, super-terrorists. They convinced a lot of people of the ridiculous Russiagate story. Is this so much more unrealistic?" Santana asked, half tongue-in-cheek.

"So, we planted a bomb on the plane in Salt Lake City, took off to Ohio as fast as the plane exploded and crashed there and hijacked the firetruck at the scene to prevent it from rescuing any survivors on board," I deduced.

"Makes as much sense as the official story of the Las Vegas shooting. There, you had a girl who had four bullet holes in her heart and two in her lungs walking down a corridor with Mickey and Minnie Mouse and a Senator the next day," Santana said. "But it helped sell those pseudo-X-ray detectors to schools, making certain sociopaths even richer and teens and children even sicker."

"These false flags are getting a little too blatant," I pointed out.

"I think Vegas was a hybrid event," Abigail said. "Some people probably died, while who knows what really happened with the rest. I can tell you from first-hand knowledge, our leaders do not hesitate to kill people and kids. Like with the drone bombings in the Middle East."

"Look. It's Evan," Bruce observed.

"My own son was killed in the crash. But I will go on in his memory."

"I'm sure there's something in that diary of Paul's that tells what a treacherous father you were," I said to the TV.

"His son wrote a diary?" my mom asked.

"It's right here," I said, pulling it out of my backpack.

"We need to put that somewhere safe," my mom advised.

"There's a safe downstairs," Bruce said. "Might be worth putting it in there while we're here."

"We should also put our money in there," Santana suggested.

Santana opened his backpack and pulled out his money. He put a few bills into his backpack and gave the sizable remainder to my mom. I pulled Shannon's money out of my backpack and handed it to her as well.

"You want to come with me, Summer?" my mom asked.

"I want to keep watching. How about if you take Emily?"

"Hey, I want to see, too."

"This is kind of depressing and this is your birthday," I said to her.

"You should be thinking happy thoughts," Bruce instructed.

"I want to see more."

"We'll fill you in on what you miss when you and Isabel get back," Santana told her.

"Darn," Emily said. She sulked towards the door.

I went over to her and gave her a hug. "Hey, we're still sisters. Later today, we'll have a party, a big birthday celebration, before you go to dinner with Alejandro."

"Can we have it on the beach?"

"Sure. And we'll get you some vegan ice cream and some more cake."

She hugged me. "I love you."

"I love you, too," I said.

"We won't be long," mom told us.

"Emily, I think Hope needs to go out. Would you give him a little walk while you and Mom are down there?"

Emily gave Hope a hug. "And to think I was once frightened of you."

Hope started yapping as if he didn't want to go out. Emily looked hurt.

"It's okay," I assured him. "You haven't had a bathroom break in a while. We'll be here when you get back."

When they had gone, Santana remarked, "She seems younger, more her correct age."

"Torture ages everyone. I think she is getting back to being herself," I responded.

"Your mom is awesome," Abigail said. "If I had a mom like that, I never would have wound up in that camp."

"I never would have either. All those years I missed her, and I didn't know how much she wanted to be with me."

"We need to get a piñata for Emily," Santana interjected, "Let her know what it's like to really be with family for a birthday."

I picked up the phone and dialed the desk clerk. "This is Jalena Sutherland in three-oh-two. I need to pick up a piñata for my sister's birthday. Do you know a good place to get one?"

"Yes, Señorita Sutherland. There are several shops on the main street. If you come down here, I can give you a map."

"Thank you," I said.

"What?" Santana reacted, watching the TV.

We looked. I couldn't make out what it was saying. It was showing footage of the ocean and divers.

"It's about the two boats that blew up. It's saying the same terrorists who blew up the plane killed six members of the National Revolutionary Police Force by bombing the boats."

"Shit," I said and covered my mouth as Santana had done earlier. "Maybe we should have picked Venezuela."

"Good thing for Maduro we didn't. Our government has tried every trick in the book and the CIA has been instituting riots there to try to unseat him. Yet, he's still popular. The people keep electing him by a landslide. Can you imagine how much more terrorism the CIA would create to try to get Maduro to hand us over?" Santana noted.

"Hopefully, the Cuban leadership has protection," I remarked.

"So, if not from the plane that blew up that boat, where did the aerial pictures of that explosion come from? Photographic thin air?" Santana asked. "Only estúpidos would buy this stuff."

"Something to consider," Bruce warned. "If the Cubans believe we killed some of their military, they will be as ready to fry us as the Americans."

"Good thing, they don't execute anyone, here, anymore," I commented.

"They might make an exception in our case," Bruce responded.

"We need to go public with our real identities. We can't be both dead and alive here in Cuba," Abigail said. "My father has to have been in on this. And I always wondered if he was in on 9/11."

The others looked as surprised by her comment as I was.

"It's time we took down Evan and my father and everyone connected with this thing," she continued.

We heard a knock at the door. "Mom, did you forget your key?" I asked, opening the door. But it wasn't my mom. It was several policemen with assault rifles aimed at us.

# CHAPTER 55

"Is there a problem?" I asked, as casually as I could, even though I was shaking. One of them roughly turned me around and prepared to slap handcuffs on me as Santana started towards me. He found himself looking down the barrel of another gun as the officer on the other end of it said, "¡Parar! !Todos ustedes están bajo arresto!"

Abigail moved quickly towards the balcony as Bruce stood between her and the police. Two other officers pushed past me and rushed into the room, pointing their weapons at Bruce and Abigail. My friends were handcuffed as the guns continued pointing at us.

"Don't worry, we've been through this before," I tried to joke to Santana.

"At least no whips, chains or electrodes," Santana attempted to return the humor.

"And we get to keep our clothes on," I quipped. "Where are the dogs? ¿Donde están los perros?"

The nearest officer looked at me.

"What? No dogs?" I asked. "I guess this isn't one of those cool torture camps."

The closest officer continued to stare at me as Santana and I were also handcuffed.

"Right," I continued. "How about you let us go? We've been through this before, and we were hoping for something less mundane."

"Ustedes venganse," the officer directed.

"With all due respect, you're boring, sir." Santana responded.

Two of the officers stayed in the room, looking through our things as we were taken out of the room. Downstairs, there was no sign of my mother, Emily or Hope. I didn't know if they had already been taken or had somehow escaped.

From somewhere outside, I heard a dog barking. Were my mom, Emily and Hope being taken? I tried to break away and move in the direction from which I had heard the sound. As I started to move, two officers grabbed me while Santana butted one of them with his head and was pushed back. I feared he'd get himself shot, but these officers seemed more restrained than most in the United States.

One of the officers who had accompanied us spoke to the hotel clerk, but I didn't know enough Spanish to make out what he was saying.

"He's asking him to check the safe," Santana informed me.

That officer stayed behind as the lead officer, and two a piece physically ushered each of us out the door. There were no sympathetic stares from anyone in the hotel as we left.

"Shannon's college fund," I lamented.

"Le exigiremos un recibio por todo lo que lleve," Santana told the officers.

The officers laughed. Not a good sign.

In response to my look, Santana informed me, "I asked for a receipt of what they take."

We were placed into the back of a police van and taken to a local jail. As we entered, I said. "This is a mistake. We're the victims, not the criminals."

Santana spoke in Spanish, repeating my words or similar ones, I presumed.

The intake officer laughed and said something in Spanish.

Santana translated, "He said, 'That's what they all say.'"

"Well, what he said is what they all tell innocent people who profess their innocence in the movies," I replied.

Abigail was glaring. The officer pushed her.

"Back off, tu puerco," she ordered.

"That's bound to endear them to us," I quipped.

"Do you see them treating us with any respect now?" she asked, and then turned back to glaring at the guy who had pushed her. "Suey, Suey. ¿Comprende?"

As dangerous as it was, if there was anyone who could lighten the mood in a Cuban jail, it was Abigail.

Santana was spouting off a bunch of words in Spanish, presumably trying to explain things to the officers. Their reaction was to laugh, again.

"At least the conditions here aren't as bad as in the camp. At least, not yet," I said. "And they haven't given us a standard police beating or choking yet."

"Wait until whoever is trying to kill us gets wind that we are in a Cuban jail," Abigail responded.

"This actually could be the safest place in the world for us," I said, optimistically. "I just hope my mom, Emily and Hope are safe," I whispered lightly to her.

"Emily's probably in their version of CPS, about to be trafficked to some sex pervert."

I feared she was right. "Yeah, we can't count on that being just an American thing. But I'm going to hope for the best until we find out more, later."

The phone in the station rang. "¿Condición?" He paused to listen. "¿Muerto?"

The word chilled me. *Had my mom fought the police? Had she and/or Emily been killed?*

As if hearing my thoughts, Santana whispered, "I'm sure they were talking about someone else. They probably have a lot of cases."

"This seems like a small station," I quietly replied.

"Don't doubt your mom. She's a survivor."

I nodded.

"Sometimes, we just have to have faith," he assured me.

"Have you gotten religious?"

"Who would have thought we would have gotten out of the camp alive, that we would have survived Marco and the dogs, Evan, the fire, the helicopters, the men with the guns, not to mention what we experienced after leaving the country?"

Santana had said something similar before. I wished I had his optimism as I thought of the lengths they had gone to cover up the truth.

"You know they can't let us live. We're proof that the crash was a false flag. And Cuba and the US were normalizing relations—even though they are temporarily worse," I said, continuing to let my worry show.

"As long as there is any tension between the two countries, there is hope we will find a sympathetic ear, here."

I nodded.

"The question is, are our parents, minus your mother, in on it or were they fooled, too?" he queried.

"At least my mom can verify my identity if she's alright and able to talk." Worry shot through me.

There was a TV on in the background and the desk officer turned it up. They were talking about the attack on the plane in the States. Some woman was being interviewed. She had blonde hair and was dressed in black clothing. A sign at what looked like a church read 'Remembrance of Summer Tanner.' Subtitled in Spanish, a reporter asked, "Mrs. Tanner, do you have a comment?"

"Who?" I asked. "I've never seen that woman before in my life. Did my dad get remarried?"

"I've lost my daughter. She was always such a happy girl and now she is gone." She burst into tears.

"She's acting," I insisted. "She doesn't even know me. Did he get her from rent-a-whore nine-one-one?"

"I think that answers the question of whether your father is in on it."

"Yeah. This keeps getting worse and worse."

"I'm going to kill my father," Abigail said. "And everyone in his F-ing Department."

"Can you take out my dad while you're at it?" I asked.

"It's possible our parents were threatened. They may have told them we're alive and that if they don't play along, we'll be killed," Bruce downplayed their likely involvement.

"My dad would give them the gun," Santana said.

"And mine would pull the trigger," Abigail added.

"And my brother would help him aim right for my heart," I remarked.

"When we get out of here, your brother is dead too," Abigail assured me, though I was certain she wasn't serious.

"Guys, they may be recording what we say. Microphones are small these days," Bruce pointed out.

One of the officers mentioned something about mañana. Santana translated. "They're keeping us here until tomorrow and then transferring us to Havana. Apparently, they are supposed to report to the investigator within twenty-four hours. They mentioned a couple of three day something or others before bail is to be decided."

"They have all our money," I reminded him.

"With our luck, they'll make it one dollar more than what they confiscated," Santana said, appearing somewhat down. He looked at me, "If it's not enough for all of us, we'll use it for you and Abigail, first."

"Guys, they think we're terrorists. They probably won't give us bail at all," Bruce noted.

"How do we know they won't just steal the money?" Abigail asked.

I wondered how much English the officers knew. We were chatting away, but if they listened to us, they might also figure out we were the real Summer Tanner, Abigail Kreskin, Santana Barillo and Bruce Jenkens. If my mother came forward now to verify who we were, would they arrest her as an accomplice or would that believe she was who she was? Were she and Emily already in custody? One thing I was certain of was that my mother would do everything she could to get us out of here if she were free. I hoped and prayed that that was the case.

And my father, he clearly had gone along with the hoax. *He'd rather have a dead daughter than me. Why did he even fight for custody of me*, I wondered. But I knew the answer. *It was to hurt my mother, separate us, make her pay for embarrassing him by letting the hospital staff find out what he had done to her.*

I thought about my brother being fine with my dad beating my mom, with me being taken to a Gulag camp and I knew how he'd turn out. I had no doubts that my brother would treat his wife and his daughter the same way our father did. I vowed, never to have anything to do with my brother, again, when I got out of this.

I was only glad that my mom was not pictured at the airport. She had been with us on the trip. That picture was taken when she was outside the terminal.

"So, from one supervillain to another, maybe we should melt these handcuffs," Santana continued to joke.

"As soon as I recover from my bout with kryptonite," I responded.

"So, are we from the Marvel comics or D.C.?" Bruce asked.

"Marvel, of course. I'm waiting for Captain American to come in and rescue us from the gang that's taken over reality. Oh, wait, you're here," I said, looking at Santana.

"So, while you are all super-heroing, do we have a right to a phone call?" Bruce asked.

"I don't know," Santana said. "If we do, who do you hate enough to call? I mean they're likely to kill anyone who knows who we are."

"If they don't have my mother, they are probably out looking for her. She's got to be okay."

"I'm certain she is, wherever she is," Santana assured me.

"My mother let him do this to me. She can eat lead, too," Abigail remarked.

"I know," Santana said. "Mine too. Let's find a way to break the Menendez brothers out of jail and enlist their help."

"Do you guys ever stop joking?" Bruce asked.

"Would crying be better?" Santana responded.

"I'm serious," Abigail said. "I want my dad on a stretcher in the morgue."

One of the guards ushered us into the back.

"Hey, remember the Maine!" Abigail shouted at the guard. "A lot of Cubans were killed the last time the U.S. pulled off a false flag. And don't forget the Bay of Pigs!"

The guard ignored her.

"I'm trying to help you," Abigail added.

Our handcuffs were removed. We were searched and everything in our pockets was removed. We were locked in two adjacent cells, one for the boys and another for me and Abigail. They apparently were not separating the men and women in separate blocks at this facility. The cells looked better than I would have expected. But this was just a jail. If we were later taken to the prison, it would likely be a lot worse.

"Well, at least they haven't separated us yet," I said.

"Where is Arnold Schwarzenegger when you need him?" Santana questioned. "Remember that jail scene in the first *Terminator* movie?"

"Wasn't he trying to kill the heroes in that one?" Bruce asked. "We don't need someone to break in here to try to kill us."

"True," Santana responded. "Too bad this isn't a Venezuelan jail."

"I'll bite. Why?" Bruce asked.

"Because even maximum-security prisoners like airline bomber Luis Posada Carilles, have been able to walk out of Venezuelan prisons with great ease."

"Long ago, after our government treated him like royalty, the California Democratic Party did a resolution demanding his return to Venezuela. The Democratic Party even posted it online. Of course, the President and Congress ignored the resolution," I said.

"Trivia question: Guess which nation in the Western Hemisphere was the first to abolish the death penalty?" Santana asked.

"Venezuela. I knew that," I answered.

"Correct. The only two nations still having the death penalty are the United States and Cuba."

"I thought you said Cuba hadn't executed anyone since 2003," Bruce reminded Santana.

"That's true, but it's still on their books and they could make an exception for us."

"I'll settle for ordinary treatment. I don't want to be special," I told him.

I looked at the cot I'd be sleeping on. I noticed some dark stains on it. "Do you think someone's bled to death in here?"

"Maybe that's why they don't feel the need to execute. They all die before trial," Bruce said.

"I want my green hair back!" Abigail exclaimed out of the blue.

"I bet you looked sensational with green hair. I'm not saying that you don't look sensational now. You do," Bruce stated, trying to put on a smile. Abigail's anger seemed to melt as she looked at Bruce. They reached across the bars and held hands.

It seemed ironic, being sent to be tortured, only to find true love and happiness. I even got to see my mom again. And Emily had found Alejandro. It would be sad if she lost him over this. How would he and his family react when he learned the truth?

On the lower bunk, I leaned back against the bars next to where Santana was lying, and Abigail did the same on the upper bunk with Bruce. We didn't get much sleep but a sense of peace settled over us. No matter what they did to us, we still had each other.

The next morning, we were escorted to a paddy wagon. They did not tell us where we were going, but from the earlier conversation Santana had translated, we suspected it would be Havana.

"That was where we were headed, and we don't have to pay for the ride," I remarked.

"An additional plus: we weren't tortured last night," Santana added.

"Yes. So far so good," I said.

"Do they torture in Cuba?" Bruce asked.

"They are signatories to the *United Nations Convention Against Torture*. But most of those conventions are a lip service thing. And like the U.S., they are not part of the ICC," I responded.

After about an hour drive, we were in Havana and were taken into some kind of prison. In this one, they separated me and Abigail from Santana and Bruce. We were forced to change into prison garbs but at least this time, it was female guards who made us strip.

"Great. We lost our translator," I said, avoiding going to tears about the bigger issue of being separated from our boyfriends. Abigail and I were put into a cell alone. I was really worried. At home, cops regularly beat up and tortured prisoners suspected of attacking a cop. We were believed to have blown up six members of a unit attached to the National Revolutionary Police Force. I didn't suppose it would help to say we were also revolutionaries in our own right. I had heard rumors about Cuban prisoners and feared they might be true.

"Hey, guards," Abigail called out. "We're communists. Fidel was our mentor. Some respect."

I heard a chuckle. "Nice try."

*They understand English. Maybe threats against the lives of some of our parents will be added to the list of charges against us.*

# CHAPTER 56

We were asked to come into a room where two female officers spoke to us in English. "My name is Elena Camino and this is Katerina Salermo. We are investigators for the National Revolutionary Police Force. We have three days to investigate this matter and submit it to the prosecutor. Then, the prosecutor has three days to decide whether to prosecute. If he does decide to pursue this, he will refer the case for judicial review as to whether you are to be held here in custody."

They seemed pleasant, but I was from a Democratic background, and I didn't trust police officers. "What will it take to get us released so we can go home?" I asked.

"I don't think that is likely to happen. You are being held in connection with the deaths of Cuban police officials. If you give us a statement, things will go a lot easier on you."

"This is a case of mistaken identity," I tried to explain. "Abigail Kreskin is the daughter of the U.S. Secretary of Defense. We were not on a plane. We were not killed. You can check our pictures against our high school yearbooks or press photos of ourselves with our parents. My father is the Chief of Staff for the Governor of California. Santana's father is Congressman Santo Barilla. Bruce's father is Howard Jenkens, the Chief Engineer for HAARP."

"HAARP?"

"It's a weather device that a contractor operates for the U.S. Government." Abigail lifted and then dropped her hands in seeming exasperation.

"We can prove who we are. Please, go on the Internet. Look up pictures of us. Some of the kids they said died on the plane really died in California at a wilderness camp. The rest of us are alive, but not for long if you don't give us protection," I said.

"Look, I've been at gatherings with the President of the United States. There are tabloid photos of me with green hair. There is a really stunning engine called *"Gagle."* Abigail rolled her eyes.

I hoped Abigail's faith in *Gagle* was justified. I knew that *Gagle* had been accused of mass censorship and erasing information. The same was true with *QuackQuackRun* and *Fakebook*.

"Our Internet access is limited here. Now, if you do not wish to give us a statement, I will have them take you back to your cell."

"May we have an attorney?" I asked.

"One will be appointed for you at trial."

"In my country, we are innocent until proven guilty."

"That is the same here."

"Give it up, Summer. This investigator is only looking for an open and closed case. She couldn't care less about the truth or saving the world, and she certainly isn't interested in protecting four teenagers from a terrible injustice."

"I assure you I will look thoroughly into this matter."

"We'll know it when you realize that we are the victims and not the perpetrators in this."

The two investigators started to get up.

"Wait. Before you go. How are our friends? Are Santana and Bruce okay? Are they safe?"

"This case will be watched. They are not in any danger," Elena said.

"How about the others?" I inquired.

"What others?"

"Were we the only ones taken into custody?"

Elena sat down. "Were there others with you?"

"I have nothing further to say," I responded. However, it seemed almost certain that they would have learned about Emily and my mom from the hotel clerk as my mom had checked us in. Maybe Elena was toying with me.

Upon returning to our cell, I rested as best I could while Abigail paced the floor and uttered descriptive phrases about her plans for her parents.

The next day, we were again called into the same room. Abigail said she didn't want to go play the game again. I talked her into coming, saying I needed her protection in case they decided to attack me. I expected to see Elaina and Katerina. Instead, seated across the table was Alonzo Martina.

# CHAPTER 57

"Have they been treating you alright?"

"Yes, if being in jail is considered alright. Look, I don't know what they've told you. We are supposed to have died in a plane crash, but we are alive, someone is trying to kill us, and we're being blamed for their crimes," I related.

"I know. Some well-informed friends of my nephew told me."

"Are they okay?"

"You can never trust your privacy in places like this, but I would not worry about anyone not in this jail right now."

"They have Santana and Bruce, too."

"Someone has gone to a lot of trouble to make you fugitives. A certain young member of my family went on something called the dark web and found proof of your identities, but he said that on the regular web, your pictures are being removed."

"How about the picture of my green hair?" Abigail asked.

Alonzo laughed. "He got that, but It's now gone from the official news sites. Whoever wants you dead has very powerful connections. A Cuban jail might be the safest place for you for the time being."

"I was saying something similar. But at home, sometimes the authorities let prisoners get brutalized, killed."

"I've arranged for your male companions to be placed in solitary, and I tipped off a friend of mine, who is a guard in the men's section, about the situation. He has promised to keep them safe. I'm going to try to bring the truth to the attention of some high officials in my government." He paused and reached out and touched my hand. "It sounds naïve to say 'Don't worry.' But know that I will be working to make sure you stay safe."

"My father is either in on it or covering for the bad guys," Abigail burst in.

"Some fake woman is masquerading around as my mother."

"A certain young man is trying to figure out who this woman is. She doesn't match the earlier pictures of your family. Your real mother does. However, as convincing as those pictures were, what I found most interesting was a certain book someone brought me."

"You have—" I cut my question, seeing his upward eye movement, presumably towards the cameras. "A book about our teen educational system?"

"I think we have a much better educational system here."

"Thank you for believing us. We were afraid to tell anyone right away with—"

"It's okay. I would have done as you did if I had been in your situation. For a sixteen-year-old girl, you are very grown up, Summer. And you are an amazing survivor, Abigail. I think we should have a doctor check your injuries to make sure they are healing properly."

"Thank you, Mr. Martina." Her voice was wavering and this was the first time I had seen her in tears since my mom and Shannon rescued us. "It isn't until almost everyone turns against you that you find out who the good guys are."

The guard was watching. Alonzo shrugged and then nodded his head at the guard and stood. Alonzo came around the table and held Abigail in his arms and then reached out and put an arm around my shoulder. "My wife and I never had children before she passed away, but if I had daughters, I'd like for them to be like the two of you and that other young lady. You are the most courageous young ladies I've ever known."

"I'm just so glad everyone is safe." I blew a sigh of relief. "Thank you for helping."

"It's my pleasure."

"I brought a book to make it easier for you to understand what is being said." He handed us an English-Spanish dictionary, a thick one.

"One more thing," I told him. "Please stay safe. These people who did this have a leave-no-witnesses approach."

"I've taken precautions. And my nephew has acquired a new guard dog. So, there is *hope* everyone will be okay."

I thanked him again, and we said our goodbyes.

Back in the cell, Abigail was more relaxed. She laid down and got some of the rest she had missed the last couple of days. I looked through the dictionary, trying to memorize as many words as possible.

I kept hoping that, somehow, we would get to see Santana and Bruce. But the night passed with no contact with our friends.

"This better not be like one of those movies where the main characters trust someone who offers to help and it turns out he's really the main bad guy," Abigail remarked.

"I think the bad guys we trusted are part of our birth families."

"I wonder if my dad was born evil."

"Politics and money can corrupt, but a person has to be willing."

The next day, Elena and Katarina came to see us.

"You need to know that the U.S. Government is seeking your extradition."

"I thought you didn't have an extradition treaty with them," I noted.

"Well, we are working at improving our relations in spite of the current political situation."

"Someone tied to the U.S. Government was behind all those killings. We need asylum, not extradition."

"It might help if you come clean about who you are and why you did what you did."

"Haven't you f—ken listened to a word we've said!" Abigail exclaimed. "We are telling the truth. They are lying. And if my government cares so much about plane bombers, ask them about the lavish American surroundings they gave Luis Posada Carilles."

I had to hold back a smile. Abigail really knew how to stick it to people in a conversation. Given that Carilles had bombed a Cuban flight, killing the entire Cuban fencing team in 1976, and the U.S. had given him the asylum of a hero, it seemed likely that his name would mean something to Cuban officials.

"Why would they want to extradite some future Posada if we won't return the favor?" Elena asked.

"I think we are done. As far as we know, you're working for the same people who blew up the boats, and you are just pretending to do an investigation," I firmly stated.

"Miss—"

"Don't 'Miss' me or her. Go F— yourself, and don't come back until you've done your job and discovered we are telling the truth," Abigail said, standing up. "Guard, can we get out of here, now, before I throw up?"

"I've been asked to take you to the infirmary to visit the nurse," the guard stated.

"She's not going anywhere without me," I insisted.

"Tell him, sister," she said to me.

"I don't have authority to take you both to the infirmary."

"Then have the nurse see me in my cell. Now we want to go back to our cell."

He shook his head. Then, he let Elena and Katerina out and escorted us back to our chamber.

Back in the cell, Abigail said, "Good call. Remember Jack Ruby."

"The assassinations of JFK and Lee Harvey Oswald were before my time, but you are talking about how he died?"

"He told them to take him to Washington to talk, or he'd be killed, and sure enough, he died before he could give them the information."

"And all these years later, the government is still covering up for JFK's assassins—as if the government hadn't orchestrated it. What do you think was the reason JFK was killed?" I asked. "Order eleven thousand to kill the Federal Reserve, the order to pull the troops out of Vietnam or his plan to dismantle the CIA?"

"I think the Bay of Pigs was more relevant than people realize. Kennedy went up against the Military Industrial Complex. He did it twice if you count his turning down Operation Northwoods. Even Eisenhower warned about the M.I.C."

"Since the government won't ever tell us the truth, I guess we might as well figure it out without them."

"I say it was the Bushes."

"Aren't they in your Party?"

"My party is the one with the beer keggers. The Bushes are in my dad's Party."

"If we get free, do you think you will ever want to go back to the States?"

"Not as long as my dad is Secretary of Defense."

"Where do you think you will go—I mean, after this is all over?"

"Greece is nice, except my dad has been part of making the Mediterranean the most radioactive sea on the planet."

"Is it more radioactive than the Pacific post-Fukushima?"

"Aren't you a surfer?"

"I've been living dangerously. I like surfing, and I keep hoping that the Pacific is large enough to absorb the radiation."

"But inside, you know it's not."

"Yeah. I guess I do. But I want to get in some surf time before there's no more surfing."

A guard brought in dinner. It appeared to be some kind of chicken and vegetable dish.

"I'll trade you my chicken for your vegetables."

"Deal," she agreed.

"The food here is better than at camp. Some time, when we aren't eating, I'll tell you what they made Ariel brush her teeth with."

"You mean Miss 'We often collected water for cooking, and we learned how to do so many cool things at camp?' She probably brushed her teeth in bird shit."

"Close. Whatever animal left it, it was brown,"

"Oohh. And she was probably so happy doing it."

We laughed. Then I remembered Ariel's real reaction and felt sad. "She went through some horrible stuff."

"But they can't take your soul unless you give it to them."

"What is it they say? 'What doesn't kill you makes you stronger?'"

"Unless you give in to it. The difference between us and them is that we never sold out who we really are. I wonder how many campers are still alive."

"The blue team is gone. Marco even shot Hillary. Part of the men's red team is dead. Their nicest purple duo is still alive. The girl's red team is part dead, part sell-out and part here in Cuba. Do you think they will go after our outside friends?"

"Who knows? Your friends at home are pretty savvy. They will probably see it coming if the bad guys try anything."

"We don't even know who the bad guys are."

"Remember Vegas? They said it was a lone gunman who shot himself, but the bullet casings and the sound effects didn't match up with that. And there were drills that night, even at the hospitals. Half the injuries were ridiculous."

"Like the guy who was running around giving interviews after being shot in the head and having an entrance and exit wound in the back of his head," I remembered.

"And instead of ambulances, the supposed victims were carted off in stolen trucks and wheelbarrows."

"I checked with my local fire department. They didn't have one wheelbarrow. They are obviously not ready for a terrorist attack," I half-joked. "Seriously. I did call and ask, but I wasn't surprised by their response."

"Did you ever watch that 'Sane Progressive' who went through all those official and unofficial videos and exposed the lies?"

"I was really young, but I loved her videos before they were censored. I couldn't let my dad know I watched her or had been exposed to anything but the official narratives. I watched her privately in my room and was cheering her on."

"I wonder if people at home have figured things out and are cheering us on," Abigail pondered.

"I don't think anyone realizes we're alive. But Bruce is right. The official story is ridiculous. I wonder if anyone is questioning it."

"So, do you think the prosecutor will do any more research into this case than the investigator?"

"I know we aren't supposed to talk to prosecutors when we are the accused."

"I keep thinking about all the people they would have had to involve in the lie: the firefighters, whose truck we stole, everyone connected with the airplane, everyone who was chasing us." Abigail let out a smile and flipped up her palms.

"Yeah. Maybe we are superheroes or supervillains. And what about the other passengers? The news reports claimed it was a major airline."

"I wonder if they called 'Rent-a-Mourner' to help with the fake funerals."

"You know about that group?" I asked.

"One of my friends found them online and asked me if I wanted to make a few extra bucks while having a lark. After we had a good laugh about the idea, it kind of freaked us out."

"One day, we should start our own party: the Truth Party."

"You think elections are real? Why do you think they flip out over accidental Presidents? They've had the outcome of every election all planned out through 2032."

"Does that mean they aren't going to start World War III before 2032?"

"It may be an underground election."

We laughed. "Hey, I had a reserved spot in one of the underground cities. I'm sure you did, too. If I still have one, I can tell them where they can shove it."

"Summer, do you think Bruce really likes me? I mean, not just because we are stuck in a crazy situation together, but because he really cares, like a forever boyfriend?"

"You didn't see how crazy he went when you had that cardiac

arrest or when we pressured him to leave the country without you. He was about to go back to get you when you arrived on the boat in Progreso. And the way he looks at you tells it all."

She leaned back on her cot. "Have you noticed how cute he is.? His eyes are so warm, and his ears are like those of an elf. And when he smiles, his whole face lights up."

"He is good-looking, but I'm too busy looking at Santana. I used to think all that forever-after love was just in movies. I never thought I would ever feel the way I feel when I'm with him."

"I miss Bruce. That's the worst part of this. I just want to be back with him."

"I feel the same. About Santana, I mean. Being apart is driving me crazy, too."

"I know I have a reputation for partying and being loose. But I've never had a real boyfriend before. It was all about rebellion, wanting to get my parents' attention and letting them know what dad did to other kids wasn't okay."

"I tried to be perfect, and I still wound up in the same place."

Despite everything that was going on, I slept that night. I dreamt of Santana and myself surfing on the beach. Then my dream turned to my mom waiting for us in the back of Santana's souped-up blue Mustang that he was able to get up past one-eighty MPH. In my dream, the police were chasing us and Santana outraced them.

---

Abigail looked rested in the morning. "I dreamed about mine. Did you dream about yours?" she asked.

"Oh yes. At least, we can have a happy ending in our dreams," I said. Then I realized I should be more optimistic as she briefly looked crushed. "It will work out. We'll have those happy endings."

"I just want to see him, again."

I nodded, feeling the same. Though Alonzo had said they would be safe, I had a sense of fear. By now, whoever was trying to kill us would likely know we were here. We could be sitting ducks.

I was hoping that Alonzo would be back with good news, but we didn't get any calls into the special room all that day. I was starting to close my eyes when I heard footsteps approaching our cell.

I sat up. It was someone in a nurse's outfit pushing a cart with what appeared to be first aid supplies.

"I'm with the medical unit for this facility," she said.

"Oh," I responded, trying not to show any reaction. "Are you here to check on Abigail's injuries?"

"Sí," she said, signaling to the guard to open the cell. "We were expecting you at the infirmary."

The guard opened it, and she rolled a little tray into the cell. Then he relocked it, staying on the outside.

"They didn't give us a map of the facilities," Abigail said. "So, we decided to stay here, and make a cartograph of our cell."

"You're, how you say, comedians," the nurse responded. "I'm Carlota Gonzales."

"Hi, Carlota Gonzales," Abigail replied.

"Nice to meet you," I said.

"If you could remove your outer clothes and lie down on your cot, I'll get a look at those wounds."

"Make Rover turn around."

The guard, probably not a Rover, complied with Abigail's demand.

Abigail removed her outer clothing as the nurse handed her a gown that she put on. "Just so long as you are better than the doctors who have been treating Mumia."

"Who?"

"Just don't kill me."

The nurse laughed. "If you could please lie down on your cot, it will make it easier to treat the injuries." Abigail complied and I moved to stand beside the nurse so I could see everything she was doing.

She removed the bandages on Abigail's arms. "They are healing, but those were bad bites."

"Dogs. Big dogs," I said.

"I'm sorry." She looked at the injury on Abigail's side and shook her head.

"Yo lo siento. It's going to heal. It must have been very painful."

Someone, probably another prisoner, called to the guard and he stepped away.

As the nurse started to dress the wound, she whispered. "I've been sent to help you."

We focused up.

"We know who you really are, and you are in grave danger."

"You think?" Abigail asked, facetiously with a scowling look.

"We have a plan to get you out of here."

"Who is this 'we?'" I asked.

"We are the Cuban equivalent of the CIA."

"Well, the U.S. equivalent is pretty nasty. How do we know you are any better?" Abigail asked, doubting the story. "Do you have any ID?"

The nurse looked around the cell. "Here is my nurse's ID," she said loudly. Then she pulled a card out of her pocket and held it with her hand covering most of it for Abigail to see. I leaned towards Abigail and noticed it had some kind of seal and words written in Spanish.

"You have to leave before anyone harms you," she whispered.

"We were told we would be safe here."

"In prison? Don't know you about the prison underground?"

"So, what is it you want us to do?" Abigail asked. "Walk out?"

"Yes. But not now. I will be back at ten tonight. By then, all the arrangements will be made."

"I see," I said.

"There's one more thing," the nurse whispered.

"And that is?" I asked.

"I need you to write a note that we can slip to your friends. Tell them to be ready at ten for someone to walk them out."

"Why don't you just show them your ID?" I asked.

"We'll need to move quickly and neither of them has Abigail's injuries. I don't have an excuse to see them."

"But you trust the person who will be taking this to them?"

"Sí."

She handed me a pen and paper as she continued dressing Abigail's wounds.

I penned a note, having reservations about what I was doing. *I could be putting our lives in even greater danger*, I thought.

The nurse finished dressing the wounds and called the guard who let her and her tray out.

"I don't trust this," Abigail said, quietly.

"I don't either. But," I whispered, "Remember the walls may have ears." I started speaking more audibly. "She seems to have done an okay job with bandaging you. So, I think she's okay."

Abigail looked dubious. I didn't trust myself not to give away my real thoughts to any hidden mikes. So, I decided not to discuss things with her at this point. I laid down on my bunk and waited.

I thought about Hope. He had sensed what was happening. He didn't want to leave us. I would never fail to listen to him, again. That was probably the yipping I heard outside. He was trying to get to me as we were taken away. Alonzo had hinted he was safe, along with Mom and Emily. My dad had never allowed me to have a dog, not since Fluffy was killed. He knew I loved animals, and yet I had to get all my pet time with other people's pets at the clinic. I thought back to my dog Fluffy, who I had some time after Cynthia. He was a cute Pomeranian. I remembered how Fluffy died. Shortly after I got him, I found him, broken, as if he was beaten to death. I was sure my dad was responsible for that, just like he was responsible for my losing my mother and Cynthia.

Though I would always love the memory of Fluffy and Cynthia, Hope was different. Fluffy and Cynthia were protective of me, but they were both small and fragile. Hope was stronger, sturdier, and had already saved my life, more than once. If Hope could have gotten to me when we had been arrested, he'd probably have attacked the officers, and they would have killed him. *In the United States, officers regularly shoot dogs. Do they do that here?*

It was great being with Abigail, but I so missed Santana. I had a horrible feeling something bad was coming down and that we had to do something to stop it. It was kind of like the feeling I had that last night at the camp.

My mind flashed back to Hillary, running, screaming and being shot, like an injured animal that some caretaker had executed. I never liked Hillary, but I felt so sorry for her. I thought of Paul, who, knowing the risks, gave us his diary for safekeeping and then died trying to save the others. If we perished in this prison, none of the families of the dead would ever know the truth.

Matt seemed so long ago. Though I only had a little time with Santana and much of it involved being tortured, I was glad Matt and I had broken up and that I had met Santana and my other friends. I felt more whole, more of a person, more human from what I had experienced and the friendships I had made since I was kidnapped to that torture camp than from anything that had happened between when I lost my mother and then.

I thought of my other friends. Were Shannon, Tiffany and Jimmy alright? Did the authorities know they had helped us? If so, would their lives be in danger?

I tried to sleep but couldn't. Dinner came and went, and still, I waited. We didn't have any timepieces, but if I strained and looked through the bars, I could see a twenty-four-hour wall clock. When it read 21:45, I turned to Abigail. "You, okay?"

"I have a bad feeling about this."

"So do I," I said. "It's 9:45."

"What if this is our last night on Earth?"

"A lot of people go through life without ever finding love or true friends. We've already lived a more fulfilling and adventurous life than most people who live to ninety-five. I can't believe that we found love only to die in this place."

"My father invoked God in killing. What kind of morality would a God have if he was helping my father? I told myself faith was nonsense. I hope I was wrong, and I hope God is a good being. I don't want to die here."

"All we've been through and how far we've come: it can't have all been for nothing. There has to be more," I said. I thought back to Santana's assurances.

"Always the optimist."

"What was your mother like?" I asked.

"She was beautiful, always proper. I think she sort of loved me when I was younger. It was the housekeeper who raised me. My mom was always too busy with social things. Philomena really loved me. She used to sing me songs and push me on the swing. She taught me how to play baseball and soccer."

"Where is Philomena now?"

"I don't know. My dad was entertaining one night, and I fell in the mud, playing outdoors. Before Philomena could take me upstairs, I heard the music and ran into the living room. My dad was so angry. His guests didn't notice, but I could hear it in his voice. That was the last night I ever saw Philomena."

Our conversation was interrupted by the sound of a key sliding into the lock. It was our nurse Carlota with a man in a guard's outfit. They handed us some maintenance worker clothes. "Get dressed."

I looked at the clothes. I thought about freedom, what it would be like to walk in the sunlight with Santana and my mom and Hope again. If I made the wrong move, I'd never have that opportunity. Did I have the right to mess it up for Abigail and the others?

"What about our friends?"

"They've gotten your note and are getting dressed as we speak. We will meet up outside in the courtyard."

Abigail looked over her outfit. "How do we know this isn't a trap?" she asked. "We go out into the courtyard, the guards are alerted and we all get shot."

"Would you rather stay here and die? Hurry."

"No," I said firmly. "Not going to happen."

Abigail looked at me, and I got that she trusted me to take the lead here.

"You want to stay here!" Carlota exclaimed, surprised by my firmness.

"I guess I'm getting used to prison life."

"But your friends."

"They will have to decide for themselves."

"Won't you feel left out if they are free and you spend your life in prison, or worse, are executed?"

"Compared to what we've been through, that's a piece of cake."

Carlota turned to Abigail. "And you?"

"The prison food isn't that bad. I'm going to hang here for a while, too."

Carlota threw up her hands. Her companion pulled out his gun. "I think you're going."

"Well, if you insist," I said. I got up. "Come on, Abigail. Time to party. It will be a kick."

"You think?" she said. "I do like parties."

"So, these are the clothes we are to put on?" I asked. I held my outfit up and quickly pushed it in the face of the guy with the gun as Abigail kicked the gun out of his hand.

Carlota went for the gun, and I jumped on her back while Abigail kicked and punched her associate. I was surprised by how strong Abigail was, given her injuries.

As Abigail and the guard struggled, I used both fists to hit the fake nurse, and then I used my legs to trip her. Quickly, I grabbed the gun. In a dangerous move, that ordinarily I wouldn't try, I threw the gun at a fire alarm, breaking the glass cover. I didn't hear any sounds coming from it, and the gun didn't fire. Carlota ran over to the gun. I jumped on her, again, and grabbed her hand as she picked it up. The gun went off. A moment later, guards were in the hallway, holding us all at gunpoint.

"They wanted us to escape!" I cried out, hoping someone understood English. "Look at the clothes they brought us. Mira la ropa." One of the guards picked up the outfits.

The guard accompanying Carlota said something to the other guard in Spanish. The guard holding the clothing motioned for the other guards to take our assailants out. Then he locked us back in our cells.

"Do you think we did the right thing?" I asked.

"You kidding? It was an obvious set-up. They were ready to kill us. But the boys—"

At that moment, we heard shots from what seemed like somewhere outside the prison wall. Abigail looked crushed.

# CHAPTER 58

"It's not them," I said. "I'm not just being positive. I'm certain they didn't try to escape. I'm just worried about what Carlota's friends did when they refused."

"You sent them a note."

"With a code, letting Santana know I believed it was a trap. He and Bruce were probably waiting for what was coming."

"Smart move. I'm impressed." We both sat down. "So, the bad guys know we're here," Abigail said. "And they are coming up with ways to get us killed right here in the prison."

"Looks that way," I agreed. "We need to be on our toes. Trust nothing."

"I know that Santana and Bruce are smart. But what if they were held at gunpoint and the bad guys shot them?"

"We can't think that way, Abigail. When we were in Mexico and heard you were dead, Bruce never believed it. I think we know if the people we truly love are still alive. What do you feel?"

"They're alive." She appeared to relax a little.

I was still worried. But when I thought about what I had written, I knew Santana got it.

Santana,

I love you. I never thought I'd ever feel this way about anyone but I love you. Remember that night we spent at the creek, the one where we found out the trustworthiness of my friend. I believe those who are helping us are as reliable and trustworthy as she was. Remember those loving words she said to us at the tree. A leap of faith can sometimes go against logic but please more than anything I want for us to be safe and have a future together.

Forever yours,

Summer

I had no doubt Santana got my warning. I only hoped that he and Bruce were able to handle whoever came to their cell. No, I knew they handled them. We did not survive all that we had been through, only for them to be taken out and executed by faux rescuers.

But it was hard to sleep. Despite my faith in Santana, I couldn't help worrying. Someone had fired those shots. The one shot in our cell block hadn't been fired at anyone. What we heard could have been a gun misfiring, like ours. But there were multiple shots. Even if it was a misfiring, someone could have been hit. The public might not believe this, but so far nobody had died from any of our hands. I really wanted it to remain that way. I already felt guilty about those who had died trying to help us.

The next afternoon, we were called into the attorney's room. Alonzo was there. He looked tired.

As we sat down, the door was opened and Santana and Bruce walked in. I jumped up, and ran over to Santana as he ran towards me. The guards moved towards us but we were faster. Our lips met and the world seemed to disappear. A guard pulled us apart. I noticed another guard was doing likewise for Abigail and Bruce.

"The prosecutor is demanding no bail as you are flight risks," Alonzo said. "I heard there was an incident last night."

"A woman claiming to be with Cuban intelligence and someone dressed in a guard's uniform tried to force us to leave at gunpoint," I said. "We refused and wound up in a struggle. Their gun went off."

"That was Venella Moreno. She is believed to be tied to the CIA, not Cuban intelligence. She's being held and they plan to turn her over to your government."

"The guard?"

"He was a real guard, but he wasn't supposed to let anyone into your cell last night. I hear they found clothes."

"Those two brought those clothes," I said.

"Something similar happened to us," Santana noted. "Bruce and I sort of disarmed our fake rescuers and they fled."

"And were shot," Alonzo said.

"The shots we heard," I surmised.

"You're lucky you didn't go with them."

"Summer saw right through them," Santana told Alonzo.

"I guess you got the point of my note."

"Well, if anyone comes in claiming to be connected to me, your mother had told me a code word you both know. Make the new code word that minus one. As I said, you are safest here."

I had to think about it a minute and then I nodded. Santana looked a little uncertain.

"It will work in your favor that you refused an offer of escape. It shows good faith on your part. I will present that matter to the prosecutor today, and see if he will grant you a release into my custody."

"That would be great," I said, shooting Santana a look as he gave me a similar one.

"Don't count on it. It is a slim possibility. Yesterday, the prosecutor was adamant. Also, I have gotten special permission for you to be in a more remote wing and in cells next to each other."

"Yes!" Abigail and I both exclaimed as Santana made a victory fist and Bruce gave Alonzo a thumbs up.

"This is highly unusual, but I argued it was for the safety of the other prisoners, given the evidence that someone had already tried to force you out of both the men's and women's sections of the prison."

"We're not adults yet. Does that count for anything?"

"It would in a different type of case. Everything about your case is unique. The U.S. is pulling out all the stops to push for extradition."

"Does that mean we might wind up in Guantanamo Bay?"

"As Americans, you would likely be sent to the mainland, but nothing is off the table in this unusual situation."

The possibility was scary. Children had been tortured at Camp X-Ray.

"It's not just ourselves we are worried about."

"There is no need to worry about anyone else. Nobody else is in danger."

I let out a sigh of relief and heard my reaction being echoed among my friends.

"Also, my friend in the government is very concerned about the information that has been related to him and about the recent actions of your government. I am hoping that some relief from up above will be coming in the next couple of days."

Before we left, Abigail and I gave Alonzo a hug. Santana and Bruce shook his hand. Multiple guards guided us to a different area of the prison and placed us in cells next to each other.

I noticed Santana looked almost happy. I went to the side of my cell between the door and a set of bunk beds, where I could reach through the bars and touch him. Our other cell had solid walls, and this was much more intimate.

"What?" I asked, trying to figure out the look he was giving me.

"You said you loved me. You said forever yours. Was that part real?"

I worried that I might push him away if I came on too strong. "If I say yes, will you get all cocky and think I'm too easy?"

"If you say yes, I will tell you that I love you to the ends of the Earth and I am your servant for life," he said, bowing. It was showy and probably overdone, but I loved it, just as I loved everything about Santana.

Abigail and Bruce were standing on the other side of the same sets of bunk beds, whispering to each other. They looked happy, too.

"I wonder how many of the inmates in this prison are as happy as the four of us are at this moment," I queried.

"I'm willing to bet, none, ever," Santana responded. "I know you're only sixteen and you and I are probably going to finish school if we survive, but I don't want to be apart. Maybe, we can go to the same school or at least be in the same town going to school."

"I wonder what kind of veterinarian school they have here."

"They have one of the best medical schools, and I bet they have a section for people who want to treat animals. If we are freed, are you thinking of living here?"

"If they free us, sure."

"Yo tambien."

I laughed. "I was just wondering what my pre-calc teacher would say about me giving up Heritage High for education in Cuba."

Santana suddenly looked serious. "They know we're here. They blew up or pretended to blow up two boats to cover up what happened at the camp. They got the CIA into the prison. They're not done with us."

"I know. I've been thinking the same thing, myself."

A guard brought us some chicken and rice. Santana looked at it. "For all we know, this is deadly."

Bruce who was about to dig in, put it down. Abigail did likewise.

"You certainly know how to make someone lose their appetite," she complained.

We pushed the trays towards the door. "I guess we're on a hunger strike," I said.

"I was really hungry," Bruce remarked.

"I don't have my earplugs. Wait until they start playing their eerie mind control sounds," Santana quipped, though it occurred to me that might come next.

The cell had four bunk beds. Two on each side. Santana and I slept on the upper bunks of the adjoining side, facing each other, reaching through the cell to hold hands. Abigail and Bruce did the same on the bottom bunks.

I dozed off with Santana watching over me.

---

The next morning, Alonzo met with us. He didn't come empty-handed.

"After reading a certain book, it occurred to me that you might be hesitant to trust anyone you don't know with your food." He handed us some sealed bottles of water, some pastries and Spaghetti.

"Spaghetti is Italian," I pointed out.

"Not the way I make it."

"You cooked for us?" I asked, surprised. "Thank you."

"You are celebrities. There is a great deal of interest in your story," he pointed out. "If a U.S. contractor plane blew up a Cuban patrol boat, that is a very serious matter that could lead to significant concerns. My government friend is going to suggest the Cuban Ambassador to the U.N. speak privately with the U.S. representative and demand answers."

Alonzo related the history of U.S. attempts to unseat the Cuban government and his government's need to gather facts and protest any proven threat against it.

"Any word on bail?" I asked.

"Officially, the answer is 'no.' There is concern over an international incident. There is also a concern about your safety and the safety of others."

"Well, thank you for arranging for us to be together. I know that must not have been easy."

"I have some connections. In Cuba, most attorneys are women and so we men have to work extra hard."

"Back in the U.S., the police regularly beat prisoners. We've been treated surprisingly well."

"The guards here know they are being watched and will be held to account if anything happens to you."

"What about asylum—if we prove we are innocent?" Santana asked.

"We can't go home," Abigail pointed out. "Our parents are the ones who sent us to be tortured."

"You are minors, and we would want the U.S. to return Cuban minors to us. But, because of your maturity and circumstances, the government may grant your request if we can prove your government's charges are false."

"The investigators seemed convinced we were guilty."

"They don't have all the facts yet. I felt it was best to keep it that way. However, I have informed the prosecutor and the judicial authority that there are extenuating circumstances that support your innocence."

I didn't want to specifically ask about my mom or Emily in case the wrong people overheard. "How is Hope doing?"

"Hope is always alive and well. There is one more concern. Pictures of you are disappearing at an alarming rate off the Internet. I understand the search engines are being wiped. I have asked that certain people take the time to review the evidence before more disappears."

"Think about it, everyone. Private corporations with ties to the U.S. Government are going out of their way to cover up the truth about who we are," Bruce pointed out.

"This sounds like shadow government stuff," Santana said.

"Maybe my dad offered them Defense contracts if they would help rid the world of his daughter."

We didn't say anything. It seemed horrid to even think that Abigail's dad might be involved in such an endeavor, but it was a possibility we had to consider. From her repeated statements, she clearly believed he was a major part of this.

"One more question." Alonzo pulled out a picture. "This man arrived in Havana this morning. Do you recognize him?"

Santana and I looked at the picture and then at each other. "He was with Senator Shemberg at the little kid's camp," Santana informed him.

"That's where the pedophilia took place?" he asked.

"Some of it. Sonja was underage, and she was at our camp," Santana said.

"Was this man with the Senator or the camp?" Alonzo redirected.

"I thought he was with the camp. He wasn't at the teen camp except with the Senator. As far as we knew, he was just with the little kids' camp," I said.

"He got video of the Senator at the little kids camp," Santana added.

"What's he doing in Cuba?" Bruce asked.

"That's what we are wondering," Alonzo responded.

"I'm pretty sure a lot of the videos were destroyed when the camp caught fire," I lamented.

"What if, instead of your parents being complicit, they are being blackmailed? What if they are told that, if the truth comes out about where they sent their kids, their careers are finished?"

"I'm sure my dad knew exactly what he was sending me off to," Abigail replied.

"My dad was a pretty awful guy to begin with," I noted. "Let's not rule out that some or most were involved."

Santana summarized the situation for Alonzo. "One thing you should understand is that camps like ours have been going on for some time. There were Congressional hearings. California, where ours was, had laws against what they did. School counselors talk rich parents into sending their kids there. A lot of kids come home in body bags. The difference in this situation is they covered up the deaths at our camp with a false flag plane crash."

"And they've been actively trying to kill five of the survivors," I said.

"I doubt those other camps had the daughter of the Secretary of Defense and the son of a Congressman at them," Abigail surmised.

"My dad knew about the problem with the camps because he was in the picture when Ricardo Lara signed the California legislation," I pointed out.

"My dad knew about Lara's legislation, and as a Congressman, my dad would have seen the testimony about the deaths presented in the prior hearings," Santana added.

"Think about the blackmail possibilities having the children of present and future world leaders at a camp like yours would provide," Alonzo said.

"We've been hashing this over," Bruce told him.

"Maybe this man," Alonzo said, showing us the picture, "who calls himself Gordon Magruder, will lead us to some answers."

"Gordon Magruder?" we asked in unison.

"What?"

"It's a bullshit name from the CIA fake name files," Santana said.

"Explain."

"Jeb Magruder and G. Gordon Liddy were part of Watergate, and both had ties to the CIA. Someone smashed their names together."

"This gets more interesting by the minute."

"It's not just Watergate, but there was evidence tying Magruder to the assassination of JFK," I told him.

"I will let my contact know. You've given us a lot of information to look into," Alonzo said, rising up.

"Guys, you are missing the overall picture," Abigail pointed out, standing with her arms crossed.

We looked at her.

"The powers that be sent one of their henchmen here while we are sitting in a Cuban prison. Do you think he is here to pick the flowers?"

Bruce crossed his arms. "She's got a strong point."

"I'll encourage them to step up security around the prison."

"Encourage?" Abigail jumped on the word.

"After last night, they should be willing," Alonzo said. "I will be in touch."

---

We were escorted back toward our cells. Before opening the door to exit the room, the guard insisted we turn over Alonzo's food to him.

"Why?" Santana asked, belligerently.

"Seguridad."

"What, not starving the prisoners is a security threat?"

"Eso es procedimiento."

"Procedure," Santana translated.

"Survival is against procedures! Wait until you're in my prison," Abigail growled at the guard.

---

"Right now, this jail doesn't seem so safe," Bruce commented as we walked towards our cell.

"I'm more than a little scared," I said.

"So, torturing me and declaring me dead wasn't enough for Daddy dearest," Abigail angrily noted.

"I will do whatever it takes to protect you," Santana assured me.

"Same with me for you," Bruce told Abigail.

"Hey, I don't want you to give your life for me. I need you, safe and alive," I told Santana.

"And I can protect myself. You need to protect you," Abigail told Bruce.

---

When we arrived at our cells, our lunch was already waiting. We laughed and set aside the trays.

"Should we check the beds for bombs?" I asked.

We laughed at the idea and then started turning over our mattresses and looking at the springs that held them up.

"So far, all clear over here," Bruce said.

"Same here," I agreed.

"After this is over, perhaps we should become superspies," Santana joked. "I mean, life could become very boring."

"I'm ready for boring," I said.

"Boring's good for me, too," Bruce seconded.

"After I Lizzy Borden my parents, I could get into boring on a beach in the Bahamas."

"I never did like Alaska," Bruce said. "Too cold. Bahamas, it is."

We looked at Santana.

"Okay, boring it is—except life with you could never be boring." Through the bars, he did his best to pull me closer to him and almost kiss me.

"I think we should alternate our sleep times, and one of us should keep watch at all times," Santana suggested.

"I'll take the first shift," Bruce said.

"Easy street. It's afternoon," Abigail teased him.

"There's something else about that camp. The brainwashing. If it had continued, would they have succeeded in turning us into Manchurian candidates?" I asked.

"Liev Schreiber's character didn't survive too well," Santana said. "I want to be Denzel Washington."

"But they implanted an electrode in his brain, yuck," I pointed out.

"And they planted chips in our wrists, and we didn't even know it," Abigail added. "You don't think?"

"No," Santana and I responded.

"Which Manchurian Candidate movie did you guys like best?" I asked.

"The Sinatra version was too dated," Santana said.

"I've always liked Denzel Washington," Bruce remarked.

"Sinatra joined my Dad's party and so I'll pick the other one," Abigail said.

"I'll make it four," I threw in.

"Oh look, a little mouse, or is it a rat, is going for our food," Abigail pointed out.

"It's a rat," Santana said. "Look at the bald tail."

"I really don't like rats," I said. "But I need to get over that if I want to be a vet."

"That's probably best," Bruce responded.

"My brother used to occasionally put rats into my bedroom when I was taking a shower."

"When I see him, is it okay if I punch him out?" Santana asked.

"I am non-violent, but I'd love to see someone punch him out. When my dad beat my mom so hard that she almost died, my brother absolutely did not care if she would live or die."

"Then I'm 'absolutely' going to punch him out."

"Guys," Bruce said.

"I know it's violent, but he deserves it," Santana remarked.

"Guys."

"I'm not going to tell you not to," I said.

"Guys."

"Lighten up, Bruce," Abigail told him.

"The rat. I think it's dead."

# CHAPTER 59

I went over to the rat that had been nibbling on my food. It looked like there was some vomit-type substance oozing from its mouth. It occurred to me it could be a sick rat, and so, I used a paper napkin supplied with dinner to pick it up.

"It's definitely dead," I said, bringing it over to the guys.

Bruce breathed a sigh of relief. "Glad I wasn't hungry,"

I examined the coloration. "It's got a slightly bluish tinge to its skin."

"Cyanide," Bruce observed, looking at it.

"I suspect the other food is also unsafe," I noted.

"I wasn't going to eat it," Santana stated, holding up his hands.

"I've lost my appetite, too," Abigail said. "We should stuff it down the throats of whoever brought it."

"What if we pour the food out, lie down and find out who was expecting us to die," I suggested.

"If we start openly pulling hoaxes right now, they might assume everything we say is a lie," Bruce reckoned.

"If we tell them, how fast do you think the evidence will be destroyed?" Abigail asked.

"I'm with the girls," Santana said.

"Okay, me too," Bruce joined in.

We poured the bulk of our food into our respective toilets (little more than holes in the floor), saving a portion of each item for evidence. "If it killed the rat that fast, it must be loaded with poison," I remarked.

Next, we stretched out like we were dead.

"Help, I'm sick," Abigail screeched before collapsing on her cot.

At first, we heard nothing. Then, we heard footsteps and Santana's door opening. I moved my right eyelid up barely so I could see through just a slit, hoping whoever had walked into Santana's cell wouldn't notice. The man touched Santana's neck for a pulse. As he did so, Santana clasped and twisted his arm and Bruce jumped up and grabbed his leg. It wasn't the guard. It was someone in a food server's outfit.

Santana dropped from his bunk, knocking the guy down and Santana and grabbed him around the throat. Bruce helped Santana shove him against the floor, facing up, as Santana's hands remained around the man's throat.

"You tried to kill us. Now, whatever I do is self-defense," Santana threatened him. "Who wants us dead?"

"If I talk," he responded weakly in gasps, "They will kill me and my family."

"Well, how many of them are working at the prison?"

"Just one other I know of. That's all I'll say."

"Who?" Santana pushed down on the server's throat, causing him to gasp further. "If you don't talk, your wife will be a widow."

"He's in administration. Even if you kill me, you are going to die, all of you."

"Why?"

"You are a threat. That's all I know."

"A threat to whom?"

"Mi familia está en peligro. Kill me if you want but I don't know anything else."

Santana relaxed his hands. The man put his hands on his throat, apparently in some pain.

"Bruce, grab the keys and call for the guard."

I joined Bruce in calling for the guard.

"¿Que bola, yumas?" the guard asked.

"Your man here tried to poison us," Santana replied, pushing the man towards the guard. "We want to see our attorney."

"Yo no puedo."

"Now!" Santana demanded. "Who do you think will get the blame if they succeed?" He repeated in Spanish. "Serás responsible si morimos."

The guard pulled out his gun and took our poisoner out of the cell block.

---

An hour later, we took the remains of the dead rat and the food dishes into the conference area, where Alonzo was waiting. Alonzo got permission to have it all bagged and analyzed. He signed a waiver for the prison officials to get copies of any lab results.

Privacy or no privacy, we had to let Alonzo know what was said. "The guy who did it said he has an ally in Administration, here. He didn't say who," I whispered to him.

"They should be questioning him now. He might give us a name."

"They've threatened his family," Bruce said.

"If he talks, they can be protected."

"Like us?" Abigail responded.

The door opened, and a police detective came in and spoke to Alonzo. Alonzo shook his head.

"Did he talk?" I asked.

"No. And they won't be getting anything more out of him."

I knew what was coming next and felt frozen.

"Why not?" Bruce asked.

Santana shook his head, sensing what I sensed.

"I'm afraid he's dead," Alonzo said.

"How did he die?" Abigail asked.

"It appears to be a heart attack. They will be doing an autopsy."

"How many witnesses died of heart attacks after the JFK assassination?" Santana asked me rhetorically.

"A lot," I responded.

Santana buried his head in his hands. "I want Summer safe. And Abigail, too."

"Hey, don't play martyr for me," I protested.

"Me neither. If someone tries to kill me again, he better have life insurance," Abigail boldly declared.

"It's important that you all be safe. Eat nothing that I don't personally bring in. Drink nothing from an unsealed bottle. Here is some more water and food." He handed us a basket with four covered plates of food and four bottles of water. We looked at the guard. "They've already inspected and authorized it."

"Thank you," I said.

"Gracias," Santana told him.

Abigail gave Alonzo a hug, and Bruce shook his hand.

"I will be making some phone calls."

"Hey, if we are unsafe in here, are you safe out there?"

"I have security that I trust. My extended family does as well. I'm not letting this go."

We again said "Goodbye," hoping that this was not the last time we saw him.

Back in our cells, we consumed the food and some of the water Alonzo had brought us. A minute later, I half-joked, "Well, we're still alive. So, Alonzo's cook must be okay."

"Time release," Santana teased. I looked at him with a "Don't you dare," to which he responded. "Just joking. He seems like a pretty good guy, and I don't think he's going to take any extra chances."

"So, what do you think is next? A bomb? Maybe Bruce's father will send us a hurricane or a firestorm," Abigail remarked.

"At least, we aren't sitting around being worried about World War III," I jested.

"Just watch. Right after we are released," Abigail commented, pessimistically.

"I guess I won't talk about the possibility of collision with a military UFO, now," Bruce said. "You do realize it is the military operating those things."

"I heard my dad bragging about those military-operated UFOs. That's in prep for an alien false flag invasion if the people turn on the government. Does anyone still think we are safest in this jail, anymore?" Abigail asked.

"I'm feeling a little like a sitting duck," Bruce declared.

Staying in here or leaving wasn't up to us. It was up to the Cuban government and I had no doubt rogue elements in my government were working overtime to make sure we stayed "sitting ducks," as Bruce called us.

---

We were hoping that Alonzo would be back later the next day but evening came and went, and there was no word from him.

When dinner came, Abigail remarked, "We should ship this stuff to Daddy."

---

I was exhausted. Bruce and Abigail kept watch as Santana and I slept. I dreamed of missiles raining down on the prison, destruction from above. When I woke up, Santana was already awake, watching me.

"You are so beautiful when you sleep."

"Wow. Thank you. What a great way to wake up."

Continuing to look at me, he said to Bruce and Abigail, "I guess it's our turn. We're awake."

"There are some nice perks to being locked up here," I said, smiling.

"I could get used to this. But I could do without these bars," Santana commented.

The door to the corridor swung open. The guard stood by it, looking perplexed. I could hear footsteps, lots of them. A second later, men in riot gear (presumably the Cuban militia or ours), were outside our cells pointing guns at us.

"From the guns, I'd say you aren't on our side," Santana posited.

# CHAPTER 60

"Ustedes, muévamse."

"Move where?" I inquired.

"You're coming with us," a man who appeared to be in charge stated.

"And we were just starting to like this place," I said.

"Did Daddy send you?" Abigail asked.

To that, the apparently lead guy used the gun as a pointer to show us he expected us to go to the door.

"Not much of a conversationalist, is he?" I said to Abigail.

"I understand big guns are needed by men who have to compensate for their small dicks," Santana remarked.

"Easy, Santana," Bruce advised. "We don't want to aggravate him."

"They're already planning to kill us," Abigail said.

"Vamamos," the head guy commanded. We went towards the cell doors as two of the men inserted keys into the two locks.

"Any chance we could talk you into turning a new leaf?" Santana asked as our cells were opened.

Following the guiding motions of the head guy's weapon, we moved out. Outside the corridor door, there were coffin-sized boxes. The head guy pointed down at them.

"Been there. Done that. I don't really like hanging out in boxes," I said. "Can we go back to our cells?"

"In," he instructed, pointing his gun between me and the box.

"You speak English. Great. There is an old rule about granting last requests before—" I started to say, stepping inside.

"My last request is to not get in the box. Oh well, I do want to stay with my friends," Santana announced as he and Bruce started getting in theirs.

"Say, please," Abigail demanded of our captors.

I watched from inside my open box.

The lead gun-guy said, "How quickly do you want to die?"

Abigail looked like she was going to argue, then stepped into her box and lay down. They closed my box as I reclined, and I could hear the other coffins close as well. I wondered if I had seen my friends or the world, for that matter, for the last time.

It felt and sounded as if something was being wrapped around my box and something was being attached to the sides. Maybe a bomb mechanism. I had no idea what they were planning—other than a quick demise for us. My box was lifted up and carried and I assumed the others were as well. Would we wake up back in another Gulag camp or dumped into the ocean to drown? Somewhere there were air holes as the oxygen supply did not seem to decrease. If they did throw us in the ocean, I figured the boxes would fill with water pretty quickly.

We were placed into some type of vehicle. I could hear it start up and feel the bumpy road beneath us as it traveled. The vehicle's engine was loud, and there was a lot of wind noise, as if we were in an open-air truck. Later, it seemed as if we were traveling down a dirt road. It was too reminiscent of going to Camp Torture. At least, these guys hadn't harmed us or tased us along the way.

I wondered what Alonzo would think when he got to the prison and found us missing. Would our bodies ever be found? If we were going to die, I would have liked to have said "goodbye" to my mother, hugged Emily and Hope and kissed Santana one more time. But it was good that Emily, Mom and Hope were away, safe. I wouldn't want them to be in any danger.

This time, I didn't sleep. Suddenly, I heard an explosion, a loud one. My box was bouncing and smacking against hard somethings. Whatever vehicle was carrying us went into a skid and overturned. My box went flying. I tried to brace myself as it landed with me face down. I heard sounds of metal smashing and glass breaking. Were we going to die in a truck accident?

# CHAPTER 61

I tried to get out of the box but the lid was strapped on too tightly. If I screamed for help, would it bring the good guys or bad guys? I heard gunshots, lots of them. Next, I heard someone rummaging through the wreckage. I felt my box being lifted and flipped right side up. What about the others? Were they being carried, too, or left behind? Which was safer. Whoever had me was moving quickly.

I heard a muffled voice. "Summer, you okay?" It was Santana, probably calling me from his coffin.

"Yes," I responded.

Then we heard a "Shh. Quiet." It sounded like the same guy who had ordered us into the boxes.

The carrying continued. I felt and heard my box being put down. It sounded as if other boxes were being placed down as well. Then, I heard what sounded like a metal door being slid shut. I gathered we were in another vehicle as I heard it being started up and driven off. It was moving over another dirt road. I could feel it move onto smoother pavement.

The vehicle finally stopped. I felt my box being lifted out and carried somewhere. It was angled down as if it was being carried down a steep slope or staircase and then placed down.

I could hear and feel whatever was wrapped around my box being removed. I heard similar noises further away, possibly the chains or wrappings from other boxes as well. Perhaps this is where the firing squad was.

The sound of shoes moving away made it to my ears. A door could be heard closing. The faint reverberation of footsteps became much more distant. It may have been my imagination but I thought I heard the echo of feet moving up a staircase.

Was there any way out? Had the wrappings really been removed? If they were gone, did I dare look out? *Why not? I can only be killed once.* I pushed the lid open.

It was dark. I got out and bumped into someone. Santana.

A second later, he was grabbing me, kissing me, hungrily, as if the world might end at any time. More sounds were audible in the background, but it didn't matter. A bright light lit up everything around me, and I was still in Santana's arms.

"Hey, guys, this is a really weird kind of prison," Bruce's voice said. Santana and I separated, still looking at each other, and then we slowly turned to view our surroundings.

It looked like we were in a studio apartment with no windows. There was a couch, a TV set, four cots and a kitchen. The boxes we came in now had labels that read, "Milk, bananas, eggs, apples." They were covered with what looked like smatterings of milk, eggs and other yuck.

"We came here in a food supply truck?" I asked.

"Food must be in short supply if they had a battle over the bananas and apples," Santana joked.

"I think the same guys who picked us up dropped us off, and so the hijacking of the fruit must have been unsuccessful," I noted.

Bruce was already checking the doors. One door wouldn't budge. Another revealed a bathroom, complete with a shower. Santana went over to the kitchen sink in the main room and turned on the water. Abigail opened the fridge. It had a variety of foods, all in packaging. Even the egg cartons had a wrapped seal around them. I opened the only remaining door. It was a walk-in closet with clothes.

"Did we die and go to heaven?" Bruce asked.

"This is a fun execution," I remarked.

"They're just buttering us up so we will trust them before they kill us," Abigail warned.

"They can keep doing that," Santana replied. "I'd like out of these prison clothes."

To our surprise, the clothes looked like they were close to our sizes. I checked the bathroom. The shower seemed to work, and it was stocked with bathing supplies.

"I don't know about you, but I think I'll wash the prison off me." I grabbed some slacks and a blouse that looked about my size, took a quick shower and put on the new clothes.

"I hope there isn't some kind of poison in the cloth," I worried.

"If they wanted to kill us, they could have just thrown the coffins in the Gulf," Santana replied as the guys let Abigail go next.

Feeling much cleaner but hungry, I pulled out a frozen pizza with a Cuban label and put it in the oven to cook. Abigail pulled sealed cold drinks out of the refrigerator.

I related, "I know that Mexico and Cuba are glyphosate-free. That's why the chem companies want to overthrow their governments."

I went with the purified water, while Abigail went with Mexican cola. Santana and Bruce decided on sealed bottles of fruit punch.

Santana found the remote control to the TV set and turned it on. It was in Spanish. Every station looked like it was focusing on a disaster.

"Isn't that the prison we were in?" Abigail asked.

"It's saying there was a massive earthquake centered in one of the wings. A whole section of the prison collapsed," Santana interpreted for us.

We all looked at Bruce.

"Hey, it was my dad, not me, who was the lead engineer for HAARP."

"Do you really think—" I started to ask.

"Well, they did make two attempts on our lives, and then, this happened. I'd say we definitely were a target," Bruce surmised. "My dad sent me to camp and I guess that makes him part of this. I don't know if he knows what they are doing. Hell, I'm sure he knows. He's not stupid." Bruce made a couple of fists.

"It's possible, it's a coincidence," I tried to assure him. The others looked at me as if I had lost it. "Okay, it's got to be HAARP."

"So those jerks who made us get in the boxes were on our side?" Abigail asked, sounding almost mad. "They could have been nicer."

"Maybe they didn't speak much English," I ventured.

The one wing looked completely devastated. "Look," Santana said. "The subtitles say there are bodies under the collapsed wing."

"So, more people died because of us," I lamented.

"I am not regretting not being one of them," Santana confessed, checking himself over as if to make sure he was still alive.

Pictures of us flashed on the screen. Despite having looked through the Spanish-English dictionary, I didn't recognize many words except for "muerto."

"It's saying we're dead," Santana translated. "Not the real we but the terrorist we. They claim our bodies are buried in a permanent tomb. Shit, and I was such a nice guy."

"You stole that line from Sam Waterston in *Capricorn One*," I accused.

"You saw that movie, too?"

"It was really good. Except I really would have liked to see James Brolin punch out Hal Holbrook at the end."

"Sí. It finished way too soon."

"So, if we are dead, what are we doing in this cellar or whatever this is?" Bruce asked.

"If you'd rather be back in the prison, we can have them return you there," Santana told him.

"No. That's quite all right."

We laughed.

We had some pizza and relaxed. "Remember that movie *Room*?" I inquired.

"This is a little bigger than that shed," Santana pointed out.

"But I wonder when or if we will be let out."

"Do you think they are still planning to prosecute us for what we didn't do?" Abigail asked, getting another cola.

"We're dead," Santana responded. "Last I heard, nobody was prosecuting dead people."

"Could you stop saying that?" Bruce, who was sitting on the couch, retorted, pulling Abigail onto his lap when she returned with her drink.

"I'm getting used to dying. We've died twice, and it's not so bad," Santana bragged.

"Do you think Mom and Emily are okay?" I asked.

"It depends on who those guys with guns were," Bruce responded.

"I figure that if we're okay, they're probably doing much better," Santana assured us. "I don't know about you, but I'd rather lighten up and party."

"Me too," Abigail said.

"Me three," I agreed.

Bruce nodded.

<hr>

Santana went through the channels again and finally found a movie. It was a Spanish-language version of *Star Wars*. It was kind of weird to hear Obi-wan saying, "Que la fuerza te acompañe," but I already had all the lines memorized and relaxed, leaning against Santana as he put his arm around me. After we finished the pizza, Abigail made some Enchiladas Cubanos from scratch.

<hr>

That night, Santana and I pulled our cots together and slept in each other's arms. It was the best sleep I had gotten since before finals. Santana and I were taking our relationship slow. Lots of hugs, kisses, holding each other, but nothing more. I remembered how Matt had tried to push me into doing things I didn't want to do. I still wasn't ready–even though I loved Santana. This time, I had picked a true gentleman who cared more about pleasing me than about himself.

Abigail and Bruce seemed to be taking it slow, too. Neither of our relationships were mere flirtations or shallow romances. They were deep. Like us, Abigail and Bruce said they wanted their relationship to last.

The next morning, the news was still focusing on the earthquake at Combino del Este, the prison that had collapsed with us supposedly inside. Abigail cooked some eggs for breakfast, and I opened up some cans of fruit. Santana had previously taught me how to play poker. I taught him and the others to play fish. I wondered when or if we would be let out.

The TV was going in the background. The scene flashed to the bombing of the home of an abogado.

"That means attorney?" Abigail asked.

"Sí," Santana replied.

We continued to play cards until a sentence on the TV set grabbed our attention: "Gao de Alonzo Martina."

# CHAPTER 62

That grabbed our attention. They had gone after our attorney. "What does it say? Is he alright?" I asked, worriedly.

"I think we missed that part," Santana replied. We flipped from station to station, but most were obsessed with the earthquake. Some said the prison had been falling down, anyway, and the earthquake just hurried it along. Some additional nearby buildings were damaged, but only the prison had collapsed.

I prayed that Alonzo was alive and that his whole family and my mom, Emily and Hope were all safe.

"Do you think they destroyed the diary?" Bruce asked.

"He said he was showing it to someone in the government. They probably have it."

"That someone may have blown up his house. We've got to get out of here and make sure everyone is safe," Abigail advised.

"I agree completely," I responded. We looked through the kitchen for anything we could use to open the entrance door to the room.

Santana found a slim knife. He looked at the door. "Its hinges are on the other side. Otherwise, we could take out the bolts and lift out the door."

There was no hole on our side for a key. Santana unsuccessfully tried to wedge the knife around the locking mechanism. He started to use the knife to whittle away on the wood. As he did so, he found there was steel around the lock, reinforcing it.

"It may take some time, but maybe we can drill a hole through the main part of the door and open it from the outside," he suggested.

We all pitched in on the plan.

"Mierda," he swore. "The outside of this door is metal. We're in some kind of safe room. Maybe this was originally a bomb shelter."

"That someone turned into a prison," I commented.

"Do you think the walls are lined that way?" Abigail asked.

"We can find out," Bruce said. "What if we burn our way out?"

"What?" Santana reacted.

"I'm not talking about a big fire. A controlled one to cut through the door-frame."

"Didn't you blow up your chem lab?" Santana asked.

"Hangars, we have metal hangars. Maybe we can slip them around the locking mechanism," I said.

Abigail and I grabbed a couple of the hangars while Santana tried to chip away at the frame.

Bruce wet some towels and threw them towards the door. Then he lit a potholder on fire and carried it in a metal trashcan to the door. It was a small fire, but he pushed it against the wooden frame to see if it would burn.

"Stop that!" a voice came across the TV.

"Shit, it's a telescreen!" Santana exclaimed.

"We're in another f-ing prison," Abigail shouted.

We backed up. "Who are you? Did you harm our attorney?"

"Guys, they've been listening to everything we've said," Bruce responded. "How many people are watching us?"

No response.

We went to the TV, unplugged it and covered it with a sheet we found in a closet. Silently we looked for other cameras and for bugs.

Finally, Santana said, "If they are listening, they are listening and there is nothing we can do about it. They brought us here while the world thinks we are dead, both our real selves and our fake identities.

Our attorney and our friends and family probably think we're dead. We are clearly prisoners."

"What's next? We've been kidnapped, tortured, almost killed again and again, framed for terrorism, and now we are being held in a soft prison for how long?" I asked.

"Didn't Alonzo say that some prisoners wait years for their trials?" Abigail recalled from our conversation in the car.

"I've changed my mind about going to vet school here," I told the turned-off, covered-up TV. "In America, we would have been arraigned by now."

"Not necessarily. Remember the NDAA, not to mention Guantanamo," Santana pointed out.

"NDAA?" Bruce asked.

"National Defense Authorization Act. Every year since and including 2011, whoever has been President has signed a bill authorizing the indefinite detention of American citizens for life without rights or a trial."

"That's unconstitutional," Bruce said.

"Has anything our government has been doing since 2001 been constitutional?" Santana asked. "Well, at least we have food and cards."

"We need to know if Alonzo is alive or dead. He's not just our attorney. He's our friend," I insisted.

"Well, let's see what I can do," Bruce said.

Bruce started examining the TV set. "I need that little knife," he commented as Santana handed it to him. Bruce started unscrewing the casing and looking inside, presumably to see if it had a transmitter in it.

"While I'm doing this, make some noise and look around to see if you can find any transmitters or receivers elsewhere: in lampshades, under the sofa, in the refrigerator," Bruce whispered to me. I repeated his whispers to the others.

"What song would you like to start with?" Santana asked.

"'American Idiot' seems appropriate."

"We should sing that in Washington while my dad is tied to a chair," Abigail remarked.

We started belting out the words as I went and turned on the hair dryer in the bathroom. *What kind of prison has a hair dryer?*

An hour later, Bruce had reversed the connections and we were looking out through the set. Instead of a room with monitors, we saw a den with sofas and coffee tables. Nobody was visible at the moment.

"I need a makeshift keyboard. Bring me the remote control." Abigail got it for him, and he started clicking away. He was looking for information on Evan Saunders. We had learned his last name from the broadcast at the hotel. At first, there was nothing. Bruce kept typing and a minute later, Evan's profile appeared on the screen in connection with an organization called Darkswamp.

"I've never heard of that agency," I said.

"They're an independent contractor." Bruce punched in some more stuff on the remote.

"¡Santo mierda!" Santana said, looking at the chart that appeared. "Our camp overseer is tied to events in Vegas, Aurora, Sandy Hook, Boston, Charleston, among other places."

Santana went back to working on the door as Abigail rhetorically asked, "Now, what do those things have in common?"

"So, they were programming us to become the next Adam Lanza or Stephen Paddock," I surmised.

"Maybe, not us. They weren't very effective with us. But Ian, Harv, Dan and Hillary. They were perfect." Santana said.

"Even Ariel," I noted. "See if Evan's connected to my dad."

"Your dad worked for Senator Madstein who has had marital ties to a military contractor, Becken, right? And guess who's on Becken's corporate advisor list," Bruce continued.

"Evan," I guessed as he nodded.

"And naturally, he has ties to my daddy if he's part of the military-industrial complex." Abigail noted.

"And your father's with HAARP, which is considered a high-level weapon," I said to Bruce.

"Can you look up Alonzo's address?" I asked. He did so quickly. "Try *Gaglemaps*. Do you have the skills to get a current satellite view?"

"This is risky. It might tip people off to our location. There are better mapping systems."

He started to visually access the general area of Alonzo's home using our new make-shift computer. "You know, the Cuban people aren't supposed to be able to do this. But I'm sure that that thug who got off the boat had the tech."

Santana waved at me from the open door and I tapped Bruce's arm and Abigail's. Bruce erased the traces of his work, and we quickly followed Santana out.

"Good job," I whispered to Santana. "You're not just good with accessing cars."

"Stick with me, and you'll find out what other skills I have," he bantered back. "Unless they are monitoring us through another camera, they will probably be busy trying to figure out how to reprogram their tele-spying access, not realizing what's happening."

We had three options: We could go up the staircase, or either left or right through the basement hallway. We followed the hallway to the left, hoping it would lead to an easier exit. It also led to another staircase.

I stepped up carefully in case it creaked, giving us away. But it was quiet. We followed it until we arrived at a door to, presumably, the main floor. I held my breath as Santana quietly opened the door at the top of the steps. Once through it, we found ourselves in a large living room. We saw a door a ways to our left In the same wall as the door we had just come through. Ahead and to our left, part way to the front of the house, was another door. As Santana carefully opened the latter door, I hoped it wasn't a door leading to our captors. It was a garage. Nobody was in it.

"Which car?" Santana asked, looking at two vehicles inside, with room for a third vehicle.

"Um, I thought there was some kind of embargo," Bruce commented.

"Well, it hasn't hit this person," Santana pointed out. "Maybe he's with the contractor. We don't know who are captors are. Normally, I'd say, 'Take the Porsche,' but let's take a more obscure car that seats four."

Santana moved towards the blue Mustang as I and the others followed. "This is a 1967. I understand Castro authorized the purchase of post-1959 American cars many years ago."

"This is more than 50 years old," Bruce noted.

"Let's see if it runs like new." It didn't take Santana long to start it up. "I don't see a garage door opener inside. See if you can press that." He pointed to a button high up on the wall of the garage.

Bruce stepped on a shelf to reach it, and a minute later, we were off through the open garage door. As the car approached the outer gate, it automatically opened. Apparently, it was set to keep people out, not in.

"Does anyone know where we are going?" I asked.

"I looked at a map of the area where Alonzo's house is, but we need to find out where we are," Bruce said.

We were on some country road with luscious vegetation, and the sky was blue rather than streaked with criss-crossed trails of who knows what in the sky. It occurred to me that without the glyphosate and trails of aluminum, cadmium and barium being dropped from the sky, the plants were bound to be a lot healthier here than in the U.S. I had noticed the absence of chemtrails in Mexico, too.

We proceeded straight, hoping not to get picked up. Before long, we saw some road signs.

"I have a general idea. Turn left on the next highway," Bruce instructed Santana. "It will take us back towards Alonzo's area. He lives in a very nice suburb. They may be socialists, but the attorneys do quite well."

Following Bruce's directions, we finally came close to Alonzo's home. We parked the car off the road under some trees and moved in the direction of the house. There had definitely been some kind of explosion. The house was in pieces. I wondered if Alonzo had gotten out.

"You didn't happen to get the address for his brother's place, did you?" Santana asked.

"Sorry. I was nervous about leaving a trail to our friends, given we want them safe."

"Good thinking," I said.

We stood under a tree, hoping to stay out of sight. Bruce advised, "Avoid being anywhere that is open to the sky."

"But they—the Americans, not the Cubans—probably could have recognized us from inside the car by satellite if they really were looking for us," Santana noted.

"Look," I said. It was the guy from the kid's camp, the one Alonzo had spoken about. "He's looking for something. Maybe, information about us or to locate and destroy any remaining evidence."

"Who is that guy?" a familiar voice asked as my shoulder was tapped.

# CHAPTER 63

"Alejandro, hi." I turned and gave him a quick hug.

"Hermano, great to see you," Santana greeted him with a hug as well.

"Is Alonzo safe?" I asked.

"He was away when it happened. The people who did this won't find anything here. My uncle was too smart to keep anything critical to your case in his house."

"I'm so sorry that we've brought him this trouble. When we heard the news about Alonzo's home, we freaked."

"The TV said you were dead. But Alonzo told us you would be protected and not to believe anything the news said about you. The TV earlier said you died in the plane crash."

"Let's hope the bad guys keep believing that and leave us alone. Someone got us out and was holding us prisoner. But I don't think it was the people trying to kill us."

"So, you escaped?"

"We couldn't just sit there when we heard about what happened here," Santana said.

"How is Emily?" I asked.

"She's wonderful. We've really been having a great time. That dog of yours is really cool, too."

"And my mom?"

"She's fine. My uncle has been trying to keep her from worrying too much."

"Your uncle seems very nice. Thank you for believing in us and taking care of everyone."

"Your family put itself at risk for us," Abigail said, giving him a hug. I could see her fighting back tears, maybe wishing her family was like his.

"Ustedes somos familia," Alejandro said. "How about you come over to our house and see everyone?"

"Good idea," Bruce joined in. "We need to regroup anyway. Can we get to your home without anyone seeing us?"

"Follow me."

"Wait," Santana said. He went back to the car, disconnected the battery, picked the lock on the trunk and pulled out a tarp and a car cover. He covered the car and brought the tarp back to us. We lifted it over our heads to make sure we were covered for any satellite imaging. It turned out the path we were taking by foot was mostly covered by shrubs and trees. Alejandro's home was a good two miles from Alonzo's place.

Alejandro took us in through the garage. I heard a barking. Alejandro opened the kitchen door, and Hope bolted through, leaping right into my arms. Emily and my mom weren't far behind.

Emily ran to us and we gave her a big group hug. Then I hugged my mom, feeling like a little girl.

"Thank God, you are okay," my mom said, tears in her eyes. I found I was crying, too. I was so relieved to see them. We moved into the kitchen.

"Hope knew something was about to happen," Emily related. "He wouldn't stop barking, and we had to take him outside before we could put anything in the safe. Then the police arrived."

"I know I should have tried to stop them from taking you," my mom berated herself. "I remembered Alonzo was an attorney and I went to get his help. I let you down again."

"No. They would have taken you and Emily, and who knows what they would have done to Hope. You did the right thing. And we are all safe."

"I've heard terrible things about the Cuban prisons. Alonzo kept assuring me that you were getting special treatment."

"I'm pretty sure we were."

"You do look pretty good for someone who has just come out of a Cuban prison," my mom observed.

"Alonzo brought us food and water. We really are fine."

"They claimed all five of us were killed in the prison. I wasn't even there," Emily said.

"We were terrified when we heard about the collapse," my mom told us. "After the earthquake, Alonzo called to tell us he believed you were safe and to ignore any reports, otherwise. That was before we turned on the TV and heard—"

"Reports of our deaths have been greatly—" I started. Knowing the end of that line, everyone except my mom laughed.

My mom smiled and then brushed back my hair. "I don't think I could have survived losing you, again."

"So, Alonzo must have gotten word that we had been removed. We don't know who took us, but they treated us really well for prisoners."

"I'm just so glad you're back with us." My mom took me in her arms again.

"Hope sensed you were coming," Emily said. "He was barking for half an hour before you arrived."

I gave Hope another hug. "Good boy, Hope."

Emily let out a broad smile. "You wanted to turn him into a vegan. Alejandro and I have been trying different fruits and vegetables on him. He especially likes avocados and watermelon."

"Then my mom tried to feed him some chicken." Alejandro shook his head and gave a thumbs down. "He wouldn't touch the meat— only the fruit."

"Awesome." I high-fived them both at the same time and then gave Hope another hug.

"Everyone could be in danger, here. We need to find a safer location," Bruce warned.

A minute later, Juanita came strolling into the kitchen.

"Thank you for taking such good care of my mom, Emily and Hope," I told Juanita.

"It was my pleasure. We don't often get house guests, and we have really enjoyed having them."

"Alejandro told us Alonzo was safe," I said.

"He was with some friend in the government when the bomb went off at his place."

We explained our concerns about everyone's safety to her.

"I know just the place," she said. Alejandro grabbed his computer bag.

"I understand you are good at searching the Net," I noted.

He nodded.

"You and Bruce would make a good team."

Per Alejandro's suggestion, Juanita got us some parkas and sombreros and drove us out of the garage in an older Chrysler station wagon. "I'm sure you've noticed that there are a lot of older American cars in Cuba."

"I'm surprised they are still running."

"Well, this one has been refurbished with a new engine and transmission."

She drove down an old country road for about an hour. My mom sat in the front with Juanita. The rest of us, including Alejandro piled into the other seats, I noticed that Alejandro and Emily were holding hands in the far back, facing forward. Abigail was on Bruce's lap. Hope spread herself out on my and Santana's lap. At first, we five fugitives were bending over in our seats so as to not show our faces. Later, we just looked toward the center of the car.

"It certainly is beautiful in Cuba," I said.

"The world has very little idea of how lovely our country is. There is so much propaganda."

"I know. My government's good at propaganda," I replied.

"Your mother says you want to be a veterinarian. She says you've always been good with animals."

"That's my plan."

"They have a wonderful veterinarian school in Havana."

"And they have a free medical school. They even pay students to attend it," Emily chimed in.

I noticed the inflection in her voice. "Do you want to go there?" I asked.

"I never wanted to become a doctor until camp. So many campers were hurt, and there was so little I could do to help."

"You did a lot, just by being there with your positive energy and love," I reminded her.

"She's given us a lot of that warmth and love," Juanita said. "We're going to miss her—particularly Alejandro."

Alejandro and Emily certainly looked happy holding hands.

"At the camp, everyone seemed to become more of what they were. If they were caring, the experience brought that out. If they were cruel, they went off the deep end with viciousness."

"Ariel got so mean," Emily recalled.

"Was that that girl who spoke on TV about you?" my mom asked.

"She started out okay, and then they did some really bad stuff to her that almost nobody could handle," I said.

"Like forcing her to brush her teeth with dog poop," Emily informed her.

"They hung her upside down by a rope attached to her feet from a cliff."

"I can see where that would affect her," Juanita sympathized.

"If they did that to her, I hate to think of what terrible things they did to you?" my mom commented.

"I never would have survived if not for Santana, Emily and Paul. And Abigail's courage and strength were so inspiring. Then there was Bruce with his scientific knowledge."

"Paul was Evan's son, right?" my mom asked.

"The last night, when Hillary's culinary tent exploded into flames, Santana and I were handcuffed to a tree and Paul freed us and gave us his jacket, which had his diary in it. After he rescued us, he tried to rescue the blue group that had been put onto a truck. One of the blues tried to take over the truck and I think the tires were shot out. Anyway, it crashed and exploded. I think there were some heavy explosives on board."

"And so, now they are covering up what happened with a fake plane crash," Alejandro elucidated.

"In our country, we call it a false flag," I explained.

"We do, too. We talk about your false flags. We've been told you have a lot of them."

"We do. And we don't know how to get them stopped."

"Where did the term come from?" Alejandro asked.

"It's an old maritime term," Santana explained. "When a ship wanted to get close to an enemy ship it was going to attack, it would put up the enemy's flag so the enemy would think it was one of its own ships. The term doesn't mean the incident didn't happen. It means the incident was created by someone pretending to be a friend."

Bruce and Abigail were relatively silent on the ride. Abigail was resting her head on Bruce's shoulder. I wondered about what Abigail's life would have been like if Philomena had been allowed to stay and raise her or if either of her parents had shown her love. All our lives would have been different, if instead of trying the brute approach to fix us, those raising us had actually cared about us at all. But then, we might not have found true love.

We pulled onto a long driveway leading through a farm and up to a farmhouse. As we got out of the car, a woman came out to greet us. She looked like an older version of Juanita.

"¡Rosa, estos son nuestros amigos!" Juanita called out, walking up to her.

"What names should we go with?" Santana whispered.

"Might as well use our real ones," I responded. "Our fake IDs are dead, and they confiscated our alternate passports, anyway."

Rosa and Juanita spoke at length in Spanish. Juanita waved to us to join them. As we did, Rosa gave each of us a hug.

"What did you tell her?" I asked Juanita.

"I told her you were the children of American leaders and were currently in the country trying to save the world. I also said that some nasty people were trying to kill you and you needed a safe place to hide out."

"And what did she say?"

"She is happy to help."

"Wow!" I turned towards Rosa, "Gracias." I turned back to Juanita. "You're related, right?"

"Ella es mi hermana," Juanita proudly announced.

"What about her familia?" Santana asked.

"She's a widow with no children. But she is loved."

Juanita and Rosa escorted us inside. Alejandro asked, "¿Mama, puedo quedarme aqui unos dias?"

"Honey, you have things to do."

Alejandro gave Juanita a really sad look.

"Bien Por pocos días. Pero no seas un problema para Rosa o sus invitados."

"Mi? No problema," he said, shaking his head. He turned to Emily. "She said I can stay a few days."

Emily smiled.

Juanita gave us each a hug before driving away.

Our group went inside and had a late lunch. Rosa didn't speak much English, but Santana seemed to enjoy his role as official translator. Alejandro assisted with that, too. Immersion was probably the best way to pick up a new language, anyway.

I did my best to say I wanted to help out, preferably indoors. Rosa agreed to let me. That afternoon, she had me and my mom baking pastries and vegetable dishes while Alejandro, Emily and Santana went to into the barn and Alejandro showed the other two how to milk a cow. Outside, everyone wore hats and scarves. Bruce made sure that Abigail was comfortable on the couch.

Rosa explained that her farm was organic and that genetically modified crops weren't allowed in Cuba. I found I could pick up enough of Rosa's words to understand her. Rosa helped by trying to use what little English she knew in communicating with us.

That evening, Alonzo dropped by for dinner. He and my mother seemed very chummy. He had gotten word that we had been removed from the prison but hadn't known who took us or any further details.

As I watched my mom and Alonzo, I felt a little jealous, maybe because I hadn't seen her in so long and now a part of me wanted to make up for lost time, just the two of us. It wasn't fair of me, though, when I had Santana. She had been alone for so long. She deserved happiness.

Before Alonzo left, he and my mom walked out on the porch to have a discussion about something. I didn't want to intrude. So, I relaxed on the couch with Santana. He put his arm around me, and it felt like butterflies were dancing up and down my body.

"Afraid your mother might be leaving the nest?" he teased.

"It's just that I hadn't seen her in so many years until she showed up with Shannon. I wonder what Shannon thinks is happening right now. With the reports saying we were arrested and then died, she's probably pretty worried."

"It would be dangerous to call her," Santana pointed out.

"I know."

Rosa had an extra bedroom for my mother, myself, Emily and Abigail. The boys stayed in the living room. My mom and I slept in the same bed as we did when I was a little girl, afraid of monsters in the closet. Abigail and Emily shared a bed.

"Mommy, do you remember that story about the maiden you used to tell me at bedtime?" I asked.

"That was a long time ago."

"Do you still know it?"

"I think so. Would you like me to tell it to you again?"

She proceeded to tell me a story about a beautiful maiden who was forced to live in the castle of a rich King who demanded she be his. One day, her fairy Godmother came and told her she could have any three wishes she wanted. The girl wished for the King to stop oppressing all the villagers, for them to have plenty and for everyone to be happy. After she made her wishes, she realized she didn't make one for herself. But it was too late to make a more personal wish. To her surprise, when the Fairy Godmother waved her wand, the girl was free, and like the villagers, she was happy and had plenty. The lesson was that when everyone was better off, each individual person was also better off.

---

I slept well. Things seemed to be going peacefully for a couple of days. We were starting to relax. The five of us who had been called terrorists continued to cover up while outside. I could feel for the women, elsewhere, who felt the need to wear burkas in the summertime. Bruce and Santana helped Rosa rearrange her living room, moving furniture to where she wanted and assisting her to sort through her supplies while I improved my cooking skills.

"Ah!" I heard Bruce exclaim.

I came out into the living room. He was looking at an old Compaq laptop that Rosa had had in storage. If we can connect this to your phone line, I can do some serious damage," he said.

"Damage?"

"Just an expression," I intervened.

We had been out of touch for some time and were interested in the latest information. "I need to do some multi-locational routing of this so the Cuban Government doesn't think Rosa's looking at any unauthorized sites."

"Which you are doing, of course," I said.

"Of course."

Santana stood, looking at what Bruce was doing. I sat down. My mom went into the bedroom to take a nap. I had time before my pastries were finished cooking. Pastries weren't usually my thing, but here, they were tastier than in the U.S. That was probably because of the lack of Monsanto.

"It will take a while," Bruce noted. "I'm going to write a program to get around the limitations and create a virtual private network."

When the buzzer rang, I went into the kitchen to get the pastries out and let them cool.

"¡Mierda!" Santana swore.

I raced back in there. "Okay, what gives?"

Abigail sat silent, not eager to talk.

"The good news is that they have accepted, as official, the story of our deaths or rather the terrorists' deaths," Bruce said. He paused.

It was Santana who continued. "The bad news is that Shannon and Jimmy flew into Havana and disappeared. It is believed they were picked up by someone. They don't know who. Their parents have demanded Washington investigate."

# CHAPTER 64

"Can you find anything more on it?" I asked.

"Nothing. Whoever took them didn't put the information online," Bruce said.

"We need to get on top of this. Our terrorist selves are officially dead, so maybe we can go as ourselves to the airport," I noted.

"Our real selves are officially dead, too," Bruce pointed out.

"How about you let me and Bruce check it out and keep you in the loop?" Santana suggested.

"No deal," I reacted at the same time Abigail said, "No F-ing way."

"We're a team," I reminded the guys.

Emily and Alejandro came in as we were saying that. "What is the team stuff we have to do?" Emily asked.

I turned to her. "We need a team member to watch Hope and Mom and make sure they stay safe."

"Why do I get that I will be missing out on all the fun?"

"What we are doing isn't fun. It's kind of mundane."

"The truth," Emily demanded.

I didn't feel like lying to her. "It looks like someone has apprehended Shannon and Jimmy at the airport in Havana."

"They came here?"

"The more of our outside friends who go to the airport, the more they might start to disbelieve the dead in the earthquake story. I really do need someone to look out for Mom and Hope, and I trust you with them."

"Emily, we can be here as backup. If they have problems at the airport, we can do more to try to help them from here than in jail or worse," Alejandro advised her. "I can hit the Net."

"Okay," she said, looking down.

"I love you, Emily. You are our sister," I reminded her. "Be glad you weren't with us last time. The food was so bad, it killed the rat."

She made a face, and we both laughed.

"I love you, too," Abigail told her. "Someone has to be able to tell our story if they get us."

Emily hugged us.

"Alejandro, can you contact your uncle and, in case his phone is bugged, find a way to get him to go to the airport without clueing in any listeners to our whereabouts."

"Sure."

"Emily, it will be okay. We'll handle whatever happens and get back here as quickly as possible," I assured her.

She sat down beside Alejandro on the couch. "Sure. But you guys promise to stay safe."

"That's the plan," I said. "Oh, wait to tell Mom until later. I don't want to worry her needlessly."

"Sí," Alejandro replied.

I went into the kitchen to speak with Rosa. I simply said we had an important errand as best I could in Spanish. She agreed to let us borrow her car.

---

An hour later, we were at the José Martí International Airport. "You know they have cameras and extra security, here, don't you?" Santana asked.

Abigail and Bruce waited outside while we walked in separately. We made sure to be wearing hats but we knew that wouldn't help with facial recognition from cameras inside the airport.

I noticed a reporter I had seen on *Telemundo* and a couple of other services. He was easy to recognize as he was carrying a microphone and camera.

Santana and I went up to him. "What is the latest on the two teens who disappeared at the airport?" he asked.

"They were Americans. Their parents are demanding answers from the Cuban Government."

"Do their parents think the leadership, here, had them picked up?"

"Nobody knows. Hey, aren't you?"

"Nope," I stated, firmly.

He looked at Santana. "Yes, you are. They said you were dead."

"I just look like someone you think you know," Santana replied.

"I was assigned to your dad as a reporter when he ran for re-election to Congress. He's a great man."

I quietly huffed. Santana responded. "Wait until you get the real story on my dad, the way he treated my mother, the way he sent his son off to be tortured at a wilderness camp that violated every law on the books, how he would rather pretend I was dead rather than own up to what he did."

"Wow. That sounds terrible. A real tabloid story." He turned to me. "And you are?"

I didn't respond.

"Maybe I could get an exclusive interview with you," he said to Santana.

"Maybe," Santana replied. "But a first requirement is that you keep it under wraps that you saw me until I'm ready for the interview and you promise to air the interview uncut."

"As long as someone doesn't out-scoop me."

"And you don't slant the story to make our parents the good guys for having us tortured," I said.

"Your dad, too?"

I nodded.

"I wouldn't do that. Deal?"

Santana looked at me and I nodded.

"Deal," he agreed.

"Do you have a card?" Santana asked.

The reporter handed each of us a card. I read the name. Diego Morinda. "And don't say anything to your news crew, wherever it is."

"I'm solo today. Budget cuts due to sanctions. I make more by working alone, whenever feasible—except when there is a need for a crew."

We were looking at the flight list when we saw him, looking right at us. It was Gordon Magruder, Evan's guy, here in Havana. He started moving towards us and we ran.

# CHAPTER 65

We leaped past the checkpoint to board the planes, and security came running after us. Magruder also leaped past them, knocking down officers in his way. He pulled out his gun and held up something that looked like a badge. Everyone ducked but nobody reacted.

After rushing outside, we ran up a ramp onto a forward doorway of some kind of plane with Magruder and airport security all chasing us. I felt lucky nobody was shooting us. I thought too soon.

Magruder was at the front door firing as we were aiming for a back exit while trying to duck around the seats on the way out. It looked as if someone in airport security had grabbed his arm and was struggling with him.

We pushed open an emergency exit at the back of the plane. There was no staircase. We heard a couple more shots and didn't look to see what was behind us. We knelt down, grabbed the floor, and jumped to the concrete. That hurt, but I didn't have time to feel the pain.

We kept moving, dodging between planes right out onto the runway. Another shot was fired, this time from outside the plane. Only Magruder was following us. In the States, a dozen sharpshooters would have flattened us by now, I suspected. Maybe they didn't shoot teens in Cuba. We avoided running in a perfect or predictable line in the hopes of missing any further bullets. He fired another bullet and missed, again.

We were heading towards a fork in the runway and were trying to decide which way to go. Somehow, maybe because our indecision delayed us, Magruder managed to get in front of us and aimed his gun directly at me.

Santana tried to move ahead of me to block the shot as I tried to push him out of the way. As we struggled for who would get shot, Magruder seemed to be watching amused. But not for long as somehow, he didn't hear the sound of an engine coming down the runway behind him over the other airplane engines in the area. He focused his gun on one of us and was pulling the trigger as he was hit from behind and thrown under the wheels, causing the bullet to go astray.

We took off fast towards an exit. As we started through the gate, I saw an emergency vehicle behind—en route to pick up the remains, I assumed. There was no way Magruder survived that. He had looked pretty squashed.

The guard at the gate said, "You can't leave."

"We'll do the report later," Santana said in Spanish. The guard looked perplexed, maybe wondering if we were with some agency, given Santana's comment. We walked through.

Diego was outside the gate, getting snapshots of us.

"You want an exclusive?" Santana asked him.

"Sure?"

"Good. Can you run, and do you mind getting shot at?"

Diego seemed almost speechless.

"This is what it's been like ever since we escaped the wilderness camp our dads sent us to," Santana explained. "And if you saw what happened on the runway, they still aren't done. Now if you don't mind, we need to get out of here. You are welcome to join us."

As we moved, I said, "Hi, I'm Summer Tanner, daughter of Marcus Tannen, Chief of Staff for California's Governor. My dad had me tased, beaten, drugged, put in the trunk of a car and taken to one of those camps on the other side of hell."

"Wow, can I print that?"

"Be my guest. But not yet. There is a much larger story awaiting you. Did you happen to get video of the guy trying to shoot at us?"

"From the gate. I think I got him pretty well with my telephoto lens."

"Oops, we have to run again," Santana said, as I pointed to our prison nurse, coming our way from the airport boarding area.

"How about a taxi?" Diego asked, pointing to one of several vehicles sitting next to the section of sidewalk we were about to pass.

"Great idea," Santana responded. He and I crawled into the back through one door while Diego climbed in through the other.

In the ruckus, we lost our hats and were visible to satellites if anyone was watching. Diego asked the driver to take us to his hotel.

As we were starting to relax, Diego looked out the window. "I wonder what that unmarked plane is."

Santana and I looked at each other. "Could you pull up under a bridge or somewhere covered?" Santana asked.

The driver complied at the next pedestrian bridge going over the roadway. Diego handed the driver a bill, presumably Cuban, and had him take off quickly.

"Wait," I called after the driver.

Santana was calling, too. "Jump,"

De je Vu had hit us. But not fast enough. A minute later, the cab was in pieces.

"We got him killed."

"Who are these people who are after you?"

"Who do you think has unmarked planes and bombs?" I asked rhetorically.

"He's coming back," Santana said. "He's going to take out the bridge."

"And everyone on it. What do we do?" I worried about how many others would die.

"I guess we run out and let them live. No, not we, I." He shoved me against Diego. "Please hold her in place," he instructed Diego, and ran out into the open.

# CHAPTER 66

Diego gripped onto me, but somehow, I managed to push Diego away and ran towards Santana.

The plane was approaching us, presumably for the kill. Suddenly to the side, we saw a fleet of planes with a Cuban military logo on their sides closing in. The unmarked plane was still flying in our direction.

As the unmarked plane fired a missile towards us, several missiles flew towards it. There wasn't time to run. I threw my arms around Santana as he pushed me into a ditch, throwing himself on top of me. I tried to push him off, but he was stronger.

We heard multiple loud explosions. One was on the ground not far from us. Two others were in the air. Debris was flying everywhere. Santana continued to cover me with his body.

I didn't want him taking the weight of anything that fell. "Please, I don't want to survive if it's without you," I whispered. Something from above hit him and he collapsed against me. I rolled him over. "Santana, Santana, I love you."

He was warm. I felt his pulse. He still had one. Diego came running and bent over Santana's chest to listen for his heart.

"Please, Santana, you have to be alright. I need you. I need you."

He moved a little. Then he reached up, put his hand behind my head and pulled me down into a kiss.

I pushed away from him. "You rat. You're okay," I chastised and then went back to kissing him.

"We were worried you were hurt and you two are just making out to fireworks."

I jumped up and gave Abigail a hug. I reached down and Santana took my hand as he got up.

Bruce slapped him on the back. "Keeping all the fun to yourselves, huh."

"Next time," Santana said, kissing me, again.

"I can get into this," Bruce said as he grabbed Abigail and kissed her.

"Looks like this will be a romance story," Diego joked and then grimaced, looking at the debris.

Releasing Abigail, Bruce stated, "That was the same plane that blew up the boats."

"Well, we don't have to worry about that one anymore, just whatever they send next," Santana responded.

"What's next is what scares me," I portended. "I sure hope they don't nuke the Island."

"Well, nuking Guantanamo Bay would be a public service," Abigail remarked.

"I'm sure the prisoners there wouldn't think so," I noted.

"On the good side, they didn't use one of those Athena planes with a silent, invisible directed energy weapon," Bruce proclaimed.

"Watch what you say. That could be next," I cautioned.

Santana still looked a little dazed. He didn't object as Bruce helped him move along.

"So, has this sort of thing happened before?" Diego asked.

"Did you hear about a Cuban patrol boat and a Mexican fishing boat being blown up?" Bruce responded with a question.

"Yes, they said it was terrorists."

"It was that same plane?"

"Who was in that plane?"

I guessed he hadn't figured it out from my earlier comment.

"Probably a contractor or an alphabet," Bruce stated.

"So, you're saying that someone connected with the U.S. Government is doing terrorist attacks?"

"Was what you just witnessed a lovefest?" Santana responded.

"Why?" Diego asked.

"Probably so we don't tell anyone what goes on in their wilderness camps," I said.

"We watched kids f-ing die," Abigail joined in. "They tortured us. They locked me in a box and fed me to dogs, literally."

"Me too. Not the dogs. They also striped me and cable-tied me to a tree. They gang-raped one of the girls and they put a noose around the neck of the son of the Deputy Chairman of the Federal Reserve. He died by hanging."

"Before you go public, we need to put everything together, get more answers," Santana maintained.

"Shannon," I reminded everyone. "We have to find Shannon and Jimmy. She's my best friend."

"I may be able to help," Diego said.

"How?" I asked.

"Did she have a smartphone?"

"Can you track it?"

"My station can. We have satellite feed."

"Look, I don't trust anyone."

"Fair enough. I won't tell the station whom I'm tracking. You can listen to my side of the call."

We accompanied Diego to his van, which was in the upper story of the parking lot. I looked for planes as we did so.

"I work for several services. One of them will help us." He made a call as Santana whispered the translation to me. "Hey, look, Javier. This other reporter is about to out-scoop me on a story. I have a cell number. If you can track the location, I can jump in and save our asses on this story." After a pause, Diego said in Spanish, "Sure. Thank you."

Diego handed me a piece of paper and a pen and whispered for me to write her number down. Hesitantly, I did so.

He gave the number to his contact. I hoped I was doing the right thing. *Telemundo,* among other news services, seemed to trust him. He had a news van and a card.

Diego offered to take us to lunch while we waited for his friend to get back to us. We left the airport and went to a little restaurant in downtown Havana that he said had unbelievably good food.

While at lunch, we related our stories to him. He had heard about George Miller's hearings and the concerns surrounding the behavior modification programs, but didn't realize the fundamental problems with the camps ran as deep as they did.

I asked him whether a person deserved to be a parent if that person was unable to train their child without the use of torture programs. He thought about it and said, "No." The use of bounty hunters to kidnap kids to take them to the camps struck him as something that needed to be criminalized.

We went back to his van to wait. He scanned for current news stories. The U.S. media was claiming that the Cubans had shot an American plane with students. They were starting to beat the drums for war.

Santana and I looked at each other and said in unison, "*Operation Northwoods.* Do they really expect anyone to buy that?"

Diego asked about *Operation Northwoods* and we encouraged him to QuackQuackRun it. We pointed out that the proposed plan involved multiple false flags, mainly recommended by the Joint Chiefs of Staff during the Kennedy Administration. One of them involved sending a plane of students to Atlanta and replacing the plane with a drone that would explode over Cuba so they could blame the Cubans and start a war. Kennedy turned down the plan.

"I got footage of the plane." He looked at us. "Sorry. I couldn't pass it up. I also got footage of your courage. The footage will prove they are lying."

"And it could stop a war, but will your network let you broadcast it?" I asked. "Wars have been started while news networks forced their reporters to sit on the truth. Remember how all the networks lied to us about Iraq, Libya, Syria and elsewhere?"

He pulled the card from his camera and started making copies.

"I'm not stupid and I work for several services. One of them will have the courage to tell the truth."

---

"You tracked her where?" Diego asked his contact as Santana, again, translated for me. "Okay. Got it." He turned to us. "We have a location. Is there a police officer you trust?"

"There isn't anyone we trust."

We sat in the back of Diego's van while Bruce played with the onboard computers. "If I had all this equipment, I'd find a way to stop a few wars," he said.

"How?" Diego asked.

"If the news media can fix elections and influence support for war, then it can do the opposite. I'd find a way to broadcast the truth twenty-four-seven."

"What about the censorship, the media consolidation and the attacks on anyone telling the truth?" Diego asked him.

"With enough equipment, we'd get our message out anyway. Well, maybe not."

"And you could make a gallant effort, right? But then, you could meet the fate of Julian Assange."

"And you? How much courage do you have?" Bruce asked him.

"I hope enough."

I was getting concerned about the farmhouse. We hadn't heard from Emily or my mom, and Rosa wasn't answering her phone. They could have been busy out in the fields. As soon as we rescued Shannon and Jimmy, I was going to make sure everyone else was safe.

---

The trip took a while. "Where are we?" I asked, getting out of Diego's van.

"In the woods, near the location. I thought you might want to make a surprise entrance."

"Do you have any weapons?"

"I'm a reporter, not a soldier."

"A distraction would be nice," Santana said.

As we neared the actual address, I stopped in my steps. "Look familiar guys?" I asked.

"Too familiar," Santana grimaced.

"Do you think this is a trap? Why did they let Shannon and Jimmy keep their cell phones?" Abigail questioned.

"To lure us in," I responded. This made me somewhat suspicious of Diego. But maybe they would have expected Bruce to be able to track the call if we hadn't run into Diego.

"How about I go up to the house and ask for an interview?" Diego suggested.

"And two of us sneak in the back while our two guys fire up a getaway car," Abigail added to the plan.

"What if we fire up multiple get-a-way cars to distract them, but don't take any of them. Instead, we get our friends out the back."

"You can do that without keys?" Diego asked.

Santana smiled and didn't answer.

The front gate was unlocked. Diego was to go to the door as Santana and Bruce worked on breaking in through the garage. If the alarm went off, Diego would rush to the basement. Abigail and I would locate and go through a back entrance, timed to correspond with when the boys went through the side from the garage. The idea was to have them distracted in so many directions, they wouldn't know what hit them. Santana went over what I would need to do to break in. We had created makeshift tools from what equipment Santana found in the news van that he felt would work.

"Okay, you ready?" I asked.

"Not really," Bruce replied. "But the longer we wait, the less ready I'll be."

I started to take off, but Santana pulled me in and gave me a kiss. Bruce and Abigail gave each other a kiss, too.

I turned towards Diego. "You sure you want to get involved? You might find yourself dodging airplanes and missiles."

"Well, at least my job will be exciting."

"One guy who tried to help us wound up dead. I can't stop feeling guilty about that."

"I'm a reporter. If they don't want to talk, they'll slam the door in my face."

"Unless they think you're involved with us."

"If I couldn't handle the heat, I wouldn't be a journalist."

I gave him a hug. He might be a ringer, but there was something endearing about his seeming courage.

When we got to the back door, we waited for the bell to ring and then counted to one hundred before acting. I wasn't as good of a burglar as I had hoped. So finally, Abigail broke a window near the back door, which opened onto the kitchen. I opened the kitchen door to the living room we had left through before. Nobody but Santana and Bruce, who had just entered from the garage, was visible on the main floor from our vantage point. Santana and Bruce were planning to check the upper floors while we went to check down below. As far as I could tell, Diego was still at the front door, ringing and ringing. The likely holding cell was our former residence in the basement. We had done a lot of damage to it, but there were other rooms down there, possibly other similar plush cells, if they hadn't fixed the door.

The entrance to our former holding cell down below had a new door and was barred shut and locked from the outside. I pulled the bars off, and unlocked and opened the door.

The lights were off. As I moved inside, I was grabbed by someone pretty strong.

"Summer?" I recognized Jimmy's voice. Abigail turned on the lights as Shannon came out of the bathroom. I thought about the closed-circuit TV that might have been fixed by now.

"We've got to get out of here," I said as Shannon and I gave each other a hug.

"I'll tell the boys," Abigail said as she started up the stairs. We turned to go up and saw that Abigail had been turned around and was being followed by Bruce and Santana. And behind them was our reporter friend and the storm troopers who may have been the same guys who released us or rather kidnapped us from Combinado del Este. They ushered us back into the room.

# CHAPTER 67

"You know this is getting really boring," I said.

"Can't you guys go bore some other people?" Santana added.

"Like maybe my father?" Abigail chimed in.

"You know, prisons we are in have a tendency to get flattened," Santana commented. "If you are smart, you will let us go. ¿Comprende?"

"Yo soy periodista. Esta será una historia de titular," Diego told them.

The men seemed unmoved and we settled down on the couch as they closed, locked and barred the door.

"Fish or poker?" I asked.

"They can't do this," Diego insisted.

"I think they just did," Bruce replied.

"So, this happens a lot to you?"

"Welcome to the den of insanity," I said.

"If you're lucky, they'll only tear off your fingernails and toenails," Abigail commented.

Diego had a horrified look on his face. Then he relaxed.

"He thinks you're kidding," Santana said to Abigail.

"At least, these guys haven't tried to kill us yet," I pointed out.

"We even had a pizza and other food that wasn't poisoned last time we were here."

"Poisoned?" he asked.

"That was earlier, before the first time they brought us here," I informed Diego. "The rat we fed our prison food to died."

Diego visibly shuddered. "So, how do we get out of here?"

"Bruce could probably whip up a kitchen explosive and blow off the door," I replied.

"I just looked in the kitchen. They've removed the food utensils. We have a lot of pre-made packaged foods. I could rig up the microwave," Bruce informed us.

"I really don't want to be microwaved. My government's already doing that to people," I said.

"Daddy actually has a plan to win wars by microwaving the inhabitants of foreign countries."

"No surprise there," I mumbled to myself. I turned to Diego. "What did you tell them?"

"I threatened them with a headline story."

"Bold."

"We need to figure out what their motivation is in holding us here. Theoretically, we're dead and so why are they holding us—unless it's because they know we aren't dead. The scenario implies the answer. Of course, they could be planning to frame us for the next terrorist act." Bruce delineated.

"How can dead people commit terrorist acts?" I asked. "The house up above isn't exactly a dump. I wonder if a Bilderberg lives here."

"They are toying with us," Abigail surmised.

"The people who picked us up at the airport said you were in danger and they were helping you. They said they were bringing us to you," Shannon informed us.

"They are clearly big liars," I said.

"They actually seemed really nice," Shannon recalled.

"That riot gear looked very friendly," I noted.

"The guys who picked us up weren't wearing riot gear. It was a middle-aged man and woman. They told us to wait here for you. A minute later, the door was locked."

"Real friendly," Santana remarked.

"Well, you did show up," Jimmy pointed out.

"Let's say the guy who owns this place is a Bilderberg. Wouldn't he be nailing himself by bringing us here if he planned to frame us for the next event?" I asked.

"Maybe it's to shut us up for the time being. These people don't want to kill us. They just don't want us to talk to anyone. Maybe it's a different government agency," Bruce suggested.

"Was anyone surprised by how easy it was for us to get away before?" Santana asked.

"It was a little too easy," Bruce said. "If you think someone is a terrorist, you don't make it easy for them to get away—unless you want them to commit an act of terrorism, but that could lead investigators to whoever owns this place and be counter-productive."

"I'm very confused," I acknowledged.

"That makes two of us," Santana agreed.

"Three," Bruce added.

"What did the woman look like?" I asked.

"She was about five feet tall, curly blonde and grey hair, not thin but not heavy either," Shannon said.

"Light skin, small bust," Jimmy added.

"Not our nurse," I noted.

"What about the guy?" Bruce asked.

"Dark hair, grey eyes, fair skin, about five foot, ten," Shannon said.

"Not Evan or that other guy," Santana remarked.

"Well, there are multiple people in on this: the riot-gear gang, the man and lady, the owner of the house and whoever told us not to burn down the door. We didn't get a look at whoever said that," Bruce noted.

"We may not have to do much. When I don't report in, my station will come looking for me and the truck," Diego reassured us.

"Do you have your phone?"

"They took it." He looked at Shannon. "We tracked your phone to here."

"The man who brought us here borrowed it before the door was locked."

"You have a phone, Jimmy?" I asked.

"I did, but it's not in my pocket. I must have left it somewhere along the way."

Shannon sat up. "Your station knows you're at this location?" She asked Diego.

"Yes."

"Then your disappearance will lead them straight here."

"Maybe our captor will send your station a fake letter like the ones they wrote at camp to our parents," I noted.

"So, you survived the prison collapse because they moved you here?" Shannon asked.

"Your friends have to be the luckiest individuals on Earth. You should have seen how they escaped a gunman and an airplane loaded with missiles at the airport."

"It was the Cuban Air Guard who saved us," I explained.

"Then, they can't think you're terrorists," Shannon pointed out.

"There were a lot of others who were at risk from the plane and I'm pretty sure our cab driver—" I couldn't finish, thinking of the explosion.

"James Bond, move over," Shannon quipped and then saw my expression and touched my shoulder.

"I can be your Q," Jimmy told Santana and me.

"And I'll be your R," Bruce said.

"You are walking targets," Diego commented.

"Shannon, did you draw a bull's eye on my back before we left the country?" I teased, joining the others in trying to lighten the mood.

"You didn't know?"

"I confess. It was me who drew it," Jimmy chimed in.

"What if you get on TV and expose what is happening?" Shannon asked.

"We would probably be received about as well as the architects and engineers who insisted the World Trade Center was brought down by controlled demolitions," Santana replied.

"Where are Emily and your mom?" Shannon asked.

I looked at the TV. "Safe, I hope."

"Oh, I have some good news," Shannon said. "I spoke with Mr. Lavery, pre-calc. He agreed to discard your final."

"But he is so strict and doesn't change rules."

"He looked over all your work from the semester. It was all A+, except for the final and he decided it would be unconscionable to give you a grade that was counter to your work from the entire semester."

"So, is he letting me take the test if I ever make it back to Heritage High?"

"No. The test questions came from the prior quizzes and work and so he is taking your original answers to those questions and treating them as if they were your answers on the final."

"Wow. You must be a real salesperson. What are the other students saying about me back home?"

"Well, Matt is talking as if the two of you were the "in" couple right up until the plane crash."

I rolled my eyes. "What a lowlife. The plane crash that wasn't."

"Operation Northwoods," Jimmy remarked.

"We've been talking about that," I said.

"It's not just this. False flags are rampant. What is your take on the reason for the camps?" he asked.

"Well, they don't have books at the Gulag camps or schools and they engage in torture at about all of them," I replied.

"Then, what are they teaching?"

"We think they may be preparing us to be Manchurian candidates. It's the most obvious possibility."

"They use standard brainwashing techniques at the camps," Bruce jumped in. "They degrade the campers, subject them to conditions where they beg for mercy and then tell them they are okay when they do what the leaders want—even if what they are told to do is to hurt other individuals. They make teens not only accept but engage in the unacceptable."

"Stockholming," Diego said.

"Stockholming," I confirmed. "It's what was reportedly done to Patty Hearst to get her to rob a bank; happens at most of those schools and camps."

"No surprise they haven't done anything to really enforce laws against the Gulag schools. There is no chance they will terminate places that they think will someday create universal soldiers," Abigail said. "In fact, my dad will encourage Congress to secretly fund places that will create lunatics who will do the bidding of the Pentagon." She made a motion like she was flinging an ax.

"All of you would make great future leaders," Diego remarked.

"But we have to wait until we have been brainwashed and given up our morality, courage and honor before they will let us lead," Santana stated.

"That speaks strongly for lowering the voting age," Diego acknowledged.

"If teens are considered old enough to be tortured, they should be eligible to vote," I remarked. I was sure Emily would agree.

"Look at the bills the so-called adults in Congress pass," Santana went on. "The PATRIOT Act, the Wall Street bailouts, wars, war-funding, bills to propagandize against foreign countries, the NDAA, attacks on our right to protest and boycott, elimination of the right to protect ourselves against the government, et cetera, et cetera, et cetera. Have you seen any of our current so-called progressive leaders prioritize single-payer health care, free college, abolition of the death penalty, nuclear disarmament, and other truly progressive issues?"

"Dennis Kucinich and Cynthia McKinney," I responded.

"Who were undermined by the power structure of their own Democratic Party." Santana continued.

"Cuba has adopted almost all of that," Diego stated.

"Which is why our government hates your country," Abigail pointed out. "Every time a country supports actual human rights, my dad can't wait to bomb it."

"Venezuela, watch out," I concluded.

"I know that the TV is bugged. But it wouldn't hurt to know what more is going on, not that anything called 'news' is real. I'd like to see more of how the news portrayed what happened at the airport," Bruce said.

A sound was audible outside. The door opened and a man and a woman in suits entered. They matched Shannon's description of the couple who picked her and Jimmy up at the airport.

"CIA, NSA, Maf-i-a?" Santana asked.

They chuckled. "None of them. We'd like you to take a trip with us."

"Well, we're tired of being kidnapped and moved from prison or storage area to prison or storage area," I responded.

"You will need to trust us," the man said.

We all chuckled and then started laughing uproariously. It was an outlet for the tension that had been building. "Does no way in hell mean anything?" Abigail asked.

"Where are your men in riot gear?" I asked.

"Is that really necessary?"

"Necessary? We've been poisoned, charged with bogus crimes, declared dead numerous times, shot at, had a missile fired from a plane at us, not to mention all the incarcerations. I think we deserve an explanation," Santana declared.

"And you will get one if you come with us."

"The last time someone offered to help us get out of incarceration, it was a trap," Abigail pointed out.

"You guys told me my friend was here," Shannon said.

"No, I said you would see your friends here and here they are," the woman replied.

"Um, we got here on our own," I corrected.

"You did?"

"Oh no," Santana wailed as we looked at Diego.

"Don't look at me," Diego said. "I'm an independent agent. I don't go around kidnapping people."

"I'm fed up with being lied to," I told him.

"All right, I was asked to find you, get you to trust me enough to tell me your story. My source also located the phone."

"Who asked you to find us?"

"My contact at the station who later located your friend."

"How did they know we weren't dead? That's what the news was saying," Santana said.

"You lied to us. Give us one reason we should ever trust you again," I demanded.

"I didn't realize they planned to lock us up. I swear. I thought everything was on the up and up. The guy at my station was someone I trusted."

"Someone who told you to lie is trustworthy? What if he's one of the bad guys who is trying to kill us? "I asked.

"Summer, most American news anchors are former or current CIA. Do you know how much money Congress authorizes annually for fake news propaganda?" Abigail asked.

"Actually, yes,"

"My dad is really proud of voting, based on those lies," Santana noted.

"My dad probably helped Dana Madstein and our Governor invent those lies."

"My dad doesn't care if they are lies. They are a good excuse for bombing innocent people and little babies. And now, it looks like you are part of the liars' club," Abigail said, turning back to Diego.

"My studio is not an arm of the U.S. Government," Diego insisted.

"That's what they all say," I chided.

"But my station isn't American," Diego reiterated.

"Would you like to come upstairs," the male captor cut in.

"What? Without chains and locks and guns pointing at us? Are you risking our taking off?"

"Actually, the riot cops, as you called them, are still in the area. But I don't think we will need them. We also want you to call your mom and Emily Hatton."

"No, thank you," I said as if I was turning down cream in my coffee.

"So that's what this is all about? Getting more victims?" Bruce asked.

We sat down on the couch as if we had all come to the same conclusion.

"We'll be back."

With that, they left.

This time, there were no sounds of the door being locked or barred.

"Okay, Diego, who at your station wanted us to talk to you? And this better be good." I asked.

"It was the director of TeleCuba. He got a call from someone who wanted me to stick to you if I found you."

"TeleCuba, not TeleMundo?" Santana questioned.

Diego nodded.

"Who funds TeleCuba?" Bruce asked.

"This isn't America, where Wall Street owns the news. Or Venezuela, where the CIA funds the anti-government propaganda news."

"The U.S. and Cuba are not on good terms," Jimmy agreed with Diego.

"We couldn't even fly out through the U.S. We went by way of Mexico," Shannon said. "We heard about the plane crash and knew that wasn't real. Later, when we heard about the arrests and the prison falling down, an armed militia couldn't keep us away. But we figured that, if they faked a plane crash, they probably faked everything else."

"I'm very lucky to have great friends like you. What about your parents?"

"They were on their way back, but we left them a note, telling them we were going to a Woodstock-type concert with friends and would be in touch," Shannon responded to me with a smile.

Bruce went to the door and opened it. "Was that a scream?"

"What?"

"I thought I heard a scream and then a loud thunk from somewhere above."

"Bruce and I will go out and check upstairs to see what's up there. If it's safe, we'll all go," Santana suggested. We followed to the open entrance near the room.

We could tell it wasn't safe when our friends opened the door at the top of the stairs and slammed it shut. Santana and Bruce came running down coughing as heavy smoke came billowing past them. "The house is on fire!" Santana exclaimed.

# CHAPTER 68

"This room is a safe room, not nuclear safe, but safe from more minor threats. We can't be sure whether it will withstand a fire. There is the way we left last time, but no guarantee that that's clear and not on fire. It looked as if the whole upstairs was ablaze," our resident brainiac, Bruce, pointed out in a surprisingly calm fashion.

"That couple!" I exclaimed.

"Let's hope they got out," Shannon said.

"Or maybe, they started the fire," Abigail pondered.

"We never finished examining the other basement rooms for a window or escape path," Santana recalled.

"If there is one, whoever did this will probably be waiting," I feared.

"The closet is full of clothes. What if we soak some, put them over us and run up?" Shannon suggested.

"A possibility," I said.

"That worked so well for Robert Wagner in *The Towering Inferno*," Santana recalled.

"Diego, did they really confiscate your phone?" I asked.

"Yes. They did. Sorry."

Bruce looked deep in thought. "We've got water."

"What if we flood the downstairs area?" Santana asked.

"That will work until it gets to boiling temperature and cooks us while evaporating," Bruce replied. "But it won't put out a chemical or electrical fire."

"Is there a fire extinguisher in the basement?" I asked.

"Guys, remember how we almost started a fire in here before. Do you think they will accuse us?" Bruce asked.

"That's absurd. You have witnesses," Diego pointed out.

"Or, in their view, accomplices," Santana predicted.

"You'll get used to being accused of things you didn't do," I told Diego.

"Heck, they'd frame us for starting a first missile strike from NORAD," Abigail added.

I knew it would only be a matter of time before the fire came through the door at the top of the stairs. We partially covered our faces in case too much of the smoke got through.

We started moving through the basement, checking the other rooms. One had a couple of computers but no windows. We followed Bruce in to check for online access. He got it. Jimmy figured the wires went underneath the house, below the basement level.

Bruce sent out a notice of the fire to the Havana Fire Department and an urgent request to rescue occupants. With his hacking skills, Bruce saw that the computer contained some files marked "Experiment." Bruce opened them up.

There was a file on each of us with current pictures, as well as pictures of Paul and Evan. It was in Spanish. Santana glanced at the contents but there wasn't time for discussion. Santana briefly translated some of the details to me. The file discussed the Pentagon's use of us and Paul, how Evan had worked to find the best approach to take control of the minds of independent thinkers, what we and others had been put through and what our reaction was. Our little group had withstood all the attempts for mind control. Evan and others had queried whether the government would find it necessary to put those immune to mind control into concentration camps or execute them.

"Are there any flash drives you can copy the files onto?" I asked.

"I don't see any," Bruce said. "I'm emailing them to myself."

Jimmy looked for flash drives while Santana continued looking at the screen.

While getting evidence was important, the fear of being cooked ran through me. Images of helpless lobsters came to my mind. We needed to get out fast. Santana and Bruce looked through the computer room as Abigail, Shannon and I continued to search for a way out.

The fire had spread below the main floor and the staircase closest to our holding room was starting to catch fire. The flames had burned through the door to the other known exit as well. With Shannon in the lead and Abigail and me following, we ran to see if there was a safe exit on the other side, past our basement holding room. As we did so, part of the staircase closest to our former cell started to collapse and almost hit Abigail, I pushed her out of the way past the stairs as I tripped. The whole staircase collapsed and I found myself hit by falling wood. I was trapped.

# CHAPTER 69

Abigail and Shannon started trying to pull boards off me. Fortunately, those boards weren't on fire, yet. Shannon called for Santana, Bruce and Jimmy to help. I could hear their footsteps moving quickly out of the other room.

"¡Dios Mio!" Santana yelled, coming to help Abigail uncover me. He ripped the boards off of me with a strength and speed I didn't know he had and started to carry me as Jimmy and Bruce rushed through the area.

"I want to see if I can stand."

He put me down. I was unsteady, injured, probably badly bruised. But I was able to put weight on my legs.

"Gracias a dios!" he exclaimed. "You mean everything to me."

"Be careful, Summer. I need you in my life, too," Shannon said.

"Later," Jimmy urged. "Survival trumps warm fuzzies."

We were all on the opposite side of the staircase from the computer room. All except for Diego. He seemed to have disappeared. The wood I had been rescued from was blazing. We were cut off from the computer room and from the exits we had entered through a little earlier. We continued on away from the only exits we knew of. I hoped

Diego had found another way out. Personally, I was having trouble moving. I leaned against Santana.

Suddenly, through the flames burst Diego. His sleeve caught on fire. Santana and Bruce took off their shirts and tried to beat out the fire on Diego's arm as he removed his shirt. They succeeded, but the burns looked like third degree and covered most of his left arm.

There was a keyed door at the end of the corridor. Santana pulled a wire out of his pocket. "I got it from the computer room—just in case we needed to break out of something again."

He wedged it into the lock. It wasn't strong enough. He doubled it, dropped it to the floor and stomped on the wire to fold and shape it exactly how he wanted. He tried it, again.

"Next time I have to break out of a burning building, I'm bringing you," I said.

The flames were coming this way. Worse than the flames were the heat and the smoke, which were making it hard to see and breathe. It felt as if my lungs were searing, even though we were covering our mouths and noses. We were all holding it together as best we could.

Diego had slunk down to the floor, seemingly in pain. I hoped we wouldn't have to carry him. Bruce and Jimmy started kicking at the door with no results as Santana tried to avoid getting kicked while still working on the lock. After what seemed like an eternity, but what was probably only a few minutes, Santana got the lock opened.

Through the other side of the door was a staircase going down. It was cement and the area looked unfinished and had a dank smell. But it was cooler. Jimmy helped Diego up while Santana helped steady me. We went down and found a tunnel. As the seven of us walked, we continued our discussions.

"As long as this leads to somewhere safe and not to a morgue with the bodies of people previously kept in that room, I'm cool," Jimmy said.

"The way things have been going, it's probably the morgue," I responded.

"The scream. I still wonder if the couple who picked us up, who left the door open, were harmed or—"

Shannon didn't finish it as we all knew she would have ended it with the word "dead."

"Hard to tell. I hope not. Maybe they got out," I said. "A lot of people have died. A lot of teens have died, not to mention the grave-yard of little kids. There was no way to the upstairs. If they were on our side, I'd hate to have their deaths on my conscience, too."

"We didn't start the fire," Santana responded. "You have nothing to feel guilty about."

"After you left us at the border, I went online and found videos of sex-trafficking victims who talked of Satanic sacrifices. One girl stated that, as she was being raped, kids were being slaughtered all around her," Shannon reported to us.

"There are reports of lunatics getting a high from dead bodies," Jimmy added.

"Necrophiliacs. There was a case involving a guy who preferred raping dead bodies," Shannon said. "He was declared sane."

"The stories from Pizzagate were chilling. Supposedly, some of the leaders think they can extend their lives by drinking the blood of terri-fied children," Abigail stated. "Pizzagate was not about a pizza parlor."

I shivered. Maybe that's what we were. Sheep, being fattened up in that room for the slaughter. But this was Cuba. I hoped our captors weren't into that.

"It's hard to know what to believe or who to trust anymore," I said. "All I know is that they were torturing and brainwashing us at the camp. The purpose behind those camps has no rational relationship to turning us into upstanding citizens or academic geniuses. What did you learn there, Abigail?"

"What it feels like to be eaten alive."

"I learned what it's like to be beaten with a chain and choked," Santana said.

"I learned what it is like to be gang attacked and have a noose put around my neck," Bruce joined in.

"Wait. What they did to Jamie, they did to you?"

"I stood there for twenty-four hours, making every effort not to move."

"Those people are really sick," Shannon said.

"No wonder they don't want any witnesses," Diego remarked with a pained voice.

Shannon continued, "I read the testimonials of kids who had been tortured in the various camps and Gulag schools. There were some horrible accounts from Tranquility Bay and several of the other so-called schools. There was also a movie put together by two people who got their son back with his head smashed in. Those parents are going to feel guilty for the rest of their lives."

"Guilty? How does that compare to how their son felt having his head smashed in at a place his parents paid for him to be at?" I asked.

"I'm glad my parents don't have a hundred thousand in extra change sitting around to pay for my torture," Shannon replied.

"I've met your parents," I said. "They actually like you. If any of the parents who sent their kids to those camps were unselfish enough and loved their kids enough to personally help them through their issues, those places would be empty."

"Imagine parents teaching their kids values, instead of pawning their responsibilities off on strangers," Shannon blurted.

"Exactly," I agreed.

"I remember at school, a lot of kids wished they were as connected and powerful as your family, but I was always glad I had my parents," Shannon said.

"And I would have given anything to be part of your family," I told her.

"I don't know your family, but I already wish I had yours instead of mine," Abigail told Shannon.

"My mom would have been cool with your green hair," Shannon responded. "I saw those pictures. You looked great that way. I don't think it would have looked good on me, but on you, it was sensational."

"I did it for a lark, but then I really liked it."

"You'd look great with any hair color, even if you had purple hair with orange polka dots," Bruce told Abigail, putting his arm around her.

"True love," Shannon commented.

"Too bad, we couldn't get a copy of that file," Santana lamented.

"I emailed it to a new email address I set up a while back for myself and to Jimmy," Bruce said. "And to an email address Diego gave me. Of course, if we don't survive to open the emails, there's no record."

"So, I guess those people who picked us up were connected with the camp and we were some kind of experiment. I heard Evan say something about the experiment when he thought I was asleep," I related.

The tunnel was long. We got to a fork. "I wonder which way," Bruce said.

"You go to the right and we'll go to the left," Santana suggested.

"I'll go with you," Diego said to Santana.

"Shannon and Jimmy, why don't you go with Bruce and Abigail, then," I said. I didn't fully trust Diego. If something funny happened, I wanted my friends to survive while I had Santana's back.

After we parted, I started in on Diego. "So, you were told to make contact with Santana at the airport, right?"

"Yes."

"And the person who told you knew we hadn't died in the plane crash or the collapse of the prison."

"Yes. But I wasn't sure if I believed it until I saw you."

"The bad guys were waiting for us, there, too," Santana commented.

"Waiting?" Diego asked him.

"I mean, the nurse, the guy on the runway, the unmarked plane. They all knew we were coming."

"Unless they got ahold of your friend's flight schedule and set up their own trap for you. I know what you are getting at. I had never seen that guy on the runway before."

We didn't say anything.

"Look, I know it looks suspicious. I am a reporter who wants to get good stories. I don't create them. I think what they did to you guys is repulsive."

I realized that anyone who suspected we were alive probably thought Shannon might be coming there to meet us. The flight information could have been hacked. Someone may have realized we had been driving Shannon's car in Mexico. Maybe multiple people put two and two together. Then again, Diego's foreknowledge was suspicious and we had no way to be sure—unless Diego pulled a gun on us or something.

The tunnel ended in another staircase. We followed it up. There was another door at the top. It was locked, of course. Santana started to pick the lock.

"Despite the circumstances, I'd really like to get that interview with you and your friends," Diego said.

"If we survive, I don't have a problem with that," I responded.

"Got it," Santana almost hooted, opening the door.

We looked out. We were in the woods. It looked like part of the route we had taken in Diego's van to the location.

"We better find the others," I said.

"Let me go get my other phone and my cameras," Diego requested.

"We need to stick together," Santana insisted.

"My van can't be far. We can all go, and you can make sure I don't do anything improper. We'll document anything that happens from here by camera."

I looked at Santana and he nodded.

A short time later, we were at the van. Diego put on a new shirt, picked up his video camera, changed video cards and handed Santana the video camera. He pulled out his still camera and switched cards on that as well. He put the old cards, along with the copies he had previously made, in a box with a combination lock under the carpet in his van. "Evidence of the plane and the guy on the runway," he told us.

We went back down into the tunnel and headed towards the split. As we rounded a corner, Jimmy came running towards us. "You have to see this."

We followed Jimmy for about half a mile of tunnel and came to an underground road, where we joined the others. The seven of us started walking along it to see where it would go. A few miles in, we rested at the side of the road. There were other tunnels opening onto the road as well.

"This looks large enough to protect all two million Havana inhabitants in the event of a nuclear war. They might not have much room to move around, but I bet this is large enough to fit them all," Santana said.

"But it's not deep enough for the occupants to survive a direct hit," Bruce noted, hearing the last of our conversation. "Unless there is an under-layer."

"I'm sure Cuba's current leaders would do what it took to protect the people," Diego said. "The philosophy of Cuban socialism is based on people taking care of each other."

"I've heard some negative things about Cuba, too. Supposedly, we were treated better than the other prisoners. There have been accusations about human rights abuses in Cuban prisons."

"And there aren't human rights abuses in your country's prisons?" Diego asked.

"According to Michael Moore's movie *Where to Invade Next*, the Norwegian prisons are the ones to be in," Santana said with a smile.

"Jimmy picked up a copy of Moore's video and showed it to me and Summer," Shannon told him.

"Norway was where the guards sang 'We are the World' to the maximum-security prisoners," Santana recalled. "Better country for stealing a car."

"Imagine a world where all the prisoners are treated like they are there," I said. "This is what my dad should be fighting for. Instead, like Senator Madstein, he is pro-death penalty and pro lock-em-up. He griped to me about California's moratorium but he didn't do so publicly."

"My dad claims to oppose private prisons," Santana said.

"But then he put his own son in a private prison camp," Abigail responded. "I wonder if it's day or night outside."

"Day," Diego said. "They didn't take my digital watch."

"Does your watch have high-speed internet?" Jimmy asked.

"What? No."

"You need a new watch," I said.

"Those things can track you," Bruce pointed out.

"How was Tiffany when you left?" I asked Shannon.

"She wanted to come. We told her that someone had to be left behind to tell the story. If she doesn't hear from one of us soon, she just might show up here."

"And then that nice couple, if they are alive, or another one can kidnap her and trap us all in another underground bunker that is catching fire," I quipped.

"Okay, now the road is splitting into more roads going in three different directions," Bruce observed.

"Roads these wide are probably long. Walking would take too long to go to the end of each direction and come back," Jimmy said.

"Diego, do you have a quarter?" Santana asked.

"Not a quarter, but—" Diego pulled out some coins.

"Heads, we keep going straight, tails we angle right and on end, we go left."

Heads. We continued on ahead.

"I understand they have a giant underground city below Denver," Shannon said.

Diego looked questioningly at her.

"The American elites have a grid of underground cities. I'm invited, or at least I was," Santana noted.

"Me too, or at least my dad was. I heard him talking about it to Senator Madstein. I think he still has access to one in California." After saying that, I realized that if my dad were to take any kids with him, it would probably just be my brother. "In the case of a nuclear attack, the elites plan to go underground and leave everyone else on top."

"Nice folks," Shannon said. "No wonder they don't care if their insanity wipes all humanity off the face of the planet."

"Remember that Weird Al Yankovic song, 'Christmas at Ground Zero?'" Santana asked.

"One of my favorite Christmas songs," Jimmy said.

Together, we started singing the lyrics. Diego looked at us as if we were crazy and then smiled.

"I just hope this road doesn't lead to Guantanamo," Shannon commented.

Santana and I looked at each other and laughed.

"I hope Mom and the others are safe," I said.

"Emily was so darling," Shannon remembered. "She really looks up to you."

"It's kind of neat having a younger sister," I said. "I feel like I've got a real family now. You're part of that family. You're my sister, too. When my dad was insane, you helped me stay sane." For a moment we got more serious. Diego was talking to Jimmy as I quietly said to Shannon, "When they arrested us, Mom and Emily were going to put the money you gave us in a safe. But the dog started barking and before they got around to it, the police arrested us. They got away, but if they had put it in the safe, the government would have confiscated it. I'd like to get that back to you so I don't have to worry about it."

"Hey, sisters, right?" Shannon said. "In all the time I was worried about you, I never once thought. 'Oh darn, there goes my money.'"

"I never had a friend like you," Abigail said to Shannon. "It would have helped."

Shannon put her arms around Abigail. "Now you do."

Santana came over to us while Jimmy, Diego and Bruce were having a discussion about their estimates of the geography of what might be above.

"I keep thinking that, if Alejandro contacted his uncle, people are looking for us."

"Maybe we should get to the top and find our way back," I suggested.

We saw some lights moving towards us up ahead. The problem with this road was there was no easy place to hide. There was some kind of maintenance area to our right. We ducked in there.

After that, we continued walking for what seemed like hours until we got to some kind of doorway in the wall. There were a couple of mini electric cars in parking places right next to it.

Santana quickly had one up and running.

"The son of a Congressman, a car thief," Shannon remarked.

"Be glad," I said.

"You want to keep walking?" Santana asked.

Diego got into the back. It was a four-seater and yet we managed to squeeze all seven of us in, awkwardly. Naturally, Santana was driving.

The vehicle was relatively open and so there was no place to hide when we passed a car going the other way. I had hoped the driver just assumed we belonged there until his vehicle made a U-turn and came after us. We made our own U-turn and aimed straight at it, passing it at the last minute. The car pulled over and then turned around and came after us. It looked as if it wasn't traveling any faster than our vehicle.

When we got back to the intersection, we turned left and followed that road. A second car seemed to come out of nowhere to follow us.

Eventually, we came to an underground parking lot with a lot of vehicles. We sped through the parking lot into a tunnel that sloped down. It led to two side other tunnels and we moved into one, hoping our pursuers would go another way. Around a curve in the tunnel, we got out. Santana sent the car continuing further down the tunnel, hoping our tails would follow the car and not us.

There was a staircase next to where we got out, and we started moving upwards, climbing several flights of stairs. Doors without handles on our side appeared to open onto the staircase, probably emergency exits. When we got to the top, there was another lock. Santana started to work on it as I watched for anyone who might be following. I was concerned about an alarm, but if there was one, it was silent.

When we got through, I was in awe. We were in some kind of museum. We began to walk through it.

"There are bound to be cameras everywhere," Santana advised.

In the museum were exhibits mostly of the revolution that had put Fidel Castro into power. There were pictures of Fidel Castro and Che Guevara. "This is the Museo de Revolucion," Diego told us.

As we passed an exhibit of a radio transmitter owned by Che, we heard a voice yell, "¡Aquí!" We turned and saw a female security guard pointing at us. "¡Ustedes se deteienen!"

# CHAPTER 70

We ran. I wasn't sure how far we ran, but we were being followed by multiple people. Nobody was shooting at us. That was good.

I hoped my athletic background would help my speed, but the guards were rushing at us fast.

Diego pointed to a staircase. We took it down. Someone was coming up from below, and we were cornered. Santana jumped over the side of one of the banisters onto the staircase below and we followed, doing likewise, bypassing our approachers. I could see Diego hurting from hitting his scorched arm against the rail.

Outside in the fresh air, we saw an engine of a Lockheed U-2 that had been shot down over Cuba during the Missile Crisis. So, there was some precedent for the plane they had shot down earlier in the day. We ran past a Jeep Willys confiscated from Baptista's army during the revolution.

"This whole area used to be part of the Presidential grounds," Diego informed us.

I wondered if the underground roadways were new or if they had played a part in history. We made it around the building to the Granma Memorial, which housed the yacht Che Guevara and Fidel and Raul

Castro had taken from Mexico to Cuba for the revolution. Guards rushed in from all sides to surround us. We were trapped.

More than two guards a piece took each of us towards a police van. They were on the radio. For some reason, they did not put us in handcuffs and they did not confiscate our camera equipment. However, we were placed in the back of the van.

The van started down a road but didn't make it too far. An explosion rocked the van, tumbling it on its side. I felt dizzy. It was a moment before I could open my eyes. The vehicle was mangled. The explosion and crash had knocked the rear door off its hinges.

Santana pulled me towards the door as Bruce and Abigail, also, exited. Shannon and Jimmy were already outside. Diego was crawling out. His injured arm looked even worse than before. The gas was leaking.

From the condition of the road, it appeared as if something had exploded in the street in front of us. Shots rang out. We ducked behind what was left of the van, moving low alongside what had been the top of the van. I moved towards the front and saw that the driver and officer beside him were unconscious.

"We've got to get them out," I said.

Jimmy returned to the open back for the camera equipment and started using the video camera to smash the windshield out. He and Santana dragged the driver out as Bruce and Diego freed the other officer. We lifted them away as a slew of shots barely missed us and the van exploded.

We ducked behind the largest of the debris, though some small particles hit me and the fumes were almost overwhelming. It was difficult to see around the flames and exploded debris, but I could hear cheers.

I moved to the side and saw that people had overpowered the gunman. Diego reached down and picked up something that had fallen next to the policeman Jimmy had rescued. But I didn't see what.

"¡Obtenga ambulancia para oficialies!" Santana shouted at the crowd.

As we took off, someone yelled, "A dónde ustedes van."

"¡Para ayuda!" Santana yelled back. Nobody tried to stop us, maybe thinking we were with the policemen we had rescued. The crowd was all focused on the bomb-throwing gunman.

In the background, I could hear an ambulance.

"How badly is your equipment damaged," I asked Diego as we moved behind cars parked near the road.

"It doesn't look good,"

"I might be able to fix it," Bruce said.

"If we can make it back to my van, I have other cameras."

In a nearby parking lot, we found an old Chevy that Santana said would be easy to hotwire. He was right, and I was happy there was no alarm. It was much roomier than the electric vehicle we had been in on the road below.

---

As we got Diego back to his van, he had a troubled expression on his face. "There is one more thing," Diego said. "It doesn't make any sense to me, but someone who was with my boss said something about winter as if winter was something significant."

"Alonzo. He's the one who sent Diego," I told Santana. I threw double fists of excitement into the air. "He's alright."

"Does that mean I still get the exclusive?"

"Sure thing," Santana said, seemingly relieved. "Right now, we're all exhausted. Give us your cell number, and we'll arrange to call you in the morning, that is if we are alive and not prisoners."

"How about I drive you to wherever you have to go? Getting caught in a stolen car won't endear you to the authorities."

"And he could be in danger from whoever is after us. He's a witness now," Bruce pointed out.

"We need to get Rosa's car," I said.

"Take us to the airport, and then Abigail and Bruce can guide you to where we are going."

When we got to the airport, the press was all around, taking pictures of the scene where the cab was blown. Reporters from international networks were standing around. I turned to Diego. "You might not be the first to report on this, but you will have the best report."

"I'll follow you out of here."

Santana drove me, Shannon and Jimmy back to Rosa's.

"I've been thinking about how those people didn't lock the door back in the room and how the officers at the museum didn't cuff us. That has to be against protocol. Why?" Santana asked.

"Maybe they've finally realized we were the good guys," I surmised. "It would be nice to know if that couple is still alive. Rosa's is going to be crowded tonight. How did they know to attack the police van?"

"Police radios," Jimmy surmised.

"Diego seems alright," Santana remarked.

Shannon chimed in. "Diego told me he couldn't imagine what you had gone through and he wanted to let the world know what heroes you are."

"That's the kind of reporter we want doing our story," I said.

"Do you think they put a tracking device on Diego's van?" Jimmy asked.

"They?"

"Well, it was parked for hours near the place where they tried to burn us out earlier."

Santana pulled off the road and stopped. The van pulled in behind us.

Santana went back and spoke with Diego. I saw them grabbing a flashlight and checking around the exterior of the van and under the hood. Jimmy got out and joined them. I couldn't resist joining the search. Shannon followed me out. I remembered that Diego had had the van locked when he wasn't driving it or getting into it, but they could have used a Slim Jim.

In his inspection, Diego opened the gas tank and used some kind of small curved mirror he pulled out of his vehicle. He put a wire down the opening and pulled out some kind of object.

Santana turned to me as I asked, "Is that a tracking device?"

"It isn't just a tracking device. It includes some explosive caps and is prepped to go off on a remote signal."

"They got all that into the gas tank?"

"It doesn't take that much to set off a gas explosion. Remote control devices can be pretty small these days," Bruce related.

Diego looked at Jimmy. "You just saved us all. Thank you."

# CHAPTER 71

After the van was re-inspected both inside and out and nothing further was found, Jimmy parked the van under a tree and pulled off the license plates. We inspected Rosa's car, next. When we decided it was clean, we took off in the two vehicles.

As we drove up to the farmhouse, Hope, Emily and Alejandro raced out to greet us. Emily practically tackled me with a hug as I hopped out of the car. Hope gave me a doggie hug with her front legs. I swooped down to pet him as I saw Mom rush out, visibly fighting back tears. Shannon joined us in a group hug.

Alejandro suggested we park the vehicles in the barn, which Santana and Diego did as Alonzo and Rosa came out of the farmhouse. Everyone was excited to greet our friends.

"We need to get that treated," Alonzo urged, looking at Diego's arm. "Miguel said he had a lot of faith in you. I see you brought the kids back safe and sound."

We all laughed.

"We were held prisoner, almost burned to death, were captured by the Cuban police and barely got out of a police van that was knocked over by an explosion before its gas tank exploded. That was before we discovered they had put an explosive tracking device in Diego's van. Typical day," I said and then realized that my comments probably scared my mom. "But we're basically fine."

"Don't forget that we were shot at by a guy who was hit by an airplane and almost struck by a missile from an unmarked plane but were rescued by the Cubana Air Guard. And, of course, there was also the car chase," Santana added.

"And for an encore, we're going to fight some supervillain on the top of an airplane in mid-air," Bruce joked, seemingly referencing *Octopussy* or some other superspy movie.

My mom had a look of horror on her face.

I put my arm around her. "We're here, safe."

"Don't worry, Katherine," Alonzo said, "If these kids survived all that, they've got skills Interpol could use."

Diego let out a breath and dropped his head and shoulders. "I'm ready for a rest. I'm exhausted."

"I emailed myself some files our captors had about us and the camp," Bruce informed them. "I think they might be connected or why would they have that information?"

"It's quite possible the NSA or CIA has an operation here, trying to unseat our President. There has been suspicion about that for quite some time. The CIA operations are more visible in Venezuela," Diego imparted.

"I know. That's where the CIA kidnapped a prior President, started riots and shot people trying to vote," I recalled from having read reports from journalist Greg Palast.

"So, you know," Alonzo said.

I nodded.

"The only person I've shared specific details about your situation with is my friend in the Cuban Government," Alonzo related. "He has a full copy of Paul's Diary. I've been trying to reach him. Right now, he's having a bit of an emergency, and I'm to be calling him back tomorrow."

We went inside and relaxed. Rosa had prepared a large dinner.

"It's always nice to eat food we don't have to test for poison," I said.

---

Dinner turned into an opportunity for further discussion. "When this is over, we should set up our own detective agency," Shannon suggested.

"Scotland Yard move over," my mom joked. "But I think I'd prefer you going back to being normal teenagers for a while."

"I think I'd like that too. But I don't want to be five hundred miles away from Santana."

"And I don't want to be three thousand miles away from Bruce," Abigail added. "And besides, I'd rather kill Daddy dearest than live with him."

Diego looked oddly at her.

"Her father is the Secretary of Defense," I told him.

"I didn't recognize you without your green hair."

"I'm getting it back!"

"Not only is he bombing other countries, but he sent his own daughter to be tortured. Not a nice guy," I said.

"There's a reason the U.S. doesn't join the International Criminal Court," Santana noted.

"Right, all our government's leaders would be in prison," I pointed out.

"They would be lucky that the ICC doesn't support executions for mass murderers," Santana added.

"We still don't know if they simply added our names to the passenger list of a plane they crashed or if the crash didn't happen at all. If a plane did crash, then they probably killed a lot of innocent people without batting an eye," I lamented.

"My daddy is good at that," Abigail acknowledged.

"My horrible monster, to put it kindly, Dad also sent me to be tortured. I wouldn't be surprised if he's involved in much worse," I said.

"Mine too," Santana joined back in.

"Both my parents agreed to it, "Emily said.

Bruce added, "Both of mine, too."

"There's always the Damen approach," Shannon recalled.

"Damen?" my mom asked.

"Damen was a kid who was raped by a dad who had full custody. At first, Damon ran away, and women who cared passed him back and forth. He even did an interview with a *Fox News* reporter, Martin Burns, while Damen was in hiding. Burns later died mysteriously. You can go online and see Damen's videos or go to his site, if it's still up. *Savingdamen.com.*"

"I think I heard about him," my mom said. "Didn't his mother form an organization called 'Safe Kids International?'"

"Yes," Shannon went on. "Anyway, after he turned sixteen, his mother went to a brothel in Vegas and offered them two hundred dollars to have one of their girls marry him on paper."

"And did that work?"

"They turned her down. But on her way out, one of the girls working there offered to do it. But she never actually charged the mother anything. After the paper marriage, Damen was emancipated and got a paper annulment. Then, he got to live with his mother until he went to UCLA. Damen is a top spokesperson for the rights of women to keep their children safe from abusers."

"I would be fine with marrying Summer," Santana said as I blushed. "But I wouldn't be fine with annulling it. I want to be with her *por siempre y para siempre*. Forever and always," he translated the last.

"I think you are a little young for marriage. That should be a last resort," my mom reproached.

"I'm not going back to living with Dad."

I noticed Alejandro taking Emily's hand softly and the two of them looking goo-goo eyed at each other.

"No. Even if we have to stay in Cuba, you aren't going back to live with him," my mom stated.

"Would Abigail and I need a parent's permission to marry? She's sixteen and I'm seventeen."

"In Cuba, girls can get married at sixteen with a parent's permission," Alonzo told Bruce. "The minimum age, otherwise, is usually eighteen."

"Could someone adopt us?" Abigail asked. "Or do they allow emancipation here?"

"Your custodial parents and your government will try to get you back, but I think you all have an excellent case for asylum."

"They'll want us back so they can finish the job of killing us," Abigail pointed out.

"After I run the story, public opinion will be against them," Diego contended.

"The U.S. Government is good at suppressing information. The power elite owns the news media in our country," Santana reminded him.

"We may have to go to the Indy press," I added.

"I'll report on it," Diego said.

"Daddy will probably order you Assanged," Abigail told him. "And they'll overthrow whatever government you take asylum in."

"If you kids can live dangerously, so can I. The truth needs to get out there."

"*Wikileaks* always had a one hundred record of accuracy and yet they completely demonized it," I pointed out. "Our leaders are a bunch of psychopaths."

"And they gave me a rough time about partying and dying my hair green while daddy dearest has been bombing and killing people and babies, newborn babies, every day."

"If other kids are like you, I can see why they have camps to brainwash and torture them. They want to stop you from fixing the world," Diego stated.

"But by the time our generation turns into adults, most will have been brainwashed in educational institutions, designed to stop them from thinking. The Gulag camps and schools are for those who resist the educational system's brainwashing," I noted.

Alejandro and Emily nodded several times during our conversation but mostly seemed to be having trouble keeping their eyes off each other. I felt like a proud big sister, watching her little sister's first romance.

Hope was happy, partially because I kept giving him servings of Rosa's dinner. Rosa's food was delicious as usual and perfect for my vegan tastes. I had several servings myself. I noticed that Rosa was speaking more English now. Immersion worked both ways.

---

Alonzo and Diego spent the night. The guys all stayed in the living room and we girls all shared the spare bedroom. It was like a big slumber party. I had missed Shannon so much. The next morning at breakfast, Diego suggested that he start filming our stories. Alonzo suggested that he include information from Paul's diary.

"Diary?" Diego asked.

"The son of the guy running the program was one of the campers. He was the one who saved us that last night, but then he died. Before he went to save the others, he slipped us his diary," I informed him.

"Mind if I look at it?" Diego asked.

Santana nodded.

"Sure," I said. But I intended to have one or more of us watching at all times to make sure nothing happened to the diary.

Diego spent the morning looking through it. "This is horrifying—the torture, the brainwashing. You say this is happening at the other camps?"

"Yes," I acknowledged. "The main difference was who was at our camp. There were rich kids at the other ones but, at ours, the campers were connected to government influencers, government leaders."

"Do you recall someone named John DeVeaux?" Diego inquired as he focused on an entry in the book.

"He was a camper. We found his body with a bullet hole," I told him.

"It says he was shot, trying to stop a friend of his from being put into a box."

"Charlie," Santana informed him.

"According to this diary, Charlie threatened the counselors later when he discovered the body and was shot, too. In both cases, a silencer was used. It doesn't say whether Charlie survived. His dad is a vice president of Nanopharm."

"I hope, at least, Charlie survived," I said. "They were both nice. A lot of the teens who died there were really nice people,"

"John's father is with the World Bank. He and some of the other parents might care."

"If they cared, they wouldn't have sent their kids there in the first place," I told him.

"Did you tell him about the graveyard?" Alonzo asked.

"Graveyard?"

"Does Paul mention the little kids' camp in there?" I inquired.

"The one where leaders are having sex with kids and then being blackmailed?" He had apparently seen information about it in the diary.

"We came across a graveyard of the remains of a lot of little kids. Dead."

"Oh, honey," my mom said, solemnly.

Diego closed his eyes. "That must have been horrible."

He leafed through the contents. "With this diary—" he started to say.

"How can we prove Paul even wrote it?" I asked.

"They could do a handwriting comparison," Santana pointed out.

"Paul's dad will block any handwriting comparison," I lamented.

"Maybe his mother will help," my mom suggested.

"But they will try to refute it anyway. And the videos were probably lost when the camp burned down."

"If only we had irrefutable proof," Mom commented.

"Proving they faked your deaths will go far," Diego said, optimistically.

"Especially bringing out the phony mom at your funeral, Summer," Alonzo remarked.

"They'll claim they got the roster wrong and that she was planning to say 'stepmother' and misspoke." I knew my dad's expertise at lying.

"Was your dad dating her?" my mom asked.

"No. Not when I left. I never saw her before she was on TV."

"Then, she is either acting—" Alonzo started to say.

"Or his next victim," Santana finished for him.

"Someday, I'd like you to tell me what he did to you," Alonzo told my mother. "Your former husband is a terrible, terrible person. If he did this to your daughter, what he did to get you to leave him must have been unthinkable."

"He claimed that being taken by ambulance to the hospital after one of the beatings was alienation. He got an order preventing me from seeing my own daughter again."

"That's something we've got to fix," Alonzo assured her. "In your country, men have forgotten how to be men. They have feigned support for the women's movement as an excuse for horrible crimes against women. As real men, it's our job to be your protectors, even protecting you from ourselves if necessary."

Mom smiled. I was happy that she and Alonzo had hit it off so well. If he meant his words, he was one of the good guys. After what my dad did to her, she deserved happiness. I liked him more each time I saw him, but I still felt a tinge of loss over having to share the mom I had just gotten back.

"If we take them to the graveyard, that will be proof," Bruce said, as he and Abigail sat down beside us.

"These guys are government contractors. The moment we go public, they'll have teams of people moving the remains and making it look like a golf course," Abigail responded. "You haven't seen my dad's friends in operation."

"Maybe we have," I said, thinking back to the unmarked plane.

"So, it's pretty much our word against theirs," Santana scoffed.

"With all the trouble they took to fake your deaths, your being alive will add credibility to your information," Diego suggested.

"Unless they claim we faked our own deaths," I said, "As part of our terrorist plot."

"What about all the attempts on our children's lives that have happened since they've been here?" Mom asked.

"Your government will deny all that," Alonzo said. "Most of what your country has said about my government is lies, obvious lies, and nobody calls them on it."

"My government calls anyone who questions their official stories a 'conspiracy theorist.'" I told him. "Even though every honest top scientist in the U.S. says 9/11 was a controlled demolition, the government has demonized anyone asking questions, even the families of the victims."

"My government has courage. I'm sure things will work out in the end," Alonzo tried to reassure us.

"Until ours takes it over," Abigail warned. "Or bombs it."

"What's this?" Diego asked, rubbing his forefinger against the inside of the front cover of the diary.

I touched it. There was an unevenness as if there were groves between the cover and something underneath. That's when I noticed how thick it was.

"May I?" Diego asked.

Santana and I nodded.

Diego used his fingernail to try to cut through the edge of the cover. His nail wasn't strong enough. He picked up a knife and carefully wedged it through the inner front cover paper and through some tape underneath that was further securing that cover in place until the bottom edge was free. Then he pulled it off. Underneath were SD cards, more than a dozen of them.

Underneath those were micro-SD cards. He found similar cards layered inside the back cover. By the time we finished counting, the cards numbered over eighty.

# CHAPTER 72

We backed them up onto Alonzo's computer, coming close to filling his disk. Diego also copied them onto large storage flash drives, as well, and gave us each multiple copies. It took the rest of the day to finish this.

Diego had to report back to his station and took Jimmy to another location where Diego was to text his boss that he had a major story and wouldn't be in until the next day. Diego used the satellite feed in his van to upload condensed images of the contents of the cards to his cloud and to his and Jimmy's emails. Diego didn't want his message to be traced back to the farm if it was tracked. Abigail and Bruce decided to hang out in the barn for some alone time while the pictures and videos were being backed up onto Alejandro's computer.

The pictures were hard to look at. Occasionally glimpsing at what the computer was copying, we could see that Paul had photographed, and in some cases videoed, the torture done at our camp. He also had pictures of top leaders in both parties with little kids. It appeared that he also managed to copy some of the videos the camp took for black-mail purposes onto some of the cards. His father may have put him there to spy on Claudio and Marco, but his conscience had forced him to find a way to expose his father's corruption.

I insisted on sending a copy to various indymedia reporters who had been the subject of censorship and attacks by our government. Alejandro sent them to several reliable sources without traces of our location to the whistle-blowing-organizations. His skills were on par with or even better than Bruce's. Our reason for sending them wasn't for political gain or money. We just wanted to let the world know what was happening to kids at these camps. Still, we knew the release might subject us to some risk from enforcement of bogus laws, like the Espionage Act, designed to punish whistleblowers.

"¡Mierda! ¡Dios Mio!" Santana swore as he watched the horrible pictures being uploaded to one of the more trusted sites.

"No wonder our leaders don't listen to the people," I said.

"With Evan's ties to the military-industrial complex and Big Pharma, they have to do his bidding or risk exposure and political ruin," Santana pointed out.

As the pictures from the little kids' camp went by on the screen, two stuck out.

"Mira al hijo de puta!"

"That was my dad!" I reacted. "So, he knew exactly what he was doing when he sent me there."

"I'm sorry, Summer," Alonzo said.

My mom was out of the room. I planned to tell her later, tactfully.

Santana gave me a hug.

"I recognized another picture," I quietly said. "Abigail's father."

Santana shook his head, clearly bothered by what he had seen.

Emily had gone quiet some time back and I noticed her complexion had turned white. "My dad's in there, too. How could he do that to some little kid?"

I went over and gave her a hug.

"No child should ever see their father in pictures like this," Alonzo told her.

Alejandro took Emily's hand. Rosa had Emily sit down next to her and put an arm around Emily. "Well, you've got a new home here and people who love you."

"Gracias," Emily said, tears in her eyes.

Alonzo went over to them, knelt, looked into Emily's eyes, and spoke softly. "And my brother and his wife love you too. If you decide to stay here, Juanita and Rosa will be fighting over who gets to adopt you. Besides, you're too pretty to have an ugly father like that guy."

"How would I ever run this farmhouse without this little angel?" Rosa asked. "Juanita will have to get her own little girl."

"Did you say your soon-to-be former dad is the chairman of the Council on Foreign Relations?" Alonzo asked Emily.

She nodded.

"They have been pushing wars for as long as I can remember," I said.

My mom came into the room with Shannon. Shannon instantly knew something was wrong. "What?" Shannon asked.

I went over and hugged my mom. "Daddy is so awful. I can't imagine what you went through. I'm so sorry for all those doubts I had about you during those years you were gone."

They glanced at the screen that was still flashing pictures of kids with various leaders. "He was there, wasn't he?" Mom asked.

I nodded. "The little kids' camp was close to our camp and run by the same people. He knew what he was sending me to and didn't care. Evan thought Paul would spy for him and must have insisted he help at both camps. No wonder he turned on his dad."

"Oh, honey, I'm so sorry. I should have disobeyed the order and grabbed you, run, and disappeared."

"They would have put out an AMBER alert and arrested you and made me live with him, anyway."

"Most AMBER alerts are women trying to rescue their children from abuse," Shannon said. "Mrs. Tanner, you wouldn't have had a chance."

"A top priority should be reforming your country's family law system so that kids don't have to go through what you and Santana and kids like you went through," Alonzo retorted, angrily, looking at me. "And if I ever get my hands on your dad after what he did to the two of you." He didn't finish but we could picture what he would have said.

When Abigail came into the house with one of the biggest smiles I had seen on her face, I didn't know quite how to tell her. This news was probably not going to make her feel any better. As tough as she came across, I knew she was hurting very badly and that the angry words were just a cover for a broken heart over her parents' treatment of her. I hugged her and held her hands. "You are my sister and I know you are hurting over what your parents did to you."

"You saw something."

"We were looking at pictures of the little kids' camp."

Abigail started to break down, crying. "I knew he was awful. If he doesn't think twice about killing kids, why would he think twice about screwing them?'

"My father and Emily's were also in those pictures."

"So, they knew they were sending us to be tortured. They must have wanted us tortured. I never want to see either of my parents again, ever." She turned to Alonzo. "Can you draw up papers to sever my family ties? Help me get emancipated or adopted by someone sane."

"I will do what I can. With what we've seen, there is no way my government would force you to go back to him."

Bruce walked in and instantly noticed the tears in Abigail's eyes. Santana whispered to him and he came over and held her.

---

When Jimmy and Diego got back, Diego informed us that some major checkpoints had been set up and cars were being examined coming into the area. "They were stopping a lot of people, and so it wasn't necessarily about us."

Jimmy and Diego had stayed off to the side to avoid the checkpoints, but had a good view and had seen checkpoints on several roads. "It's as if they are looking for someone coming in this general direction," Jimmy said.

Alonzo kept trying to call his friend, but his friend wasn't answering. Finally, his friend called back and said to sit tight until the next day. We hoped that things would not go crazy by then.

"Of course, I will keep them safe," Alonzo said to him. "Thank you for informing me."

"What is it?" I asked.

After the call, Alonzo turned to us. "He thinks you might still be in danger."

"From whom or rather which whom?" Santana asked.

"He didn't say."

Diego was disappointed that we had already sent pictures to other newsmen.

"By the time they verify everything, you'll have gotten your exclusive and if anything happens to us, the truth will come out anyway," I told him. "Besides, you have us, and they don't."

Later that evening, Juanita arrived to pick up Alejandro. "I managed to get around the checkpoints. I put some scratches on the car, but they were worth it."

Alejandro gave Emily a hug. "I don't want to leave them, Mom."

"Yo no quiero decirle a tu papa que te deje en peligro."

"She doesn't want his father to kill her," Santana related.

"You sure you'll be safe leaving?" Alonzo asked. "Do we know we can trust whoever is running those checkpoints?"

"I know where they are on the route. It shouldn't be a problem as long as I stay off the road, going by them."

That night, as we continued to work, we felt relaxed and safe. Suddenly, gunfire erupted from various directions in the distance. We had no way of knowing whether it was the good guys firing at the bad guys or the bad guys firing at the good guys. Juanita suggested we take refuge in the cellar.

"What about you?" I asked as she and Alonzo chose to stay up above.

"We'll deal with whoever comes. Someone needs to be a lookout. It will be suspicious if Rosa isn't here and I can't risk anything happening to her." Alonzo showed us that he had a gun.

"I thought the Government had disarmed the people and that nobody was allowed to have guns here, outside of the government and obviously the bad guys," Santana commented.

"When I gave my friend in government the copy of the diary, he handed me this for protection. It is a rare exception."

As my mom started to go down into the cellar, she gave Alonzo a warm hug. "Please be careful," she said.

"I will," he replied softly.

Diego was the last of us to go down into the cellar. We had already hidden the diary, cards, and some copies in various places. Diego brought a copy into the cellar.

I looked at Mom, "Are you thinking of settling down here in Cuba?"

"I'll go where you do."

"You really care about Alonzo, don't you?" I asked.

"Very much. But you are my priority."

I hugged her. "You deserve happiness, too."

"You like him, too, don't you?" she asked.

"He's great. When we were down and out in prison, it was Alonzo who believed in us and helped us. So, yeah, I like him a lot."

"I'm sorry, I couldn't come to you."

"Didn't we have this discussion? By staying away, you paved the way for our freedom. I know it was hard for you, but we wouldn't be alive and well and in possession of all that evidence but for how you handled everything."

She hugged me, again.

"I've gotten to dislike basements," Bruce said.

"It's probably the sitting duck feeling," Santana commented.

"Remember the last time we were in a cellar," Bruce reminded us.

# CHAPTER 73

"Maybe we should go for the fields," Jimmy said.

"Or for the road," Diego suggested.

"It might take Alonzo and Rosa off the hook as they wouldn't be protecting us," I noted.

Diego knocked on the cellar door. Alonzo opened it. "We took a vote," Abigail said. "We're leaving."

"We wouldn't want to bring any harm to Rosa," I said.

"Using me as an excuse?" Rosa asked. "Stop!"

"The last time we were in a basement, they burned down the place. If they set Rosa's place on fire, we'll be trapped and she'll lose her farm."

Alonzo nodded. "Okay, I know a place where you can hide the van and still watch the farmhouse from a distance."

Rosa gave him some binoculars. "I use these to look for coyotes."

Alonzo was reluctant to leave Rosa. "I'm going to lead the way and then come back. She shouldn't be alone."

Alonzo and my mom led in his car and the rest of us took the van into a grove of Sierra Maesta pine trees and several palm trees on a hill overlooking the farm. "The royal palm is my country's national tree. The Sierra Maestra pines are endemic to Cuba," Diego told us.

Our parking spot had a good view of the farm but was hidden by the trees.

"This really is a beautiful country," I said, getting out of the van. "I know it has a ways to go with respect to human rights, but my country, now, has even further to go."

"We're trying. For instance, quite some time back, Raul Castro declared that there would be two Presidential terms of five years and the country is sticking to that. I've been covering elections and they are much more accurate than—never mind," Alonzo said.

"I wish we had real elections in our country," I lamented. "And real organic farming, not the fake organic farming that includes glyphosate and oil fracking wastewater."

"As informed as you are, it's crazy that you don't have the vote," my mom commented.

"Do you think Rosa will be alright?" I asked.

"At least, we're where we can see the farm," Diego observed.

Alonzo gave my mom a hug and turned to me. "Take care of yourselves and your mother." With that, he handed the binoculars to Santana and took off to protect Rosa. The rest of us got back into the van.

"If anyone goes after Alonzo and Rosa, we move in and help out," I said.

"The goal should be to keep you kids safe," Diego argued.

"I don't want anyone else to die because of me," I responded.

Diego looked questioningly at me.

"A boy named Jason died at camp because he tried to protect me."

"Summer, it's not your fault. It was Marco," Santana stated, firmly.

"Marco got torn apart by dogs. He doesn't have to live with what happened."

"You can't accept responsibility for what those people did. I've read the diary. I've seen the pictures. You were up against some very evil people." Diego countered.

"Jason wouldn't want you to feel bad about what happened to him," Santana went on. "For a while, I was jealous. He managed to be your friend before I did. He chose to risk his life. You never asked him to help you. He had more courage than I did."

"You risked your life for me, too. I completely misjudged you. You were the one who gave me the water when I was in the box. I'm alive because of you and what you risked." Santana looked so sweet, I had to add, "Besides, you're the hottest guy I've ever met."

"Biased," Jimmy teased.

"Jimmy, you and Bruce are hot too," I threw in.

Somewhere behind us, we heard an explosion.

"That doesn't sound good," Brue acknowledged. "Evan and company are good at blowing things up and usually someone dies when they do."

# CHAPTER 74

"This van may be hidden, but we are still sitting ducks," Santana pointed out.

We exited the van. Diego pulled out a camera that could shoot infrared as well as regular video and also one that did both stills and video. All recording indicators were covered. We split up and climbed some of the shorter trees with each other's help. Santana and I helped my mom and Emily into one of the trees. Shannon and Jimmy joined their tree. Santana helped me up another tree, then handed me Hope and climbed up to join me.

As Bruce lifted Abigail into our tree, we assisted her from above and then he joined us. Diego climbed a separate tree on the other side of us with his cameras. We all kept watch and were close enough to still speak to each other. From the trees, we had a good view of the farmhouse.

We heard more gunfire. It was on the far side of the farmhouse from our location. "That sounds a lot closer to the farm than before," Bruce said.

"If there is total gun control in Cuba, who is shooting at whom?" Emily asked.

"If it's getting closer to the farmhouse, maybe we should walk back in that direction," I suggested.

"Darling, the idea is to keep you alive," my mom responded. "I realize you have survived a lot, but it's not wise to run towards so much danger."

"Alonzo and Rosa could be hurt."

"I'm scared for them, too. But at least Alonzo has a gun. We all want you kids safe."

"I'll be safest if nobody else dies protecting me."

"I'm heading in," Abigail announced, climbing down from our tree.

"Me too," I said, landing on the ground.

"I can't speak for anyone else, but I'm in," Santana joined in, following me to the ground.

Bruce gave Santana a friendly punch on the shoulder as he landed next to us. "You know I'm in."

"I'm going where the action is," Diego declared as he joined us.

I turned to Shannon and Jimmy. "Please stay here and take care of my mom, Emily and Hope."

"What? Why don't I get to go?" Emily pouted.

"We need someone to protect the van. It's got satellite communication and Jimmy, you're a techie. This may be where all the action is. And Emily, we need you to let the world know what happened," I said.

"Again?" Emily complained.

"And we may need you safe to rescue us later," I added.

My mom shuddered.

"Trust me, I plan to survive," I told her.

Santana handed Jimmy his binoculars. Diego pulled extra cards, a video camera and a still camera out of the van and handed them to Jimmy. "Anything you film will go into my report. You cool with that?"

"Naturally."

Diego and his other cameras joined us.

"Take care of our heroes," Shannon instructed Diego.

We started moving out towards the farm, keeping down. While watching the farm, we made it to Rosa's orange grove. A second later,

Hope was at my side. "Guess we're a team," I whispered to my dog. I turned to Santana. "There are more orange trees in Cuba than in Orange County, California."

"I remember my last trip to Orange County before the camp. We were trying to locate the lone orange tree after which the county was named."

We heard more gun fire. It sounded even closer to the farm than before. Next, we heard loud blasts from the directions of the checkpoints.

We continued moving. So far, it looked and sounded as if nothing intrusive had reached the farmhouse.

We paused again, a couple hundred feet from the farmhouse. We continued to use the orange trees for cover. Suddenly, a nearby explosion rocked the ground around us, knocking us all down. Even Hope was knocked on his side.

The barn was in smithereens.

# CHAPTER 75

Alonzo was helping Rosa out of the farmhouse. Her car and Alonzo's, which were inside the barn, were undoubtedly destroyed.

"Alonzo," I called out. He and Rosa ran our way. We all moved back towards the hill where the van waited. As we proceeded, the ground seemed to be rippling around us.

"HAARP?" Santana asked Bruce.

"Maybe."

Next, lightning started striking the crops not far from us. We ran in a zig-zag pattern, trying to avoid the lightning strikes. Hope ran at my side. I had thought dogs feared lightning, but Hope kept up like nothing mattered except being next to me.

We continued to try to use the orange trees for cover but they weren't much help. The trees were catching fire around us amidst more lighting strikes.

Then came the hail. I pulled off my jacket and fastened it over Hope to protect him from the falling ice cubes.

"In Cuba?" I asked. It was summer, and we were being hammered by the onslaught.

"Didn't they do this with Luke and Laura in General Hospital?" Abigail asked.

We looked at her. That was long before any of us were born.

"Hey, my mom watches soap opera reruns to keep from going crazy while my dad is bombing kids in other countries. The five martinis a day probably help her more than the soap operas, though. And then there are the Death in the Afternoons. That cocktail was created by Hemmingway and so she calls that her literary drink. She usually has six of those in a setting. Oops!" she reacted, as a bolt of lightning hit the tree right by her.

The lightning strikes seemed to be aiming at us as we continued running. We tried to stay under the branches of the orange trees to avoid the hail while not touching the trees to avoid the lighting.

"Oh!" Rosa exclaimed. She had slipped on the ice and fallen on her knee. Alonzo helped her up. As he did so, sheets of hail struck his arm causing him to drop his gun. Santana went for it as lighting blocked his path to retrieving it. This was followed by buckets of rain and them more hail.

"I don't see it," Santana said.

"Let's get out of here, " I encouraged.

"I'll carry you," Alonzo told Rosa.

"Yo estoy bien," she said, but I could tell she was in some pain.

"Diego," Bruce called out, "Are you catching this on video?"

"Yes, and my camera has weather sealant on it for use in hurricanes."

"Well, I'm not concerned about a hurricane at the moment, but is that a tornado up the hill?" Bruce asked.

"¡Mierda!" Santana exclaimed. "And it's too close to where we started running. We need to draw it away from that area before it hits the others."

Santana and I started moving into the open. The tornado started coming in our direction as the lighting and hail seemed to aim for us. We ran back towards the burning trees.

The hail was putting out the nearby lighting fires as more lighting lit more trees on fire. With the sky dark from the strange weather and smoke or steam clouding things around us, everything was almost invisible on the ground between the bursts. We tried to make our way back to where we thought the rest of our group was.

I tripped over something on the ground that was hidden under some fallen branches and soil. "What is this?" I asked, feeling something metal underneath the dirt as Santana knelt down beside me.

Rosa responded. "It's a bomb shelter. It was built well over half a century ago when we were afraid your country was going to bomb us." She, Alonzo and Diego closed the short distance between us.

"Wise move. I mean, wise move to build this," I said. The entrance seemed to blend in with the dirt that was covering it.

"The opening device should be over there," Rosa said pointing to the base of the tree we were under. It was one of the few that was still unburned. Alonzo helped her over to where she was pointing and they dug with their hands into the ground for a box, opened it up and then Rosa pushed some buttons. "When I was a little girl, my father taught me to open this if we went to war."

We heard a click and some kind of handle popped up. We lifted the door just enough to slip through. My friends insisted I be first to climb down the ladder going down as bursts of fire and ice continued to threaten all of us up above. After reaching the floor, I caught Hope as Santana leaned down and lowered him. Abigail followed and then Rosa, Bruce, Diego and Santana. As Alonzo, the last one, slipped in, the tree above the opening caught fire and then exploded. He pulled the door down quickly to block the flames from entering.

It was pitch-black inside. Diego took a flashlight out of his pocket. Rosa located and pulled a lever on another of the walls and I got the impression that the door sealed securely. The area inside was a small room.

"I used this for my private playhouse as a child." Rosa took us to one of the walls. "My father showed me how to get through, here," she said. She pulled up a brick on the floor next to it, and a section of the wall opened. On the other side was a staircase that led into a room with another doorway.

"There is an underground network of passageways on the island," Alonzo said. "I haven't been down in it, but I've heard about it."

"So like Russia, Cuba will beat the U.S. in World War III," I commented. "Hey, only a tiny percentage of Americans have any idea where any bomb shelter is located."

"Isn't Russia prepared to have every citizen in a bomb shelter within half an hour?" Abigail asked.

"That's what I've heard," Santana replied.

"Mom and the others are still up with the van," I reminded them.

"We drew the tornado away from them and they are covered by the tree branches, but they could still be in danger," Bruce responded.

"What do you think the shooting and blasts before were all about?" I asked.

"That concerns me more than the weather. There could be an assailant or a team of assailants on the ground up above and the others could be in extreme danger," Santana warned.

"We've got to get them down here too," I said.

"Unless I am getting turned around, my guess is the hill is in that direction," Diego related, pointing towards the far doorway.

We moved through the exit into a tunnel that led in the direction he had suggested and followed it.

"There might not be an exit where the others are located. But, if we can get past there, we might be able to come back to them on the other side," Diego continued.

"Santana, do you have anything to pick any locks we come across?" I asked.

He pulled a twisted-up wire out of his pocket. "I made this last night—just in case."

Rosa was looking at him oddly.

"We've been locked in so many rooms that I figured the odds were in favor of winding up in a locked room again."

We kept moving. There seemed to be no exit close to where we estimated the occupied tree was. Finally, we found a passage up. Santana opened the ground plate to the outside. When we looked, we found we were in a grove of palm trees. We kept looking around and saw what looked like an explosion had hit the nearby road. Debris from cars, along with body parts were visible.

"Shit," Santana said.

"It's a checkpoint," Alonzo told us, moving over to the vehicle debris and finding a piece of a license plate. "If the Cuban government figures out who did this, they should be on our side. If they can trace it to your government, it's an act of war."

"As if the attacks by the unmarked plane weren't," Abigail remarked.

"Clearly you aren't going to war with the U.S. What will your country do?" Bruce asked.

"We can go to the United Nations. But there is a downside. Remember you were blamed for the prior explosions," Alonzo pointed out.

"Right. They could accuse us," I acknowledged.

"I'm sure my dad will lie," Abigail remarked.

"Which direction do you think the farm is from here?" I asked.

"Well, if we look at the glow from over there, I'd say that direction," Alonzo pointed into the trees that were on a hill above with a glow coming from the other side. Apparently, we had crossed under the hill. "And at the top of the hill should be where the others are waiting."

We had some cover. The assailants might have thought when we disappeared, that they had killed us—especially if they didn't see further movement above ground. That was our best hope. Rosa was moving better at this point. Diego wasn't letting his burn injury from yesterday slow him down. We had all been injured at times but had managed to survive and not let the injuries stop us.

Santana put his arm around me as we walked. He knew how worried I was about my mom, Emily, and my friends. Even though I tried not to show it, I was close to terrified about them. I loved them all and I couldn't lose any of them.

"I'm sure they are fine. They are probably really worried about us," Santana said softly as if reading my mind.

"I'm sorry about your barn," I told Rosa. "And your orange grove. We've brought you nothing but trouble."

"You've brought me a reason to feel needed again."

"This is a communist country. Our government and our people will help repair the damage," Alonzo reassured me.

"In our country, we rely on insurance companies that deny the claims and leave losses uncovered," I pointed out.

"Don't forget the organizations that collect money to help out with disasters and then pocket it?" Santana said.

"Oh, you mean like the Clinton Foundation," Abigail noted.

I hoped everyone would still be close to the van and that nobody had tried to go after us.

When we got to the trees we had been in, nobody was there or in the van. We moved to the tree they had been on and found an attached note. It read:

*"I will trade your mom and friends for you. Farmhouse."*

# CHAPTER 76

Back, downhill to the farmhouse we went. The lightening had stopped and the hail and buckets of rain seemed to have put out most of the fire.

"You do know, I'm not going to let you trade yourself," Santana told me.

"We have to find a way to save them," I responded. I looked around. Diego and Alonzo were on their phones. I didn't hear the discussions, though.

As we approached the farmhouse, Evan was on the porch with a gun to my mother's head. "I will trade one of my hostages for one each of you," he said to our group. "And I will decide the order. First, the mother for the daughter."

"Don't do it, Summer!" my mom yelled. I stepped forward, avoiding Santana's grasp.

Evan turned his gun to aim at me. As he did so, my mom struggled with him. The gun went off as it hit the porch. In a moment, Hope was at their side, growling.

Santana was trying to pull me back as I worked to get free of him. Evan knocked my mom down and picked up the gun to shoot her.

I could hear a shot, but my mother was still moving. It was Evan who fell down cold, the top of his head covered in blood.

As Santana released me and I ran to my mom, I could see that Evan's eyes had a glazed, lifeless look. A second later, Hope pounced on Evan and treated him like a chew toy. By the time I pulled Hope back, Evan was covered in both blood and holes.

Alonzo rushed to my mom, helped her to her feet, pulled her into his arms and held her tightly.

"I've always supported the gun control views of my government. Maybe it's time to rethink them," Diego said, putting his gun down. "I got this from the officer I rescued. The way things were going, I thought it might come in handy."

"Gun control has never stopped the criminals in my county or even put a dent in their mass shootings," I noted.

"So, what do we do now?" Bruce asked. "They know where we are, and who knows when we'll next be hit with twisters, hurricanes and whatnot?"

---

We spent the night in the bomb shelter after I checked the location where we had buried Paul's diary and originals of the SD cards, along with some copies. They were safe. I took a copy of everything into the shelter. Fortunately, none of our evidence had been hidden in the barn. Diego stayed up much of the night editing the footage he had gotten and doing a descriptive voiceover of sections that needed explaining. He included pictures of the camp and of the leaders with the little kids. He asked our permission to use our fathers' pictures in his video. Without hesitation, we gave it.

"Take them down," Abigail declared.

I nodded.

"They deserve to go to prison, even my dad," Emily retorted in her soft way with a real sadness in her voice.

The next morning as were leaving our underground haven, a helicopter landed. It belonged to the Cuban Revolutionary Police.

"Not again," Santana whispered.

# CHAPTER 77

"It will be alright," Alonzo said.

All of us, including Hope, were escorted onto the copter. We were asked for evidence but didn't know if these guys could be trusted. Diego brought a camera and a copy of his footage. Like us, he was worried about the loss of any evidence and left the originals behind. We also brought a copy of Paul's diary and his SD cards.

Instead of prison, the helicopter flew us to the Presidential Palace. We were greeted by the couple that had come down to the basement where we had been held prisoner.

"My name is Emelia Sanchez, and this is my husband, Ricardo Sanchez. I understand why you didn't trust us," the woman said. "In our position, we wouldn't have trusted anyone, either."

"Why did you hold us prisoner?"

"It was, how do you say it in your country? Protective custody. It will all be explained to you in a little while."

"I'm sorry about your house if that was your house," I said.

"Actually, it belonged to the person you will see next."

"The scream? I heard a scream."

Emilia explained. "After you refused to come with us, we had to leave for a meeting about the situation. Jakinta, a woman on the security detail stayed to keep an eye on you. When the men who were after you broke into the house, she screamed to let you know something was happening as she rushed out the back to go for help. This is Cuba. There were no guns in the house. Before she got back, the place was on fire. When we heard about it, we rushed back, but the firemen wouldn't let us inside until the fire was put out. By that time, we learned you'd been spotted at the museum."

"What about the armed men?"

"They assigned to protect you during your transfer and also your friends until your arrival. They left before we arrived."

"They didn't seem particularly friendly."

"They wouldn't have known the reason for transferring and protecting you."

"The walls have ears," I murmured.

Emilia nodded.

We were escorted to a large office. A distinguished-looking gentleman entered the room. "Hello, Juan. I'm sorry about your house," Alonzo said.

"It will be rebuilt. The important thing is that these brave chamacos are safe now."

"I can't guarantee someone won't reactivate HAARP," Bruce noted, grimacing.

"Is that the device they used on the prison?" Juan asked.

"I don't know, but HAARP's patent says it can have the impact of an earthquake or atomic bomb. They could also have used one of those directed energy weapons."

"We'll have to call them on that," Alonzo said.

"Is Juan your contact?" I asked Alonzo.

"As a matter of fact, yes," Alonzo informed us. "I promised to keep his name out of everything until an investigation was done."

"The men who brought us from the prison. Were they yours?" I asked Juan.

"I can't take credit for that." Suddenly, Juan's attention was focused on the door.

"Señior Presidente, es un honor," Alonzo said.

Before us stood Miguel Diaz-Canel, Raúl Castro's successor. I didn't know whether the Cuban tradition was to salute, shake hands or bow, so I decided to curtsey. Emily and my mom did likewise. Rosa clasped her hands to her mouth. Abigail just stood there.

"Estoy felize de conocerte," Santana said, formally bowing.

"Por favor. El honor es mío," the Cuban leader said. "We can speak in English. You don't get into my position without knowing the universal language."

"Sir, then you realize who we are?" I attempted to confirm.

"I recognized your green-haired friend from the start. I was actually an admirer of Señorita Kreskin and her exploits, showing up your government's misdeeds. Señiorita Kreskin, tú tienees tanta energía y espíritu."

"Gracias," Abigail said.

"With your government seeking your return while pretending you were dead, Miguel and I thought it was best to play along. When we saw the copy of the diary and information that Señor Martina presented, we knew that some very peligroso hombres as you Americans say, were 'gunning for you,'" Recardo Sanchez explained.

"We were transferred from the prison just in time to save us. How did you know?" Santana asked.

"After the attack on you, we moved you into the special wing for your protection. It was evident the assassins had inside information. When our intelligence picked up a communique about a plan to flatten the prison, we got you out and prepared to evacuate the rest of the prison."

"And so, you had us taken to that residential basement?" I asked.

The President nodded and looked at Ricardo Sanchez, who continued with the details. "When your friends arrived, we felt they needed protection, too."

"And the unmarked plane?" Diego asked.

"Our men got a call right before our patrol boat was blown up that an unmarked plane was in the area. They watched from a distance. There might have been an intervention if they had realized the plane was about to attack," Mr. Sanchez explained. "Our observers believed they used some kind of particle beam or direct energy weapon, as you mentioned."

"Your investigators seemed to think we were guilty," Santana noted. "And the police called us terrorists."

"We thought it was best to keep everyone on a need-to-know basis. The police and prison guards were told to treat you with the utmost care."

"We were told one of the prison administrators was in on the attempts on our lives," I said.

"After the poison attack, we did background checks on all our personnel. I think we found the administrator who was involved. We are continuing to look to see if there are more."

"Do you think you have them all?" my mom asked.

"We can't be sure," Sanchez told her.

The President added, "But we are continuing to watch and we won't take any chances with these valientes chamacos, or rather brave children."

My mom seemed to relax, some.

"Last night, we heard gunfire and explosions," Santana recalled.

Sanchez continued. "One of our checkpoints was blown up. Another was nearly destroyed. The gunfire was between our forces and two men who accompanied Evan Saunders, the man Mr. Morinda shot. The Revolutionary police wounded the two accomplices and they are in custody. Saunders got away from them only to die trying to kill you."

"This is quite a contrast to the American police. When they start shooting, survivors aren't common," I noted.

"I've heard about some of the police abuses in your country." The President said. "I hope you will find the rest of your stay here more enjoyable."

Diego inquired, "Could we make use of your facilities for an international broadcast with the kids?"

"Certainly. We will assist you in whatever way we can."

"Does that mean you will be part of the interview," I asked.

"I'm afraid not," Miguel said and then explained. "If we are part of it, they will assume it's a propaganda piece. We want them to treat this matter with the seriousness that is involved. If you wish, I can have the head of the Revolutionary Police give a statement about the attacks that took place after they pursued you here."

"Usted es muy inteligente," Alonzo said to Miquel.

"Gracias," I replied to Miguel.

"Jimmy and I are just friends of Summer's and the others," Shannon stated. "But I am very honored to meet you."

"The honor is, again, mine," Miguel replied.

"Me, too," Jimmy added. "I watched Michael Moore's movie *Sicko*, about how you have a better health care system than we do. I wish my government would adopt some of your reforms."

"You are more than just friends," I said to Jimmy and Shannon. "You are family. When nobody else was there for us, you were."

Emily went up to Miguel and hugged him. At first, I worried he might not like hugs, but he hugged her back and reached out for all of us to join in the hug. We did. I had never hugged a foreign leader before. Here, I felt safe for the first time in a very long time.

I heard a barking. In ran Hope. A woman came in behind him. "I'm sorry, sir. He wouldn't stay in the room where they put him."

"¿Is this the Famoso Hope?" Miguel asked, leaning down to pet my friend. "You are always welcome in my home and in the Presidential Palace. If necessary, an executive order will be given to that effect." Hope licked him and then curled up at his feet.

I reached down and hugged Hope. Then, we all gave Miguel another group hug as Hope barked approval.

# CHAPTER 78

When the cameras were set up, we started our part of the presentation that was being broadcast live internationally to countries around the world. We sat in a circle, each prepared to tell our story.

The cameras focused on Abigail.

"My name is Abigail Kreskin. You may recognize me. If you don't, I can always get a green wig until my hair grows back. My parents sent me to a behavior modification, also known as a Gulag, camp.

"What really happens in these camps is torture. If you have read any books to the contrary, they are lies, propaganda pieces, aimed at promoting and justifying the torture of kids."

I was really glad she wasn't talking about doing a 187 (the penal code section for murder) and had toned down her comments for the camera. But I wouldn't have blamed her if she had 187ed her parents. She was speaking like a leader, and I could picture that she would have a very bright future if she went into politics—if America ever started having free and verified elections.

Abigail continued, "Even if any constructive learning is going on in these camps, and it isn't, that wouldn't justify the torture of teens. It doesn't justify this." She lifted up her blouse to show the healing bite marks on her side. She rolled up her sleeves and the legs of her pants to show the injuries there as well. "These were done by dogs at the encouragement of the camp counselors. Intentional injuries like these have happened to teens at other camps as well. I was put in a box for days with no food and water. I almost died. Too many teens have died at these camps. It's past time to regulate them. It's time to close them down."

The cameras flashed to me. "If people cannot raise their children without sending them to places to get fixed, those people shouldn't be parents. There should be an automatic removal of the rights of parents who do that. The poor and lower-middle-class parents aren't sending their kids to these places. These camps cost parents thirty to one hundred thousand dollars or more. Our custodial parents didn't just send us there. They spent large sums of money to have us tortured. They can't claim ignorance. It was their duty to find out what they were paying to have done to us. A friend of mine, Sonja, was gang raped. A boy not much older than me named Jason was very kind to me. To punish him for his kindness, they electrocuted him. Jamie couldn't handle what they forced him to do to a girl at the camp because it didn't fit with his moral code, which was much higher than those of the camp counselors. They put a noose around his neck. He died by hanging. His father, the deputy head of the Federal Reserve, sent him to camp because he was ashamed his son was gay. The fix killed Jamie, and being gay isn't something that needs to be fixed anyway. Another girl, Hillary, tried to live up to the demands of the leaders. She died at the camp. Paul Saunders, who saved my life and Santana's, tried to save other campers and died in the attempt, along with other campers. His father knew how and where he died and lied about his having died in a plane crash, elsewhere.

"I was stripped naked and tied to a tree, out in the sun as well as in the cold of night. I was beaten, starved, forced to go without water and am lucky to be alive. My father was the Chief of Staff for a U. S. Senator and for a Governor. He thought I needed to be fixed because things didn't work out between me and the son of a man he wanted to finance his future Lieutenant Governor's bid." I paused. The cameras almost moved away, and I waved them back.

"The father who sent me there beat my mother and put her in the hospital. I wasn't allowed to see her for years because the family court system has an automatic policy that any allegations of abuse against a father are alienation, no matter how true. So, children like me are forced to live with abusers and the parents who love us are not allowed to see us again. Millions of children are living like this. The abuse teens are subjected to, isn't just in the camps. It's in their own homes, where kids are raped and beaten and subjected to abuses that should violate the law. But the courts give a green light, banning evidence of the abuse and then claiming there is none. Do all children have to get married and emancipated like Damen of SavingDamon.com in order to free themselves from abusers? My father belongs in prison for what he did to my mother. I saw her beaten and I called 9-1-1, but they later dragged her away from me. I wasn't allowed to testify to what I witnessed, and I lost the chance to be raised by someone who loves me."

Santana reached out and held my hand. I hadn't realized it until then, but tears were streaming down my face.

The cameras moved to Santana. "My father is a congressman who believed I was an embarrassment to his reputation. Like others at the camp—" He looked at me. "I was kidnapped in the middle of the night by someone using brutal force. At that camp, I went through some of what Summer went through. I was also beaten and forced to engage in brutal fights with the other campers. Kids died. If it weren't for Paul Saunders, who stood up against his father, Evan Saunders, I wouldn't be alive today. He didn't just save us. He gave us the evidence you will see later because he opposed what was happening at his father's camp."

The cameras moved to Emily. She looked at Alejandro, who had come to support her. He smiled at her and nodded. She hesitated and then turned around with her back to the camera and pulled off her blouse, showing the welts that were still visible on her back. She put it back on and turned back to the camera.

"There were no books, no learning, only torture. They didn't care about us. They laughed at our injuries. In the end, they started handing out Bibles and going over Bible verses, but they weren't

Christians. They raped and killed kids. If you have lost someone you love at a camp, find out what happened and how they died."

The cameras focused on Bruce. "A school counselor convinced my parents that I would have a great future if only they sent me to a behavior modification program, also known as a Gulag School. From the school I was sent to the camp. The schools engage in much the same kind of human rights abuses and torture that take place in the camps.

"Counselors are getting kickbacks for sending teens to be tortured. All their promos and that stupid book that was recently written as a promo for the camps are lies told by people with no conscience. We didn't have any rights. We were in California, where there was legislation banning the practices that took place. We got phones with no batteries. When we were injured, there were no doctors. Abigail was nearly killed when they gave her an antibiotic to which she was allergic. One girl bled to death. Other campers died of dehydration before Summer arrived.

"Those running the camp didn't care. The leaders kept starving and dehydrating teens. We were all hogtied at points, particularly when we didn't do everything we were ordered to do. The deaths are a natural progression from the way these camps are run. Abigail is right. The camps should be shut down. Summer is right. Any parent who would send their child to one of these camps or schools should instantly lose custody. I know I don't want to go back to my parents and none of the others, here, want to go back to the parents who sent them to be tortured."

Diego stepped into view of the cameras and spoke. "These are very brave kids. They have endured more than most Americans do in a lifetime. Even worse, they had to endure the cruelty of being sent to be tortured by those they trusted, their parents. Those running the camp tried to cover up what had happened by either faking a plane crash or simply claiming these kids were on board some plane that crashed but as you can see, these campers are alive and well. Hopefully, others declared dead will turn up alive."

Diego showed excerpts from Paul's diary and photos taken by Paul of the torture. We had decided that the exposé on the kids' camp should be in a second segment so it did not detract from the issue of the torture taking place at the teen camps.

# EPILOGUE

The reception to the broadcast was amazing. Support came in from all over the world. In some cases, the support came from world leaders and current and former members of our government back home.

We were allowed to stay in the Presidential Palace while we decided what to do. Abigail and Bruce talked about traveling the world. Santana and I wanted to go back to the States, but we didn't want to go back to the parents who had sent us to be tortured. Our mom had really hit it off with Alonzo but insisted on sticking with me, whatever my decision was.

Cuba offered us all asylum. Alonzo filed an action in the U.S. Courts to overturn the family law decisions that placed Santana and me into the hands of the men who had turned us over to the camps and to have our fathers, as well as Abigail's, Bruce's, and Emily's parents, declared unfit. We didn't know whether the result would be in our favor, but there was hope. And I had Hope, who had been welcomed by the Cuban leaders. We were told they might make him Cuba's new national mascot.

Juanita and Rosa both wanted to adopt Emily. Rosa pointed out that, because Alejandro was Emily's boyfriend, it would make more sense for Emily to be raised by her and visit Juanita when she could.

Alejandro was pushing for his mother to win so he could see Emily all the time. Juanita was surrounded by family while Rosa was living alone at the farm, though she had unrelated workers who adored her and treated Emily like a princess. In the end, it was decided that Rosa would adopt Emily and Juanita would have her over for extended stays as her aunt.

Shannon and Jimmy's parents let them stay for a couple of weeks, with the condition that they return home at the end of that time.

"Shannon," I said, frowning. "I am so going to miss you."

"Me, you too. Promise you'll text and call and email."

"I promise."

"I'm going to talk my parents into letting me come back here. Maybe, we can go to college together."

"That would be great."

"You are the best friend I've ever had. Any time you need me, let me know, and I'll be on the next flight," Shannon said.

"Same here," I responded. "Give my love to Tiffany."

"I will."

"The Pacific is getting radioactive. The reports say it's safer to surf the waves out here. Maybe you can talk Cuba into making surfing the national sport," Jimmy suggested.

We all hugged.

<hr />

A few days later, I was having lunch with my mom when the President's secretary came in. "You have a visitor, Mr. Pandar Tanner. He is waiting for you, down the hall on the first floor, third door."

I looked at my mother. "I don't want to see him. After all you did for him, he almost let you die, and he never showed any remorse over what Daddy did to you."

"You can't let my situation affect your relationship with your brother."

"He was also okay with Dad beating me and sending me to camp."

"I'm sorry. You deserved better. I remember when Pandar was born, he was so sweet. It was a tough pregnancy. The doctor was going to put my life first, and I demanded he protect Pandar before me—even if it cost me my life. It's my fault for pampering him and not finding a way to teach him to be more caring. I didn't know how to stop him from viewing your father as a role model. Perhaps if I had been a better parent."

"You were the best. You couldn't have been better. When there is abuse, kids often follow the abusers and not the people who care about them. I saw that at camp. Teens would fear the abuse, and then they would learn to crave doing the abusers' bidding."

My mom hugged me. "If there is any hope for him, it is through love. Please, at least, speak with him."

I walked from the dining area to the first-floor hallway and over to the third door. Before I opened it, a hand reached out and grasped my arm.

"Are you sure you want to do this?" Santana asked.

"I need to. It will be alright."

"Do you want me to go with you?"

"I need to do this, alone."

"I'll be waiting outside the door in case you need me."

"Thank you."

"I love you," he said in his sweet way that made me want to forget about going through the door.

"I love you, too."

I opened the door. "Sis, it's great to see you." Pandar came up and gave me a hug. I didn't react, not even to hug him back. "Dad and I have missed you. I hope they've been treating you well, here."

"Why are you here?"

"Dad and I would like you to come home. Daddy got you a new puppy. His tentative name is Snuggles,"

"I have a dog. His name is Hope."

"I'm sure you can bring him home. Isn't Hope an unusual name for a boy?"

I didn't respond to that. I wasn't doing small talk.

"You want me to come home after you let Dad beat me and send me off to be tortured."

"It was a mistake. We're both sorry, and we want you back."

"Did Dad pay for your plane fare or send you here on a private plane?"

"It was a private plane. It's ready to fly us both home."

"I'm not going anywhere with you."

"Sis."

"I don't want anything to do with either you or Dad ever again. But you know who does want something to do with you Pandar?"

"Who?"

"Our mother. Even though you stood there and let Dad beat her, again and again, nearly to death, and even though you refused to help her get medical help when you could have, she still loves you."

"She's poisoned your mind?"

I laughed coldly. "Poison? Poison? No, that's what abusers do. Not those who are abused. And you know what? As much as she loves you, I hope you never give her another chance because she deserves better than you. You are no better than a pile of horse manure. She was there for you. She loved you so much, and you would have been just fine with Dad killing her. In fact, I've remembered a conversation where you told her just that."

"That's not how it was."

"That is how it was."

"She asked for those beatings. She brought out the worst in Dad."

I started to react and then controlled myself. "Pandar, I never want to see you again as long as I live. As far as I'm concerned, you are no longer my brother. I have a new family and a new life. But this is what I will do. If and when you get married and if and when you abuse your wife, which you will if you get married, I will let her know that I will side with her against you. Now get out of my life, and never try to contact me in any way, ever again. Get out."

Santana came in and tried to take Pandar's arm to escort him out. Pandar shook him off, started to walk out and then looked back. "You know, Dad lost his job because of you. I would expect you to have some remorse."

"Remorse? Daddy belongs in prison for life, and I'm going to help make sure that happens."

Pandar turned his face away, looked straight ahead and walked out the door.

I went with Santana back to see Mom.

"Did you resolve your family differences?"

"I'm with the only family I want," I said, going over and hugging her like I never wanted to let her go. "I am the luckiest girl in the world to have a mother like you, and I will never, again, forget how much you love me."

We hugged again.

I turned to Santana. "You are another part of this family. Forever?"

"Forever," he said as my mom and he hugged me.

---

The Cuban President called our group, along with Alonzo, my mom and Rosa back into a conference to discuss developments. We learned that quite a number of people had called for Abigail's father resignation, but he was ignoring all the criticism. My father had been fired and was in seclusion. With pushing from the Democratic Party, my Dad withdrew his name from consideration in the next California Lieutenant Governor's race. Santana's father was refusing to resign from the House.

Emily's dad was still Chairman of the Council on Foreign Relations. Torture and killing weren't a big thing to the CFR, anyway. As far as we knew, Bruce's father still had his job. As we couldn't prove that HAARP was involved in the attacks, neither the Cuban government nor Diego's station discussed the possible connection, publicly.

The United Nations was considering a resolution calling for the closure or monitoring by human rights observers of all teen wilderness camps, boot camps, and behavior modification programs. We had been asked to go to the United Nations in New York before the vote.

Mom was worried. "A lot of the people who tried to kill you are in Washington. I don't think it's safe."

"The Cuban Government is also worried about you," Alonzo said. "You are a threat to certain people in your country's intelligence community."

"Hey, we've survived kidnapping, torture, beatings, starvation, dehydration, brainwashing, fires, being chased by police and killers, attacks from the air, a prison collapse, and more. Do you really think there's anything the bad guys can throw at us that we can't handle?" I asked.

"As you can see, this girl needs me around to keep her safe." Santana smiled, putting his arms around me.

Abigail flexed her knuckles. "I'm ready. Emily?" Abigail asked.

"Ready!" Emily excitedly jumped with her arms in the air as she replied.

I started, working on coming up with a reason for Emily to choose to stay home in Cuba. I wanted her protected, and I think my reluctance to take her showed on my face.

"You are not leaving me behind. No way," she declared, firmly.

"Emily, we would be lonely if you left," Rosa told her.

"I love you, but I need to do this if I'm to stay here," Emily said.

"There's a lot of stuff we can handle, but what about our custodial parents?" Santana asked.

"I'm being adopted," Emily said. "That will hold, won't it?"

"Shannon kept talking about Damen," Santana noted. His enthusiasm for the idea of what Damen did to be free made me a little nervous.

"He's the one who got emancipated by getting married, wasn't he?" my mom asked.

"Mrs. Tanner, I'd be happy to marry your daughter," Santana said. "If she'll have me."

"You're asking me to marry you?"

"Whoa, whoa," my mom said. "Summer and you are only sixteen."

"I promise to treat her well."

"You want to get married too?" Bruce asked Abigail. "I mean, for real. Or for paper, like Damen, if you prefer."

Emily looked at Alejandro as he took Emily's hand. "You're are too young. Period," Rosa strongly objected.

"Wait," Alonzo advised "You are all a little young to be considering this. There are rules that wave the eighteen-year-old age with parental consent, and we could theoretically do adoptions on all of you who don't have a parent here. However. If your country doesn't accept the adoptions, they might not accept the marriages and emancipations."

"And my daughter is not getting married at sixteen, no matter how much I like you, Santana. I would be happy to have you for a son-in-law—later."

"If you want, we could do paper only," Santana compromised.

"No!" my mother put her foot down.

"So, what is the solution?" I asked.

"I have a thought," Alonzo said. "What if we do all the prep work here? Your custodial parents are under fire and might not try anything. If they do, you will be staying in the Cuban consulate while in New York. You can finish the ceremonies there if necessary and by necessary, I mean, there is absolutely no alternative."

"Alonzo!" my mom reacted in a scolding tone.

"Only if that is the only way. In fact, they don't have to know you aren't married. You could wear wedding rings when you go there to speak and let them assume you've gone the way of this Damen boy."

"But no sex," my mom insisted.

We laughed.

Santana nodded, looking a bit fallen. As much as I loved him, I was a bit relieved. I really wanted to wait and have a big wedding when I was older and it would be more than a paper one.

Abigail looked a little relieved, too.

The secretary came in. "I've got some envelopes for the group from the California, Alaska, Florida and District of Columbia Departments of Education."

We had taken our GEDs, even Emily. Being from well to do families, we had grown up with access to the best education available. I held my envelope and closed my eyes, hoping and saying a little prayer. Santana opened his and looked at me as I opened mine. "Passed!" I exclaimed, reading the results.

"Me too," Santana said.

"Me three," Abigail announced.

"Four," Bruce added in.

We looked at Emily, who was still holding her envelope. She was fourteen and the youngest. She could always do a retake if there was a problem. Slowly she opened the envelope. Her eyes went wide and she started jumping up and down. "Five!" she exclaimed.

---

Later that evening, Santana and I looked out on the Gulf. "You were actually asking for permission to marry me?"

"I would marry you anytime, anywhere, you want. I love you."

"I love you, too. I'm nervous, though. I don't think I'm ready to get married. After what happened in my parents' marriage, I'm a little frightened of the institution."

"I understand. I wasn't going to push you into anything. How about this? We take it slow and whenever you are ready, a year from now or ten years from now, I'll be waiting."

"Then the answer is 'yes,'" I said, jumping into his arms. As he kissed me, it felt as if the Earth was moving and the stars were whirling around us.

As he whispered in my ear, "Forever?" I had no doubt that it would be.

"Forever," I whispered back.

# ACKNOWLEDGMENTS

The family law portions of the story were inspired by tragedies commonly suffered by children and by protective parents who lost their children to violent sexual predators in kangaroo-type proceedings in family courts.

The National Youth Rights Association has worked over the years to educate the public on the horrors of teen behavior modification programs AKA Gulag camps, Gulag schools and Gulag treatment facilities.

I would also like to thank former U.S. Representative George Miller, who held hearings when he was the chairman of the House Education sub-committee for the purpose of regulating what both sides of the aisle in those hearings determined was torture. Greg Kutz of the Government Accounting Office presented the details of a number of the deaths in these programs. Many of the incidents depicted in this book were reflective of the actual kinds of abuses and deaths inflicted in the various behavior modification programs as related by survivors and in the hearing. In those settings, teens were dehydrated, starved, hog-tied, forced to brush their teeth with toilet water and to drink their own vomit, placed naked in dark rooms or boxes, often raped or subjected to other sexual abuses, had nooses placed around their necks and were subjected to electric shock treatment, forced fights and other forms of torture. Quite a number have died from reported suicides and from being shot trying to escape. Though George Miller pushed legislation through the House of Representative to regulate the camps and schools, that legislation never was adopted by the U.S. Senate.

In California, after the deaths of a number of teens in these camps within a one-year period, Ricardo Lara (who was then an assemblyman and is now California's Insurance Commissioner) introduced legislation to regulate these facilities and camps. It passed both houses and was signed into law in California.

Natasha H., the former President of the Orange County Chapter of the National Youth Rights Association, compiled the following partial list of known youth deaths at American Gulag schools: **Lorene Larhette, Joy Evans, Jonathan S. Lenoff, Peter Cooper, Connie Munson, Robert Doyle Erwin, Lyle Foodroy, Robert Zimmerman, Charles Lucas, James Lamb, Bernard Reefer, Eric David Schibley, Tammy Edmiston, Philip Williams Jr., Mario Cano, Leon Anger, Gregory Owens Jones, Carey Dunn, Leroy Prinkley, James Tomas Roman, Joshua Ferarini, Wauketta Wallace, Roxanna Gray, Danny Lewis, David Sellers, Shawn Diaz, Ryan McCandless, Diane Harris, Michelle Lynn Sutton, John Vincent Garrison, Kristen Beth Chase, Brad Glickman, Anthony Green, Geoffrey Alan Vorhies, Paul Choy, Christy Scheck, Dawn Marie Birnbaum, Dawn Renay Perry, Jason Tallman, Casey Collier, Aaron Wright Bacon, Thomas Mapes, Jamar Griffiths, Shinaul McGraw , Lorenzo Johnson, Carlos Ruiz, Jonathan Avila, Jeffrey Bogrett, Earl Smith, Dawnne Takeuchi , Bryan Jones, Eric Roberts, Will Futrelle, Bobby Sue Thomas Rochelle Clayborne, Melissa Neyman, Jimmy Kanda, Chris Campbell, Robert Rollins, Sakena Dorsey, Jeffrey Demetrius, Kelly Young, Dustin E. Phelps, Laura Hanson, Mark Draheim, Nicholas Contreras, Matt Tappi,  Chris Brown, Ashley Shaddox, Andrew McClain, Tristan Sovern, Mark Soares, Edith Campos, Chad Andrew Franza, Kristal Mayon-Ceniceros, Jerry McLaurin, Brandon Hoffman,  Joshua Sharpe, Michael Ibarra-Wiltsie, Sabrina E. Day, Randy Steele, Willie Wright, Candace Newmaker, Kevin Niel Rider, Joseph Douglas Bolt Jr., William "Eddie" Lee, Dionte Pickens, Tanner Wilson, Stephanie Duffield, Ryan Lewis, Angela Miller, Tony Haynes, Valerie Ann Heron, Aaron Albert Grey, Katherine Lank, Victoria Petersilka, LaTasha Bush, Matthew Goodman, Erica Harvey, Kiley Michelle Jaquays, Ian August, Isiah Simmons, Jeremy Gaulin, Charles "Chase" Moody, Jamal Odum, Autumn Sun Bear, Orlena Parker, Corey Baines, Daniel "Danny" Jack Matthews, Jerry Trivett, Omar Paisley, Maria Mendoza, Ian**

Mulhare, Karlye Newman, Matthew Meyers, Roberto Reyes, Garrett Halsey, Travis Parker, Linda Harris, Shirley Arciszewski, Kasey Warner, Kathy Warner, Willie Durden, Christening "Mikie" Garcia, James White, Martin Lee Anderson, Joey (Giovanni) Alteriz, Richard DeMaar, Angellika Arndt, Lenny Ortega, Natalynndria Lucy Slim, Dillon Peak, Elisa D. Santry, Rocco D. Magliozzi, Alex Cullinane, Har,ry Tyrone Rutledge, Christopher Ladell Hill, Darryl Thompson, Caleb Jensen, Brendan James Blum, Ashlie Bunch, Katherine Rice, Faith Finley, James Richard Shirey, Sergey Blashchishen, Alexis Evette Richie, Levi Snyder, Carnez Boone, Shanice Nibbs, Grace Christine James, Grace Christine James, Roger Eugene Benson, Astrid Valdivia, Dyskeha Streeter, Benjamin James Lolley, Caitlin Lee, Daniel Huerta, Anthony Parker, Corey Foster, Joseph Winters, Paige Elizabeth Lunsford, Matthew Loebach, Kenneth Barkley, Khalil Todd, Cristian Cuellar-Gonzales, Alec Sanford Lansing, Nicholas Grant, Logan Volpe, Del'Quan Seagers, Shaquan Allen, Janaia N Barnhart, David Hess, Another kid named Paul Choy, Jeremiah Flemming, Raven Nichole Keffer, Andrew Potter, Diane Ramirez, Kayla Neal, Kirsta Simons, Cornelius Frederick, Naomi Massa Wood, Monrius Rendon, Timmy Montoya-Kloepfel, Jared Camacho, Clay Hensley, Rylan Harris, Mia Gabrielle Fontana, Angel Lynn Rolph-Jackson, Svetlana Hope Cyphert, Joshua Hancey, Sofia Soto, Connor Bennett, Ja'Ceon Terry, Summer Rose Lambert, Raiden Toms-Moonin, Taylor Goodridge, Kamryn Meyers, Sitlalli Avelar, Arianna Duenez, Dee Rutzen, Alegend Jones, Zy'Kiria Bell and a number of unidentified teens and younger.

I would also like to thank six-term Congresswoman Cynthia McKinney, eight-term Congressman Dennis Kucinich, Gold Star Mother for Peace Cindy Sheehan and journalist Greg Palast for educating me on issues related to Cuba and Venezuela. Since the writing of this book in 2017, Max Blumenthal and Anya Parampil of the *Grayzone* have become top reporters on the subject of Venezuela and it would be a major omission to fail to mention these courageous reporters.

I am grateful to Rosie de Guzman, a wonderful writer in her own right, who proofed the novel, and to Susan Estrella, who assisted with the Spanish translations.

Lastly, I would like to thank my mom and dad for being positive and loving role models as parents.

This book and the sequel were drafted in 2017 during NaNoWriMo. A minor change was made to the original draft to reflect some changes in foreign leadership.

# ALSO BY NATALIE TRIUMPHS

**Coming Soon**

**The Adventure Continues: Summer Heat II**

How far will the government go to silence the escapees and to continue the torture and brainwashing of America's teens? As Summer and the other escaped campers return to the United States to call for an end to the teen torture programs, they again find themselves the targets of a well-funded military industrial complex that is willing to pull out all the stops to hide the truth. Summer Heat II, which was also written in the 2017 Camp NaNoWriMo, predicted the 2020 plandemic and vaccines, government attacks on college students and more events that have since come to pass.

**Best Sellers Now Available**

**Kakistocracy of the Technocrats: Amazon Best Seller #1 in Young Adult Politics & Government and #1 in Young Adult Fiction Alternative History**

As White House researcher for a non-existent department that oversees a demented robotic President, Karissa James finds herself in the middle of a string of murders, fires, earthquakes, embassy bombings, assassination attempts, bribes, wars and an Administration that can best be described as a Kakistocracy.

**Everything: Amazon Best Seller #1 in Human Rights Law, Number 1 in Young Adult Adventures and Adventurers and #1 in Young Adults Politics and Government**

After the deaths of her parents, Meadow Clarkson finds herself woven into the world of child trafficking, false flags, mass disappearances, rogue government agents and secret government operations. Her primary companions are a two-hundred-and-fifty year old talking dog named Everything and Cal, a mysterious guy who keeps appearing in her life as Meadow fights to save children from capture and slaughter, to protect her canine companion and other dogs from a dog-killing frenzy that has swept the nation and to discover what has happened to curious people who have suddenly disappeared.

**Also Coming Soon:**

**Everything II:** Meadow, her talking Papillion Everything, Cal and their friends continue their adventure as they work to save the lives of dogs and other animals in and a world that will forever be changed by judicial corruption, murders, dognappings and trans-species experimentation.

# ABOUT THE AUTHOR

Natalie Triumphs is an attorney, private investigator, educator and best-selling author. After learning of the deaths and injuries at America's Teen Gulag Camps, Schools and Programs, Natalie worked to encourage legislators in Congress and in California to close down or at least regulate these torture programs. She has fought to reform an extremely biased family law injustice system that has destroyed and often ended the lives of those who most need protection. Natalie continues to be a strong advocate for persons unjustly targeted by the criminal justice system.